DATE DUE

THIS **B**OOK
IS IN THE **C**ARE OF

_____

_____

FAIRFAX PUBLIC LIBRARY
313 Vanderbilt Street
Fairfax, IA 52228
319-846-2994

Wingfeather
Tales

THE WINGFEATHER SAGA

BOOK ONE: ON THE EDGE OF THE DARK SEA OF DARKNESS
BOOK TWO: NORTH! OR BE EATEN
BOOK THREE: THE MONSTER IN THE HOLLOWS
BOOK FOUR: THE WARDEN AND THE WOLF KING

Also by Andrew Peterson

Music

Carried Along

Clear to Venus

Love and Thunder

*Behold the Lamb of God: The True
Tall Tale of the Coming of Christ*

The Far Country

Resurrection Letters Vol. II

Counting Stars

Light for the Lost Boy

After All These Years: A Collection

The Burning Edge of Dawn

For Children

The Ballad of Matthew's Begats

Slugs & Bugs & Lullabies
(with Randall Goodgame)

Dragon Hunters.
Mysterious Trees.
A Father's Redemption.
And the Thieves of Yorsha Doon.

Wingfeather Tales

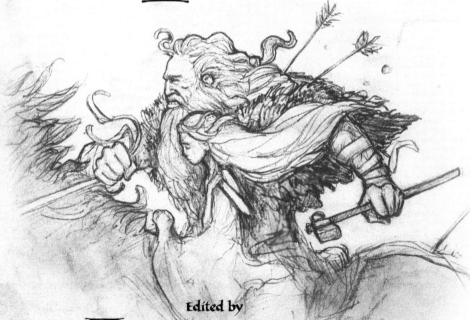

Edited by

ANDREW PETERSON

FX: 01-19

RABBIT ROOM
— PRESS —

WINGFEATHER TALES © 2016 by Rabbit Room Press

Published by
RABBIT ROOM PRESS
3321 Stephens Hill Lane
Nashville, Tennessee 37013
info@rabbitroom.com

All rights reserved. No portion of this book may be reproduced, stored in a retrieval system or magical cabinet, or transmitted in any form or by any means—electronic, mechanical, slinking courier, photocopy, recording, scanning, raggant, or other—except for brief quotations in critical reviews or articles, without the prior written permission of the publisher and Oskar N. Reteep, lest you find yourself begibboned (and utterly so).

Special thanks to Laure Hittle (a.k.a. Madame Sidler) for knowing more about Aerwiar than I do. Your help was invaluable.

Cover design by Brannon McAllister and Ron Eddy
Cover illustration © 2016 by Nicholas Kole
Map © 2016 by Justin Gerard
Illustrations © 2016 by Joe Sutphin, Aedan Peterson, Cory Godbey, Doug TenNapel, John Hendrix, Justin Gerard, Nicholas Kole

ISBN 9780986381898

First Edition
Printed in the United States of America

Contents

This book is lovingly dedicated to
Kenny Woodhull and his family.

Foreword

"Are you going to write more Wingfeather books?"

"I certainly hope so," is my typical answer.

But if you're asking whether or not I'll write about what happened *after* the epilogue of *The Warden and the Wolf King*, the answer is a definite "no." The canon is closed. I have my reasons, some of which are literary and some of which are theological, and they boil down to this: whatever hope or longing might have woken in you when you finished the book is better by far than anything I might have written. If, however, you're asking if there will be more stories in Aerwiar, then the book you hold in your hands is the answer.

It took about ten years to write the four books of *The Wingfeather Saga*, and I grieved when it was over, not just because of the bittersweet ending. I grieved because I came to love the characters and knew them intimately, and also because the world of Aerwiar had become a pleasant place for my mind to wander. Taking a cue from Orson Scott Card's helpful book *How to Write Science Fiction and Fantasy*, I spent a lot of time early on building the world—which is sort of like spreading compost in a garden, treating the soil where the story will grow. If the ground is fertile, then the characters will have strong roots. The tale itself will be more robust, its fruit will have deeper color and its leaves a wider and wilder spread. No one did this better than J. R. R. Tolkien (and I doubt anyone ever will). Half the reason we read and re-read *The Lord of the Rings* is thanks to the vividness of Middle-earth. It reads like history, and the feeling that it all might have actually happened is part of the delight. Tolkien believed that the building of imaginary worlds is one of our highest callings as image-bearing children of God, and he bore that image well.

So I started with a map. I drew the coastlines and then let my imagination run wild, naming continents, rivers, oceans, mountain ranges, towns, forests, and plains. I felt like I was twelve again. Then I started to wonder what sorts of creatures might inhabit those places, which of course led to toothy cows and sea dragons and thwaps. Then I realized that if Janner were to buy a sugarberry bun at the Dragon Day festival then he'd have to pay with *something*. Gold? Jewels? Coins? And if he used coins, then that meant there was a mint somewhere, and it also meant that the coin probably bore someone's likeness. Whose? A governor's? A king's? And if there were bad guys named Fangs, then where did they come from? What did they want? If the villain is named Gnag the Nameless, then why? (I had to sit on the answer to that question for almost a decade before I had the immense satisfaction of revealing it.) World-building isn't just part of the fun (and it *is* fun), it's crucial to writing fantasy. One of the surest ways for a tale to run out of steam is to skimp on the setting. When book four was complete I knew I wasn't finished with Aerwiar because there were castle ruins and cities and jungles full of trolls that I hadn't yet explored. Young Safiki, for example, in my story "The Prince of Yorsha Doon" (illustrated by the great Cory Godbey and Nicholas Kole), gave me a first-hand tour of a city that I ached to visit while writing the saga but never quite reached. There are more ideas knocking around that I hope to write about when

I get the time. The garden, after all, is already fertilized, and all these unexpected seeds keep sprouting.

So when my brother had the idea for a volume of Wingfeather short stories by some of the authors in the Rabbit Room community, I had no idea it would lead to a book this expansive or varied. I expected a few fun little stories, and worried that it wouldn't be long enough. I'm so glad I was wrong.

The first tale I read in this collection was by Jennifer Trafton, author of *Henry and the Chalk Dragon* and *The Rise and Fall of Mount Majestic.* One of the best compliments I can pay Jennifer came by way of my daughter. When we finished reading George MacDonald's *At the Back of the North Wind*, little Skye said, "He writes like Aunt Jennifer." Her writing is full of whimsy and warmth, and there are sentences and words in her story "The Wooing of Sophelia Stupe" that crackle like sparklers on Fourth of July. ("Besqueeblined" comes to mind.) Her tale features an illustration by one of the finest artists in the world, the great John Hendrix, whose work you can see in everything from *Sports Illustrated* to *Paste* to *Books and Culture*, to his own books, like *Drawing is Magic* and *Miracle Man.*

Next came A. S. "Pete" Peterson's epic and heart-wrenching "From the Deeps of the Dragon King," in which we see what it was like for a younger Podo Helmer to actually hunt a sea dragon. "Epic and heart-wrenching," come to think of it, are two adjectives that pretty well sum up what I love about Pete's Revolutionary War novels *The Fiddler's Gun* and *Fiddler's Green*, as well as his stage play *The Battle of Franklin.* Not only is Pete a former U. S. Marine, he spent quite a bit of time on a ship in the Adriatic Sea, has built boats, and can even now be found sailing with his wife from time to time. It's no surprise that he wanted to write about a pirate who hunts sea dragons. Illustrator Doug TenNapel, whom we have to thank for Earthworm Jim and graphic novels like *Cardboard* and *Ghostopolis*, contributed an epic and heart-wrenching (of course) illustration of a dragon hunt.

N. D. Wilson, storyteller *extraordinaire*, took time out of his crazy writing and filmmaking schedule to write yet another story about young Podo Helmer—and it's a story that helps explain Ollister Pembrick's somewhat mysterious entry in the *Creaturepedia* about his encounter with a raggant. If you've never heard of a raggant, it's time you read Wilson's wonderful *100 Cupboards* series. Joe Sutphin, whose illustrations in *The Warden and the Wolf King* elevated and inspired my own writing of that book, offered up two timeless illustrations for this story. You'll recognize Sutphin's work from *Critchlore's School for Minions* by Sheila Grau and James Patterson's *Word of Mouse*.

My dear friend Jonathan Rogers, author of the Wilderking Trilogy, *The Charlatan's Boy,* and my personal favorite Flannery O'Connor biography *The Terrible Speed of Mercy*, along with a host of other books, put on his comedic bard hat and wrote "The Ballad of Lanric and Rube," which you may remember from a footnote in *On the Edge of the Dark Sea of Darkness.* The poem is illustrated by Justin Gerard, who not only drew the pictures for *On the Edge* and *The Monster in the Hollows*, but is one of the finest fantasy artists in the world.

Douglas Kaine McKelvey is a man of mystery. He's the author of *The Angel Knew Papa and the Dog* and *The Wishes of the Fish King*, two hauntingly beautiful books for families. He (along with artist Jonathan Richter) created the utterly unique mash-up of art and poetic captioning called *Subjects Without Objects*, and is writing the forthcoming Rabbit Room Press book of everyday liturgies called *Every Moment Holy.* So when he agreed to write one of these short stories I knew it would be prosaic and meaningful. I had no idea (and neither did he) that "The Places Beyond the Maps" would be a novella that's almost as long as the first Wingfeather book. I marveled at Doug's towering prose, his deft use of archaic words, and his vast imagination, sensing as I read that he was exploring not just Aerwiar but some deep and broken part of his own heart. Then came Aedan Peterson's gritty and mournful illustrations—his finest work yet, in my humble opinion.

Aedan was 14 or 15 when he drew most of the beasts in *Pembrick's Creaturepedia*, and it's apparent with these new illustrations that he's on his way to becoming a master of his craft.

By the time I read all five of these stories I realized that *Wingfeather Tales* was more than just a nostalgic romp through Aerwiar. This was a legitimate collection, the imaginative and heartfelt expression of a group of excellent writers and illustrators, as much a part of the mythos of the Wingfeather world as anything I had written.

I wish I could say that you'll enjoy reading these as much as I did, but that wouldn't be true. No one else on earth will experience these stories the way I did, and here's why. Imagine building a big, rambling mansion from the ground up. Imagine drawing up the architectural plans, overseeing the construction, living in it for years and years, giving people regular tours of every nook and cranny. Now imagine inviting a group of writers and illustrators over for dinner. One at a time they politely take your hand and lead you down hallways you didn't know existed. They open magic doors that lead to secret passages that lead to cavernous chambers or hidden cellars or castle towers that you would have sworn weren't there before. These friends give you the gift of their own magic—magic that cost them a great deal of time and creative energy—and they turn the house you built into an enchanted palace. As I read these stories, Aerwiar became more real, more mysterious, more dangerous, more beautiful than I ever would have dreamed. And that is a rare gift.

So it is with my deepest gratitude to you, Jennifer, John, Pete, Doug, Nate, Joe, Douglas, Aedan, Jonathan, Justin, Nicholas, and Cory—and to you, dear readers—that I beckon you down this dusty hallway, remove a portrait of an oddly beautiful woman who might have once been a tree, and reveal a secret door on which is written the words *Wingfeather Tales*. To open it, all you have to do is turn the page.

Andrew Peterson
The Warren
October 17, 2016

THE PRINCE OF YORSHA DOON

Written by Andrew Peterson
Illustrated by Cory Godbey and Nicholas Kole

South of the Killridge Mountains, west of the Chasm, north of the Jungles of Plontst, and east of the Dark Sea of Darkness lay the broad and blighted wasteland of white stone and red sand called the Woes of Shreve. The Woes were lethal. No human could survive there because the blistering sunlight would sizzle their skin and bake their bones in a matter of minutes—no human, that is, except those who managed to slather themselves with bloodrock dye, which was very expensive and very hard to come by. Hard to come by unless of course you owned one of the few bloodrock mines which were well-guarded by all manner of deadly things like assassins and mad Fangs (who survived the war) and packs of slidder vipes whose needle-teeth could skin a tahala whole in the time one could say, "Oh my, I'm all out of bloodrock dye and we're hours from shelter. It was nice knowing you."

But there was no need to venture into the Woes of Shreve if you had the sense enough to live in Yorsha Doon. West of the Woes, on the edge of the Dark Sea of Darkness, the sprawling city of Yorsha Doon adorned the desert with bright spires and the blues and greens and purples of flags fluttering and robes billowing and turbans bobbing along the thousands of narrow streets. *Butaar* music played, tahalum gruttled, merchants shouted, children laughed in the streets while in the nearby maze of piers hundreds of ships creaked as waves slapped hulls and gullbirds squawked and eels shrieked. Historian and basket critic Hodar Von Voodicum described Yorsha Doon as "that chaotically exquisite collision of the Doonlands."[1] It was hot and sandy, but close as it was to the sea no bloodrock was needed there, and so the city was quite safe. Safe, that is, except for the clandestine guilds of thieves and assassins, the constant crush of traffic, the danger of being trampled by a tahala or lost in the labyrinth of passages and alleyways and high rope bridges slung between windows. A dagger, a steady hand, and a quick eye was quite useful in Yorsha Doon, though it must be said not every one of the millions of people, trolls, and occasional ridgerunners was a wicked thief—some of the thieves were in fact quite friendly.

There in the heart of Yorsha Doon, somewhere south of Prince Majah's palace, a boy in black leggings and a billowy blue patchwork shirt climbed barefoot through the second story window of a pleasant white building and woke a wrinkled old woman from her midday nap.

"It's me," whispered the boy.

"Safiki," the old woman said as she stirred. "Where have you been?"

The boy glanced out the window at the dusty city and the spires of the palace. He wouldn't know where to begin, and he didn't want to worry her. "All over," he said, grateful that today she remembered who he was. Some days she greeted him as a total stranger.

"You would tell your grandmother if you were in trouble, wouldn't you?" She lifted her a trembling hand and touched his face. Her white eyes looked in his direction but he knew they couldn't see a thing. "Have you bathed?"

"Yes, Mamada," he said. What he didn't say was that it was four days ago and it was only because he had been hiding from the port

---

1. *Why the Sorry Weave? A Musing of Basketry*, Hodar Von Voodicum (Laxfirth Press, Ban Rugan, Green Hollows, 3/245).

warden. Surely, he thought, leaping from the deck of a ship and swimming under the pier with his pockets stuffed with plumyums counted as bathing. He had at least entertained a passing thought about his grandmother's insistence on cleanliness after he had climbed out of the sea and spread out on the roof of the warden's *badaan*, listening to the gullbirds and the shouts of the shipmates as they searched hopelessly for him among the many ships. The plumyums had been delicious. "That reminds me," Safiki said, "I have something for you." His grandmother grinned, revealing her single tooth and her wonderful rumple of tanned wrinkles made deep and soft after years of smiling. "I brought you this." He removed a plumyum from one of the folds in his shirt and offered it to her with a bow of his head.

"Safiki, my dear one, you are so kind to your *mamada*!" She took the fruit and smelled it rapturously. "These *umamri* only feed me soup," she grumbled with a glance in the direction of the door. "What they don't know is that I have the most fearsome tooth in all of Yorsha Doon." She winked a blind eye at Safiki and reached into her mouth, wrenching the old yellow tooth to and fro a few times before removing it altogether with a crunch that made the boy wince even as he stifled a laugh. She wiped the false tooth on her sheets and held it up to Safiki as if he had never seen it before. The bottom end of the tooth had been ground to a point and its edge was sharpened like a blade. "Hah!" she crowed, then she clapped a hand over her mouth and lowered her voice to a whisper. "Your *mamada* could eat a flank of charred tahala rump if she wanted!"

"Then next time I will hide a whole rump of tahala in my shirt." Safiki laughed as he sat on the edge of the bed and watched her arthritic hands make deft work of the plumyum, slicing it into tiny pieces with the tooth and popping them into her mouth. "Will one be enough?"

"Yes, my boy." She sucked noisily on the fruity chunks. "Whatever you bring me is always enough."

"The *umamri* are treating you well?"

"Well enough," she said between slurps. "They are good people. But they don't give me plumyums." She finished eating, replaced her tooth, folded her hands, and faced him as if she could study his features. Safiki adjusted her pillow and stood to leave. "What will happen to you, my boy?"

"I'll be fine."

"Why don't you stay here? The *umamri* will give you a home."

Safiki sighed. "You know what I'll say."

"That you don't want to spend your life in a robe caring for old women like me?"

"I care for you, Mamada. But I would go crazy here. All they do is sing and read. My *papada* was the same. You said so."

"Ah, your *papada* was a fool."

"But you loved him."

"I loved a fool." Her face softened and she looked with unseeing eyes out the window toward the spires of Yorsha Doon. "A wonderful old fool. All he did was talk about everywhere else. The Killridge Mountains, the troll kingdoms, the Chasm. He never stood still long enough to see the beauty under his boots." She closed her eyes and flexed her fingers. Safiki's heart swelled for her. How many sarongs, how many turbans, how many draperies and quilts and pillow fringes had she fashioned with those hands—how many tunics and leggings for Safiki?—while her wonderful fool of a husband peddled them day after day at the markets, always returning home with rumors of the faraway, always with another map or sea chart? Now, Safiki thought, her memory was fading, she was blind, too feeble to work, her husband was dead, Safiki's parents were dead—and all she had left was this boy who only came to see her when the noise of his conscience was too loud to bear.

"Mamada, will you tell me about my parents?"

She worked her jaw and squinted her eyes for a moment, then she shook her head. "I'm sorry, dear boy. I have tried and tried to remember.

But my mind is like a broken mirror. I cannot see their faces anymore. Sometimes I dream that I remember who they were, what they were like, how they died, and when I wake it vanishes. But I was already very old when you were born, and that part of my memory is gone. That is why the *umamri* must care for me."

She took his hand and they sat for a while without speaking. The silence was broken by the sound of voices on the other side of the door.

"Go!" said the old woman, shooing him away and brushing the sheets to be sure there were no remnants of the plumyum. "And be *safe*, Safiki. Find a home. Maker knows I won't always be here to love you."

Safiki hopped to the window and perched on the sill.

"I'll be back soon, Mamada," he said.

The door opened. A man and woman in white robes entered with a pitcher of water and a bowl of soup, and with a flutter of the drapes the boy was gone.

Safiki dropped from the sill to a ledge, edged along it to the end of the whitestone building, then dropped two stories and landed on a canvas awning. He grabbed the supporting pole and spun down to the ground just as a tahala pulling a cart lumbered past. He had done it a hundred times before, but he was beginning to think he was getting too big for such acrobatics. In the last few months he had found himself thinking twice before making leaps that used to come easily. He didn't want to get any bigger. Half the fun of swiping fruit and bread and whatever else he could lay his hands on was the thrill of scrambling up the sides of buildings or leaping from one wagon to another or creeping under the tables at the market without being seen. But he couldn't think about that now. Now he had to think about food. He had just given his grandmother his last plumyum, and his stomach was already muttering.

"Safiki," said a familiar voice.

The boy dusted off his knees and turned to face the entrance to the *umamri* house. A man stood in the doorway in a white robe. His face was leathery but kind and clean-shaven, and his dark eyes watched the boy with amusement.

"How is she?"

Safiki took a step backwards. "I think she is doing well, *umam* Falam."

"Did she like the fruit?"

Safiki decided a lie would be pointless. "Yes, *salah*. She's getting tired of soup." He stepped out of the way as another tahala cart rumbled between them, followed by a short woman herding an annoyance of gambloats.

"She worries about you," said the man as the bleating faded.

"She has no need to worry. And neither do you, *salah*."

"Why don't you stay here with us? We don't eat like princes, but we eat. Every man needs a home."

"You forget," Safiki said, standing up straight and spreading his arms, "I am not yet a man. And Yorsha Doon is my home. All of it."

Falam smiled, but there was sadness in his eyes. "You will be a man before you know it. I am here if you need me, Safiki. Maker keep you."

"And you," Safiki shouted over his shoulder as he slipped into an alley and ran, relishing the wild freedom of the city. He wound through passageways and hopped over henbirds, pausing only to swipe an apple from a passing cart. Ignoring the shouts of the fruit merchant behind him, he ducked under a lumbering cart, dashed into an alley, climbed the rocky face of an old sandstone building, and huddled in the shade of the roof ledge to catch his breath and munch the apple. When he was finished—core and seeds and stem—he shielded his eyes and looked out over the rooftops of the city. The sun was dipping towards the glittering sea in the west, and the whitestone buildings had begun to deepen to a buttery yellow.

This was when he loved Yorsha Doon the best, when the haze of the heat faded and the bustle of the streets gradually lazed into the living silence of the sleeping city, like some great dozing sea dragon on whose back Safiki would climb all night. By sundown there would be no more merchants, and therefore no food to swipe so easily, but neither would there be the constant danger of kidnapping, of port wardens, of angry merchants ready to stab the hands of swipers like Safiki. Under cover of night he could walk the streets in safety until he found a district he had never haunted. There he would do as he had always done. He would find a secluded corner on a *havala* roof or a forgotten alleyway or a pile of splintered boatwood and would make a nest until he sensed it was time to move on—which was usually when people began to recognize him. Safiki liked to be invisible. He liked to be anonymous. As soon as he lost his anonymity, he lost his freedom. He could be days or weeks in one place, then he would migrate. The city was large enough that he figured he could live the rest of his life that way and never run out of nests, never run out of food, never need a soul other than himself. No one but his grandmother and a few of the *umamri* knew his name. He had no friends. He saw no need for it. As soon as you had friends, he reasoned, things got complicated—you had to make hard choices, you had to find food for more than just yourself, and worst of all, you were *visible*. Safiki had his grandmother, and that was enough.

Safiki's eyes grew heavy, as they usually did before sundown, and he surveyed the rooftop to be sure he was safe and alone. *Alone*, he thought to himself, *is safe*. He stretched out in the lengthening shade of one of the distant palace spires, locked his fingers behind his head, and drifted into dreams.

When he woke, the streets of Yorsha Doon were fast asleep.

Safiki sat up and peered over the edge of the roof. The city lay blue and cool under a gibbous moon and a spray of stars, like a reflection of the lights of the million lanterns glowing in the city's windows. Faint clouds feathered the east where the southern edge of the Killridge Mountains descended for fathoms into the mystery of the Chasm. The mountains were a jagged but indistinct blackness on the horizon, like the memory of a bad dream. Safiki heard the echo of someone mumbling drunkenly to himself in the streets below, probably a husband who had lingered too long at the bibery after his day's work. The palace towers to the north stabbed at the moon, and along the palace wall he spied the turbaned silhouettes of the guards as they moved to and fro, their spear tips glinting in the torchlight.

What were they guarding? Safiki wondered, as he often did. The palace was the heart of the city, and like all hearts it was a mystery. No one was ever allowed in. No one was certain how Prince Majah and his court ate because the gates had never been raised as far as Safiki knew. It was rumored that there were secret passages, entrances that had been kept hidden for epochs, and for a thousand years the kings had gathered their treasure hordes and lived in splendor. If the gleaming spires that sprouted into the heavens beyond the wall were any indication, the treasure was vast. The prince was only ever seen from a great distance, standing on a balcony of the center spire and waving at the masses that gathered to glimpse him. Still, the city loved him. Whenever there was a drought, the prince provided food by lowering it in baskets over the wall. Whenever there was an attack by the Symian pirates, Prince Majah's warriors appeared in the streets as if from nowhere to fight them back. The palace was a city within a city, and as long as the prince was safe, so was Yorsha Doon.

When Safiki was certain the way was clear, he hopped over the ledge, scrambled down the way he had come (past an open window where he heard a family's murmured conversation and smelled their dinner), and landed without a sound on the sandstone cobbles, his back to the wall. He looked to his left and right, and saw in both directions shadowy doorways and canvas awnings rolled up tight, piles of tahala dung speckling the silent streets.

"Which way tonight, Maker?" he whispered with a glance at the stars.

"Right," a woman said, and Safiki almost jumped out of his shirt. Her voice had come from inside the house.

"I am telling you, Reela," said a man, "the shiptain made me stay until I was finished with every last rope." The man burped, and Safiki thought his words sounded a little slurred.

"Right," the woman repeated. "You say that every night, Damolek."

"Please believe me, my love," the man said with another burp, and the woman stomped up the stairs with the man stumbling after.

"Right it is, then." Safiki smiled up at the stars. "I thank you for your direction, Maker."

He wandered along streets he didn't know, though he wasn't far from the district where his grandmother had raised him. Every turn brought more of the same, and yet everything was different, like new verses to an old song. Ancient buildings that he knew by the rugged stone at the foundations were as old as the city itself; newer buildings that stood as many as eight stories tall, made of stone so smooth and polished he could see his moonlit reflection when he passed; shacks built of driftwood and the planks of decommissioned ships. The carvings of stone faces, worn smooth and nearly featureless by hundreds of years of sandstorms, grimaced or grinned or looked on stoically from archways and pillars. Rope bridges spanned the high windows where laundry swayed in the night breeze. After a while he came upon an empty square with a round stone well pool at the center and realized he was terribly thirsty.

Safiki stopped at the edge of the square and listened. Where there was water, there were usually people, and where there were people, there was danger. When he heard nothing, Safiki crept as silent as the moon to the pool, sat on the edge, and dipped his hands into the cool water. He drank with his eyes wide open, scanning the four corners of the square for movement.

He didn't think to look in the water itself.

A hand shot out and pulled him under. Safiki struggled, and though the assailant's hands weren't strong, they were quick enough to keep him busy. He sputtered and gasped and kicked until he was free, then he jumped out of the fountain and backed away, shaking the water from his eyes. All he saw was a shadow—a small shape, dripping and motionless, hiding under the ledge formed by the flat rim of the pool. Safiki knew better than to investigate. He turned to run.

"Wait!" the shadow said with a loud whisper.

Safiki took a few steps and stopped. "What do you want?"

"*They're coming*!"

"Who's coming?"

"The palace guard. And worse."

"Why?"

"Shh! Listen!"

Safiki heard movement to the north and saw the glow of torchlight down one of the streets. It was getting brighter. Then he heard footsteps. He spun around and saw that down two of the other streets more torchlight approached. He thought about sprinting for the other street, the only dark one, but he doubted he would cross the open square before the nearest of the guard—or worse, whatever that meant—emerged. It didn't matter that he wasn't the one they were hunting. He would be chased, and perhaps caught and interrogated—and likely thrown into a workhouse with the rest of the orphans too slow to survive on the streets. Safiki knew exactly how to hide in a crowd, but now he felt exposed, so he slipped into the pool as quietly as he could and pressed himself against the side, his face just above the water, hoping he was as invisible as the well's other occupant had been.

"My name is Saana," the shadow whispered.

"A *girl*?" Safiki said. "Why are they after you?"

"I escaped the palace."

Safiki forgot he was hiding and whispered, too loudly, "The *palace*?" He had never spoken to anyone who had seen the inside. "What's in there? Is it as lovely as they say?"

"Yes. Well, it used to be. Before Roduin came."

"Roduin the Bloodbrute? From the Woes?"

"Keep your voice down!" Saana whispered.

The guards sounded like they were in the square now, searching the perimeter. Torchlight illuminated the faces of the buildings, but the girl was still just a vague shadow on the opposite side of the pool. "Listen. I need to tell you this now, in case they catch me. A year ago, Roduin and his mercenaries found a way into the palace and captured Prince Majah."

"Why?"

"For the treasure. Roduin's hoarding it in one of his bloodrock mines somewhere in the Woes. The prince and his whole court have been in the dungeon ever since. My father is the kitchener, which is the only reason we're not in the dungeon, too. Our family prepares the food."

"But what about all the palace guards? I see them on the wall every day."

"The real guards are in the dungeons. They killed the prince's personal guard. I'm telling you, the palace is overrun with Roduin's men. And his Fangs."

Safiki's stared at her. "You're lying."

"Why would I lie?" Safiki couldn't see her face, but he could feel her eyes. The guards were getting closer.

This, Safiki thought, *is why I like to be alone. As soon as you know someone's name, things get complicated.*

"I can't help you," Safiki said. "I'm sorry. I wouldn't even know what to do."

"You can hide me. You can help me find someone who is brave enough to do something."

Safiki pretended he didn't hear her. The voices of the guards drew ever nearer until they stood in a circle around the pool. He could see, just above where Saana hid, the bearded faces of the guards glowing in the torchlight—and for the first time he could see her. Her eyes were wide with panic, and her dark hair clung to her cheeks. She was trembling. Then it occurred to Safiki that if he could see the girl by the glow of the torches, then she could see him—and so could the guards. He tried not to move. He tried not to breathe. All the guards had to do was look in the right place.

"Nothing?" asked a man with a long black beard. The guards shifted their weight and shook their heads. The man with the beard spat into the fountain. "Do you smell anything, dog?"

Just above Safiki's head a rasping voice said, "She passed this way." There was a sniffling sound, followed by a ragged cough. "Not long ago."

Safiki sensed with dread the slow realization that was dawning on the guards, which was dawning on him too: the girl was about to be caught. He wondered for a wild moment if he should do something to help her, but his instinct for survival triumphed and he merely pressed himself hard against the wet stone of the well and prayed that he wouldn't be seen. Then the awful silence was broken by an even more awful growl. Something leaped into the pool. In the explosion of water and screams, Safiki saw a Grey Fang, its hairy tail whipping the surface as it wrenched the girl from her hiding place and lifted her by one leg. She flailed and screamed as the wolf bared its long yellow teeth in her face, and Safiki thought for a horrible moment that it would gobble her up. But the leader of the guard cracked a whip and the Fang whimpered, tucked its tail between its legs, and climbed out of the pool. Safiki had seen Fangs before, but never up close. This beast was as wretched as a mangy dog, pale and splotchy skin glistening where there was no fur, and ribs heaving with each of its ragged breaths. It handed Saana to the one of the guards and slunk away. She no longer struggled, but merely wept as they carried her off. Just before she was borne out of sight her eyes met Safiki's.

It was a look that would haunt him for weeks.

The next day Safiki found an abandoned alleyway near the eastern edge of the city and spent hours constructing a cozy nest out of boat planks and crate wood, taking great care to make it look like a pile of trash on the outside while the inside was clean and comfortable. He scavenged some old torn sheets from a trash pile behind a seamery and lined the floor and walls of the nest, thinking as he did so that his grandmother would be pleased.

He struggled to forget the girl. Every time he remembered the look on her face it seemed to be less a look of terror and more a look of accusation, so he spent more time on the nest than he needed to, trying to distract himself from her (he refused to call her Saana) and her story. A part of him wished he were as forgetful as his grandmother so he could get on with his day of carefree swiping. Besides, how could he be sure she was telling the truth? He heard many things on the streets of Yorsha Doon, and had never caught the slightest hint that the situation at the palace was anything but ordinary. He had seen the prince with his own eyes, waving from the distant turret. Nothing seemed amiss. The guards looked the same as they always did: sentries posted on the wall, companies of guards marching through the city to keep peace or to announce the prince's appearance from time to time. It seemed impossible that a year could pass with Roduin in control without anyone noticing.

But why would she lie?

In an effort to quiet his doubts, Safiki slipped out of his nest, inspected it from the outside to be sure it looked inconspicuous, then struck out into the city. He wandered aimlessly, sneaking food whenever he wanted it, exploring districts he'd never seen, riding secretly on the roof of tahala carts into undiscovered markets and neighborhoods, creeping through deserted ruins. He was happy—except that he wasn't. He couldn't get the girl's name out of his mind. Saana. *You could help me*, she had said. Toward noon, without exactly meaning to, he found himself in a river of traffic at the foot of the palace wall. He told himself that since he was there anyway he might as well investigate. He crossed through the ever-moving crowd, stepped over fly-ridden piles of dung, clambered onto a wagon parked opposite the palace wall, and hopped up to a second story window. He crouched there, looking over the heads of the crowd at the high wall and the sentries posted there, watching for several minutes and trying to imagine that the guards were impostors, that they were Roduin's cronies pretending to be guards. How would he even know the difference? They were all big men with big beards and black turbans. They all held spears. They all looked fierce as they scanned the crowds below. Something about it did, in fact, seem odd, but he couldn't imagine what.

"I'm a fool, just like Papada," he said under his breath. Then he climbed the rest of the way up the building to the roof where he could better see the palace itself. Nothing seemed out of the ordinary. Just more guards here and there on the turrets, all watching the streets below. "Roduin the Bloodbrute, in the palace," Safiki said with a roll of his eyes. "I'm not the fool—*she* is, for thinking I'd believe such nonsense."

At last, Safiki's conscience cleared. The girl was crazy. Or she had stolen something important and probably deserved to be caught. Safiki shook the previous night's events from his mind, took a deep breath, and smiled. The city seemed normal again, a teeming cluster of endless adventure, just the way he liked it. He got a running start, jumped from one rooftop to another, then climbed a stony wall to a rope bridge that led to a balcony, which happened to open onto a kitchen. He waited until the woman inside wasn't looking, then he slipped in and silently snatched a fried plonkfish from a tray. He held it in his teeth as he climbed higher, stole across another high bridge, and lost himself among the rooftops till late afternoon.

He was happy to find that his nest was undisturbed. Safiki climbed into the cool dark, lay on his back, and settled in to sleep until the night was deep. Just before he drifted away he sat up. "They didn't look bored," he said aloud. The palace guards ordinarily looked like they'd rather be anywhere else, especially in the heat of the day. But these had all been scanning the crowd, as if looking for trouble. Safiki lay back down slowly and closed his eyes. It was too late, anyway. Even if the girl—*Saana*—had been telling the truth, there was nothing Safiki could do for her. *Saana*. He couldn't singlehandedly invade the palace and rescue the prince or the girl—*Saana*—or anyone else. He was Safiki, which meant everything he did was singlehanded.

Saana.

It took a long time for Safiki to drift into a fitful sleep.

After several days of roaming Yorsha Doon, Safiki slept as well as he ever did, and he managed to forget everything about the girl.

Except her name.

Three weeks later, Safiki decided it was time to visit his grandmother again, and he didn't want to show up at the *umamri* house without a gift. He peeked out of an alleyway into the harsh, dusty sunlight as a stenchulous grobble of trolls thudded through the chattering, churning mass of people. Doonlanders were glad for the trolls because they brought massive shipments of fruit and meat and the finest over-sized cookware in all of Dang, but the trolls also brought with them an odor that lingered for hours—weeks if someone actually touched one, Maker forbid. The throngs held their noses or covered their faces with the bright cloth of their robes and waved with pained smiles as the trolls waded the thoroughfare. When Safiki was sure that all those watering eyes were on the trolls he slipped into an empty basket next to one of the finest food stalls he had ever seen. The table was heavy with strips of dried slidder vipe meat, dried apples, dried plumyums, and dried herbs, all of which were carefully arranged into little mountains of deliciousness. The display was so appealing that Safiki almost hated to swipe from it. His mouth watered as the market regained its pleasant bustle. Soon merchants were once again shouting prices at passersby and passersby were shouting at merchants as birds squawked and *butaar* music played and beasts grunted and Safiki listened to it all, relishing the secrecy of his hiding place. Another moment of distraction for the merchant, and the boy would be free to swipe as many delicacies for his grandmother as he could carry.

"Where did you say you were from?" asked the merchant. He had a perfectly curled mustache and wore a bright blue turban. Safiki couldn't see the customer's face through the cracks in the basket, but he could tell by his boots and breeches that this fellow was new to Yorsha Doon. "Forgive me, *salah*, where did you say you were from?"

"Ban Rona," the customer answered with a nervous chuckle. Safiki's curiosity overcame his prudence and he shifted his weight and eased the wicker basket to one side to get a glimpse of the stranger's face. It was useless. All he saw was a belly. But what a belly! No wonder the merchant was being so friendly.

"Ban Rona!" said the merchant. "You have come very far, *salah*. That is in the Green Hollows, no?"

"Indeed! In the words of Doylie the Funeralist, 'It's a long way from here to there.' Have you been to the Hollows?"

Safiki had heard of the Green Hollows. They sold fruit, of course, but they also sold soil. Their ships arrived in the port from time to time, and the sacks of rich, dark earth were always gone before the crew had even debarked. Someone made a lot of money on that dirt.

"No, *salah*," the merchant said. "I have never seen the Green Hollows. My wife—Maker bless her with a thousand robes of meepish fur!—would never allow it. If I am late for dinner by even a seven-beat of her heart she refuses to feed me. Ban Rona, I am afraid, is a place only known to me in books."

At the word "books," the large man loosed an excited chortle that sounded like a tahala retching on a nettle. "But what a magnificent way to know a place! I have never set foot in the Jungles of Plontst, but Grillby's most excellent *Somewhat Approximate Troll Atlas* fills me with the most exquisite jigglies. I daresay that I'd prefer to visit Plontst from my armchair at the Great Library with the aid of Grillby's volume than to sweat and bug-smack my way through the darkest jungle in Aerwiar." He added in a teacherly voice, "If I may quote my own incomplete history of the Wingfeather War, 'Reading books is neatest of all.'"

"Of course, of course," said the merchant with a wave of his hand. "What can I offer you from my humble stall, *salah*?"

"Goodness gravy," murmured the large stranger, and Safiki heard, over the racket of the crowds, the rumble of the man's stomach.

Safiki's sense of swipery told him that his moment was fast approaching. As soon as the fruit was handed over and the merchant was paid, he would turn to place the coins in his safe box, and Safiki's hand would slip out of the basket as quick as a whip and snatch a bellyful of food. The tips of his fingers tingled.

"I think I'd like one of everything," said the large man. "No, make that three. Three of everything."

The merchant gleefully gathered the items on the table. The large man hummed to himself and Safiki saw his chubby hand reach down to the satchel at his side and flip open the cover. The musical sound of coins jingled from within, and the tingle in Safiki's fingers increased. Perhaps there was a better prize to be had than a few plumyums, he thought. The stranger clearly had no idea how treacherous were the streets of Yorsha Doon, and it would be an easy thing to swipe the satchel—assuming Safiki got to it before any of the other thieves did.

"And what brings you to Yorsha Doon, *salah*?" asked the merchant as he counted the items.

"I'm here to trade books with Prince Majah!" said the man in a loud whisper. "But you mustn't tell *anyone*. He's giving me his first edition of *Tales of the Battles of the Wars of the Woes of Shreve of Dang of Aerwiar* in exchange for the only known copy of Amagri the Wise's famous recipe book, *Feasting in the Woes*."

Safiki's grin vanished.

He had never read a single book, but even he had heard of Amagri's *Feasting in the Woes*. Everyone had. It was more than just a collection of recipes—legend had it the book contained a secret map of the palace, including all the hidden passageways, escape routes, and long-lost treasure hordes. If it fell into the wrong hands (or the right ones, depending on how one saw it) the palace could be infiltrated.

Saana.

"But you mustn't tell a soul, my friend! The prince insisted on the utmost secrecy. His letter warned that the wrong chef would make a botchery of the meals therein!"

"Of course, *salah*!" the merchant said with barely concealed eagerness. "I would never tell a soul. That will be twenty *renn*, if you please."

As the stranger rummaged in his satchel, Safiki glimpsed the book. The leather cover was ornate and bejeweled, and in flowing *renari* script were the words, "Feasting in the Doonlands." Whoever this man was, he had no business traveling to Yorsha Doon alone with such a treasure. Then Safiki heard the familiar whisper of a dagger drawn from its sheath and watched with mounting horror as the merchant stepped casually from behind his table, concealing the blade beneath the sack of food.

"Let me help you," said the merchant kindly.

"Ah! Thank you, friend," said the old man, with an obliviousness that Safiki found infuriating. Half of him wanted to stay hidden, but the other half couldn't get the girl out of his head—the girl and the terrible feeling in his gut when he had stood by and watched as she was snatched up by the Grey Fang.

Before he could stop himself, Safiki burst from the basket and shouted, "Stop!"

The stranger yelped and jumped so violently that several *renn* coins slipped from his fingers and clinked onto the sandstone cobbles. His face was large and kind, and a swath of white hair peeked out from a red turban that was soaked with sweat. His spectacles were fogged and had slipped to the end of his nose.

"Why, hello there, young man," he said with a smile, turning his back to the merchant. "My name is Oskar."

Just as the merchant thrust the dagger, the old man bent over to retrieve the coins. The knife stabbed the air and Oskar's rump bumped the table, spilling several of the dried plumyums to the ground. The merchant stepped forward for another jab but he stepped on the fruit and wheeled his arms before thudding to the ground. The knife clattered away as the old man, once again as oblivious as a digtoad, apologized to the merchant and straightened, holding the coins triumphantly in one hand.

"Come on, you fool!" shouted Safiki as he toppled out of the basket. He grabbed Oskar's hand and tugged him away.

"Whatever is the matter?" Oskar said as he rubbed the condensation from his spectacles with the back of one hand.

"Run!" Safiki shouted as the merchant retrieved his dagger and spun around with a snarl.

Oskar's wide eyes went from the knife to the merchant's leering face to the satchel, then back to the knife, and at last he seemed to understand. He clutched the satchel to his chest and gasped. With a speed Safiki would have thought impossible, the old man turned and ran, shrieking through the crowd and knocking down people and carts and tables of wares. Safiki, dumbstruck by the man's thundering velocity, slowly realized that the merchant's sinister gaze had settled on him.

"You wretched little thief," the man growled, apparently untroubled by the fact that he himself was a thief, or was about to become one. "That book would have bought me a herd of tahalum!"

The merchant lunged, but Safiki rolled between his legs and raced after Oskar in the wake of his destruction. The old man's turban had come undone and trailed behind him like a flag, which made him easy to follow. The boy darted between people and under tahala legs and around trolls and over upturned crates until he at last was sprinting with Oskar's jelliful girth beside him.

"Do you know where you're going?" panted Safiki.

"Away!" Oskar still clutched the satchel to his chest. "Away!"

Safiki had seen galloping tahalum, he had seen racing trolls, but he had never seen anyone—or anything—so large move with such power. The old man's head didn't bob, but remained more or less level with the ground, while the rest of him moved with dizzying speed. His meaty legs pumped up and down with uncanny agility; his magnificent belly sloshed in five different directions at once, slapping the tops of Oskar's knees one moment and folding itself momentarily over the satchel the next. His jowls were splotchy red and they trembled with each magnificent step, the way a bowl of soup might if someone were pounding the table with a hammer. But it was the face that delighted Safiki the most. Oskar's eyebrows were raised so high that they seemed to rest on the top of his pate, and his eyes, floating above the rattling spectacles, were open wide enough that Safiki could almost see the man's brains.

By now the cacophony of shouts behind them had warned the crowds ahead, so the center of the main market street was clear and the people watched in confusion as the unlikely pair hurried by. "You're going to want to turn left at the next alleyway," Safiki said between breaths. The boy was fast, but even he was running out of air.

"Why?" Oskar shrieked.

"Because this . . . is a dead end," Safiki huffed. The dead end was actually a long way off, but Safiki needed a break. "And . . . that merchant . . . will have . . . gathered his friends . . . by now. We need . . . to lose him."

Without warning, Oskar veered left—nearly trampling the boy—and entered a narrow alley. He probably would have kept running for another five days if Safiki hadn't shouted, "Stop! For the Maker's sake stop running!"

It took a full arrowshot for Oskar to slow himself down to a halt near an empty wagon. The old man doubled over and wheezed. Sweat cascaded from every pore and speckled the dusty cobbles. Safiki found enough breath to laugh and paced the alleyway, shaking his head with wonder. "Who *are* you?"

"My name is Oskar N. Reteep," he wheezed, "appreciator of the strange, neat, and/or the yummy." He looked up at Safiki and smiled. "Also, an appreciator of friendly help when it's needed." He straightened and dabbed his glistening forehead with a handkerchief that was immediately soaked through. "In the words of Namulus Croddle-Norton in his seminal treatise on wagon sculptures, 'Please don't steal my book, young fellow. It doesn't become you.'"

"Don't worry," Safiki said with a wave of his hands. "I only swipe things that no one will miss after a few hours. That thing is dangerous. But I won't protest if you offer me a few *renn*."

"I would be delighted, young man. On one condition."

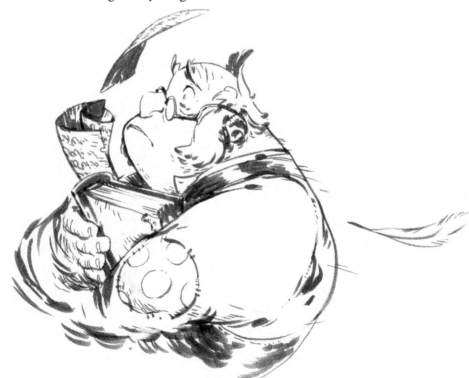

"What would you like?"

"I'd like to know your name. It's hard to be your friend if I don't know your name."

"I don't have friends, *salah*. Friends are as dangerous as that book."

Oskar looked at the boy over his spectacles. "I know we just met, but I must say that you are greatly mistaken. I would likely be dead right now if not for your kindness. A friend is one of the Maker's finest gifts."

Safiki folded his arms. "Ah, but if we had never met I would be eating plumyums in the sun right now, happy as a meep."

"But instead, you have a friend."

"No, instead I am out of breath and must avoid this market for many months because that merchant knows my face. Imagine how much worse it would be if he knew my name. "

"You're a sharp lad. Names indeed have power. Where I come from that is widely known." Oskar patted his belly and thought for a moment. "Then what if I swore to tell no one? After all, I'm leaving the Doonlands as soon as I get the book to the prince. Whom would I tell?"

Safiki paused. "You would tell no one?"

"I swear it. I only want you to see what it feels like to trust someone."

The truth was, Safiki liked the old man and felt a strange inner compulsion to break his own rule. He looked up and down the alley, then back at the strange man. "Very well." He bowed and said, "My name is Safiki."

Oskar put a hand over his heart. "I am truly honored, Safiki, to make your acquaintance. I wonder if you might help me with just one more thing?"

Safiki sighed. Of course. There was always just one more thing. He was already annoyed with himself. "What is it?"

"I wonder if you would help me escape those men."

Safiki spun around. The alleyway was blocked by seven men—which turned quickly to ten, and then twelve. They all held scimitars or daggers or clubs, and they all looked ready to use them. The merchant shouldered his way to the front and smiled wickedly while he curled his moustache. "Yes, Mufalu," he said. "That is the one."

"And you say he has the book?" asked the tallest of them in a deep voice. His dark beard was braided and he wore a black turban with a blue gulpswallow feather pinned to the front.

"Would your cousin lie to you?"

Mufalu nodded and raised his sabre. The others did likewise, and the alleyway became a small forest of blades. "Stranger, if you want to leave Yorsha Doon alive," Mufalu said, "drop the book and sail home."

Safiki ducked behind Oskar. He had no intention of getting sliced into little pieces over a book—or a stranger for that matter, even if he knew his name. And yet, even as he inched deeper into the alley his mind raced to think of a way to help the old man. He felt bound to him somehow. The alley was littered with empty crates. All the doors—back entrances to shops and dwellings—were closed and probably locked. Above were plenty of windows, but all were shuttered. Their only hope lay beyond the deep end of the alley where a small archway led to a labyrinth of narrow streets called the Heshibal District.[2] It was possible for Safiki to escape, but it would require a great deal more agility than the big man had, however fast he could run.

Mufalu pointed his sabre at Oskar and stepped forward, and his small army followed. Oskar let out a whimper and tightened his grip on the satchel.

"Give me the book," Safiki whispered.

"What?" Oskar said out of the side of his mouth.

"Give it to me." He placed his hand on Oskar's sweaty back. "They want the book, not you. There is an *umamri* house near the

---

2. Known to Doonlanders as the "Wormway" because, in a city of densely clustered buildings, its buildings were even more so. Believed to be the oldest part of Yorsha Doon, it was an intricate, twisting, and all but impenetrable maze. Some older citizens claimed to have lived their whole lives in Heshibal because they'd never managed to figure out how to leave.

south gate of the city, next to a bloodrock stall. Ask for Falam, and tell him I sent you. I will meet you there at sunset." Safiki paused. "You can trust me, *salah*."

"Old man," Mufalu snarled as he moved closer, "you and the boy—Safiki, was it?—do not need to die today. Give me the book." Safiki closed his eyes and gritted his teeth. They had heard. What had he been thinking? Why had he given in? Oskar lifted the strap over his head clutched the satchel in both hands. He looked at it longingly, then back at the advancing men. "Good," Mufalu said. "Now put it on the ground and be gone. Don't try to run. Word travels fast in the Wormway, so I swear we will find you."

Oskar bent over with an involuntary grunt and placed the satchel gingerly on the sandstone cobbles. "I trust you, my friend," he whispered to Safiki, and the boy's heart kicked in his chest. He had never heard those words before. In one swift motion, Oskar slid the satchel backwards between his legs and charged the men with an ear-splitting squeal. Safiki snatched up the satchel and ran. As he passed through the archway he saw Mufalu and the merchant and the rest of the swordsmen slam into the walls as the largest, strangest man Safiki had ever met barreled past them and into the crowded streets of Yorsha Doon.

It should have been easy. Safiki knew that if he bore generally to the right, which was north, he should eventually emerge from the Heshibal District near the west wall of the palace. There would be plenty of people there, and it would be a simple thing to disappear. As soon as he was out of sight of his pursuers, he ducked under a pile of refuse and lay perfectly still until Mufalu and his men ran past, shouting and waving their curved blades. Safiki waited till it was quiet and then crept out and sped down a different alleyway. He didn't realize how much trouble those few minutes would cause. Word spread so quickly that in minutes every brigand in Yorsha Doon was hunting for a boy with dark, shaggy hair and carrying a gray leather satchel.

And they knew his name.

Safiki skidded to a stop where three narrow alleys intersected. Four young children played a game of Cat Punch[3] down one lane. A sheepling bleated mournfully in another while an old woman tried to feed it a sandwich. The third was empty except for a rain of food scraps splatting on the cobbles from a high window. When he turned around he saw a boy not much older than himself sneaking toward him.

"You are the one with the book," the boy said, cracking his knuckles. Safiki backed away.

"He is Safiki, the one with the book," said another voice, and Safiki saw the three children stand up from their game of Cat Punch.

"You," said the old woman with the sheep sandwich, "have the look of a boy with a rare and precious book."

The satchel suddenly felt as conspicuous as a third foot. "I don't know what you're talking about," Safiki said.

"Get him," the woman barked.

The four children chased him to a dead end, which was fine since Safiki was an excellent climber. He shimmied up one wall and hand-walked along a laundry line to the opposite wall while the children threw trash at him and jumped to try and grab his feet. He swung through an open window and interrupted a family gathered around a table to eat a meal of ferno-on-the-bone. The father looked up from his prayers and gasped, "It is the boy with the book!"

"Safiki!" said the mother.

"Get him!" screamed the three young children.

Safiki jumped onto the table and danced across it, dodging hands and swiping a bite of roasted ferno lizard leg in the process, then tore through the house while the family shouted curses behind him. He

3. No actual cats are harmed in the playing of Cat Punch.

burst from their front door onto a narrow walkway above the street. Residents from the other houses poked their heads from windows and doorways. "What is all this fuss?" they shouted, and then, "Get him! He has the book!"

Safiki edged along the railing, squirming and twisting out of the grip of many hands, until he reached a set of stairs at the end. A crowd had already gathered in the alley below, so he had no choice but to climb another flight. He reached a rope bridge to the next building, which was several stories taller than the last, and climbed again, higher and higher as the people of the Wormway grew in number and anger, until at last he reached the flat rooftop and felt the lowering sun on his face.

To the north were the spires of the palace. To the west, the Dark Sea. He couldn't go to the *umamri* house or he would lead the mob to his grandmother's doorstep. Besides, he couldn't face her like this. She would scold him, fret over him, or worse, be disappointed in him. She needed to know that her grandson was safe, not that he was the most wanted soul in Yorsha Doon. He had to find a place to hide, a place where no one knew his name or his face, and he had to find it fast.

He had run out of time. Doonlanders poured onto the roof and screamed his name. Safiki ran like a desert wind, planted a foot on the ledge, and launched himself to the next rooftop. He knew he would make it. The alleyways were narrow enough for that. But the problem, it turned out, was not the distance—it was the small army of men waiting for him on the other side. In the center was the large man from the first alley—Mufalu—and he was smiling as the boy arced straight toward him. Safiki wheeled his arms as if he could undo his leap, then landed in the firm grasp of many rough hands. He struggled, but it was futile. Mufalu jerked the satchel from him, then someone struck Safiki's head with the pommel of a dagger and the world went black.

When Safiki woke on the floor, he heard voices that seemed to come from the other side of a wall. His feet were bound. His hands were tied behind his back. His jaw ached and he was gagged with a strip of cloth. By the glow of a lantern in the dim room he saw the swordsmen gathered around a table, studying the open book and speaking in hushed tones. The hilts of their swords glinted in the lamplight. *This is what happens*, he thought, *when you make a friend. You fail him. And you get your head clobbered, too.*

"The boy is awake," one of the men said.

All eyes turned to Safiki. One of them stood and strode toward him with a wicked sneer. It was the merchant with the curled mustache. He prodded Safiki with the toe of his boot.

"Safiki the thief is awake!" he hissed. "I should cut off one of your toes. What were you doing in my basket, eh? Planning to swipe my hard-earned food? Do you know that I have a wife and a daughter? Do you know that they are my soul's delight? How can I feed them if all my food is stolen?"

"Enough, Hofaan," said the big one, Mufalu. "You too have swiped, have you not?" The merchant spat on the ground and kicked Safiki halfheartedly before slinking back to the table. Safiki looked at Mufalu and grunted, hoping that they would at least remove the gag so he could plead to be released. "Quiet, or we will find a way to make you sleep again," said Mufalu.

Safiki rested his head on the cool floor and looked around. He seemed to be in a cellar with a low ceiling. There were no windows, which was rare in Yorsha Doon where the heat required as much of a breeze as possible. A stairway on the opposite side of the room led up and into shadows. It seemed to be the only way out.

"Is he coming?" Mufalu asked a man with a gray beard and a jewel in the center of his turban.

"Yes. He said he would be here soon."

Mufalu closed the old book and leaned back from the table. "We can do nothing until he arrives. This book is useless without him."

"Patience, Mufalu. We have waited many months for an opportunity like this. We can wait a few moments more."

A short while later, the door opened at the top of the stairs and Safiki squinted into the light as a figure descended. Mufalu and the others stood and greeted him. When the door shut and Safiki's eyes adjusted he saw that the man wore a white robe and had a leathery but clean-shaven face. *Falam*? Safiki felt a rush of relief. Falam would tell the men to release him. Falam was an *umam*, and the *umam* were gracious. But what was he doing with these thieves? Why wasn't he at the *umamri* house caring for his grandmother? Safiki grunted again and Falam looked his way. But if he recognized the boy he didn't show it. Falam walked to the table, bowed, and said, "Mufalu, my friend, it is always good to see you." Safiki froze. Falam was *friends* with this brigand? All those years of Falam's white robes and kind smiles were a lie. He was a traitor and a fraud. How many other of the *umam* were assassins or spies or whatever it was these men were? The thought of Falam feeding soup to Safiki's dear *mamada* made him sick. The spark of relief blazed to anger, and he set his eyes on Falam with the fiercest gaze he could muster, as if his eyes could set Falam's robes on fire.

Mufalu looked from Safiki to Falam. "Do you know this boy?"

Falam pulled a chair up to the table. "We care for his grandmother at the house. He is harmless. Show me the book."

The men all sat back down with a clatter of swords and scooting chairs. Mufalu slid the book to Falam, who paused, took a deep and reverent breath, and opened the book to the first page. "It is as I thought. Old *renari*. This might take a while."

"But Padimar said you knew it!" Mufalu said.

"I do know it, *salah*, but I still must translate. And then I must decipher the code."

Mufalu sighed and folded his arms. "Well, get on with it. Word travels fast in Yorsha Doon."

At first the men leaned forward and watched Falam with interest, but as the minutes passed with only a nod or a mumbled, "interesting," or "how strange," from Falam, followed by the scratching of notes on a piece of paper, they grew restless. Some stood and paced the room, fidgeting with their weapons and stroking their beards. Three of the men sat in one shadowy corner and played a game of Miners and Mice with a set of small, colorful stones. Safiki grew bored as well, and he spent his time listening for each of the men's names, learning what he could of them for no reason other than curiosity.

Bukaar, the skinny one with the stringy beard, made stringier by the way he tugged at the strands whenever he was losing at Miners and Mice. Ufarik, the quiet one with the bowed legs and the odd gait. He was always smiling. Zu'udar, who, as far as Safiki could tell, had no teeth. What he lacked in mouth, however, he gained in eye. His eyes bulged and he never blinked, which gave him a look of constant surprise. Then there were Imann, Padimar, Sharaanu, Bahbi, Ramalama Odokh and his brother Adokh. At first Safiki was merely passing the time, but soon he realized that he enjoyed watching the men interact, listening to their murmured jabs at each other, their hushed laughter, their shared memories—and to his surprise, Safiki began to like them. Safiki may as well have been invisible, bound and gagged on the floor as he was, and for perhaps the first time in his life he *wanted* to be seen, to be acknowledged by the men and even welcomed into their companionship. Safiki had to remind himself that these were bad men, that they had kidnapped and wounded him, that they were planning to infiltrate the palace to do Maker knew what.

At last, Falam leaned back from the table. "Mufalu, I think I have something." Mufalu and his men scrambled to the table and waited. "There seems to be a passage beneath the dipping well near the north wall. Someone will have to climb inside, find a black stone, remove it, and activate some sort of mechanism using this code." Falam pointed at a page in the book.

"That looks like no code," Mufalu grunted. "It is a recipe for dag-gerfish chawbry sauce."

Falam smiled. "Yes, but if you turn the book this way," he rotated the book, "and substitute the four old *renari* flimners for the numbers of our modern alphabet, you will see that it is also another word."

Mufalu bent over the book and studied it for a moment. "C . . . O . . . D . . . E. That spells 'code.' What does it mean?"

"I think, Mufalu, it means there is a code."

Unconvinced, Mufalu beckoned his men to inspect the recipe. "What do you say, my friends?"

"I think he is correct," said Bahbi. "It must be a code."

The others agreed.

"Then someone should go and inspect it," Mufalu said, and all the men stood at attention. "Zu'udar. You can see best in the dark. Go, and report back. Hurry."

Zu'udar grinned a toothless grin and bound up the stairs. The men fell back to their conversations and games while Falam continued his study of the book. A short time later, the door opened again and Zu'udar squelched down the stairs dripping wet.

"Well?" said Mufalu.

"Yes. It is a well."

"I know that, you oaf. What did you find?"

"A well, sir."

"*Inside* the well. Did you use the code?"

"Yes, *salah*. I removed the black stone and there were four let-ters carved into the stone, along with four latches." Zu'udar bowed and edged closer to the game of Miners and Mice, glancing from it to Mufalu and back again.

"What were the four letters?" shouted Mufalu.

"E, O, D, and C."

Mufalu stroked his beard, deep in thought. "Maker only knows what that could mean!" He grabbed Falam's collar. "Surely you can do

better than this! What are you *umamri* good for if you cannot decipher recipe books?"

"I triggered them in order of the word CODE, *salah*," said Zu'udar
said over his shoulder as he crouched and rolled the dice.

"And what did you find?"

"A tunnel," Zu'udar said as he moved a blue stone from one part of
the game board to another.

"And?"

"It was too small for me, *salah*. I'm sorry. It's your turn, Odokh."

"Too small." Mufalu kicked a chair, and his men winced. "Falam,
find another way in."

"It could take some time," Falam said.

"We do not have time!"

"I'm sorry. This is an ancient book, and no one knows how many
secrets it holds. This could be the only one, after all." Falam looked at
Safiki. "May I suggest a solution?"

Mufalu sighed and sat down wearily. "What?"

"The boy. Safiki."

"How could a boy translate the book if you cannot?"

"Perhaps the boy could fit in the tunnel. Perhaps he can infiltrate
the palace and open one of the gates."

Mufalu and the rest of his men stopped whatever they were doing
and turned as one to look at Safiki. He nodded and smiled as well as he
could through the gag. Of course, he had no intention of letting these
rogues into the palace, but it would be an easy thing to escape once
they untied him. Mufalu and his men huddled around the table and
discussed the idea in whispers. After a moment they came to an agreement and Bukaar with the stringy beard approached Safiki. He pulled
him to his feet and half-carried him to Mufalu.

The big man leaned down and put his face in Safiki's, studying
his eyes. Safiki could smell his beard. "Can I trust you, boy?" He met
Mufalu's eyes and nodded. Mufalu tugged the gag away. "Say it."

"You can trust me." *You can trust me to run away as soon as I get the chance*, he thought.

Falam approached and said, "Safiki, do you know who these men are?"

Thieves. "No, *salah.*"

"They are Prince Majah's personal guard."

Safiki's eyes bulged almost as wide as Zu'udar's. "Then it is true," Safiki said.

"What is true?" Mufalu asked.

"Roduin has control of the palace. But I was told that all the guards are in the dungeon."

"The rest of them are. We escaped the night Roduin attacked," Mufalu said. "How did you come to know this?"

"A girl. Saana told me."

Mufalu and all of his men chattered with surprise. Shaaranu grabbed Safiki and spun him around. There were tears in his eyes. "She lives? You saw her?" Safiki gulped and told them what had happened all those weeks ago, careful to leave out the fact that he had refused to help her. "She is my niece," said Shaaranu, wiping his cheeks. "My brother is the kitchener."

"Will you help us?" Falam asked gently. "Your grandmother would want you to. You know that."

Safiki could hardly believe his own ears when he said, "I will do whatever you ask."

Minutes later, under the cover of night, Safiki was being lowered into a well to rescue Prince Majah from Roduin the Bloodbrute. With one foot in the bucket and one hand clutching the rope, Safiki lifted the lantern up to the glistening wall of the well and saw where Zu'udar had removed an odd shaped black stone and left it on a small ledge. Inside the opening were the letters

E O D C

each corresponding to a rusty iron latch. Behind him, on the opposite wall of the well, a mossy iron gate had fallen outward, revealing a rough hewn tunnel not even as big around as the basket Safiki had hidden inside earlier that day. He held his breath and listened, but all he heard was an ever-present dripping and the whispers of Mufalu's men far above. He placed the lantern in the tunnel and bellied his way in headfirst. He tried not to think about the bright freedom of the city above as he inched forward, scooting the lantern as far as he could and then squirming toward it again and again. The tunnel soon went from damp to dusty, and little pale skitterbugs that had never seen light crawled over the cobwebby stones. He wasn't sure how long it was before he sensed a slight decline in the tunnel, but his knees and elbows were bruised and raw and he was sweating profusely. After several minutes of the downward slope the tunnel opened onto a vertical shaft that looked like the one he had left behind. This one had no rope, but there were footholds carved into the stone. He worked his way out, careful not to drop the lantern, and peered up into complete darkness. With a heavy sigh, Safiki began the climb, trying not to think about how far he would fall if he slipped. He reached the top at last, and climbed into a small, empty chamber that looked like it hadn't been used in ages. A thick layer of dust covered the floor, and his footprints were the only sign of disturbance. He inspected the low wooden door. Next to the handle was another set of letters:

N E P O

Safiki laughed to himself at how confused Mufalu would have been. He triggered the O, the P, the E, and the N, and heard a satisfying click. Safiki listened with his ear to the door and heard nothing, then carefully turned the handle.

He peeked out onto a wide courtyard under a sky bright with stars, and Safiki was so happy he promised himself he'd never go underground again. His heart lurched when he looked up and realized that this little chamber was a part of the palace. He was standing at the base, and above him rose those magnificent towers he had only ever seen from a distance. He was pleased to discover that it was more, and not less, impressive up close. He slipped out and eased the door shut, standing with his back to it as he scanned the courtyard for movement. When his eyes adjusted, he saw, scattered across the cobblestones, at least fifty figures asleep on the ground. The ones nearest to him were snoring, and he could tell by the rotten odor that some of them, at least, were Grey Fangs. All his life he had wondered what it would be like to enter the palace, and he never would have dreamed it would be like this—climbing through a secret tunnel into a sleeping garden of assassins and monsters. But he felt more excitement than fear, because he knew how to sneak. He just had to do as Mufalu had instructed: avoid being seen by the guards along the top of the wall, get to the corner where the east and south walls met, unlock the door, and let in Mufalu and his men. They would do the rest. He hadn't asked what was supposed to happen next.

Safiki tiptoed past the huddled forms, working his way across to the perimeter where he planned to follow the palace wall to the door. One of the Fangs growled in its sleep as Safiki stepped over its leg and he had to wait until he was certain it was snoring again before he moved on. He finally reached the wall and waited in the shadows, watching Roduin's guards move to and fro, comforted by the fact that all their attention was on the streets outside.

Safiki slinked to the corner where the door was supposed to be, pleased with himself that things had gone so smoothly, when out of the near darkness a voice barked, "Where do you think *you're* going, boy?" Safiki froze, as if by doing so he might become invisible. The voice laughed a grating, wolfish laugh, and Safiki knew that it came from a Grey Fang. "We can see in the dark, you know. I've been watching you.

You're quite an impressive sneak."

Safiki's stomach shriveled. He couldn't see a thing, but he sensed the Fang just a few feet away. "Please, just let me go," Safiki whispered. "I didn't take anything. I'm just trying to get out."

"You'd like me to open this door and let you escape?"

"Yes, sir."

The Fang laughed again. "So you can tell the whole city that Roduin the Bloodbrute is in the palace?"

"I—I don't know what you're talking about."

"Of course you don't." The Fang took a deep, rattling breath. "You're going back to the dungeon with the rest of the court." The Fang leapt out of the shadows with a growl, and Safiki bolted. He felt the scrape of the Fang's claws on his shoulders as he ran back to the well chamber, hopping over the sleeping forms in the courtyard. Then he heard an ear-splitting howl. Every man and Fang in the courtyard sprang up in confusion. It was as if a forest had grown up around him in an instant. Safiki dodged left and right, spinning away from some as they tried to grab him and squirming out of the clammy grips of others. He broke free and reached the door to the well, twisted the handle and—it was locked. By the starlight he could see beside the door another set of letters:

K L N C U O H T D E I T E H O C W

"What?" he shouted. "How am I supposed to—" He jiggled the handle with frustration and threw a wild look over his shoulder at the small army gathering behind him. Many of them were still groggy and confused, but the Grey Fang was shouting, "Get the boy!" Safiki looked up at the sheer wall of the palace and saw just enough cracks in the stonework that he might be able to climb. "Maker help me," he said, and he jumped for the top of the door, placing a toe on the handle and launching himself as high as he could reach. But he found no purchase. He thudded to the ground so hard his teeth clacked together, but he had felt what he was looking for. Just a little below where he had reached was a slot between two stones. As the Fangs and angry men bore down on him he jumped again and slid his fingers into the crack. He found another with his other hand, then another with his toe, and heaved himself higher as the pursuers gathered below. The men shouted and jabbed with their swords while the Fangs jumped and clawed at the wall, but Safiki had managed to climb beyond their reach. He inched his way higher, telling himself all the while that this was no different than climbing any other building, though in truth it could not have been more different. Not only was the face of the palace smoother than most buildings in the city, not only was this wall ten times as high as the highest structure in the Doonlands, but there were monsters and murderers waiting below. All of his attention was aimed upwards. He could see no opening, no ledge, no landing to aim for. The whole of his vision was the spangled heavens and the flat, bluish black of the palace wall that seemed to rise forever. If he had looked a mength to his left, he would have seen a girl peeking out from a narrow window, and would have been much less startled when she said, "It's you!"

Somehow, he didn't fall.

"Saana?" he asked when he had recovered.

"Hurry!"

It was more difficult to climb sideways than up, but soon Safiki reached the window and tumbled in. He collapsed on the floor, dripping with sweat, and lay there staring at the ornate vaulted ceiling of Prince Majah's palace.

"You came for me!" Saana said. She knelt at Safiki's side with one of his hands in both of hers. She was prettier than Safiki remembered—or maybe it was that now she wasn't drenched with well water. She smiled down at him. "I knew you would come. What is your plan?"

"Plan?" Safiki sat up and wiped his forehead. He didn't want to disappoint her, and though he had, in fact, thought of her when he had agreed to sneak into the palace, she wasn't the real reason he was there.

"We have to let the guards—the real guards—in."

"What real guards?"

"Mufalu. Your uncle and the others."

She squealed and stood up. "They're alive! Roduin said they had all been executed!"

"Keep your voice down!"

"We have to let them in," she whispered.

"That's what I've been saying. But we can't. There's a bit of a problem in the courtyard. You may have noticed."

Saana rushed to the window as if she had forgotten what had brought her there in the first place. "This is very bad." She wheeled around and grabbed Safiki's hand again. "Come on. We have to get to the kitchens."

The two children sprinted down a long hallway that was finer than anything Safiki had ever seen. Statues stood guard along the walls, leafy plants flowered in bejeweled pots, paintings adorned every surface, lamps in wall sconces flickered lazily. They raced down a flight of wide, curving stairs and through several enormous rooms whose walls were hung with paintings and tapestries and weaponry, then the dining hall which boasted sheets of fine bright cloths dangling from the domed ceiling. A long table stretched from one end of the room to another, and the remnants of the evening's meal were still scattered on the plates. Saana tugged Safiki through a narrow door that was painted to blend with the wall, and they burst into the kitchen. A thin, weary-looking man stood at a large basin with a towel over one shoulder. He plunged a platter into the water and without turning said, "Did you find the source of all the noise, my dear?"

"Yes, Papi."

The man scrubbed the platter and heaved a sigh. "What was it?"

"It was the boy. The one I told you about."

"I hope he was not captured by the Fangs. They are worse than Roduin's men."

"He was not captured."

Saana's papi stopped scrubbing the platter. He dried his hands on the towel and slowly turned. One of his eyes was swollen and bruised, and his nose was crooked, like it had been broken and had healed badly. But when he smiled Safiki saw that he had Saana's kind face. "Saana told me she met a heroic boy who would some day come and rescue her. I am honored to meet you. What is your name?"

Safiki looked at the floor. "That doesn't matter."

"Fine. You may call me Rumii. Or Saana's papi. Or you may call me the finest kitchener in Yorsha Doon, and you would be telling the truth. Whatever you call me, we need to hide you. Get in the kettle, quick."

"The kettle?"

"Now." Rumii lifted Safiki onto the counter and shoved him into a kettle big enough to sleep in. Thank the Maker, it was empty but for a few inches of cold broth. The top of the pot clanged overhead and Safiki once again found himself in a dark, cramped place. Before he had time to grumble, however, angry voices filled the room.

"Have you seen a boy?" boomed an angry voice.

"No, *salah* Roduin," answered Saana's father. *Roduin the Blood-brute*! The top of the kettle came off and the cook shook salt and pepper all over Safiki. "I am only a cook. As you can see, *salah*, my daughter and I are preparing tomorrow's soup. The palace is large, and a boy could be many places other than here." Safiki was battered and poked by a long wooden spoon while Rumii pretended to stir the soup. Then he replaced the lid.

"I know that, kitchener. Do not tell me things I already know." There was a crash, and a whimper from Saana. "If you see any sign of the boy and you say nothing, your daughter will pay for it."

"What would you like for breakfast, *salah*?" said Rumii quietly.

"Henmeat. And toast."

Safiki heard the door shut, and the lid of the kettle came off. He climbed out as quietly as he could, brushing salt and pepper out of his hair. Saana stood near the wall with tears running down her cheeks. Her father's lip was bleeding. He wiped away the blood with the towel, sat wearily on a stool beside the great oven, and looked at Safiki. "Now tell me, young man, how you got inside." Safiki explained how *Feasting in the Woes* had been discovered and Rumii's eyes widened. "Amagri's lost recipes! By the Maker, the secret codes are only half of the treasure of that book!" When Safiki told him about Mufalu and the rest of the guard, Rumii stood up and paced the kitchen. "We must find a way to let them in. The treasure stores are nearly depleted, and there is no telling what Roduin will do with us then. They call him the Bloodbrute for a reason."

"He could sneak into the dungeon and free Prince Majah and the court," Saana said.

"Yes. That's good, Saana dear! And you can show him the way. And even if the boy is captured, he will distract Roduin's men and then perhaps I can make it to the door in the outer wall." Rumii rubbed his hands together. "Mufalu and his men are great warriors, and they will catch Roduin by surprise. Even if one of us fails, the other stands a chance. It is like a good recipe. Sometimes the best meals are discovered when the cook improvises upon a mistake. But we must hurry. Soon the pot is going to boil over." Rumii hugged his daughter tightly and looked into her eyes. "Tonight, my girl, we will free your mother and sister." He bowed to Safiki. "Your courage is great, young man, whatever your name is. Maker bless your sneakery with swift and silent feet."

Safiki blushed and felt again the odd compulsion to tell them his name. But the moment passed. "Thank you, *salah*. I will try."

Saana peeked through the kitchen door, beckoned to Safiki, and sped away with him at her heels. They wound through the corridors of the palace, stopping at every doorway to listen before slipping through the next room. Safiki was utterly lost. It was like wandering a new district of the city except he had no sky, no palace spire to tell him which direction he was going. Twice they heard voices and had to hide beneath a table or behind a frondy plant while Grey Fangs and vicious looking men marched past them. Some of the rooms were torn apart as if they had just been searched. Soon they came to another, smaller kitchen with a narrow stair in the back, and Saana paused.

"These stairs lead to the dungeon. I don't know where the keys are, or how to open the doors, or how many guards are posted."

"Stay here," Safiki said with a smile. "Warn me if someone is coming."

He glided down the steps without a sound, like a ghost haunting the passageway. The ceiling was low and smooth, and reflected the faint glow of torchlight somewhere below. As he drew nearer he smelled the bitter musk of Grey Fangs and his heart beat so hard that he was afraid they might hear it. At the bottom of the steps was a long corridor with torches spaced along the walls between barred cells. The commotion in the courtyard had apparently not reached the dungeons because the three Grey Fangs meant to guard the prisoners were curled up on the floor at the far end, sleeping like monstrous puppies. Safiki edged out into the passageway and crept closer to the Fangs, hoping to spot a lever or a key or another series of latches that might release the prisoners. He passed the first cell and saw several people sleeping on the floor. The second cell held the same. The third cell on his right, however, was empty but for one figure chained to the wall. Safiki peered inside and saw that it was a young man, naked to the waist and skinnier than anyone he had ever seen. His wrists were shackled to the wall so that his arms were outspread, which made his ribs protrude like cages.

"Prince Majah?" Safiki whispered with a glance at the sleeping Fangs.

The figure stirred and struggled to raise his head. Dark locks of ratty hair hung around a gaunt face. "*Help me.*"

"Are you the prince?" Safiki asked, though he knew somehow that it was.

His voice was ragged and barely audible. "*Yes.*"

Safiki bowed his head without intending to, and when he looked up the prince's head hung low and motionless again. "I'm here to help you, *salah*. But I don't know how. Tell me what to do." There was no reply, but the bony ribcage expanded with each breath. "Prince Majah, *please!*"

"The . . . code . . . "

"What code? Where is it?"

Prince Majah's head swung in the direction of the Fangs at the end of the corridor. "In the floor. Under . . . the Fangs."

"But what's the code?"

"Under the . . . Fangs."

"The code, *salah*!"

"Don't . . . know."

The prince was unconscious. Safiki looked back down the corridor and realized that several of the prisoners had awoken and were watching him with desperate, sunken eyes. He held a finger to his lips and motioned for them to wait, then tiptoed up the stairs to where Saana waited.

"I saw the prince."

"He is alive?"

"For now. Saana, I need you to draw the Fangs away. Can you do it? Will you be all right?" She nodded hesitantly. "I'll hide here. Get them to chase you and I'll free the prisoners." Safiki hid behind a cabinet and waved her down the stairs. A moment later he heard her shout, followed by the growls and howls of the Fangs, and then she burst through the door with the wolves at her heels. It had worked perfectly. Safiki descended again and found the prisoners awake and all speaking to him at once. Where the Fangs had been sleeping the stones were warm and the air was rank, so Safiki had to hold his breath as he inspected the floor. A rusty iron ring no bigger than a coin was bolted to one of the stones. He hooked it with his finger, lifted it, and brushed the spider webs away from yet another set of latches and letters.

D M O E R E F

"Help us!" the prisoners shouted.

"We haven't eaten for days!"

"Please, let us out!"

"I'm trying to," Safiki snapped. "But I don't know the code!"

MORE FED? The prisoners were hungry, so it made a weird kind of sense. He flipped the triggers and tried one of the doors, but nothing happened. He had to think, but the people were clamoring and he felt that at any moment the Fangs, or the assassins, or Roduin the Blood-brute himself would appear.

RED FOME? Safiki shook his head. FEED MOR?

"Please!" shouted a woman in the nearest cell. "Set us free."

Safiki looked at the letters again and laughed. He triggered them in the correct order, heard a wonderful metallic clank, then every door in the dungeon swung open with a triumphant creak. Men, women, and children poured out of the cells and nearly crushed Safiki with hugs.

"Listen! Mufalu and his men are alive!" he shouted. "Rumii is trying to let them in through the outer wall. If any of you can fight, join him in the courtyard. Hurry!"

"Come on!" shouted one of the men, and, haggard though they were, a small army of the prince's true guard ran up the stairs. Safiki pushed through those who remained and ran to the prince's cell. The unlocked shackles dangled from the wall, and he lay on the floor like a pile of sticks. Safiki knelt at his side and lifted his head while the rest of the court crowded into the cell.

"Prince Majah, you are free."

"Thank you . . . my friend." The prince smiled at him. "What is your name?"

Safiki did not hesitate. He felt no desire to disappear, no desire to run. He was, for the first time, more afraid of being alone than of being known. "Safiki. My name is Safiki."

Later, Saana told Safiki that by the time her father had reached the courtyard, it was empty of Roduin's fighters and Fangs. He let Mufalu and his men through the wall but there was no one for them to fight. And by the time the prisoners from the dungeon had streamed through the palace with whatever weapons they could find, the palace was empty, too. Roduin the Bloodbrute was gone, along with whatever loot was left. No one knew how he had infiltrated the palace in the first place, and no one knew how he had escaped. Even the Fangs that had pursued Saana, once they realized that the rest of their gang was missing, gave up the chase and scattered into the secret bowels of the palace, never to be seen again.

The palace came immediately to life, with guards scouring every room for possible stragglers, members of the court returning to their chambers after a year of captivity, servants cleaning the mess that Roduin had left behind. The treasure stores had been plundered, but no one seemed concerned about it. There was food, and freedom, and life once again. As the sun rose, Safiki found Saana and her family in the kitchen preparing a broth for Prince Majah. Saana squeezed him and whispered, "I knew you would come."

"He wants to see you," Rumii said. "Come with me." He handed Safiki a carafe of water, loaded a tray with a bowl of soup and a loaf of bread, then led the boy up many flights of stairs to the prince's chambers.

Prince Majah lay in a large, canopied bed in the center of the room. The drapes of the tall windows were drawn so that the morning light streamed through and illuminated the bright blues and yellows of the lush carpet. Mufalu, along with Zu'udar, Bukaar, Ufarik, Imann,

Sharaanu, Bahbi, Ramalama, and the brothers Adokh and Odokh, stood at the perimeter of the chamber, hands resting on the pommels of their scimitars. They smiled proudly at Safiki, and Mufalu saluted him. The prince sat up with great effort and thanked Rumii for the soup, then he beckoned Safiki closer. Even these few hours later, the prince looked healthier. The bejeweled copy of *Feasting in the Woes* sat in his lap.

"Welcome, Safiki," he said, and the boy knelt.

"Rise, my friend, and come closer." Safiki approached the bedside. The prince sipped a spoonful of the soup and wiped the corners of his mouth. "If not for you, we might have been killed by Roduin, or left to rot. Mufalu says you are the one who found the book."

"Your majesty," Safiki said, "I only helped the fat man."

Prince Majah looked confused. "Of whom do you speak?"

"A stranger. Oskar, from Ban Rona. He said he was bringing the book to you."

The prince laughed. "So he came! He wrote to me two years ago with the most magnificent tale of the defeat of Gnag the Nameless and the restoration of Anniera. Marvelous things have been happening in the far corners of Aerwiar. He said he had discovered *Feasting in the Woes* during the repair of Ban Rona's Great Library. I wondered if he was telling the truth. Now I see the Maker's hand in all this."

"All I knew, *salah*, was that he needed help. He said he trusted me."

"And he was right to do so." The prince studied Safiki's face, then looked at his ragged clothes. Safiki felt underdressed and shamefully exposed to be the thieving street child that he was. "Where do you live?"

"Yorsha Doon, your majesty."

The prince laughed again. "Yes, but where?"

Safiki stared at his bare feet and shrugged. "Everywhere, *salah*."

After a moment, the prince stretched out his hand to the boy and made a sign in the air which caused Mufalu and his men to drop to one knee. Safiki did likewise. In a formal voice with which only princes truly know how to speak, Prince Majah declared, "I grant Safiki of Yorsha Doon full access to my palace whenever he wishes it. He shall never lack a bed, or a meal, or the friendship of the court. From this day hence, Safiki is, and ever shall be, my friend."

Safiki wiped his eyes and stood. "Thank you, *salah*." He was overwhelmed, and could think of nothing else to say, which seemed to please the prince.

"You shall never need to steal again. Do you understand?"

"Yes." Safiki struggled to meet the prince's eyes.

"Now is there anything you want? You have but to ask."

Later that morning, Safiki stood outside the *umamri* house and waited for a family of trolls to pass before leaping from the top of a cart to the edge of the awning. He pulled himself up, crawled onto the second story ledge, and hopped through his grandmother's window. He expected to have to wake her. What he didn't expect was to find a very large man with spectacles sitting beside her bed. Oskar held a plate of soft, wet bread in one hand and was feeding pieces one by one to the old woman. Next to him was a makeshift desk piled with papers, along with an ink bottle and a quill.

"My boy!" said the old woman, turning her blind eyes his direction.

When Oskar saw the satchel slung over Safiki's shoulder he looked like he might faint with relief. "Good gracious grobblins!" Oskar said. "Safiki, I feared I'd never see you again."

"Don't worry," Safiki said with a wink, patting the satchel. "I brought you some plumyums, Mamada." Safiki reached into the satchel and handed them over. His grandmother spat the bread onto the floor, clapped like a little girl and, to Oskar's horror, wrenched out her bottom tooth and began cutting the plumyums into pieces.

"Thank you, dear one!" she said. "I've been telling Oskar here all about your sweet mami and papi, and how they used to sneak onto the slave ships of the Pirates of Symia to free the prisoners, and how that awful Captain Scarjaw caught them and killed them both when you were little. Have I ever told you about them? Thank you for the plumyums."

"It's a wonderful story," Oskar said, patting the stack of pages. "Your parents were remarkable. It's all here."

Safiki was stunned. Suddenly he wanted nothing more than to gather up those pages, climb onto a rooftop, and read every word. "This is for you," he said to Oskar, handing him the satchel.

With trembling fingers, Oskar removed the book and gasped with confused delight. "*Tales of the Battles of the Wars of the Woes of Shreve of Dang of Aerwiar*! But how did you—I mean, where did you . . . ?"

"The prince sent it with his best wishes. And he thanks you for *Feasting in the Woes*. He says it has already been most useful."

"Oh, I knew it!" Oskar giggled. "The recipes are quite legendary, are they not?" The old man opened his new book to the first page and he slumped back in his chair with awe. "He *signed* it. To me! The prince of Yorsha Doon autographed the first edition of his personal copy of *Tales of the Battles of the Wars of the Woes of Shreve of Dang of Aerwiar*. For me!" He adjusted his spectacles and read, "'For Oskar N. Reteep. I look forward to reading your history of the Wingfeather Wars upon its publication. Are the stories true?' Signed, 'Prince Majah of Yorsha Doon.'"

Safiki was thinking of his parents as he watched his grandmother eating her fruit, so he didn't actually see the moment when Oskar fainted. But when he heard the thud and looked, the old bookseller was splayed on the floor with his eyes closed and his spectacles askew. The old book rested on his belly and he wore a rapturous smile.

"Safiki," the old woman said between slurps, "I won't always be here to love you, you know. Will you be all right? Where will you live?

Who will care for you?"

"It is a good question," said another voice. Falam stood in the doorway. "What will you do, Safiki? You need a home."

"Yorsha Doon is my home," Safiki said. He looked out the window at the palace spires and smiled. "All of it."

THE WOOING
OF SOPHELIA STUPE

Written by Jennifer Trafton
Illustration by John Hendrix

A letter from Ollister B. Pembrick,
dated the 5th day of Sixmoon, Year 222, Third Epoch

To the illustrious sirs and madams of Annieran University Press, formerly known as Graff Publishing, mysteriously transported from the Green Hollows to the Shining Isle sometime between the writing and the printing of my book *The Inexhaustive Creaturepedia: Skreean Edition*, and particularly to my editor Thaddeus Glapp, though you did not bother to read the manuscript the first time and can hardly be expected to read this letter (professional mockery! rudeness! but no matter), and most especially to the generous donors who allow the Press to continue printing books at all, though in latter times it has been forced to print primarily dog food labels in order to avoid insolvency in these illiterate days of Dang—

Greetings, and forewarnings! This promised report of my recent travels is fraught with such heartbreak and, yea, toebreak, that even I, partly-maimed, half-gobbled, and ferociously-nibbled as I am, have never known its equal in tragedy. But this tragedy is mixed with an enormous dollop of hope and even unexpected pecuniary blessings (that is, a fat purse of coins) and so I send them to you—coins, hope, and tragedy, sealed in a single envelope—with trust that you will greet my story, and my subsequent plea, with your fullest sympathy and aid.

And so to my tale.

The circumstances that sent me on my current journey hardly bear repeating (but nevertheless! I repeat!). After years of calamitous exploration on foreign shores, engaged in lengthy scientific sketchery and at repeated peril to my innards, not to mention my outards, I enjoyed the relative peace of my hometown in Anniera while I prepared the manuscript of my bestiary. But the quiet life of a scribe and occasional greengrocer soon galled my very gizzards. How I longed once again for adventure (frenetical!), discovery (frumious!), disguisery (frolicking!), and tiny deluded umbrellas (frivolous!). How oft my thoughts did fly to the unexplored Jungles of Plontst, the undocumented trollish lands, the unsketched animals still waiting to be espied! It was therefore with intense nail-biting anticipation that I awaited the publication of my first *Creaturepedia*, knowing that any future explorations and *Creatupediae* were dependent upon its immediate success. Alas, my nails were bitten in vain.

The graceful green volume, while indibnibly eruditious in content and pulchritudinous in form, entered the world like a mustachioed thwap, preened to near-perfection only to find that no admirers were readily available. (None except my Aunt Sewsin, that is, but aunts are notoriously unreliable judges of mustaches or of literature.) I say "preened to *near*-perfection" because, as you know well (since I have repeatedly pointed it out, to no avail), a stenchiful and ill-placed typographical error mars the second page, inserted no doubt by a mathematically blundering copyeditor. Though the book was *in fact* published in the year 221 of the Third Epoch, you have unfortunately broadcast to its readers the false impression that it was published several centuries hence—namely, 342 of the *Fourth* Epoch, which fateful and far-off year I pray I will not live long enough to see. I am afraid many potential customers concluded that, since the book was apparently *published* in the future, they had no need to *read* it until the future. Such are the career-destroying implications of an ill-placed typographical error.

But I am not so ungenerous as to place *all* of the blame for the *Creaturepedia*'s unpopularity on the recipients of this present letter. Indeed, I could hardly rely upon your own generosity (so necessary now!) if I did.

For in truth, I had vastly underestimated the popularity of my Uncle Bahb, otherwise known as The Gobbled. I had further underestimated the wanderlust-killing effect his grisly fate would have on the Occasional Greengrocer's Alliance and their friends, relatives, customers, suppliers, and fan clubs across the length and breadth of Dang. (It was, of course, Uncle Bahb's death by blazzrod that inspired me to research and write the *Creaturepedia* in the first place, so that I could help other greengrocers, and indeed non-grocerous readers as well, to avoid being begobbled on future vegetationary expeditions. Of which, I'm told, there will now be none.) I had also vastly *over*estimated the number of people with the time and leisure to read books in the midst of daily skirmishes with the unscrupulous pirates of the Symian Straits—those mortal enemies of the peace of Anniera and the Green Hollows.

In short, devoted fans of Skreean zoology are regrettably few on our side of the Dark Sea of Darkness, where marauding buccaneers are plentiful and adventurous grocers are dead.

And so, laden with unsold books and with (vainglorious, I admit!) dreams of fame and fortune in kindlier climes, to Skree I sailed.

My previous travels in Skree had been confined mainly to the forests, the wildlands, the cliffs, the rivers, the caves, the burrows, the gullies, the sinkholes, the mudbanks, and the hovels where dwell the creepers, crawlers, squatters, chewers, gnawers, etc. that fill the pages of my

Creaturepedia. I had met few humans during that time except some lazy, burping soldiers, the kidnappish Stranders, and more than one comely infirmary nurse who healed my broken limbs and broke my lonely heart. It was therefore with some trepidation (for I am a bashful man without my sketchpad) that I this time turned my face towards those bepeopled regions (noisy! chatterous!) I had hitherto avoided.

At first, what wonder was mine! For Skree is in the grip of such a thriving artistocracy that one cannot throw a stone without hitting a poet, a painter, a storyspinner, or a songmaker. Indeed, I tried several times, and nearly nockled the eye out of a passing accordionist with my pebble.

Believe it or believe it not, my rude and doubting editor: there is a publisher on nearly every street corner (aye, the rumors are true!), printing not merely dog food labels but cartloads and cartloads of shiny new books, quite as pulchritudinous (though not nearly as eruditious) as my own. In fact, there are so many volumes that people have begun gathering them into *shops*, much like a greengrocery, except with shelves of literature instead of bins of totatoes. It is quite marvelous! I chortled to myself: What good fortune! What a blappy mood I am in! If there is any place in all of Aerwiar where my literary industry and eloquence will be aptly appreciated and suitably repaid, it is surely here in Skree.

Oh, how quickly hopes are dashed! How disastrously fate flops upon the noggin of the naive dreamer!

But I leap ahead of my tale.

My first destination, after I had spent several days wandering in a pleasureful haze, was the little town of Glipwood. I had an old friend there (old in acquaintance, though young in years). Edd Helmer was an indispensable help when I was preparing to explore the nearby Glipwood Forest years ago. Recently, he had written to me indicating that he had personally arranged a signature affixation ceremony for my *Creaturepedia* at the new book shop in Glipwood.

When I arrived, however, Edd was nowhere to be found. What was to be found was the lofty wooden skeleton of a shop-to-be, with carpenters squatting on the roof and sawdust raining down from their hammering hammers. A sign above the doorless doorframe said "Books & Crannies," but there seemed to be far more crannies than books.

A side-whiskered man was climbing through an empty window frame while trying not to drop a tall stack of leather-bound volumes. He stopped when he saw me standing there with my little wooden cart of *Creatupediae*. "Can I help you?" he said.

"Good sir," I answered cheerfully, "you *can* help me, but more importantly, I believe I can help *you*. I am Ollister B. Pembrick."

The shopkeeper (as I assumed he was) stared back at me with polite befuddlement. The poor fellow was evidently highly allergic to carpenters, for his eyes were so pitifully puffish, his visage so oozily runny, that he reminded me of the miserable snottamus I once happened upon in the Dolgrannon Canyon. He put the pile of books down, tore out a page of *A Comprehensive History of Sad, Sad Songs*, and sneezed into it.

Ever-so-slightly daunted, I continued, "I am the author of the *Inexhaustive Creaturepedia* . . ."

"Ah, you've written a *book*," cooed the shopkeeper, somewhat sniffingly. "Well done."

I once had a grandfather, as many do. "Why, Ollie-wolly," he would say when I brought him early samples of my sketchery, "did you dwaw a wittle kitty cat? It's a cutesy-wootsy wittle kitty cat, yes it is! Can you dwaw a doggy-woggy now? That's a good boy."

The shopkeeper's words can be roughly translated into grandfatherese thusly: *Awwww, you wote a cutesy-wootsy wittle booky-wooky. Good boy.* He reached up and patted my head. "Keep on writing! Keep your chin up! Everyone has to start somewhere."

This is indibnibly true. Everyone *does* have to start somewhere. I started in the dry and dutiful village of Pennybridge, Anniera, only to find myself later trapped in the squelchy and flappulous mouth of a bumpy digtoad (sticky!). I started in the golden-haired glow of youth only to grow prematurely grey from the strain of being quilled, munched, nibbled, pocked, snicked, poisoned, impaled, assaulted, enswelled, engrowled, and betrayed (squeeblinly!). I started with two hands, two elbows, two feet, and ten toes, only to be de-handed, de-elbowed, de-footed, and de-toed. Yes, I started well, and I have injuriously continued. But I will gladly keep my chin up, as long as I am allowed to keep my chin.

"I was under the impression—" I started. "I had expected—" I stuttered. "My dear friend Edd Helmer made it quite clear that he had spoken to you about—" One of the carpenters cursed far above our heads, and the long-suffering owner of Books & Crannies glanced upwards in quiet despair. In the nick of time I remembered the best method for ingratiating oneself to a lachrymose snottamus, and (I hoped!) a leaky-nosed shopkeeper: sympathy. Namely, in this case, a large, well-washed handkerchief, which I pulled out of my pocket and handed to him. "I am here to present my recently published work to the fine community of Glipwood and to affix my signature to any purchases."

The shopkeeper grabbed the handkerchief gratefully and blew his nose into it. "Ahhhhh, I do apologize. What was your name again?"

"Ollister Bahbert Pembrick, esq., the Partly-Maimed, Master of Disguisery, President of the Occasional Greengrocers Alliance of—"

"Pembroke, Pembronk, Pembrelly . . . Are you sure your name isn't Ponkbelly? We do indeed have several authors here today for the purposes of signature affixation, but I could have sworn one of them was named Ponkbelly. Well, no matter. I don't suppose you would mind sitting on the ground if he shows up? I'm told he's quite a favorite around here."

I assured him that, of course, if an *important* author arrived, I would not mind at all giving up my comfortable seat in favor of a damp corner of the bare earth amidst the sawdust and bent nails and swarming nittleflug nests. After all, I'm a naturalist, and I only have three and a half toes left. I've endured far worse.

Sneezing bountiful sneezes, my phlegmatical host led me through the forest of wooden beams and half-built bookshelves to a room at the far end of the bookshop, where a sizeable crowd was gathered. At his direction I took an empty seat at a long table. A man and a woman were already bent over several huge piles of books, affixing their signatures with great aplomb while eager customers awaited with handfuls of coins.

In my short acquaintance with other authors, I've determined that, as a species, they fall somewhere between the jovial saggy hound (affectionately stretchy! prone to itching!) and the strong, lumbering tahala (persevering! competitive! distractible by toys!). At the far end of the table, the tahala variety of author was represented by a young woman with flame-colored hair and a determined jaw whose books were apparently well spiced with popular pirate yarns. An even longer line of customers stretched out before the saggy-houndish author sitting next to me, whose large and colorful book was primarily filled with drawings of kittens inspired by the feline spires of Palace Torr in Torrboro. Indeed it was the cutesy-wootsiest wittle kitty cat booky-wooky you've ever seen, and I swear to you on Uncle Bahb's grave that the author himself was the spitting image of my grandfather, and smelled of a similar beanish smell.

I am perhaps more hortubinous than the common species of author, but in any event, when I unveiled my own long-traveled *Creaturepedia* before the crowd, the effect was immediate and damperific. Oh, woe! Grubby fingers grubbled the covers, rovering eyes roamed the pages, and hecklish mouths heckled so fecklishly I could hardly insert a courteous word of my own.

"Is this a pirate book too? I like pirate books."

"Well, I do mention pirates on page 10, but—" I began.

"It's another pirate book! Blaggert, come see the new pirate book!"

"It is *not* a pirate book, I'm afraid, but—" I began again.

"It just looks like *information* to me. What fun is *information*? I like a good gut-ripping story, myself."

"Hey. The second page says this book was published in the *future*. Why should I read it *now*? I'm a busy man!"

"Everyone knows there's no such thing as a raggant, or a tricorn. Is this a work of fiction?"

"Bumpy digtoad . . . gargan rockroach . . . limberwolf . . . these aren't even living creatures. These are *extinct*. No one has seen a quill diggle in, well, an eternity!"

"They are most definitely *not* extinct!" I spluttered. "I myself encountered the quill diggle's squishy countenance not two autumns ago. I escaped unscathed, but I assure you my shin skin did not!"

"Here's a bright idea: if you don't want your shins to be scathed by diggle quills, *stay inside*."

"Why do I need to know about horned hounds and toothy cows when the rangers and hunters take care of them all for us?"

"Hear, hear! The only interesting flabbit is a *dead* flabbit."

(You must imagine this harassment going on for quite some time, patient readers, but I will spare you most of the woeful utterances. The point is this: I discovered, to my surprise and aghastitude, that these artistocratic Skreean folks, in their recent years of peace, prosperity, poetry, publishing, and accordion playing, had all but forgotten the very creatures that once plagued their vegetable gardens and haunted their daydreams. So enthralled had I been with exploring sticky sinkholes and treacherous hovels, I never realized that the very citizens I'd worked so hard to preserve unmunched had given no thought at all to the possibility of bemunchedness. As the heckling grew, so did my aghastled state of mind.)

"You should write more about kittens. What's not to like about a kitten? Why didn't you include a kitten in your *Creaturepedia*? People care about kittens, not about fazzlenubblewhatevers."

"Your words are too long, but your drawings are so pretty. Have you ever considered making greeting cards? Like, maybe this cute little tailhanded thwap fellow could be holding a sign with his tail that said, 'Missing You,' with hearts around it. You'd make *so* much money!"

"Have I ever considered?" I spat. "Have I have ever considered?" I choked.

My positude was conquered at last. The indignity of expecting to be expected and then unexpectedly not being so, of being head-patted like a grandchild, of being fecklishly heckled by pirate-lovers and kitten-lovers, all left me with no choice. I proceeded to spontificate with much gestural vexation.

"Have *you* ever considered that your heroic rangers and hunters might one day fall asleep, or slip into laziness, or otherwise fail in their duties? Have you ever considered that, loving your own lovely creations so much, you have shut your eyes to the Maker's makings in all of their flappulant glory and, sometimes, their twisted corruption? You are a continent of gulpswallows, poofishly beautiful yet oblivious to the dangers besetting you on all sides! You are a people entirely without fear. My Uncle Bahb had no fear. My Uncle Bahb was gobbled. Hence goeth the fearless. Your soldiers think themselves so invincible they've taken up *knitting*! You go home to your dinners imagining you are the only beings in Aerwiar with teeth. But hearken to Ollister B. Pembrick, lest someday you yourselves be dinner!"

At this highly inopportune moment, one of the carpenters cried out in warning and a massive beam began to wobble loose from the ceiling. The crowd screamed, I leaped out of my chair, and the wooden beast splatted squarely and agonizingly upon my left foot, shattering three of my three-and-a-half remaining toes.

The shopkeeper reappeared stricken with horror, then with relief. "Oh, thank the Maker! I forgot it was only *you* sitting there. I thought the beam had fallen upon Mr. Ponkbelly."

There are many things that might have occurred in the wake of this lamentable incident, but the one thing that did occur was the very thing I did not see coming.

I did not see *her* coming. Not until the crowd parted silently, almost reverently, and she approached the table in a gown of pale chartreuse. Behind her walked three (scrupulously!) well-dressed and well-mannered children—a girl and two boys.

She was the Lone Fendril, or as close as a human being has e'er come to impersonating that majestic and elusive bird. With the glidingest of movements she glode, like the queenliest of queens, and she seemed not to notice the sad deference paid to her by the other townspeople, or the fact that their eyes averted themselves from her face so as not to appear to espy it.

But I did espy. It was a face like a cratered moon, or a furrowed field, or a quill-scriven shin. Its age was beyond guessing, for the pits that riddled its surface and the deep grooves that criss-crossed its curves had not been placed there by years, but by a sorrow that leaves its scars behind.

The fendrilady picked up each book on the table, thoughtfully balancing it on the palm of her hand as if measuring its weight—first the pirate book of the flame-haired woman, then the kitten book of the saggy hound, then my much-heckled *Creaturepedia*. Finally, she turned to me and held out a bag of coins. "Eight, please." When I did not immediately step forward (for I was still besplatted and affixed to the ground, not to mentioned shocked speechless), she laid the money on the table and pick up the books herself. "Thank you. They are exactly the right size and shape for our posture practice," she said sweetly.

And then she smiled.

I could not have moved even if a mere feather were crushing my foot.

The fendrilady placed two Creaturepediae atop the girl's head, two atop the short boy's head, two atop the tall boy's head, and two atop her own. Then the four unlikely customers with their unlikely hats turned, with perfect poise, and disappeared once more into the crowd.

When they were gone, the author of the kitten book leaned toward me and whispered, "That was Sophelia Stupe, poor lass. Taken with the direful turkeypox as a tot and nearly perished along with her unfortunate mother. Her face never recovered, nor did her old papa's heart. They live up at Anklejelly Manor where she runs a Betterment School for Unpolished Children, which is all she'll ever do, I 'spect, unless she marries a blind feller who can't see the face he's a-kissin.'"

You might expect, persevering readers of this letter, that after all of the disappointment of the day, the use of my precious bestiary for the purposes of correct posturing would be the last straw of disgrace. You might expect that I would despise the scars of another, as painful reminders of my own. You might also expect that I would care about nothing more at that moment than extracting my broken toes from the weight of the fallen beam.

But if you expect such things, you vastly underestimate the beauty of a dignified smile in the face of suffering. I felt as if I had beheld an unearthly vision (illuminous!) right there in the ill-built innards of the new Glipwood greengrocery for literature. And no matter for what purpose, this unearthly vision in pale chartreuse had bought *eight* of my books.

In short, I was undone.

There are those who are lucky enough to find someone to love in this world. There are also those who are lucky enough to lay hands upon the plappy flesh of a cave blat while flootching through a pitch-black creek.

I am the second kind of lucky.

You may recall from my book, or you may not recall, since at least one of you didn't bother to read it, that I am tragically acquainted with the grief of thwarted romance. There was the lovely Dugtown lass who, alas, objected to my occasional stenchious aroma. There was the Kimeran maiden who could not follow me in my quest to espy a snickbuzzard's belly button. There was the Fithyhoopian nurse, and the Erwailian lover of fine poetry (though not thwapperflies). But the more I have been nibbled and gobbled and munched and maimed and scarred, the rarer have been those amorous glances in my direction.

How impossible, how unfair, how heart-sundering is the choice between a lovesome life of domesticity and a lonesome life of adventure! between a pair of fair eyes and a promise of fairer skies! between the mysteries in the soul of a beamish woman and the mysteries in the sole of a beastish foot! I am a wanderer, a sketcher, a seeker of the strange, the streaked, the squawking, and the squillious. I have neither the time nor the toes left to pomple a waglis, or a cockledrop, or a waltzyhoop, or any other kind of dance, with a wifely one.

For all of these reasons I endeavored to banish the image of Sophelia Stupe from my mind. Yet I couldn't! Yet I tried again. Yet I failed!

The morning after my dilapidatious debut in Glipwood, I tarried a while in my room at the town's Only Inn, uncertain of my course. The signature affixation ceremony was over, though a stack of *Creaturepediae* was still at the bookshop in case there was any change of heart or sudden outburst of zoological passion amongst the hecklers. My broken digits were swaddled in bandages, and I had found a stout branch from a plumyum tree to use as a cane. I needed to speak with my friend Edd Helmer, for in the same letter in which he had invited me to Glipwood, he had also hinted about a new concoction he'd cooked up that would help me greatly in my expeditions. But he was still missing (mysteriously!). His shop next to the Shipshape Tavern was closed up, with an assortment of signs hanging on the locked door:

Edd Helmer, apothecary: OUT

Edd Helmer, dentist: GONE TO LUNCH

Edd Helmer, fishmonger: WILL RETURN SOON

Edd Helmer, wedding officiant: COME BACK TOMORROW

Edd Helmer, boot salesman: THOSE GABNUBBABLE PIRATES

Though I was unsure what this last signage signified, it was clear I would not see Edd today.

Meanwhile the Only Inn was filling up quickly as travelers were pouring into Glipwood for some sort of festival that, as far as I could tell, involved painted faces, dueling accordions, and elaborately dressed farm animals. I admit I did not much care what fashion Skreeans preferred for their hens, since my mind was distracted by quite another dress, of a certain pale chartreuse hue.

If only I could see her once more! If only I could make a sketch of her smiling face and carry it with me in a concealed pocket next to my heart, to give me courage and joy in the midst of future travails and travels! I had brought no sketchpad or quill with me, but my eyes happened upon the bill for my room, blank on one side, and a stub of pencil (remarkable Skreean invention!). I pocketed both thoughtfully.

Then a commotion in the street drew me to the window. Two men were struggling to steady an enormous, unwieldy cart full of topiaries. The tall bushy plants were expertly pruned into the shapes of laughing soldiers, frolicking fiddlers, and fruit-laden donkeys, all so lifelike yet so green they could have passed for a company of seasick travelers on a lurching vessel.

"Gentlelike, you dumblustering flod!" cried one of the men as the cart stumbled over a pebble in the road. "Stop doinklin' about! These here got to make it to Anklejelly Manor without a single squibblin' leafsplat. Sir Brimney Stupe *deploores* an imperfectly leafed topithingamigary."

Oh, Maker-sent inspiration! Oh, gladful gush of pruning!

And that is how I, Ollister B. Pembrick, Master of Disguisery, arrived at Anklejelly Manor later that morning in the perfect likeness of a perfectly leafed topiary.

My disguise worked to perfection. I was carried, along with the rest of the topiary delivery, into the great hall of Anklejelly Manor and set in a corner beside some statues without any arms or legs, which interested me exceedingly. (The Manor itself did not interest me exceedingly, for I have never been one to go blappy over architectural grandiosity. It smelled of clamcurdle biscuits and chamberpots. It was, in short, a house that dearly wanted to grow a curly mustache.)

I quickly deduced that the great hall was the home of Sophelia Stupe's Betterment School for Unpolished Children, for there was Sophelia herself in the process of bettering a dozen children in various states of polishment. She was wearing a different (but equally comely!) pale chartreuse gown, and her hair, nearly as pale as her gown (like the glistening underbelly of a baby sea dragon!), was swept up into a regalish thingamapoof away from the puckered and pocked ruin of her (adorable!) face. I quelled the flutterings of my heart.

"Nikledos! Dimtree! Artemy!" she called to the two boys and the girl who had accompanied her to the bookshop. They were still wearing their *Creaturepedia* hats as they paced slowly back and forth across the room. "Noses high, shoulders back, spine strong! Never slouch, my dears. Never. Slouching is for those ashamed of who they are. But you are the Maker's little sculptures, and he has chiseled your chins to greet the world with joy." Elsewhere in the great hall, children practiced patiently cutting henmeat with silver forks and knives, reciting (and quietly listening to) extremely long epic poetry, politely taking turns on a rubbery jumping contraption, and sharing their toys without screaming. Sophelia glode back and forth and to and fro, leaving each child in turn with a word of encouragement, a tender squeeze with her arm, or the briefest blossom of a smile.

While Sophelia and her pupils were engaged in betterment, I was engaged in secretive sketchery. It was, indeed, tricky to sketch a portrait while also maintaining the perfectly still pose of a topiary, but I managed to do it well enough to please even my own scrupulous eye.

I captured the queenly contour of her posture, the cratered moon of her countenance, the pale upswing of her thingamapoof. Then I noted underneath, as was my custom,

Weakness: children.

Demeanor: sorrowful, yet dignified, yet smileable, yet stately.

Taste . . .

I paused and gazed again at her gown of glowing chartreuse, simple, modest, practical (buttons!), and perfectly befitting her person. I wrote, "Impeccable."

A ghastly and woefully miserable moan suddenly broke the peace of the great hall. The children turned (murmurously!) towards an archway at the far end, through which an exhausted-looking maid was pushing a large man into the room on a wheeled couch. I could not guess, at first, which of these two miserable personages had been the source of the moan. The man appeared to be about the same size, paunchiness, and wheezy disposition of a Skreean bomnubble. Yet so pale was he from sickliness that he seemed two huffs away from being the *ghost* of a bomnubble. This must be (I surmised!) the very Sir Brimney Stupe who deploores imperfect greenery . . . Sophelia's papa, whose heart never recovered from her poor mama's demise by turkeypox . . . in short, the illustrious lord of Anklejelly Manor.

He pointed a long, shivery white finger in my direction and wheezed, "That one." My bowels froze, until I realized he was pointing at the somewhat shabbily pruned green pirate next to me. "It is wrong. It is all wrong. Take it away."

Sophelia sighed and nodded to one of the boys, who picked up the offending topiary, walked to an open window, and tossed it out.

Sir Brimney laid one hand on his forehead and groaned, "Ooooooooooooooohhhhhhhhhhhhhhh!" Quite plainly, the ghastly moaner was he. "I am ready for my soup, daughter."

The furrows on Sophelia's cheeks grew deeper and she closed her eyes for a moment, then opened them again and knelt beside the couch.

"Papa, I am in the middle of school right now, remember? Cook can make you soup."

"No! It must be you! Your silly school is about to give me schooliosis."

"You know very well that Cook makes an *excellent* henmeat stew."

"I do not know it! My growlulous stomach does not know it! She stews the stewbroth so long that the meat's as brizzled as a scorched sponge and I can barely bear a nibble. No, you are the *only* one who makes soup correctly. It's your soup that saved me thirteen times from dying of clumpatitis—"

"They were only headaches, papa."

"—*and* the galloping phnood."

"A mere cold."

"If only you could have made soup for your poor mama, she would still be alive and unpoxed today. It's very disappointing that you were too short to reach the spoons back then. Ahhhhhhhhhhh, sadness! Ahhhhhhhh, woe! Ahhhhhh, pain! I feel I have a touch of navalrot coming on, and I am so hungry, too."

Sophelia sighed again and nodded to her pupils. "Nikledos, you're in charge of lessons until I return." Relieving the miserable maid, she wheeled Sir Brimney's couch around and began pushing it back through the archway.

"Darling, I do so much *enjoy* my soup."

"I know, papa."

"What a kind daughter you are. What a kind, sad, poxified daughter. Oh, grief! Oh, sorrow! Oh, woe!"

As I strained to see where they were going, I spotted, out of the corner of my eye, a small wooden door hidden in a little alcove to the right of an elegant staircase. On the door was a bronze plaque with raised letters that caught the light of the chandeliers. The plaque said only this:

The FLABBIT ROOM

I was (to put it mildly!) intrigued. As quietly as I could, I hopped (for obviously a topiary could not be seen walking) along a shadowy wall towards the alcove. This unfortunately caught the attention of the girl named Artemy, who peered at me suspiciously. However, I (quite cannily!) tweeted like a bird in order to prove my unsuspiciousness as a piece of innocent greenery, and she went back to her posture practice.

You may imagine my flutterful trepidation as I opened the ominously-plaqued door. But no flabbitous skin (stretchy!) or claws (sharpish!) greeted me on the other side. In fact, what greeted me instead was a burrow of a very different sort. The room smelled dusty, sweetly moldish, bookish, and with good reason! For its walls were as bookish as its smell. Shelves and shelves of books enwraptured the room in a wordly embrace. There were paintings too—of the Plains of Palen Jahb-j, the Stony Mountains, and the Phoob Islands—and old yellowish maps of far-off places (one of Anniera itself!)—but it was the books that called my name.

I forgot my topiarical posture. I forgot the pain of my crushed and swaddled toes. *The Chomping of the Skonk*! By Bip Thwainbly himself! Long had I coveted this rare volume, far had I searched (in vain!) for one of the last remaining copies, and—what! *The Codex of Snollygaster*, right before my very eyes!—painstakingly handwritten by a scribe who had gotten so bored halfway through that he'd filled the remaining pages with doodles of cavorting trolls. I could hardly believe my extraordinary fortune. Shelves and shelves of such ancient tomes that the pages would crumble to dust if I merely breathed upon them!

I circled and circled, and circled again, until I found myself in the center of the room, where a weathered old desk was covered with more books, and scattered with parchment paper from which the scent of fresh ink arose. A glance at them made my already blappish bosom nearly burst in wonderment. They were letters, all affixed with the mysterious signature "From a Concerned Reader." And yet, the dignified slant of the handwriting, the stately feminine swooshes, the punctuary polishment of its very commas—there could be no question (none!) that this was the hand of Sophelia Stupe herself.

"Dear Mr. Ponkbelly, I regret to inform you that your latest book, *Bonked*, is an embarrassment to truly knowledgable gardeners everywhere. It is lucky for you that your abundant readership includes so few of them. Please allow me to point out the difference between a *tubular tonkblossom* and *tonquish tubicularus* . . ."

"Dear Mr. Nolittle, With your recent *Compendium of Roundish Stuffs*, I'm afraid you may have set Skreean scientific progress back a century. But all is not lost, for your writing is actually quite lovely . . ."

(It appeared that unpolished children were not the only ones Sophelia was bettering!)

"Dear Mr. Flibbleton, It pains me to say this, for I eagerly awaited the publication of *Doors of Mystery, Doors of Myth*, having greatly enjoyed your previous work, *Tricorn: Truth or Fiction?* But your descriptions of these rumored magical passageways, or portals as you call them, are (forgive me) complete rubbish. I have seen one myself (as well as its jubilant eight-eyed doorkeeper), and they do not look like that at all . . . "

Mysterious portal! Eight-eyed doorkeeper! Was it possible that Sophelia had beheld a *raggant*? No one (to my extensive knowledge) had ever seen one but myself. Indeed I will never in all my days forget the moment when, wandering alone in the unpeopled Linnard Woodlands, I laid my two eyes upon the small, grey, leather-skinned creature with its harmless horn and flapperful wings, its octovisual perspicuity, its squeakish jubilance, its otherworldly cuteness. *Raggant*, I thought immediately when I saw it, though I knew not whence the name had come into my brain, and I conjectured (guessingly!) that the strange animal had emerged from one of the doors some say the Maker has planted among us, to tickle our hearts with mystery and keep us humble and vigilant.

Surely such a sophisticated and seemingly practical lady as Sophelia Stupe was not (like me) a believer in so-called fairy tales! Surely she
did not mean she had *seen* such a door. Yet on a tall pile beside the letters lay a well-thumbed copy of the book *Come With Me: A Treatise
on the Exploration of Other Worlds*, and as I turned to the title page,
my eyes rested upon a scribbled notation in the same swooshy script, a
single word that struck me to my deepest soul:

"Someday."

I am not sure which amazed me more: the melancholy hopeful-
ness squinched into that one word, or the impertinence of permanently
scarring the precious innards of book with *writing*. While I was medi-
tating upon these things, I espied the corner of a familiar green cover
peeking out from under the pile of letters. I pounced.

My *Inexhaustive Creaturepedia*. With tremblesome palms I
opened it, and there, in the margins, from the beginning of the book
till the end, were scrawled Sophelia's elegant notes. But this time I did
not pause long enough to be shocked at the marring of my pulchritudinous pages, so absorbed was I in the content of her scribblings.

"A most unfortunate typographical error. The editor should be
fired."

"Contradicts Bloge's *The Taming of the Creepiful Wood* at several
key points. It will fall to others to determine whether Bloge was blind
or Pembrick deaf."

"A fair observation, though somewhat offensively punctuated."

"Many a poisoned herbologist would argue otherwise."

And so on, and so forth, until the final page—

"Lacks polish, but shows great promise. I hope there will be
another."

You might expect, unperceptive readers, that I would resent such
disparages upon my grueling literary labors, but you expect wrongly!
There is nothing (nothing!) so flattering as the just criticism of a reader
who takes one's work seriously. Those notes were, indeed, the highest

compliment anyone had yet paid my (much-rejected!) little book. And the last words—

I hope there will be another.

Be still, my palpitatious heart!

A sudden commotion in the great hall outside *The* FLABBIT ROOM drew me to the door, where I pressed my ear to listen.

"But we will only be a few hours at the festival, papa. You know how much the children enjoy having their faces painted, and it is such good practice in the polished art of sitting still."

"You are determined to leave me alone. You are bent on abandoning me. What would I do if you vanished forever? I would shrivel up from the prolongulated pestilence without you."

"Why don't you come to the festival too, papa?"

"Horror! All of those people, those filthy hands, those foul breathings! What maladious ailments would I catch in such a place! I can't believe you would even put yourself and the children at such risk—"

The voices faded, and soon the scufflings and preparations in the great hall stilled and the Manor was silent.

My heart was wrung by the tragical circumstances of Miss Sophelia Stupe. Denied amorous suitors because of her deformed, scarred countenance (yet how beautiful to a kinder eye!). Denied the paths of discovery and adventure because of her malingering papa and his needlesome demands. Forced to splunder her brilliance in anonymous letters and marginal mutterings instead of in companionable conversation. She was not just a fendril but a *caged* fendril!

Shame on me, sketching her from afar as if she was merely another creature in my *Creaturepedia*! Shame on me, as affixed on her queenliness as others were affixed on her plainness, none of us seeing the cavernous deeps of the mind beneath! My resolve was now resolute. I would no longer hide behind disguisery, no matter how well-pruned. I would speak with her face to face. I would tell her of my newfound but unplappable love. Today! At the festival!

I hopped all the way back to town on my one unbroken topiarish foot, without losing a single leaf.

I hopped right smack into Edd Helmer.

"Ollister!" he cried.

"Edd! How did you recognize me?"

"By your missing elbow flesh, of course."

I blushed as I realized the fatal weakness of my disguise and thanked the Maker no one else had espied the missing flesh under my perfect foliage.

In a swoop of words (for Edd's chatter was as swifty as a sweeft) my old youngish friend apologized for not greeting me in town upon my arrival and explained that he had been detained for the last week in Lamendron, awaiting shipments of boots from the Green Hollows ("Skreeans pay a pretty coin for foreign footwear!") as well as several exotic ingredients for his apothecarial mixtures and medicines. "Those gabnubbable pirates! I'd like to round up the whole sea of them, slap them into my dentist chairs, and give them agonizing root canals, one by one. There has never been a Helmer gone piratical, and I swear to you there never shall be! I lost an entire shipment to their marauding villainy (I hope they enjoy their new boots, the ruffians), and the pungent piccadrool blossoms of Phoob never arrived either, so I had to search half the beaches of Shard Harbor for an acceptable alternative . . ."

I began to shed my topiary leaves impatiently, for I could see the crowds gathering in the Glipwood Commons and, as glad as I was to see my friend, I would be even more glad to see a chartreuse gown followed by a bevy of polished children.

" . . . but knowing you'd be eager to continue your travels, I was on my way to the Only Inn to bring you this." Edd handed me a small bottle of a pinkish hue, with a lacy ribbon adorning its cap. "It's disguised," he added with a wink, "as expensive lady's perfume (since you like disguisery so much). No one will ever know it is in fact the most powerful medicinal concoction I've ever concocted!"

I took the bottle with great interest and peered at its murky pink liquid within. "I believe you said, in your letter, that this would make my presence pleasing to wild creatures, so that they would approach me in friendliness instead of ferocity?"

"Precisely! At least, I believe so. I am quite confidently almost certain of it, though the regrettable theft of the Phoobian piccadrool forced me to change my recipe slightly, though I have little doubt, only a little, that the effect will be exactly as I expect. It should last as long as your adventures shall continue, for only a drop will be enough to protect you for a year or more . . ."

There would be plenty for both of us. I could take Sophelia with me, without ever having to worry about risking her innards or her out-ards in perilous creaturely encounters. I could show her all the places she'd only seen in her paintings and read about in her books. I could teach her the ways of a wandering adventurer.

But her papa. She would never be able leave her papa!

" . . . completely waterproof, soapproof, sweatproof, mudproof, droolproof, oozeproof, gooproof . . ."

Aha, the limberwolf! I once made an exact replica of my form and duped the limberwolf into attacking *it* instead of *me*, while I sketched safely in hiding. Surely Sir Brimney Stupe was as dupiful as the lim-berwolf. I could construct an exact replica of Sophelia to remain at Anklejelly Manor while the real Sophelia and I went forth together in expeditionary bliss!

But the soup. Could I make a Sophelian replica skilled in the cookery of soup?

"However, and this is extremely important, I must warn you not to use any more than a drop at a time, for an excess of perfume could skiddlypop the cartusian fripperfoozle and I cannot guarantee your gordian glamfuzz if you squip squap piddly plap the bottle cap's safety spring bozobibblehootensplat then you must winderhoppen immediately!"

That is not exactly what Edd said. I do not know exactly what Edd said (though, looking back now, I can guess). For, readers, I was not listening. I was thinking only of Sophelia, and I was not listening.

Alas, I, Ollister B. Pembrick, who had so long beseeched others to hearken to my warnings, did not hearken to the warnings given me by another.

So much in life dependeth upon a good hearkening. Remember that, and beware.

I now come to the crux of my tale, the crucible, the crowfly in the ointment, about which I shudder to write. But I must! For if I do not I will never finish this letter, and then you will never read it, and then I will not have the aid I require in order to—

Breathe deeply, Ollister. Just pluck that crowfly out of the ointment one oozy feather at a time.

I went to the festival, which was, as I expected, perplexingly filled with garishly decorated noses, musical competitions, and fashionable fowl—as well as a few poets reciting ballads while balancing on tiptoe. I know not to what purposes these Glipwood festivals pertain, but apparently they are quite popular in Skree, for there were folks from Torrboro, Dugtown, Lamendron, and many other parts toting their pet chickens, ducks, and turkeys all bedecked in formal attire—the chickens, ducks, and turkeys, that is. The people themselves appeared (like most Skreeans in my eyes) to have dressed themselves, as usual, in flamboyantly artistic pajamas.

But I ignored the pen of ducks in black stovepipe hats, the accordion duel, and the man in sackcloth prophesying something about an army of Teeth, and walked straight up to the tall figure in pale chartreuse standing with her perfectly poised students in the largest tent, where farmers were parading their exquisitely dressed hens before a squinty-eyed judge.

"Madam—" I began as soon as she turned her head, for I had wasted many a long year in partly-maimed loneliness and intended to waste no more. "Madam, I am at your slicelong lervice, er, longlife slervice. I mean to say, your speck and gall—kick and ball—beck and call—Ah! Your beauty has betwitched me gizzard and sole. What I mean to say is, in short—" But there was no short, nor long, in my love-twisted tongue, but only a middlish mength of bare truth. "I adore you, Miss Sophelia Stupe."

The students giggled, and the queenly, brainly object of my besottedness blushed from scar to scar. "I must say, your adoration is quite sudden," she murmured, peering at my face suspiciously but also (for I did see a hint of something else there!) hopefully. "When did this unexpected betwitching start? I only just met you yesterday."

When? I opened my mouth, then closed it again, shamed into silence. *When I read your anonymous letters and bookish marginalia while trespassing inside your house in the guise of a perfectly leafed topiary* is not exactly the thing you want to say to impress the woman you love.

So I said the only thing a wanderer, a sketcher, a seeker of the strange, the streaked, the squawking, and the squillious could say in such a moment. "Danger!" I cried. "Woe!" I croaked. "Run!" I crooned. For in the farthest, squinchiest corner of my left eye I espied, behind the woman I loved, a most perilous and stenchiful treachery. "That is not a hen! That's a squeeblin!"

The crowd under the tent did not run. Instead, they stared at my pointed finger, then at the roundish, furry, spine-shivering ball of vicious sweetness—the betrayer—the anti-hen—to which my finger pointed. It was adorned in a lacy baby gown, with a beribboned bonnet, much like the other hens in the tent.

"A *what?*" asked the judge, squinting at me.

"A *squeeblin*. I cannot make out, beneath all those ribbons and lace, whether it is the fuzzy, the softish, or the verbose variety of squeeblin, but a squeeblin it most definitely is. You can tell by its pure and innocent countenance that hides a darkly perfidious heart. *Never trust a squeeblin*, especially one disguised in hennish garb."

Sophelia bent quickly and gathered her students in her arms. "Children, you must trust *me*, right now, and I must trust *you*. Run to your homes. Run as fast as you can. Nikledos, lead the little ones. Dimtree, don't slouch, even in danger. Artemy, sprint like the wind. Shoulders back! Chin high!"

The children had been far better bettered than the grown-up Skreeans in the tent, and they ran without question. But the woman holding the squeeblin turned to me and retorted, "Who are you calling a skeepoople? This is my very own Bessie-boo, who laid me an egg just last week—already scrambled and scribbled on a sammyich, too!"

"Madam, I once trusted a squeeblin and suffered dearly for it in a way that pains me to remember and shames me to mention. But I turned my bitterness into warning. I was betrayed so that others might not be. That's one of the many reasons why I wrote my *Creaturepedia*."

"I knew I recognized him from somewhere," called a man in the crowd. "It's that crazy author from the bookshop! The one who believes in *quill diggles*!"

"Hey, have you seen any *flabbits* lately? Ha ha! What a joke."

"I bet he *still* hasn't put a kitten in his book."

Hecklers are everywhere in Skree. Even at festivals.

"Not a hen, says he?" said the squeeblin's gullible owner, red-faced and furious. "Well, let's ask her. Bessie-boo, honey, you *are* a hen, aren't you?"

Out of the innocent furry mouth came a perfectly reasonable and entirely unsuspicious "BWAAAAK."

"You see? She's a hen!" said the woman.

"You poor deceived lady, of course it says it's a hen, because it's a *squeeblin* and you *cannot trust a squeeblin*."

"He's right," said Sophelia. All eyes turned towards her, some to stare, some to immediately avert themselves from her disfigured face and look at her perfectly polished shoes. "Despite a few minor flaws and an egregious typographical error on page two, which was not his fault, his *Creaturepedia* is absolutely correct and far more trustworthy than any squeeblin. That hen" (she pointed to the black-hearted furball) "is a fraud."

Readers, I grabbed her outstretched pointy finger and I kissed it thrice. At last, my love (staunchiful! beatitudinous!) could pour itself out unhindered by secrets. "Darlingest! Sweetingest! Fendrilest! You read my book!"

"Of course I did. What did you think I was going to do with it, wear it on my head every day?"

"But—but—you *liked* it? You didn't find the punctuation somewhat—er, offensive?"

"Terribly so. You will drive your readers into exclamatory exhaustion if you aren't careful."

At that moment, in a flurry of lace and ribbons, the black-hearted furball leaped straight at Sophelia's elegant thingamapoof, screaming as it flew: "Blah! Blahbitty blahbitty bloo bloo blooblooblooboo BLAH! Ba ba blah blippetty blip blop bloop ba ba BLOO blah blee. BO BO BO BO! Beepitty bleepetty BLAHbittybittybittybittybittybittybitty-bittybitty BOOBOO!"

Apparently this was the verbose variety of squeeblin.

It landed on her head, toppling her to the ground, but her face showed only startlement, not fear.

"Sophelia!" I cried.

"Bessie-boo!" cried the squeeblin's tragically duped former owner. We both fell upon the two combatants on the ground, I trying to disentangle my adored one from the wilyish fuzzfury of a deceitful squeeblin, the woman trying to disentangle her erstwhile hen from Sophelia's regally coiffed hair. Suddenly the poor woman jerked her hands back, blood spurting from her pinky finger. "B-b-b-b-Bessie-b-b-b-boo! How could you?" She jumped to her feet and stumbled out of the tent, face buried in the folds of her dress, heartbreak and betrayal in her wake. Alas, I knew that heartbreak all too well.

"A pencil!" Sophelia gasped as the squeeblin's fuzz-hidden flesh-hooks thrust themselves through lace and ribbon towards her nose.

Brilliant girl! The squeeblin's one weakness is its highly pokable eyes. I searched my pockets, but I must have dropped my pencil during my topiarish hopping in Anklejelly Manor. "A pencil, a pencil!" I yelled to the puzzled and slightly horrified onlookers. "Doesn't anyone in this ridiculously artistocratic festival have a pencil? Find an author, quick!"

My entreaty was in vain. "Mad hen! Mad hen!" they cried, scattering quickly and taking shelter in a neighboring tent with the far more peaceful and less dangerously lacy dueling accordionists.

And then my fearless fendrilady, the sweet chartreuse stealer of my soul, screamed. The squeeblin's fleshhooks had found those lovely poxed cheeks, that fair furrowed brow, and torn a fresh river of suffering across the dear cratered face that had haunted my waking dreams for a full twenty six hours.

Now I beg you, impatient yet gracious readers, have some pity on this smitten, lonely, long-wandering naturalist. Remember that I had swum with daggerfish, I had belched at armadillers, I had escaped from a rockroach's gobblish gully, but I had never in all my misadventures been lucky enough to rescue a beloved lady in distress. So who can blame me for an overdose of heroic zeal? Who can blame me if, in the swirl and scuffle of passionate gallantry, I overdid my rescue just a tittle? Who can blame me if, having in my possession a perfume that could prevent creaturely belligerence with a single drop, I bit the safety cap off with my teeth and poured *the entire bottle of it* over the top of my true love's besqueeblined head? I ask you, who can blame me?

Edd Helmer, that's who.

"What have you done, you gabnubbable plunkhead?!?" came his thundering voice behind me. And that was the moment when (alas! too late!) I remembered his urgent warning about skiddlypopping the cartusian fripperfoozle and wondered if I might have possibly mishearkened.

A strong, sweetish, and slightly vegetative scent filled the air inside the tent. The squeeblin ceased its furry fury and dropped to the ground. I fell back, as Edd crouched breathlessly beside me. Sophelia sat up, her hair soaking wet, her face bleeding and glistening with perfume that ran down her cheeks and neck, yet filled with wonder as she stared at her assailant. "Look," she said quietly. The fuzzy, toothy pillow of perniciousness was staring back at her with what can only be described as awe. Then the creature bent over awkwardly and—kissed—her gown-draped knee. "I think it likes me."

She held out her hand tentatively, as if to pet it, but I wrapped my arms around her and pulled her away. "DON'T TRUST IT! DON'T TRUST THE SQUEEBLIN!"

"It won't hurt me," whispered Sophelia. "Just look at its eyes."

"They are the eyes of treachery. In those eyes lie only heartbreak and sorrow. Believe me, I know."

"Eh—Ollister," said Edd, pointing away from Sophelia. I looked up, and surrounding us was a slowly closing circle of roosters wearing bow ties. Thankfully, they were actual, non-squeeblinish, trustworthy roosters. Strangely, they were crowing in croonly harmony, and the plaintive pleading of their warbles sounded much like my own lovestruck heart would sound if my heart could crow croonishly. Ominously, they were all heading straight for Sophelia. And abruptly, a wave of belaced and beribboned hens broke upon the circle of roosters in a fit of jealous pecking.

Edd's eyes widened in alarm. "We need to get her home—now."

I picked up Sophelia (light as a sweeft's feather!) before she could protest and followed Edd through the swirling sea of henpecked roosters, hobbling as quickly as I could and wishing I had not left my plumyum cane in the Only Inn (you may have forgotten, readers—though my beswaddled toes have not—the damaged condition in which I found myself on that fateful day!). As we left the tent and started half-running (the Edd half), half-hobbling (the me half) towards the main street of Glipwood, the wind caught our backs and swept the aroma of Sophelia's perfumed scalp high into the air, like a sweetly stenchious cloud that spread over the rooftops and teased the nostrils of the very sun above our heads. Then the sky darkened, and Edd called, "Hurry!" and I could hear a distant flapping that grew rapidly nearer.

"Put me down!" commanded Sophelia, and I put. Immediately we were beset by such a winged tempest that for a moment I could not tell whether we had stumbled into a geef's nest or into a gaggle of garrulous and overheated ladies all waving their fans at once. The situation become more clear as an enormous flock of fazzle doves began to swirl wildly around Sophelia, and another flock of gulpswallows dove right into them with cute splattering sounds, and a hundred floating selbrils rained down upon our heads.

For a moment I could hardly even see Sophelia, so thick was the whirling chaos of wingish things around us, and then I thought I saw her holding out her arms widely, as if to embrace them all (foolish yet bewitching gesture!). Then the downpour paused and Sophelia was beside me, pulling me and Edd into the shelter of a selbril's umbrellish tail. The floatsome rodent itself was rapturously hugging her stomach upside-down. "That should save our hairdos, at least," she said cheerfully. Under the cover of the tail, while fazzle doves and gulpswallows (and a few other selbrils) bounced off harmlessly, the three of us continued running down the main street of Glipwood. If I didn't know any better, I would have suspected that Miss Sophelia Stupe was enjoying herself immensely.

"Edd, what is going on?" I yelled above the squashy sounds of the bouncing birds.

"What is going on? What is going on is that you defied my warnings and used too much perfume. What is going on is that a single
drop was carefully formulated to draw the creatures to you in pleasant
friendship, but I can only guess horrifically inaccurate and sickeningly
speculative guesses what a million drops has the power to do. What is
going on is that we've got to get Miss Stupe inside Anklejelly Manor as
soon as possible and hope beyond all hope that my waterproof, soapproof, sweatproof, mudproof, droolproof, oozeproof, gooproof perfume
might be not dungeonproof, and we can hide her where nothing more
can smell her."

"Nothing *more?*"

"That scent will travel for miles. *Miles.*"

The Glipwood festival was already in turmoil as tents collapsed
under the weight of the falling critters and panicked ladies with painted
cheeks began running to protect their hats from dove droppings. All over
town folks scrambled for umbrellas and slingshots. The sky was raining
rodents. It was gulping swallows. It was fazzling doves. And since none
of the flying creatures were very bright (or skillful in their aim at the
fleeing Sophelia), the town received a good and thorough pelting.

But when we had left the little town far behind, we felt a rumbling
beneath our feet, like distant thunder slowly rolling through the earth
itself, and before we'd even come within sight of the Manor, we were
met on the road by a huge crowd of men wearing fur hats and hunting
gear and running towards *us.*

"Turn back, turn back!" the men called. "They're coming!"

We stopped in confusion. "Who's coming?" Edd yelled.

"Everything!" said a passing ranger, who paused to catch his breath.
"Everything that ever moved or slithered or crept or crawled or gnawed
or galloped or squatted or squealed in the entire Forest and beyond! It
is an invasion! It is an apocalypse! It is a terrible day!"

"Then let us make haste to Anklejelly Manor," I cried, "for its walls
are as thick as they are grandiose, and—"

"It's already overrun," said the ranger.

Sophelia's hand flew to her mouth. "Oh, no! Papa!"

"A cook who escaped said the Lord of the Manor and his servants were safely stowed in an underground catacomb, though with much wailing because an entire courtyard of very fine topiaries had been trampled." The ranger glanced behind him, eyes wide with horror, and sprinted towards Glipwood with the rest of the men.

"You are *hunters*!" I called after them. "You are *rangers*! Go range and hunt!"

"I only signed up to knock off an occasional toothy cow or two," another hunter called back to me, "not an entire army of them!"

"Bosh and biddesticks!" My patience was by then in an utterly brizzled state. "Glipwood's sole protectors! The heroes of Skree! The reason no one even believes in quill diggles anymore! Fleeing like—like—

"Ollister—"

"Like cowardly flabbits!"

"Ollister!"

I looked at Sophelia. She was looking at the horizon, where a long line of darkness had crested the hill, and the darkness had hoofs and horns.

We ran, readers, we ran. All the way back to Glipwood we ran. Trailing a selbril umbrella behind us we ran. The pain in my broken toes was nothing compared to the peril that pursued us.

As we reached the edge of town, Edd glanced backwards and exclaimed, "What in Aerwiar—does that bird have a *bellybutton*?"

Sophelia halted in her tracks and spun around to look at the sky, where a paunchy and nefarious shape hovered. "A snickbuzzard? Truly? Oh, let me see it! I have *longed* to see a snickbuzzard's bellybutton my whole life!

"My love!" I chirped. "So have I! And I did! And I will again! With you! Any time you like!"

"*Hurry up!*" Edd yanked us both by the arms, and we kept running. I thought I heard the faintest giggle of glee from Sophelia, but I must have mishearkened once again.

If the rainstorm of fazzle doves, gulpswallows, and selbrils had tipped the festival into a fine kerfuffle, the arrival of the terrified rangers and hunters had multiplied the kerfufflity a hundredfold. Glipwoodians, Torrborians, Dugtownians, Lamendronians, and other festivalgoers were running helter-skelter, unsure what exactly was coming or where to run to. Ahead of us the skeletal frame of Books & Crannies towered over the other buildings, and we could see carpenters leaping from the roof beams into the trees and scurrying away. "Quick!" I said. "There are crannies! Crannies are for hiding in!"

"I'll meet you there in two shivers of a sneed's whisker," answered Edd, running towards his own shop.

I had no time to wonder what a sneed was, where its whiskers were located, or why Edd had not told me about them in time to include them in my *Creatupedia*, for Sophelia and I had already reached the doorless doorframe of the bookshop and bumped into the frazzled shopkeeper I had met yesterday. His face sank in disappointment. "Oh, it's you again. If you're looking for your little green books I put them in the far back corner, for I hadn't sold a single copy after—"

"Pardon me, my good sir, but we have need of the shelter of your bookshop, and I suggest you take shelter as well. A veritable monsoon of pernicious yet pulchritudinous beasts is hotly pursuing us as we stand talking."

"No, no, no, you can't lead them in here! I am aaaaaaa-CHOOOOO allergic to a-a-a-aaaaa-PHHOOOOEY to animals!" I handed him another clean handkerchief from my pocket, and we ran past him into the shop. Without finished walls or roof it was perhaps not the ideal hiding place I had imagined, but I blocked the open doorframe with several bookshelves, and we managed to find a quite serviceable cranny between two more bookshelves that I immediately began to surround with a barricade of heavy books. It took me a few minutes to realize that Sophelia was not helping but standing erect and dignified, with her arms crossed over her chartreuse gown.

"My dear, we must hide you!"

"No."

"*No?*"

"I am *not* hiding! I've been hiding my whole life. I've been hiding behind *books* my whole life. I've been squished into the cranny of a stuffy Manor while a world whizzes by, full of wonders I long to look upon, mysteries I yearn to unravel, places I ache to explore. Ollister, I want to *see*. Don't you understand? All I've ever wanted to do is *see*. I have read—so, so many books!—and I have learned and I have wondered and I have taught and I have even written—letters, at least, not books, not yet. I know you will be surprised at this—" (Oh, how little she knew of what I knew!) "—but even while I am dutifully bettering those lovely unpolished children, my thoughts wander far away, even to the explored Jungles of Plontst and the undocumented trollish lands!" (Oh heart, oh shiversome heart, be still!) "Do you think I'm afraid of a few more scars? Life has already done its worst to me. What if the *best* is a foot full of broken toes and a mind full of adventure, of discovery, of passionate inquiry into all the Maker's makings? No, Ollister, I am done hiding."

I felt as if my innards had split into twoards, so torn was I between admiration and perplexation. Indeed, I should have rejoiced, and yet her composure almost irked me, for I had had a high view of her wisdom until this moment, but it did not seem to me that she was taking the situation nearly seriously enough. Fear has saved many a life and limb in the past, and if the foolhardy fearlessness of my Uncle Bahb taught me anything, it's that there is a time for harvesting aromatical vegetables, and that time is *not* during the Fifthmoon a fortnight after a sandstorm.

This time was not during the Fifthmoon a fortnight after a sandstorm either, but that was beside the point. In my imagination I had

dreamed of a fair and faithful companion for my frenetical life of wanderings, but in my flesh, at that moment, all I wanted was to see her
whole, hale, and unmaimed in her FLABBIT ROOM, surrounded by
scholarly tomes and writing a letter, with no threat of actual flabbits
anywhere near her.

I answered not knowing whether it was truth or lie: "We will go to
all of those places. Together. I promise. But right now, it is *your* smell
the creatures are following. We must see what we can do to block you
from view—er, scent."

"But didn't you see what happened to that squeeblin? How it
looked at me? Whatever this perfume is doing to these poor animals, I
am not afraid of them."

"*You cannot trust a squeeblin.* But you can trust me, and I swear
(solemnly!) on the gobbled remains of my Uncle Bahb that I will keep
you perfectly safe!"

"Miss Stupe is the only person in this entire town who *is* perfectly
safe!" yelled Edd above our heads. He was peering down at us from one
of the open patches in the unfinished roof. "It's my own skin I'm worried about. And yours. And *theirs*." He nodded his head towards the
main street, where the sound of screaming mingled with the thunder
of hoofs growing ever louder.

"I'm not sure I understand."

"You will. Now get up here, Ollister. I can't fend off these beasts by
myself. Sophelia, for the sake of everyone else in Glipwood, *cover yourself up with whatever you can find.* See if you can muffle your stench."

With a longing glance toward the windows, Sophelia obeyed and
ducked behind the little book fortress I had built. Though I was loathe
to leave her undefended in her cranny, I had already beheld the conse-
quences of not hearkening to Edd Helmer, so I climbed up a bookshelf
and through the hole in the roof to the beam where he sat. And just
in time—for what a sight and what a clamor did then assail our eyes
and ears!

The squelching! The squawking! The scrambling! The squattering! The snorting! The snapping! The slapping! The squishing! The swishing! The spitting! The snuffling! The snickering! The snorting! The snaggering! The skittering! The stampeding in that unprotected, unsuspecting, unmunched (yet!) town was—well, I must leave the full depiction of this stamposity to your imaginations, dear readers, for I cannot attempt it without a great many more s's than even my own abundant vocabulary can afford.

Edd began pulling an assortment of items out of a large sack. "These are the best I could find for weaponry," he sighed. "I'm a pacifist under normal circumstances." Alas, so was I (so are all scientifically curious sketchers!), but since normal circumstances had ceased to exist several hours ago, we began hurling boots at toothy cows with unpacific gusto. When the boots were gone, we threw everything else we could get our hands on. Edd threw a large wooden apothecary scale at a gargan rockroach that was trying to squeeze through one of the bookstore windows. *The Wedding Officiant's Official Guide to Bowing and Vowing* became permanently lodged in the hornly crown of a galloping gambloat (I hardly had time to ponder the significance of the normally sluggish and lopeful gambloat's sudden urge to gallop), and I managed to bust the snap out of a snapping diggle with a particularly lethal-looking metal tool of dentistral torture used (Edd explained) for tooth extraction.

"My entire livelihood, cast like pearls before a herd of smitten swine!" he groaned. "I'll never be able to build that cottage for Yamsa now, and I'd almost very nearly gotten to the point of thinking about making the decision to ask her to marry me. That gabnubbable perfume! You gabnubbable hero!"

"Sophelia! Are you still safe within your cranny?" I called down to her.

"I am quite safe," she called back.

Meanwhile, people were gawking with peepiful curiosity from their windows, or gathered on the rooftops of the Only Inn and the

Shipshape Tavern, and some foolish few were still in the streets, alternately whacking thwaps and pointing in giddy disbelief at the beasts they had thought only existed in old stories and rangers' tall tales. I was (I'm ashamed to say!) ever-so-slightly amused at the sight of a quill diggle flinging quills at the very heckler who had denied its existence yesterday. Yet I could not resist dispensing a few pertinent pieces of advice from my lofty perch, so pitiful was the Skreeans' zoological ignorance.

"Put out that fire immediately!" I bellowed to a Glipwoodian who was waving a torch in the spiteful face of ferno lizard. "There are horned hounds on the loose, you blimpnoggin, and they are drawn to flame like big, nasty, horned moths! Haven't you read my *Creaturepedia*? Oh, no, of course you haven't. You bought a pirate book instead."

"No, no, no, you cannot sweet-talk a yimp," I yelled to another. "Do you want to be gooed by its squirtical belly? You must look indignant! You must be annoyed at its annoyance! You must swap offense for offense! Is that your most snobbulous face? Scowl, man, scowl! You would know all of this if you had only read my *Creaturepedia*."

I saw another man running away with a dozen wexters under each arm, their tiny umbrellas hanging lifelessly. He no doubt intended them for stew. I wanted to warn him not to wait too long, for if you are foolish enough to eat an unfresh wexter . . . but he was out of earshot, and I will never know whether that man ever began singing love songs to his barn door or not.

Here lieth the tragic impasse of an author's art. You can pour all of your hard-won wisdom into a book, but you cannot make people read it and learn. That part is solely up to them.

But my attention was diverted back from the town to the safety of my beloved lady when the blocked door of Books & Crannies abruptly gave way, and a hundred creatures flooded into the shop below.

I hurled myself through the hole in the roof and landed on top of the bookshelf above Sophelia's barricaded cranny. But her barricade of books had already been toppled, and there was Sophelia, sitting calmly surrounded by the pages of my very own *Creatupedia* come alive in tooth and horn and stinger.

And then, finally, I understood what Edd had meant when he said she was the only perfectly safe person in the whole town.

An armadiller struck a contemplative pose (so fetching to female armadillers) and gazed deeply into her eyes.

A bumpy digtoad shot out its oozing tongue towards her face, but instead of wrapping itself around her and pulling her into its mouth, it laid a sticky flower in her lap.

A grobblin shyly dumped a sack of hand towels and spoons at her feet.

A mustachioed thwap preened its handsome lip hair, bowed, and gallantly kissed her hand.

A guggler tried desperately to hug her before realizing its armless rotundity prevented the possibility of huggishness, and then it wept heartbrokenly into its flowy hair.

A quill diggle (looking, as all quill diggles do, disturbingly like my Uncle Bahb) leered at her with patronizing affection.

A saggy hound sat on a pile of kitten books and meditatively chewed them while a slobbery grin snuggled the wattles of its cheeks.

A snickbuzzard snizzled a long, pining, buzzardly snizzle through its skywardly pointy nozzle-tooth, which is a snickbuzzard's most puzzling feature, umbilical ambiguity aside.

A toothy cow began to moo moonishly and batted its brazen lashes at her.

A flabbit recited a lengthy, florid, flappy, yet eloquent poem in a language I can only describe as *snoutish*, and which was accompanied by syncopated *fwops* of its foofy tail.

And behind those came more, and more, and more, crowding into the dense forest of wooden shelves and leather books, creeping as close as they could to the glodious, cherished presence in the middle.

The creatures were not attacking Sophelia at all.

They were *wooing* Sophelia.

She was being swallowed up not by ravenous beastly gulps, but by an abundance of grufflish, stabbish, ploppish, hortubinous, snifferous, huppitous, flapperful *love*.

My editorially astute but romantically ignorant readers might now be thinking, "Aha! You tricked us into believing this was a tragic story, but indeed it is not! All peril is an illusion! All danger is a dream! For there is only, at the center of your unforgivably long tale of woe, a lonely girl who has found some animals to love her. Isn't that charming? And if they love her, she can surely tell them all to behave nicely and not hurt anyone and go back home."

For a moment I, even I, fell prey to this fleeting mirage of a happy ending. The sight of my Sophelia's ravaged face softening with tenderness over the beasts around her, much as it had softened over the children in her school, filled me such a wellitude of affection that I knew, beyond doubt, that all would be well. She began to speak to them, as she had spoken to Nikledos and Dimtree and Artemy and her other students, lecturing them gently but firmly on their slouchiness and admonishing them to suck in their paunchy guts and to lift high the chins and beaks and horns and snouts the Maker had given them.

Yet something rankled within me. You see, I had pitied the lady of Anklejelly Manor once (how long ago it seemed now!) for her lack of amorous suitors. But I did not want her to have a thousand suitors, especially not the kind with claws and quills. I only wanted her to have one. Me.

The problem was, every single lovesick flabbit, limberwolf, toothy cow, horned hound, gargan rockroach, bomnubble, and skonk in that town felt the same as I did. And jealousy is a monster of such unsketchable monstrosity that even my *Creaturepedia* can not do artful justice to its wrath.

Already, as Edd and I hunched on our haunches atop the book-shelves watching the menagerie below, the brittle peace was breaking. The creatures further back began to stomp and squish and swallop and squanch those in front of them, each vying for a coveted place in the perfumed lady's immediate presence, each resentful that any other being in the world should share it with them. Alas, so near is love to hate.

"They will tear each other apart," said Edd, "as well as anyone else who stands between them and Miss Stupe. That includes everyone in Glipwood who attempts to drive the hoards of invading beasts out of town. And that includes you, too, as soon as they catch a whiff of your devotion to her."

"Then we must find a way to get her back to Anklejelly Manor immediately! Perhaps a chorkney will fall in love with her and fly her back, and then she can hide in the catacombs along with Lord Brimney Stupe—"

"I will not," said Sophelia from her cranny. She was struggling to separate two thwaps as they wrestled over which one had the right to lick her shoe. "I will not go back there and put my papa in danger, and he will never leave. And what would life be like, buried underground, without even the children to teach anymore? No, I cannot go home again."

"Aha, I have it!" said Edd. "She could lead all the wild creatures out into the Linnard Woodlands, far away from civilization, so they will never bother Glipwood again!"

The very idea filled me with sickening pity and dread. "But I would have to accompany her! She could not live out in the wilderness alone!"

"And how long do you think you would last against a thousand jealous beastly beaux who gobble elbows and squirt poisonous goo?"

"Are you certain *nothing* will wash off the perfume? Couldn't you make another perfume to remove the scent of the first perfume?"

"Sure, if you can figure out how to unskin a sackyderm, unsqueeze a dirigiblous floxmelon, and unmix a beetle's saliva from the ear wax of an aboriginal Phoobian postman."

"But the smell must surely wear off eventually. How long?"

"Who knows? My calculations were based on a dosage of only one a drop at a time. Two years? Ten years? A hundred years? Who knows?"

I beat my breast (guiltily!), I pounded my head (repentantly!), I flogged my eyes (painfully!) with the tips of my thumbs (a form of penance practiced by noble gunkees). "I am sorry, Sophelia Stupe! I am so sorry I poured this calamity upon your innocent (saintifical!) head. I loved you in foolishness, not in wisdom. I wish I were in a cave somewhere, so that no one would ever look at me again and I could die in my shame. I thought I was a crafty and heroic adventurer, a benefactor of the unsketched and untraveled masses, but I am not! I am a cave blat!"

"My darling Ollister," said Sophelia quietly, looking up at me with the faintest dimple in the smallest crater of her left cheek, "love means never having to say you're a cave blat. Besides, I know where I can go. I know where the animals will not be able to smell me."

Edd shook his head dismally. "Miss Stupe, my perfume is specially formulated to work on any creatures in Aerwiar. There is nowhere you can go."

"Any creatures in Aerwiar. Yes. I know what to do. There's a tree behind Books & Crannies—a fat, squat one, with five branches outstretched sideways like the stubby fingers of a hand waving goodbye. I see it every week when I come this way. I used to climb it as a little girl. I know it well. Can you spot it?"

I was already on the roof again, peering over the heads of the creatures who pressed hungrily against the walls of the bookshop. "I see it!" Around me on the unfinished roof, amongst the carpenters' discarded tools, flying things perched on every beam—fazzle doves and selbrils, gulpswallops and snickbuzzards, ickaws and midgeons, all basking in the Sophelian scent that drifted through the rafters—and there, at the very edge, poised like a feathery topiary glistening with dew, was the Lone Fendril. I blinked several times to clear the blur of disbelief from my eyes. That most majestic of all birds, set in motion by the Maker himself, seen only in the highest clouds at the turning of the seasons, was right there in front of me, waiting quietly, its swanlike neck dipped in deference to the fragrant queen beneath us.

Edd, who had poked his head up beside mine, looked at me and smiled.

Ten minutes later we had each lost a pinky finger and suffered multiple peckings, slicings, snickings, and munchings from the jealous suitors below, but we had Sophelia on the roof, and in two jumps after that the fendrilady was climbing onto the back of the fendril, with me close behind her, and Edd in the rear. On a magnificent wingspan of four mengths we rose into the sky.

There are those who are lucky enough to find a life of settled, unsquillious domesticitude in this world. There are also those who are lucky enough to soar on the back of the Lone Fendril behind a woman whose face has been furrowed by suffering and whose mind has been sown with hope.

I am the second kind of lucky.

I suspect that the Lone Fendril wanted that flight to last as long as I did, for it did not head straight to the tree immediately but rose high (so high!) and circled around the little town of Glipwood first. We could see the Books & Crannies shopkeeper leaping from a window into the bushes below, sneezing spectacular sneezes into my handkerchief. We could see the people gathered on rooftops with the gulpswallows, gazing down in awe at the beastly multitudes in the streets. We could see, as we rose even higher, the hoofish and wingish and tailish shadows of more creatures fluanching toward Glipwood from the farthest edges of the forest and from the great River Blapp and from the rolling grasslands stretching to the Plains of Palen Jahb-J. How far could the scent of a powerful perfume carry in this wind? Was all of Skree falling in love?

Up there in the heart of the wind, hidden by wings, my arm was wrapped around a pale chartreuse waist. Sophelia leaned back against me and whispered in my ear: "Promise me something, Ollister. Promise that if anything happens to me, you will make sure my papa gets his soup."

"But—"

"He will be scared. He will not want to come above ground again, but you must make him. And give him plenty of soup. Promise me."

"Of course I promise! But nothing is going to happen to you."

And I believed it when I said it. Oh, readers, I believed it deep down in my swoonious soul.

The Lone Fendril landed lightly (so lightly!) on one of the five fingerish branches of Sophelia's tree, and the three of us slid down into the palm of the tree's gnarled and farewelling hand. I was confused, perplexed, doubtful even, for I could see no way of escaping the creatures here. But I did not dare question my fendrilady, for her face was flushed and eager, yet with a glint of fear in her eyes. "Funny," she said, with a half-laugh that sounded almost like a sob, "I have dreamed of this for so long. I have felt such longing that I thought I would turn inside-out. And now the time has come, and I am frightened."

"It's a *tree*," said Edd, scratching his ear.

"I used to sit here often as a girl," Sophelia continued as if not hearing him, "cupped in the hand of this tree, and I would tell it all of my secrets, all of my sorrows. I would lay my cheek against its bark and weep here until my eyes and my heart had run dry. And then one day I saw—"

She paused and looked at me, then rested her hand briefly on mine. "I am ready now."

And without giving me time to raise her fingers to my lips, she pressed both of her palms upon a hollowed place in the tree's ancient bark, lowered her head, and breathed upon it.

Here I must impress upon you, readers, that I am still your very own Ollister B. Pembrick, born and raised in the town of Pennybridge on the Isle of Anniera, trustworthy and levelheaded president of the Occasional Greengrocer's Alliance, and friend of all that is true and factual and sketchable in this world. I remind you of these things because I know you will suspect me of a most pernicious deceivery when I tell you what happened next. But I do not lie.

The palm of the five-fingered tree, in the spot where she breathed, shimmered, shivered, and rippled outward until it became a glassy pool of water—except it was not water—and in the pool was a perfect mirrored reflection of the world, just as you would see looking back at you if you gazed into a lake on a sunny day—except it was not the world. At least, it was not Glipwood we saw mirrored there, or Books & Crannies, or the cloudy sky of Skree, with its lingering flocks of fazzle doves above our heads.

In that rippling pool we saw a lumpish green mountain with the ruins of a castle on top, and before it stretched a forest, but it was not Glipwood Forest. No, here were graceful willows, and mangrove trees that appeared to be *walking*, and amongst them leaped enormous turtles like nothing I had ever beheld in Aerwiar. Where the trees faded into grass, a cottage stood, with a warm glow in its windows and a thread of smoke rising from its chimney.

And all around that mountain the sky burned a million flames of violet fire, but it was another fire than the one that burns above me at the close of every day. For I swear to you, on all my ungobbled Uncle Bahb knew to be good and holy and whole, that we were gazing upon the sunset of a different sun.

Without a word, Sophelia dove into the water that was not water, and I saw her rise, dry and unharmed, on the grass beyond it. "Sophelia!" I cried.

She turned towards me, her shoulders thrown back and her chin held high. Her smile was the silver glow of a cratered moon. "Come with me," she said.

"With all my heart!" I swung my swaddled toes into the pool.

A force like jubilant thunder struck me back again and sent both me and Edd tumbling onto a lower branch.

I saw a pair of flappery wings on a grey body. I saw a single harmless horn. I saw eight eyes that stared back at me in gentle rebuke, as if I had happened upon a child's secret journal no other eyes were meant to see. I felt the tree around us shiver and ripple and turn to water, and we splashed to the ground in a rush of melting light. And then—and then—there was only the creeping and crawling and squatting and squishing and leaping and flurrying and scattering and galloping of the heartbroken, confused creatures of Skree, chasing after a scent that had vanished from the world.

The raggant was gone, and so was its door, and so was my beloved.

Illustrious sirs and madams of the Press, my incompetent but loyal editor, generous donors, I forewarned you of tragedy (unequaled!) but also of hope and of unexpected blessing. No doubt you have already emptied this envelope of its trove of coins and spent them all on Annieran butterpuffs with snoozeberry jam, but allow me a few more words to explain their presence amidst such a ponderous tale of distress and misfortune.

There was a long, sad, shufflesome exodus from Glipwood when the creatures realized the adored bearer of the smell was no more to be found. The digtoads returned to their hovels, the rockroaches to their gullies, the thwaps to their gardens. A few of the animals seem permanently more polished because of Sophelia's betterment. I overheard a chorus of flabbits singing snoutish ballads together on a lonely night while I strolled, dejected, through Glipwood Forest, and at least one grobblin locked himself in the town jail, weeping shamefacedly over a pile of stolen spoons.

But even as the sudden passion of the wild creatures of Skree faded into slumber again, something in the Skreeans themselves seemed to awaken—two somethings, in fact (though I do not know that there is a great deal of difference between them): a respectful and most deliciously-shivery-in-the-belly sense of fear, and a new dawn of wonder. Soon after the invasion it was common to hear folks on the streets of Glipwood discussing the difference between the fuzzy, the softish, and the verbose varieties of squeeblin (all equally untrustworthy!) or debating the implications of a snickbuzzard's bellybutton. And within two days, the owner of Books & Crannies found me at Anklejelly Manor to deliver some utterly surprising and strangely bittersweet news. All of those little green books he'd hidden in the back of the bookstore were gone. *Bought.* And there was a line of people the length of Main Street outside of his bookstore asking for more.

In short, my *Creaturepedia* is a phenomenon. A sensation. A heckler-proof humdinger. It is currently the bestselling book in all of Skree, and I have enclosed with this letter a list of bookshops from Torboro to Lamendron demanding shipments of additional copies immediately for their waiting customers. I have also enclosed (as promised) the Press's share of the proceeds I have earned so far, which, as you can see, are far and above what we had ever dared to hope for.

You might expect that, having previously bitten off my nails in (vain!) anticipation of its publication, I would feel nothing but gleeful, gratified merriment at the runaway success of my eruditious and pulchritudinous volume.

You might expect that, having sought—and found!—fame and fortune in the continent of Skree, having seen my literary industry and eloquence repaid a hundred times over, I would be delivering this news to you with the most exclamatory punctuation my weary pen could muster.

But (as usual!) your expectations are entirely false.

I said that the Books & Crannies owner found me at Anklejelly Manor, for indeed that is where I have been living since Sophelia's disappearance. I have spent the past 36 days, 17 hours, and 45 minutes in the company of Sir Brimney Stupe, and I have determined, finally, definitively, and without a doubt, that I detest the cookery of soup. I also detest posture. Though I have done my best to fill Sophelia's shoes and continue teaching her students, I can assure you that it is the most difficult task in the world to keep your balance walking across a room with shoulders back, nose high, and books piled on your head when you have only one half of a working toe left.

But when the children go home and Sir Brimney retires again to wail and moan in his new underground bedchamber (the trampling of his topiaries and the loss of his daughter did indeed send him into a pro-longulated pestilence), then I am free to take refuge in *The* FLABBIT ROOM, *her* place. I have sought comfort in the stately swoops and punctuary polishment of her letters. I have tried to sniff her sweetly vegetative perfume amongst the moldish aroma of old leathery tomes. I have gazed upon the paintings and the maps of the regions she yearned to explore. And most of all I have endeavored to read every book she read, learn everything she knew, and discover any clues about where she might have gone and how I might find her again. Why did the raggant let her dive into the waterish tree-door, and not me? Where are the other raggants? Where are the other doors? Sophelia's knowl-edge of Aerwiaran mythology and legend was apparently prodigious, particularly in relation to the presence of and passage to other worlds, and it will be weeks before I decipher all the marginalia she scrawled in the pile of the books on her desk alone, especially as I keep getting distracted by the *The Chomping of the Skonk* (rare! thrilling! bloody!).

Which brings me at last to my request, the very reason for this long and lamentiful letter to you.

I beg you, my persevering and magnanimous publisher, to impart unto me a contractual agreement for a sequel to my *Creatupedia*, and to send me the means for continuing my adventuresome journey into parts hitherto unknown. Though Edd Helmer is able to procure much of the necessary equipment for further scientific expeditions, I have urgent need of the items listed on the back of this paper, in particular my personal sketchbooks, quill pens, and disguises hidden under a secret plank in my home in Pennybridge, to which my list will lead you. Please send these to me on the next ship to set sail from Anniera, and we will hope together that the Symian pirates are seasick on the day of its voyage.

Meanwhile, I will fulfill my promise to Sophelia: I will find the best cook in Skree to make soup for her bereaved and bedridden papa. I will polish these children till they gleam in the sunlight and till a more suitable and adequately toed teacher can be hired. And then, when all is ready, and when I can leave this town of my greatest heartbreak behind me at last, I will explore the unexplored Jungles of Plontst, the undocumented trollish lands, and even far beyond, and I will not rest until I have breathed upon every tree that is not a tree and dived into every pool of water that is not water. For I, Ollister B. Pembrick, hunt the eight-eyed raggant, the keeper of the doors, and for the sake of my relentless quest I have already done that which I never before dared: I have marred the innards of a book.

On the title page of *Come With Me: A Treatise on the Exploration of Other Worlds*, I crossed out Sophelia's swooshy, melancholy, yet hopeful "Someday."

And underneath, I wrote in my own shaky but steadfast left-handed scribble:

"Soon."

Yours truly nibbled,

—Ollister Bahbert Pembrick, esq., the Partly-Maimed, Master of Disguisery, President of the Occasional Greengrocer's Alliance of Pennybridge, Isle of Anniera, and Temporary Soup-Maker and Headmaster of the Betterment School for Unpolished Children, Anklejelly Manor, Skree.

WILLOW WORLDS

Written by N. D. Wilson
Illustrated by Joe Sutphin

Some places in this world just can't tell a lie. Oh, I've wandered in woods that could deceive the very wind, and I've been lost in my fair share of fog-swallowed swamps. I've been led astray by snarled city streets and unbounded deserts and a mountain maze or two. I can't even remember the last honest thing the saltwater sea told me. But from the very first time I knelt between the ancient willows on the soft southern bank below Bylome Falls and felt her sweet icy melt on my cracking lips and her cool mist on my face, I knew I'd found the taste of truth. In that place, I set my roots for a time, and every time I drank, I dreamed, and every dream was true.

It was there, on a bed of moss, in an ancient stone hermitage with strange winged creatures carved into the walls, that I first saw how the world had been divided into many. It was there that I saw that the many were all woven into one. I learned what the trees have always known—through root and branch, twig and bough, there are hidden roads and secret ways connecting every leaf. And so it is with the one world . . . and the many worlds within it.

I listened to the Bylome roar. I filled my lungs with cool wet air, and when I closed my eyes, she told me her stories, stories from every world her water had ever seen, stories her water was constantly etching in the grain of the willows around me.

I saw a strange man seeking the falls in another time. His dusty beard drooped below hollow cheeks and his old eyelids seemed too small for his gaping bloodshot eyes. He was tall but bent, and his long coat fell past the top of high muddy boots. Behind him came a struggling donkey, carrying a drooping, bound young man—no more than eighteen years old—like saddlebags and pulling an overloaded wagon covered with brown oiled canvas. Mist from the falls beaded on the cloth as the wagon approached the southern bank between ancient trees. The boy hung as limp as death over the beast's back, his legs and arms swaying like stockings stuffed with mud.

The man halted the donkey and wagon beside the river and stood on the very edge, watching the water swirl past his boots. Flaring his nostrils, he sniffed at the air and then smiled.

"No lies from you here, strander."

The young man on the donkey didn't move.

"Boy!" the man snarled. "D'ya hear me?"

With surprising swiftness, the man snapped the top off of a young willow sapling and whipped it across the back of his prisoner's drooping legs.

The young man yelped. Jerking into consciousness he overbalanced, slipping backward off the donkey and landing hard in the moss and the mud. He had straggly, untrimmed hair and his once white shirt was stained and torn, but his young, hairless jaw was strong, and his eyes were bright with anger.

"It's time for the truth, lad." The man pulled at his beard and grinned. "One way or another. Is this where you felled the wood for

Growlfist's little treasure box?"

"Growlfist," the young man sneered. "Growlfist the Strander King and he'd sooner fry your liver for breakfast than shake your hand. You're a dead man. The deadest I've ever seen."

The man laughed. "Boy, I've lived through nightmares that'd make your Strander King wet his straw-stuffed bed. I am a world walker. He is no more than a brigand." The man crouched down, and scooping up water in one clawlike hand, he lifted it to his lips. He slurped the water down, and drops spilled down his beard as he turned back to the young man. "Tell me your name."

The prisoner sat up. "Untie me."

The man sidled closer to him, still crouching, and drew a long curved knife from his belt. With a quick flash the bonds parted between the young man's wrists and then his ankles.

"Now tell me your name." The man rose to his full height, spinning the knife between his fingers.

"Arthrum," he said, rubbing his wrists. "Arthrum Spuddock. I'm from Dugtown."

The man shut his eyes, lids smooth and taut over his bulging orbs. After a moment, he shook his head.

"You're no Arthrum." He flipped the knife, catching it by the tip, and then opened his eyes. "Did you not just see me take a drink? You can't lie to me with the taste of the Bylome on my tongue."

"The water is poison," the young man said. "It will make you mad."

"Poison, no," said the man. "Mad, maybe. But I am mad already. Mad as a toothy cow in May. Now try again, with the truth."

"Would you believe Welsleyham?" the young man asked. "No? Well all right then." He climbed to his feet and squared himself up to face the taller man. "I am called Helmer. Podo Helmer. Now tell me who you are and where you're from, and why you knocked me on the head and packed me out here like a sack of stolen grain. You don't want me as an enemy, I'm warning you, and you haven't started things well if you want to be friends."

"Podo." The man seemed amused by the name. "Well, Podo, you can call me Wyle. I have wandered farther than far. I am from another place, one that you will likely never see, nor even hear named. And when I am done here, my load and I will be returning through roads you cannot take."

Podo looked back at the cloth covered wagon, behind the donkey glumly chewing on willow shoots.

"Your load?" Podo asked. "What is it?"

"Did the wood for Growlfist's treasure box come from this place?"

"Why does it matter?" Podo asked. "Are you hoping to make one of your own?" He looked at the loaded wagon. "Do you have treasure that needs boxing?"

Wyle scratched his cheek with his knife. "Boy, the box is worth more than any loot that grubby fool puts in it. Yes, I want my own. I want as many of my own as I can shape. I would fell every stick of timber beside these falls to gain just one."

"You believe the stories, then?" Podo asked, crossing his arms. "You call Growlfist a brigand, but you believe the tales of his bottomless box?"

"Do you not?" Wyle asked.

Podo shrugged. "The box is no bigger than two fists. Maybe he has a hoard hidden within, and maybe he doesn't. Maybe it's story he doesn't mind being told."

Wyle nodded. "Aye. Could be," he said. "But in all my wanderings, the only clues I've ever followed are such stories. Tales in inns of bottomless drawers, of cupboards with backs that come and go, of things gone missing and of new things arrived. And in all my collecting, such tales have usually grown from a seed of truth. And they have always been worth the journey."

The tall man strode to the wagon, quickly sliced two strands of twine and then threw back the heavy oilcloth, revealing his load.

Podo's curiosity was stronger than any fear he had of the blade in the man's fast hands. He moved toward the wagon and rose onto his toes.

The bed of the wagon was a jumble of…cabinetry.

"Cupboards?" he asked.

"Indeed," Wyle said. "Hutches, boxes, traps, cupboards, and drawers. Forty-one collected in twenty years spent walking worlds with my ear to the wood. To some folks, I'm a carpenter with a love for doors. To others, I'm a wracker and a timber-haul. And to more than I care to admit, I'm a no-good thief." He patted a worn glossy door, perfectly square with a tarnished brass knob. "This was my first. Once it was set in one end of a bar in a tavern just north of city called New Orleans beside a muddy river that'd put your River Blapp to shame. I spent one long night quietly working a wet saw through that old wood until—just before the sun rose—I slipped out the back with one drawer and one cupboard in my arms." Wyle's bulging eyes sparkled with the memory. "The innkeeper had been complaining of magical rats somehow stealing his cheeses from inside a locked and sealed cupboard." Sheathing his knife, he reached into the wagon and pulled the cupboard out of the jumble and turned it in his hands. It was maybe sixteen inches up, down, and deep, and sealed shut on every side. A box with brass knob and brass hinges. Podo could see the uneven cuts where it had been removed from something bigger.

"Go ahead," Wyle said. "Feel it. You see any place a rat could get inside?"

Podo traced the sealed joints around the back. He touched the cold hinges and knuckle-tapped the top. A piece of paper was tacked to the wood with a handwritten name that Podo couldn't make out.

"What's inside?" he asked.

Wyle grinned, holding the box with flat palms on both sides. His eyes grew even wider. "My world," he said. "Open it."

Podo looked into the man's wild eyes, and then down at the brass knob in front of him. It had to be a trick, a joke. Maybe a clown on a spring would explode out and startle him. Or maybe a viper. Wyle was obviously crazy enough to kidnap one of Growlfist's men, and crazy enough to drink from the Bylome. Maybe watching Podo die would be hilarious to him. Or maybe he was completely mad and truly believed that he held another world in a box in his hands.

There was only one way to find out.

Podo gripped the brass knob in the center of the cupboard door and tugged. With a pop, the door opened.

No clown on a spring. No serpent hissing. There was absolutely nothing in the box. Nothing but darkness.

Podo looked up into Wyle's still wide eyes and then back down at the empty darkness in his hands.

"No offense," Podo said. "But your world is a bit small. And dark."

And then he felt the air moving across his skin, a breeze crawling out of the box. And the smell of salt reached his nostrils and he heard the crash of waves and the creaking of timbers and the cry of gulls and men. All of it together strummed hidden strings in his soul, waking something in him he had never known was there.

"The sea," Podo said. "A ship."

"Aye," said Wyle. "And dirty cheese-thieving rats. Put your hand in it."

Podo hesitated, thinking of traps and snakes and tricks. But he couldn't resist. Slowly, he slid his left hand into the cupboard, spreading his fingers defensively. His hand disappeared. Then his wrist and half his forearm. He stepped closer and reached further. He should be touching Wyle's stomach by now, but instead, all he felt was a temperature change...and sunlight on his knuckles. Groping around, he found a wet rope, and a slick timber deck, rising and falling like a slow swing.

Podo pulled his arm out and stepped back.

Wyle snapped the door shut, smiling.

"Wait," Podo said. "How does it work? I don't understand."

"And that's where I was hoping you could help me," Wyle said. "Of all the stories of heard, of all the cabinets I've hacked and sawn and thieved, all seem to have this power only by happenstance."

Podo looked back at the wagon, and its strange freight struck him very differently now. He wanted to open every little door immediately.

"But then I hear of Growlfist's box," Wyle said. "A box that stores a hoard. A new box, milled and crafted for such a task, and a drunk strander tells me a young fella drew the shortest straw and was sent all the way to Bylome Falls for the timber. Alone, because the poisonous water gets in the air and will drive any man mad." Wyle smiled. "And that fella was you, Podo Helmer. Show me where you gathered the wood and how. I must know everything that you did and more. If I can learn to craft such doors, I will have no more need to scavenge."

"But Growlfist's box might not be like these," Podo said. "Even if it isn't a lie, it still could be something completely different—changed with spells or rites or some stolen charm."

"A bottomless box?" Wyle laughed. "No. If the fool has a hoard at all, it is hidden in another place and that place has a bottom where things are stacked and piled. His treasure box is a doorway, or a lie. Show me where you cut the wood and I will know soon enough."

Podo looked up at the falls, and then around the willow grove. The last time he'd been in this place, the sun had been setting and he'd been in a rush, holding his breath to try and avoid ingesting any misty poisons. He'd tied a pony to a rotting stump well downstream, and then he'd raced around with a small ax and a rusty saw until he'd found a forked willow with a small trunk, just big enough to suit.

Two hands by two hands
green leaf free
branchless, budless,
feet length three
trunk wood and no other
ye wee daft fool.

That's the rhyme that Growlfist had spoken—although Podo was pretty sure that the end hadn't been part of it. And that's exactly what Podo had found in the dim light below the Bylome, and that's what he'd hacked and sawed and lugged away on a pony.

"If I show you where I cut the wood," Podo said. "Will you let me keep one of the cupboards in the wagon?"

Wyle snorted in surprise and moved his hand onto the handle of his knife "No lad. I wouldn't make such a trade for anything under the sun. But I'll let you keep your life, and that's more than I might."

Podo looked at the wagon full of boxes and then back into man's wild eyes. Why would Wyle let him live at all? Why had he been willing to tell him so much already?

"Fine." Podo nodded. "I'll show you. But I want to know where the other doors lead."

Wyle pulled at his beard and shook his head.

Podo didn't give up. "Do they all connect to your world?"

"No," Wyle said. "Not all. Every world has doorways. Even Aerwiar. How do you think I reached this land, if not through a doorway?"

"Right," Podo said. "Well, follow me if you want wood for more." Turning sharply, he began to run upstream toward the falls.

"Boy!" Wyle leapt into motion after him. "There's no rush, lad!"

Podo accelerated, slicing through ferns and hopping logs, veering through trees to break Wyle's line of sight. He could hear the man crashing through brush and trampling rotting limbs behind him, and he ran faster, scanning the ground for anything he might use to defend himself.

"Helmer!" Wyle shouted. "Stop or I'll carve a second smile in that scrawny throat of yours!"

Podo stopped. An old willow limb, about his own height, lay at his feet. A mossy stone cottage quietly possessed the clearing in front of him, but he didn't have time to be curious.

"Here it is!" Podo yelled. "Right here!" Scooping up the heavy limb with both hands, he slipped behind a tree and tried to hold his breath.

Wyle crashed loudly toward him, and as he emerged into the clearing, his eyes were fixed on the cottage in surprise.

With a whoop, Podo launched himself out from behind his tree, already swinging his rotten, mossy club. Spilling beetles and worms, it exploded against Wyle's brow, and he tumbled through the ferns like a thrown doll.

Laughing with relief and pleasure and surprise, Podo dropped what was left of the limb and raced back the way he had come.

What would Growlfist say when Podo arrived with a wagon full of magic doors? What a hero's welcome he would receive beside the fire tonight! Had anyone ever stolen so much? Had anyone ever stolen so much that could be so easily used to steal so much more?

Podo slid to a stop beside the still-chewing donkey and grabbed her bridle.

"Come on, girl!" He tugged. Then he tugged harder.

The donkey chewed.

Podo didn't know if Wyle was unconscious or dead or no more than woozy, and he didn't intend to wait around and find out.

Climbing up onto the wagon, he snapped off a willow switch from the tree above him, and then flicked it sharply against the donkey's rump.

The donkey chewed.

"Go!" Podo yelled. "Now!" And he whipped. Hard.

The donkey's ears twitched. Her tail swung gently.

"Helmer!" Wyle's bellowing voice echoed through the wood. "Helmer!"

Podo whipped wildly. "Godonkeygodonkeygodonkeygo!"

The donkey heehawed, reared forward onto its front legs, and kicked the front of the wagon with both rear legs.

The hitch snapped. Podo rolled backward into the loose cupboards, and the wagon began to bounce and roll down the bank toward the dark eddying pools of the Bylome.

The rear wheels hit water. The wagon began to ease into the current.

"I'll sell your skin to the Fangs for slippers!" Wyle shrieked. "I'll use your giblets for marbles!"

Podo flailed, trying to sit up. The cupboard next to him might be big enough to wriggle through. He could disappear, but into what world? He pulled it open and tried to slide his head and shoulders inside.

As his head passed through the cupboard, he was suddenly looking down an attic wall of tiny doors in a dark, warm room. On a bed below him, a boy was sleeping in strange clothing. His sheets were covered with rubble.

Wrong world. Everything felt wrong about it.

Podo wriggled back out and stood up in the wagon. It was completely in the water now, and floating downstream. Not floating. Sinking. But sinking while moving. Cupboards were beginning to float around his feet.

The donkey was still standing where Podo had left her, but Wyle had returned. He was running along the river bank, a knife in each hand, his lips curled, his eyes wilder than flame.

Podo focused on the biggest cupboards. A strange yellow one with a wide green grain caught his eye and he snatched it out of the rising water.

PLONTST was written on a soggy paper tag attached to it.

Podo knew that word. He'd heard about in stories told around the strander fires. A faraway forest or jungle or something. But definitely in his world. A curved knife flashed past him and plunged into the door.

Grabbing the hilt, Podo used it to pull the door open.

No time to smell. No time to think. Wyle was splashing toward Podo and the flock of floating boxes. He was raising another knife.

Podo raised the open cupboard up above his head, and then he let it drop, slithering his arms and head and shoulders and ribs into a sweaty foul smelling heat.

The box dropped all the way to his feet and he was suddenly falling, but not far. He landed immediately in something soft. And sticky. Slowly, nervously, he opened his eyes and looked around.

All at once, Podo remembered the story he had heard about Plontst. It had been about trolls.

FROM THE DEEPS
OF THE DRAGON KING

Written by A. S. Peterson
Illustrated by Doug TenNapel

It ain't true."

"Is so. Seen it me own self. With me own eye."

"Then how is it you ain't drowned and dead?"

"*That* is a fine question. And deserves a finer answer." He tilted up his cup and drained it, then tapped it thrice upon the table. "Innkeep! Fill her up. I've got a tale for this one."

Then he leaned forward and took a deep breath.

He said:

In the days before the Ban, a dragoneer's life were a high life indeed. We went where we wanted go. We said what we wanted to say. And we had gold enough to want things most folk never dreamed could be wanted at all. High castles? Aye. Caves full of gemrocks? Them too. Slick, black, low-riding wagons with twenty horses of power, and quilted seats? Believe it. I once knew a man that wanted a hundred-weight of fazzle-dove gizzard just so he could feed Fancy Francis, his wee baby gupple-fuzzard, the fanciest of fuzzard food whilst it rode around on his shoulder. Now who ever dreamed of that? A *dragoneer*. That's who. And we got what we wanted. Every time.

But a life of luxury has got to be lived at somebody's expense, don't it? Does indeed. And it was dragons what paid for it. Every scale was worth a fortune. An ounce of wyrmblubber was worth more than gold. Painters the world over bargained their lives away for a single dragon's whisker, for there was no finer brush in the realm for creating their silly pictures. The prize of every army in Dang was its dragonpikers, and where do you think they got their dragonpikes? That's right, dragon's *teeth*—the sharpest and stickiest stickers that ever stuck. I tell you, every kibble and giblet of a dragon is a treasure. We wanted it all. And we wanted it hard. And we wanted it as quick as it could be got.

That's what drawn us to our doom—and it was Podo Helmer led us there.

See, it ain't dragons a dragoneer hunts. It's young'uns. Most folks never know there's a difference. A young'un be the size of this inn with a head like a mountain boulder. But a grown'un? A grown dragon is the mountain itself. A dragoneer ain't fool enough to go looking for that kind of trouble. Nope, you got to find them young. And that's the pickle of a dragon hunt. A biddie don't wander far from its hen, does it? Neither do a sqwyrm, that's what we call the little ones. Most folk call them all dragons, see? But the males? Them are drakes. The females? Them are wyrms. And the babies? We call them sqwyrms. No self-respecting dragoneer would ever call hisself a sqwyrm hunter, though, would he? Course not. A word like *dragoneer* has got some swagger to it. And we like our swagger. Even if it's really sqwyrms we're after.

It's a dangerous business, as you'd imagine. Once we find a sqwyrm and tag it and bag it and get its bits stowed aboard the ship, we run for port as fast as the wind will take us, 'cause it ain't but a small matter of time before mama wyrm comes a-slithering around looking for baby. And you can imagine how she gets in a rage when baby can't be found. That's the trick of it—finding a sqwyrm in the wild, alone and unwatched, yet close enough to a harbor that you get safe before mama comes running.

As I said, dragoneers is a vain lot. Land-living folk think we're heroes of the sea, when mainly we just snatch little ones and run for cover. It begins to look cowardly if you think on it much. But it does pay well. Fazzle-gizzard, remember? Sometimes a man has got to have some fazzle-gizzard for Fancy Francis. And dragoneering is a sure way to get it.

So when Podo Helmer, the infamous pirate, sauntered aboard the *Gilded Whilly* and said he had a plan to harvest sqwyrms without the threat of mama wyrm giving chase, you'll understand why he had the captain's attention.

He said, "Tell me something, Whilly. How long you been snatching sqwyrms?"

Captain Whilly was a nervous man—odd quality in a dragoneer, but it kept him alive—and he wasn't quick to answer. He didn't care for pirates, and he cared for infamous pirates least of all. Especially Podo Helmer. Whilly shuffled around the deck a bit and kept a wary eye on Podo's legs. Finally he answered him short and sweet. "Four years."

After he said it, he tensed up and squinched his eyes shut, afraid he might be kicked for his trouble. You've heard of Podo Helmer's legs, I assume. The man had legs that would make a crowd stop and stare. They was pure muscular. They rippled in the light, and he always kept his pants rolled up so folks could admire them. Such fearsome legs— and he knowed how to use them. If he spotted a man on his crew that didn't seem mean enough to inspire the fear a pirate ought, he'd kick him overboard. Some say he kicked a hundred men over the rail before he'd instilled a proper scowl into everyone that dared to sail with him. When he needed to call the deck to order, did he ring the ship's bell like any ordinary captain? Blimey, no. He stomped a foot on the deck and shuddered the whole hull. Sent men stumbling out of the belowdecks like they'd been staggered by a cannonblast. Marvelous legs, they was. And Captain Whilly was right to be wary of such terrible appendages.

But Podo had no need of kicking his gams on the day he come to the *Gilded Whilly*. He asked, "In them four years, how many sqwyrms has you caught?"

"We've the best record of any dragoneer crew this side of the Dark Sea. We've brought in two a year. Enough to enrichen every man on my crew, I can assure you." Whilly gulped. "Sir."

"So eight in all?"

"Yes." Captain Whilly gulped again, feeling he may have answered incorrectly. "Yes, sir."

Podo leaned in and appraised Whilly with one of his fearsome eyes. Whilly squeaked ever so slightly.

Podo huffed in amusement. "Eight? In four years?"

"We can check our records to be sure, but I believe my account is accurate." Whilly squeaked again before adding. "Please don't kick me—sir."

"What if I told you I could bring in that many of the beasts, and do it in a single day?"

When he made that claim, the entire crew went shifty and eyed one another like they'd heard something that didn't quite line up. These men was dragoneers. They knowed their trade. And they didn't give credence to a pirate who claimed he could do it better.

A nervous chuckle escaped Whilly's throat. "Why, that's impossible."

"Is it now?" Podo turned away and paced the deck with a grin. He tapped one foot thoughtfully, an alarming sight, and several sailors backed away in caution. "But if it *was* possible. How much might that be worth to you? Quite a lot, I'd reckon. Am I right?"

"If such a thing were possible, we'd be richer than any men in Aerwiar."

Podo winked at a crewmen. "Aye. And maybe even richer than that." This seemed to confuse Whilly, but he kept his thoughts to himself. Podo scratched his chin and then nodded decisively. "I'll do it for half."

"Excuse me? Do what? For half the what?"

Podo smiled wide. "I'll help you bring in all the sqwyrms you can stomach. And in return, I get half the gold. Maker knows I got no use for half the sqwyrms."

Whilly sputtered and gibbered for a moment before he could answer. "Ss . . . sir, I don't think you—"

Podo stomped his foot and the deck quivered. "*Furthermore*, I'll take command of this here vessel until the deed is done."

Whilly's mouth open and closed three times but nothing came out.

"Don't you worry, Whilly. You can be me first mate and I'll have her back to you without a scratch. Them's my terms. Take them or leave them."

Whilly took a bold step forward and found his voice. "Then we shall lea—"

"*But if you leave them*, be sure that I'll have no trouble finding another wheedlely bunch of sqwyrm-stealing blubber-jobbers to take under me wing and make rich as the Maker and famous as fame itself." Podo raised one eyebrow and the icy blue eye that glared out from beneath it stabbed a pang of terror into Whilly's heart. "And you can be sure I'll let them know what a cowardly heap captains the *Gilded Whilly*."

Did I mention that dragoneers is a vain lot? Well I should have. We can't stand to have our trade belittled, nor our personhoods wrongly besmirched. I reckon that made us an easy mark for the piratical wiles of Podo Helmer, but such was our fate. And we swallered it whole.

So a week before the Dragon Day Festival, we sharpened our sharpoons, we knitted our nets, we pitched our hull, we buffed our brasswork, we said goodbye to our biddies and huggables, and we set sail. But where was it we sailed for?

A fine question.

Even Whilly didn't know. "We're clear of the harbor, sir. What course shall we set?"

Podo looked around at the horizon and sniffed at the air. Then he turned and scowled back at the dwindling wharf behind us. After a few minutes he seemed to satisfy whatever misgivings haunted him and he told us to set a course southeast.

Captain, now First Mate, Whilly wrinkled up his face. He seemed to think this an ill-advised course, but he kept his thoughts to himself and shouted "Set a course south by east!"

"South by east, aye!" cried Billy Munken, the helmsman. He spun the wheel, the *Whilly* lurched to port, the yards creaked above us as the crew adjusted the tackle, and we was away.

Three days later, Whilly was a nervous wreck—more than usual. He paced the deck at all hours. He sweated through his coat. He mumbled to himself. And he kept a fretful eye trained toward the northwest, toward home. When Podo ventured out of his stateroom to appraise our progress, Whilly approached him.

"Sir, we've kept southeast for three days and are far beyond the safe reach of any port. If we attempt to take a sqwyrm this far asea we're doomed. Its mother will catch us up. We'll have no hope of outrunning her. We'll be crushed! Eaten! Chewn, sir. We shall be *chewn*! Perhaps even gnawn!" At this point Whilly became so distressed that he could scarcely prevent himself from outright tears and he had to leave off from further speech in order to master himself.

"If any chewing's done, it'll be us that does it, laddie. Just you keep southeast and trust Podo. And get you some rest, Whilly. You look right peaked. We'll have arrived in another couple days and you'll need your strength."

"Arrived? Arrived where? There's nothing out here!"

Podo winked at him. "Just you leave that to me, Whilly."

Whilly buried his face in his hands and tottered toward the nearest hatch. When he'd safely gone out of sight below, Podo went into his

stateroom and reemerged with a wooden chair. He carried it onto the
poopdeck where he placed it thoughtfully, sat down, kicked his legs up
on the rail, leaned back, and proceeded to stoke up his pipe. "It's a fine
day for sailing, ain't it, boys?"

The crewmen standing nearby looked at one another nervously,
then looked at Podo's legs even more nervously. "Yes, sir," said Hodd,
who was the bravest of them. Podo winked at him and spent the rest of
the day surveying the sea with apparent pleasure.

First Mate Captain Whilly spent the rest of the day poring over sea
charts. And the endeavor only distressed him further. The south seas
are rarely sailed by dragoneers. And the east seas even rarlier. So you
can imagine that the prospect of sailing a *southeastern* sea was not one
that provided Whilly a smidgen of relief.

I take it you've seen the maps and know what I'm referring to.
The east side of the Dark Sea is the domain of the Symian Pirates.
I've already told you that Whilly didn't care for pirates, and for Podo
Helmer least of all. But Podo Helmer was the fearsomest pirate in all
of Skree, not necessarily in all the sea itself—there's pirates elsewhere
too, and of all them that is, the Symian Pirates is generally considered
the worst. Folk say they tattoo themselves with misspelled words just
for the horror of it. They say they swear off vegetables and eat only
the rarest and bloodiest of meats. They say their women got bearded
bellies—and *no eyebrows at all.* They even say when a Symian Pirate
is born, it comes into the world with a wee biddy knife clutched in its
wee biddy teeth. That's right. Symian Pirate babies got teeth. And they
know how to use them for terrible deeds. So Whilly, of course, weren't
anxious to sail east.

And the southlier seas is the waters of the Dragon King, Yurgen
himself. They say him and his kin churn the seas white as snow. They
bash it and slash it and slather it up until it's no more than a hoary
foam terrible to behold, for the dragons are angry still from grudges
old as the mountains themselves, and naught can assuage their grief

over losses that men have long forgot. To sail the seas of the Dragon King is a mad dream indeed. And so Whilly could find no respite from his worry in the thought of waters further south.

And beyond them worrisome dangers is the possibility of running afoul of a Trollian Armada—a fleet of stone-carven vessels beaten out of the earth by the Trolls of Plonst and kept afloat by ruinous magiks. They ply the seas and prey upon the Symian Pirates, their sworn enemies. But trolls is scarcely able to tell one human from another. They're as like to squash an innocent merchantman—or dragoneer—as they are a Symian sloop of ill repute. And not only trolls, but there's legend of the Gyres of Pnumb, great whorls hundreds of paces wide that drift across the sea and suck down all they can pull into their dreadful throats. Pnumb Floo, the great cartographer, was the only man to ever return alive from being gyre-swallered and he was dizzy the rest of his life. Never walked a straight line again. Apt to fall down with no warning at all. Every map he drew after he come back was squiggly and useless. A terrible fate.

And there's more dangers, as you well know, the Bright Squalls, the Sea of Spouts, the Languishing Deep, the Haunted Smoldrums. All these was on Whilly's mind as his beloved ship slipped further and further southeast under the command of Podo Helmer.

On the seventh day of the voyage, First Mate Captain Whilly could take it no more. He screwed up his courage, took up his charts, and approached Podo with a sense of purpose that he'd rarely shown in his life. With his charts stuffed under his arms and a fat bead of sweat rolling down his nose, he proclaimed, "We must turn back!"

Podo calmly puffed on his pipe and said, "How's that?"

"We must turn back while we can. I don't know what this plan of yours is, but you have no notion of what it takes to harvest a sqwyrm, and you'll kill us all if you press forward with this madness."

Whilly looked as if he could hardly believe he'd spoken so harshly to a man he so thoroughly feared, and almost immediately he began to apologize. "Forgive me, sir. Mr. Helmer. But these men are my responsibility and—"

"You ever hear of a woman named Nurgabog, Whilly?"

"Nurga-what?"

"Bog. Nurga*bog*. Sounds like a swamp gas, but it ain't. It's a woman."

Whilly looked around at us for help, but everyone merely shrugged.

"And not just any woman neither. A dangerous kind of woman. The sort that's gnarled as an old tree, but clever as a hungry ridgerunner. Fiesty too. Maybe it's hard for a feller like you to understand, but for a feller like me, it's a mighty desirable set of qualities. I courted her."

"You courted a nurgabog?"

"Not *a* nurgabog, laddie. *Nurgabog*. That's her name. She's a Strander." Several of the crew nodded in recognition—not of Nurgabog, mind you, but of Stranders. "Filthy. Wily. Ugly. Ignoble. Half toothless—and *all* woman, nappy head to wretched toenail."

"That sounds very fine, sir. But the ship—"

"Every man of the Strand had his designs on her. But it was Lunker Jim that had her. He was what Stranders call a big'un." Podo turned to Whilly and raised an eyebrow. "You know why that is?"

"No, sir."

"'Cause he was *big*."

The crew gathered around let out a collective "ahhh" and nodded their heads.

"But wouldn't *anyone* call that a big'un?" asked Whilly.

"And he was mean as he was big. Whenever some other feller came slinking around and making eyes at Nurgabog and her wondrous ugliness, Lunker Jim would pitch a fit. He'd hop up and down and charge about and terrify whoever it was that had come with their designs. Men tried all manner of ways to get to her and catch her eye and lure her away, but Lunker Jim had a keen eye for keeping what was his. And Nurgabog? She loved it. She loved to see him whack and wail and carry on and send the other fellers running. So what do you think I did?"

Whilly looked over his shoulder hoping the question had been addressed to someone else. When he decided it hadn't been, he hurried to answer. "I don't know, sir."

"I waited. And I watched. I bided me time until I had me a plan to woo her. I slunk outside the shack where Lunker Jim lived and I made his business my business. I followed him where he went and I learned his ways and learned to think like him until I found the answer I was after. You see, there was one thing in the world Lunker Jim loved more than Nurgabog. What do you think it was?"

"His ma?" shouted one of the crew.

"His pa?" shouted another.

"Nope," said Podo.

"Whackin' fellers?"

"All You Can Eat Night at the Windy Monkey?"

"Nope and nope."

Podo looked around at the whole crew and when he was sure there were no more guesses, he leaned forward and raised his bushy eyebrows and said, "His birthday!"

The crew seemed to agree that loving one's birthday more than one's Nurgabog made a whole heap of sense, though First Mate Captain Whilly seemed to become more annoyed with every passing moment of Podo's Nurgabogian epic.

"And who here knows how Stranders celebrate a birthday?"

Silence. A few of the crew turned up their eyes and fingered their chins in thought, but most merely shrugged and awaited Podo's answer.

"A Strander is a thief and a rogue through and through. But it's on his birthday that he's got to prove it. See, a Strander believes that when he's born he steals his life from his mother, taking a little bit of hers to be his own. So once a year, on the anniversary of that first bit of thieving, a Strander has to go out into the world and steal something he ain't never stole before. Some Stranders simply go out and get themselves a new rock and claim 'Oh, but this one's not like any rock I ever saw' or they put in as little effort as they can muster and pluck something silly from a Torrboro merchant's stall. But others, those like Lunker Jim, they take the business as serious as can be. Lunker Jim spent all year plannin' his birthday heist. He aimed to be sure that no one forgot he was the most devious, most theivious Strander to ever crawl the banks of the Blapp. And on the year that I laid my wooing eye upon Nurgabog and her womanly charms, Lunker Jim had planned a terrific heist indeed. He aimed to steal the crystalline eyes of the Torrboro Castle Kitten. Gems the size of lumpkins they are, and worth a king's fortune."

By this time, the crew had gathered around Podo and many had even taken their seats at his fearsome feet. They looked up at the pirate in rapt attention and awaited the unfolding of his tale. All but Whilly, who had dropped all his sea charts to the deck, save one—and this he studied intently while Podo spoke.

"So on the evening of Lunker Jim's birthday, he called the whole Strand together and laid out his plan. He would slip across the river through an ancient tunnel he'd lately uncovered. Then he'd steal through the sewers and emerge inside the castle courtyard. Simple so far, and any fool could figure that much. But once inside the castle, the guards would be swarming and looking for such as a Strander come lurking. And the Kitten's eyes are the prize of the city. They're lit from below by great watchfires and guarded by Troll mercenaries trained to sniff out cat burglars and squash them flat. But Lunker Jim had laid his plans for a year and he had it all figured. When he emerged from the sewers, he gave the signal and blew out the tunnel he'd found under the river. The whole mighty Blapp swirled and gurgled down into the ancient sewerways and backed up the entire system. In no time the city streets was awash with the smelliest, rottenest backwashed water you ever smelt. It was chaos. And the stink of it plugged up the trolls' noses till they went *smellblind*. The rushing water rose up and put out the watchfires and the Kitten went dark. In all the ruckus and stink, the Stranders run amok through the town distracting the guards from Lunker Jim's purpose. The guards was running this way and that and slipping in the water and being washed away like rocks in a gulley. And in all that madness, it weren't nothing for Lunker Jim to scurry up the Kitten and pry out its eyes. Once he had them, he leapt into the water and let it wash him back down to the river where he had but to swim to the far side and make his way home in victory.

"But Lunker Jim weren't the victor that night. And who do you think was?"

Podo leaned forward and let his sly grin settle in while the sailors wondered.

"Nurgabog?" someone asked, and Podo raised an eyebrow.

"Hmm. After a fashion, I suppose you could look at it that way. But let me tell you something Lunker Jim didn't know. It wasn't just him that had a birthday that night. In fact, it probably never occurred to the big lunk that two people could be born the same day. And it certainly didn't occur to him that the other person would be Podo Helmer. Hah! That's right."

"So you're twins?" said a skinny old sailor named Gnut.

"What? No, you idiot. We just got born on the same day."

"Then how come you ain't twins?"

Several of the crew nodded thoughtfully. Podo waved his hand in the air and continued.

"I ain't no Strander by birth. I fell in with them later. So not one of them ever wondered about my birthday. But I reasoned that if I was to have Nurgabog for my own, I'd best act like one of them and live by their ways. And that meant thieving something I ain't never thove before. And can you guess what it was?"

"The Kitten's eyes?" asked Gnut.

Podo stared at Gnut as if he might kick him overboard. Once Gnut seemed properly quieted, Podo leaned forward in his chair and said: "Nurgabog."

"I knew it was Nurgabog," said Gnut victoriously. Podo eyed him down and Gnut whispered once more to the man sitting next to him, "I *knew* it was Nurgabog."

Podo ignored him and kept on. "I waited until Lunker Jim slipped into his tunnel. As soon as he and the rest of the Stranders was gone, I sauntered into Nurgabog's tent and said, 'Nurgabog, I aim to steal ye.' She batted her lazy eye at me and said, 'What if I don't aim to be stole?' and I told her, 'I can't live without you no more. Your skin is crusty as the bark of a moldy oak and I can't go on without its touch. Your eyes is the color of a milktoad's tongue, and I don't want to live without their gaze. Your brain is like a varmit trap that lays in wait for unsuspecting critters and snaps shut without remorse or pity, and I long to be snatched in its embrace. Will you agree to be stole?' I asked her.

'You ain't even appreciated my hair yet, nor my teeth, nor my odor, singing voice, lips, nor toes. No man can steal me without he can sing praises of my crooked toes.'

"So I went on with my praises of her unsavory yet blissful qualities until at last she was mine. I gathered her up and we made for the coast where I had a ship waiting to carry us away. We was long gone by the time Lunker Jim come home with his kitty eyes and found himself robbed of a greater treasure than he'd ever known. It was a beautiful thing, I tell you."

"What happened then?" said a wistful sailor with dreamy eyes.

"We sailed the seas together, a pirate and his pirate lass, until she came to long for the Strand and all she'd left behind—all except Lunker Jim, that is. In the end she went back. But I knowed I never could. If Lunker Jim was ever to find me, I'd be done for. I did mention he was a big'un, right? That was the last I ever seen of Nurgabog. Aye, but a man can dream, can't he? Nurgabog . . . Nurgabog . . . just the sound of her makes me shivery."

By this point, First Mate Captain Whilly had reached the extent of his frustration. He stamped a foot (a daring move in the presence of Podo Helmer's legs) and shouted, "What has that got to do with us?"

Podo patiently turned to look at Whilly. "Ain't you heard a word I said, Whilly?"

"Yes! Yes, I heard every useless word of it! And none of it has anything to do with the fact that we are sailing directly toward the Sunken Mountains!" He held up his chart and thrust a meaty finger at an area of the south seas surrounded by red warnings, capital letters, exclamation points, and a large frowny face.

Podo smiled at him. The crew looked around at each other in uncertainty.

"The *Sunken Mountains*?" Whilly went on. "Are all of you addled? He's leading us directly into the Dragon Kingdom. Yurgen's kin! He'll have us eaten and chewn!"

Podo got up from his seat and put his arm around Whilly.

"Do I look like the sort of man who would sail out to be eaten and chewn?"

The blood-drained out of First Mate Captain Whilly's face as he began to regret his tone and offense. "No. No, sir."

"And did you listen to my story, Whilly?"

"Yes, sir."

"Nurgabog, you see, is the sqwyrms. And Lunker Jim? Who's he?" The entire crew scratched their various chins, heads, ears, and cheeks in bafflement. "Great Maker, you are a thick bunch of skulls. Lunker Jim is mama wyrm. See? And what's Jim's birthday?"

Gnut's face lit up. "Dragon Day!"

"Aye. The Dragon Day Festival. Good lad. Do you see it now, Whilly?"

First Mate Captain Whilly did not see it.

"Try to pay close attention, Whilly. We're headed for the Sunken Mountains. And what's in the Sunken Mountains?"

"Dragons."

"You'd be right every day of the year—every day but one."

Whilly's face began to unfold in the growing light of revelation. "They all go to Fingap Falls!"

"Now your noggin's noggin! They all go to the falls and the prize is left at home. Only *we* aim to be there, and we'll be long gone before anyone comes a-slithering back to find our mischief."

"It's genius!"

"Why, thank you. I thought so meself," said Podo as he preened his beard. "Now hustle up, boys. Let's get ready to do some dragon hunting. We'll be in the Sunken Mountains come dawn, and I aim to catch me a big'un!"

Having learned where we was bound, and what it was we intended, you might think we turned our minds to our work and left our worries behind, but that weren't the case. Not even a wee bit. For we'd set our aim to trespass in Yurgen's Halls, and for dragoneers, there's no place in the Maker's many seas that fills a mind with more forboding and fear—for you see, it's always Yurgen we've trespassed against, if not in geography then in deed. We've made sport of his young and ground them in the mill of commerce. So the last place in the world a dragoneer wants to find himself is asea in the Sunken Mountains, the very throneroom of the great granddrake of them all.

"But are you sure they've *all* gone to the Falls?" asked Whilly once his excitement had worn away.

Podo shrugged off the question. "Yes, Whilly. They *all* go."

"But how can you be sure? If there's even one that stays behind..."

"I know cause I been there."

Whilly shook his head and looked annoyed. "You've *been* there? To the Sunken Mountains? That's impossible."

"Aye. A year past. We'd run afoul of a Symian buccaneer named Horvath and thought if we set a course for Yurgen's Deep, he'd leave off the chase. We was right, but we was also unlucky. A squall blew up and before we could get clear of it, we was blown right into the heart of the Sunken Mountains. We made our peace with the Maker and resigned ourselves to being gobbled whole—but when the sun come up, we was unchewn. The surface of the water was calm and smooth like a mirror. There was no sign whatever of the churning and foaming an ear hears tell of. But we had no want of enjoying our stay, so we set our sails and pointed the ship west.

"All was quiet and peaceful till along about noonday. That's when they began to breach. Young ones. Sqwyrms. All around us. They'd leap up out of the water to spin and fall back with a great slap and a spray of water. We was terrified. Were they warning us off? Were they attacking? Were they calling Yurgen to come and swallow us whole? We didn't know. But we sure didn't like it. And then one come near the ship and swam alongside it for a spell. We was in a fit of fear, so we brought out our sole, rusty sharpoon—pirates got little use for sharpoons, and littler skill at throwing them—and the first mate took aim. But just as he was about to heave it, the critter rolled over and looked at him and—"

Podo paused and frowned.

"And what?" asked Whilly.

"It smiled at us."

Whilly threw up his arms and shook his head. "A dragon? *Smiled?*"

"Now don't get you excited. I seen what I seen. I tell you the thing slithered over on its side and smiled a big toothy smile right at us. It give our first mate pause, and before he could regain his wits and fling the sharpoon, the beast dove and was gone. And that's when we realized what it was. They wasn't attacking. They wasn't warning us. They was playing. Just like young'uns in a treehouse or a swimming hole. And there wasn't no grown'uns to be seen.

"We sailed through them as they frolicked for most of the afternoon until we left the mountains behind.

"We scratched our heads and kept our thoughts to ourselves for a long time. None of us knowed what to think of what we seen. But as the sun crept low, we saw something terrible on the horizon. The sea frothed and boiled and a great swell of water was heaped up like a blanket throwed over a hilltop. It was Yurgen's kin. Their coils heaved out of the water like mountains. Their fins beat the sea and whipped it white. They was so many they was uncountable. As far as a man can spy there was nothing but angry sea and dragonflesh.

"We thought we was doomed, but to our relief, they didn't notice us no more than a bomnubble notices a phleabug. They rushed past us all through the night and we could hear them churning the sea and singing their eerie songs in the darkness. When the sun come up, they was gone.

"A few days later we tied up at the wharf in Torrboro and the whole town was just getting home from their Dragon Day festivities. Don't think nobody else thought too much on what had happened. But it wouldn't leave me alone, and it didn't take too long to put three and three together to come up with six. So I bided me time and told meself that come Dragon Day the next year, I'd find me a hearty crew of dragoneers, and I'd be ready.

"So *yes*, Whilly! I been there. And *yes*, they'll *all* be gone. You satisfied?"

First Mate Captain Whilly didn't appear satisfied. He appeared distressed. But he said, "Yes, sir."

And so it was we come to the Sunken Mountains. An eerie place, it is. Here and there a jagged peak juts up out of the deep like a gravestone. The water beneath the ship turned clear as glass and we could see down into the yawning chasms between the peaks. The sea was so calm and clear that you felt you was aloft in the air and floating through the Killridge. There was sheer cliffs below us and smaller peaks stretching up like they was drowned men reaching one last time for the surface. And at times you could spy dark caverns burrowed into the sides of the mountains where Yurgen and his kin delved into the earth in the elder days. They burrowed and tore at the mountains, looking, some say, for secret stones of great power with which to rend the world. Others say they were stricken by a woeful grief and tunneled so deeply that they begged the peaks would fall down and cover them up and assuage them of their pain. I don't know. You sail the seas long enough and you hear all manner of tale, but I tell you this—I seen the dragon hollows in them mountains, and I feared what might have been looking back at me from within their watery dark.

"All right, boys. Let's get to work," said Podo. He looked out over the stillness of the sea and for the first time since he'd come aboard, he seemed uncertain. His humor was gone and his jaw was clenched and he looked like a man steeling himself for a fight. And it's a fight was coming, make no mistake—though he had no idea what a fight it would be.

"Quod!" cried Whilly. "Get aloft! Set the dragonwatch."

First Mate Captain Whilly has thus far in me tale seemed an odd fit for a dragoneer, but now he found himself in his element. He'd not have been a captain of a dragoneer if he didn't know the way of the work. And now that Podo Helmer had led him to the greatest hunting grounds a dragoneer ever dreamed of, he set himself to his craft with singular skill.

A sailor name of Pea Quod was the first of the dragonwatch. He skimpered up the mainmast and settled into the buzzard's nest with his peeperglass. From high up in the nest, he could see anything that stirred the sea for miles about and he set to glaring this way and that in search of sqwyrm-sign—that's what we call the peculiar stir and roll of the sea when a sqwyrm is swum up near the surface and readying itself to breach.

Meanwhile, the crew busied itself with the dragonboats. The *Gilded Whilly* had six of them. Each thirty feet long and crewed by ten oarsmen, a skipper, and a sharpooner. The boats was lowered. The 'poons was sharped and fixed each to six hundred feet of rope. The crew took their positions, and then we waited.

A dragonhunt is mostly a business of boredom and waiting, see? We get ourselves settled in a likely spot, and then we ready our gear and we wait for the cry from the dragonwatch. At any moment the call can go up and the chase can commence, but in the meanwhile, you sit and you wait, and you wonder if this is the hunt that'll be your last.

All morning we waited. We stared up at Pea in the nest and watched him watching the water. The sun crawled high and beat down with a terrible heat. Podo paced the deck, and as the day wore on he stomped his magnificent legs harder and harder and we could feel in the shudder of the ship that he was impatient and nervy. First Mate Captain Whilly on the other hand was calm as a digtoad on a sillypad. He stood on the foredeck with his hands clasped behind his back and appraised the sea before him as if it were his pupil.

Come noonday, some was getting slap-happy, and the rest was getting nappish. I was hanging my head and feeling the need of a few minutes to close me eyes when I heard the old call to battle: "Yonder she breaches!"

It was Pea in the nest and he was jumping up and down and shouting it over and over again. "Yonder she breaches! Yonder she breaches!"

"Bearing?" asked Whilly.

"Due east, captain. A league and a half again."

Podo and Whilly ran to the port rail and strained their eyes to the east.

"Launch the boats!" cried Whilly, and we were off.

I was in a boat called *Sea Beater*. Our skipper was an old hand named Dodger Thew, and our sharpooner was a tall lanky boy called Eddy McFeal. Eddy had notched three kills on his dragon iron over the years—his sharpoon, that is—and he'd gained quite a reputation for his hurling arm. It was an able crew, and they was a pleasure to pull an oar for.

All six boats rowed east as fast as their crews could pull them, while Podo and Whilly commanded what was left of the crew aboard the ship and spotted for us.

The peculiar thing about crewing a dragonboat is that you got no idea where you're going or when you'll come upon the beast. Down on the water, all you can see is the waves about you and the *Gilded Whilly* behind as they yell and point and do their best to aim the skippers toward the breaching sqwyrm. So you pull them oars for all you're worth and try not to think about how you might be swallowed whole in an instant.

On that first sighting, I reckon we drove hard for an hour before Pea lost sight of the sqwyrm. That's how it goes. The beast comes up and does his dance on the surface, but before long he tires and sounds—dives, that is. He descends back to the deeps to do whatever it is dragons do.

Three times we repeated that tale. A breach. A chase. And a disappointment.

If we had any sense about us, we'd have give up the game and gone home. But Podo wouldn't have it. He'd come for the harvest, and he wasn't one to leave before he'd got what he come for.

We was all tired. We'd sat under the sun for hours, and pulled at the oars till our arms had gone jellified. It was like the sqwyrms knew it. Like they was waiting for it. Like they knowed if they got us tired and irritable we'd be easier playthings, for just as we was sitting nappish and grouchy and thinking of dinner, we spotted it—sqwyrm-sign.

Some hundred yards distant, another dragonboat was drifting as sleepily as we was, when the sea around it began to swell and stir. It's not a frightful looking thing. It's more just odd—you'd think it lovely even, if you didn't know what it portended. The water begins to swuzzle and whirl and well up like a grey belly. Normally, it's a thing you'd be glad to pause and take a gander at, but mind you, this was taking place with an entire dragon boat slap in the middle of it. Their skipper yelled and hollered and the oarsmen heaved. They got the boat in motion and it slid off the swollen spot of water just as the head of the beast broke the surface. It shot out of the water like a boulder attached to a great tree trunk. The thing rose up, up, up over the boat and then—*sqwaaplooosh*—it crashed down beside them and sent a wave of seawater coursing over the gunwales.

For a moment you could see the crew was stone still in shock. I think they scarcely believed they'd lived through such a thing. But the shock didn't last no more than a moment, for the skipper howled, "*Give her the iron!*" And the sharpooner's arm shot forward like a catapult. He plunged four feet of dragon-iron into the flank of the beast. The creature writhed in pain. A great loop of it lashed up out of the water, and then it coiled itself and sprung away in a flash of speed and blue scales.

The oarsmen pulled in their oars and as the rope attached to the sharpoon paid out behind the fleeing sqwyrm, a crewman looped it around the tow-pole. He pulled the rope tight and looped it again and again, taking in the slack until the boat jerked to life and sped away— dragged behind the sqwyrm. This is what we call being dragon-bound. Once bound, the crew has only to hang on tight and wear the beast down. When the sqwyrm tires of the chase, the crew reels themselves in, draws up alongside, and the sharpooner takes up his heart-pike—a long, slender iron made to pierce deep—and hurls the killing blow.

That's the way of it. Then it's a business of drawing the *Gilded Whilly* alongside the slain beast and cutting it up for storage and the trip home.

You should have seen how Podo Helmer jumped and danced while he watched that first sqwyrm taken. I expect the whole ship was a-shudder as he stomped his magnificent legs across her deck. We could see him smiling a mile away, and I could even see in First Mate Captain Whilly's gait that his spirits was coming up for air.

As that first sqwyrm was being towed back to the ship, Pea got to hopping and hollering again. "Yonder's a breach!" This one was on the far side of the ship and we couldn't see that one at all. We let the other boats be bothered by it while we bided our time and watched our own patch of sea.

But as the other boats went out of sight on the far side of the *Whilly*, we began to feel mighty lonely, like we'd been abandoned by our brethren. A dragoneer only sees a few sqwyrms in an entire year, and maybe only harvests one or two of those. But here we'd already seen two in a day—more if you count the three Pea spotted that got away—and Podo had told us there was lots more than that even. So when we found ourselves floating our own patch of sea with all our mates gone off, we felt small. And it weren't too long before we began to feel watched as well. It were uncomfortable.

And then, from far off on the other side of the *Whilly*, we heard the sounds of splintering wood. And after that the sounds of men yellering in fear.

You ever wonder what an ant is thinking just before you step on it? Like when you raise up your foot, but just before you stamp it down, the little feller stops and looks around like he knows something terrible is about to come thundering, but he can't quite tell where it's coming from or what it is? And then—*sqwaamp*! He's nothing but boot jelly on the cobbles.

That's how the crew of the *Sea Beater* felt while we waited and listened and worried.

Then come the boot.

Sqwyrm-sign. Bigger than I ever seen. The water turned to a boil all around the boat, and before a one of us could utter a word, we was gone up, up, up into the air. I looked over the rail and seen Pea staring back at me from the *Gilded Whilly*'s buzzard nest—we was both up in the air and looking straight across at one another. The beast had come up under us and we was balanced on its boulderous head as it towered

out of the sea. But just as I was meeting Pea's eye and his jaw was falling open, the creature flopped back into the water and we tumbled down with it. The boat landed upside down and bobbed like a turtle as the crew tried to climb onto the hull.

As I clenched a hand onto the keel and hauled meself out of the water, I seen Eddy McFeal, our sharpooner, climb to his feet, sharpoon in hand. He wobbled and tottered and clenched his jaw and had a murderous look in his eye as he raised his iron. I turned and saw the beast had come around. It was barreling through the water at full speed—right toward us. Just before it struck, Eddy flung his 'poon. 'Twas one of the daringest sights I ever seen. The 'poon flew like a stab of lightning and pierced the beast betwixt its eyes. Eddy's throw drove the pike brain-deep, killing with a single hurl—a thing unheard of in the world.

It's a shame it killed Eddy too.

As the rest of us jumped away, Eddy hadn't a chance. He stood in the path of the monster to see his blow strike true. I doubt he had time to appreciate that it had. As the charging beast died, it smashed into the *Sea Beater* and poor Eddy was smashed along with it.

It wasn't until I scrambled up onto the dead sqwyrm's back that we got a count of the crew and discovered there wasn't but six of us left. The rest had either drowned or been smashed along with Eddy—or worse. It's hard not to think of the worst when you just seen a mouthful of flashing dragon-teeth racing toward you.

When I looked around for the ship, I seen three more sqwyrms. Two had boats bound. The third had a sharpoon jutting out of its flank and a line trailing behind it—but no boat. There was a single unfortunate sailor caught in the tangle of the line and the poor boy was skipping along the top of the waves like a toy. I never seen what become of his boat or crew.

We knowed by now that we'd got in too deep. We had more sqwrym already than any dragoneer had ever seen in a year. We'd two of them killed and ready to harvest, and two more on the line. That's as many sqwyrms as we'd taken in the past two years combined. Time to get back to the *Whilly* and get home while we could.

If Podo Helmer had figured the same, maybe me tale would have a better end. But it's got the end it's got, and here's how it all gone down.

A couple hours later, we had four sqwyrms tied up alongside the *Whilly* and ready to stow. In the short time we'd been on the hunt, Podo and First Mate Captain Whilly seemed to have become the best of friends. They was arm-in-arm, dancing in circles, singing of the gold they was going to spend and how they was going to spend it. You'll understand this display didn't set too well with the crew, many of whom was now dead. But it weren't more than a few minutes before Whilly quit off his dancing and took on a mournful air.

"A fine job, men," he told us. "A fine job indeed. Now let's honor our lost by finishing the job and sailing safely home."

Podo nodded as he listened but looked at Whilly sharply when he mentioned getting home. "You don't mean to leave off now, do you? We got but four! We'll haul in another four by sundown if we keep at it."

The crew shuffled their tired feet and looked around at one another. Whilly read them well. "We cannot, sir."

"What!?" cried Podo. He stomped a mighty foot and glowered.

"Sir! We have lost nearly half the crew, and we have only three able boats left to us. "

"Then we set them out for three more sqwyrms! Launch the boats!"
The crew stood still.

"Sir. If you please—"

"If I please, what?" Podo took a threatening step toward Whilly, but to Whilly's credit, he withstood it.

"It will take us some hours yet to harvest what we have and stow it aboard. We need the men for that. We cannot take on another kill until we've dealt with what we have. I am ten years a dragoneer, sir. I beg you to heed me."

Podo slunk up next to Whilly and put his gaze upon him. He studied Whilly's face and sniffed at it and considered it grimly in terrible silence. Whilly trembled and squeaked and sweated but he held his ground until Podo felt he'd terrified him enough. Then Podo looked around at the crew and relaxed.

"All right, laddies. You heard the man. Get them dragons stowed!"

Everybody jumped and went to work. We got out our bone-saws, and fin-hammers, and heart-scoopers, and tail-cleavers, and eye-hooks, and belly-skinners, and scale-rakers and we sawed and hammered and scooped and clove and hooked and skinned and raked until we had the hold so full of dragon-flesh, wyrmblubber, whisker skin, eye juice, tailspines, dragon ivory, bellybrine, and heartsblood that we'd run out of room to store it all.

And another thing.

By the end, they was the glint of gold in every eye. You've never seen such a fortune, for not only had we taken better than two years worth of sqwyrm in a single day, it was the finest sqwyrm we'd ever seen. It was bigger, and tastier, and pointer, and glamourouser, and expensiver than any harvest a dragoneer has ever took. We was going to be kings—every one of us.

But as we finished hauling in the last of the catch, Pea started hopping again. "They's something—captain?"

We all turned to look, and some distance out we seen a passle of sqwyrm slithering through the water. They wasn't charging. They wasn't breaching. They was just swimming peaceful-like, and coming toward us. What did we think of it? We'd never seen nothing to liken it to. We was no small bit afraid, but we was also held by a powerful curiosity. There was dozens of them. Maybe a hundred even. The sea was rolling and wavering as they humped up and coiled round each other and there was a quiet rustling as their scales slid and scraped and rubbed one against the other. It cast a spell on us. They came on until they parted around the ship and surrounded us. The ship's timber began to murmur as they passed and slid along the hull. We was breathless, all of us.

They swirled around long enough for any fear we had to give way to wonder. Their great bodies coursed through the water in every direction, and now and again a head rose up and peered at us quietly. They was studying us—same as we was studying them. A dragoneer knows a dragon, sure enough, but all he knows is how to stab it, how to chase it, how to kill it, how to cut it. Few of us has ever took time to stand still and wonder at the fearsome beauty of the beasts the Maker wrought. They shimmer with scales of blue and gold and green and every color you ever seen in a gemrock, their great whiskers ripple in the air, their fins sway to and fro and catch the light like stained glass, their eyes—deep as any sea—stare back with something you'd swear was the knowing of things men has yet even to ponder. Silly, I know— but at times I thought one of them might open its great toothful maw and begin to *speak*. And under it all the deep rumble of the creatures' breathing, like a distant thunder that makes you want to lie down and rest while the rain comes and washes you clean. And to think, these was but *sqwyrms*. Think you now: how would it be to stare into the baleful eye of a great drake? I believe it would either drive a man mad—or transfigure him. Maybe end him outright—maybe make him into something else entirely. What man can say? Not I.

It was Podo Helmer broke the spell.

"She smiled at me," I heard him whisper. He was standing at the rail and staring down at the waterline.

I looked and I seen one of the beasts lying on its side by the ship. Its head was rolled over so that it stared straight up at us with one eye, and Podo was right—the creature's mouth was opened ever so slightly and it seemed to be grinning at us. As eerie a sight as I ever beheld.

"The beasts are laughing at us!" said Podo.

Now I hadn't considered this possibility. I was too caught up in the oddity of the moment to ascribe it much in the way of meaning. But when he said it, it seemed suddenly true. And once we'd made up our minds that the smile was laughter, it didn't take but a small step further to see laughter as mockery. And that turned us away from our wonder and back toward our fear.

"Give her the iron," said Podo.

Everyone heard. But no one moved.

"I said give her the iron. I don't aim to be laughed at by an overgrowed fish!"

The crew kept silent and looked to First Mate Captain Whilly for guidance. Unprepared for the burden of having to disagree with Podo Helmer at such a moment, Whilly shrunk into his clothes as if he could hide there.

"I'll do it meself."

Podo strode across the deck and snatched up a sharpoon.

Whilly took a step toward him. "Sir, is this wise?"

"Wise? I aim to teach it a lesson."

Podo steadied himself on the rail with one of his magnificent gams and then drew back his arm and hurled the sharpoon at the grinning dragon.

When it struck, the beast recoiled like a parted line. For a moment, the air was filled with a sharp hiss as every sqwyrm about the ship froze and drew in its breath. Then they was gone. They sounded and left the ship bobbing and lonely in a settling sea.

I think we was all too scared to move until we was given leave. We looked about suspiciously until the order came. "Set us a course west," said Whilly.

"West, aye," answered Hodd at the helm.

Podo didn't protest. He stared into the distance and muttered under his breath.

The crew trimmed the sails and before long we was making good headway toward home. The crew began to breathe easier and you could read relief in every man's eye. But just as we was passing out of the Sunken Mountains—

Pea began to scream.

It were a terrible sound. Like he was trying to talk and yell and cry and cackle and gurgle and hiccup and whimper all at the same time. And when we turned to look where he was pointing, every man on deck began to make pretty much the same exact sound.

Let me translate that sound for you. It's the sound a dragoneer makes when it comes home to him that the fox has been caught in the henhouse. Not a league behind us a *wyrm*—no sqwyrm, this—had breached like a volcano and was hurtling right toward us.

Have you ever heard of a dragoneer surviving a disagreement with a full-grown sea dragon? No? Well there's a good reason for that. It's never been done.

Lucky for us—if you can call us lucky—this one weren't grown. It was something in between. I figure it stayed behind to watch the little ones, while all the rest had gone for Fingap Falls. But no matter, it was three times as big as any sqwyrm I ever saw, and plenty big enough to make a sad wreck of the *Gilded Whilly*.

As we was looking at the beast and measuring the likelihood of living through the next hour, Podo Helmer clenched his jaw, snatched up a pike, and said, "Looks like we got us a big'un."

"Sir! It's impossible!"

"Quiet, Whilly. You're itchin' my concentration."

Podo kicked open a stowage locker and hauled out a coil of rope. He dragged it to the foredeck and then shimmied out onto the bowsprit.

"Gimme that rope," he said.

Whilly did as he was told.

"Now pass me that heart-pike."

Whilly did and watched in bafflement as Podo tied the pike fast to the bowsprit such that it struck out ahead of the ship like a lance.

"Sir, this is madness."

"You got a better idea?"

"We cannot *ram* a dragon!"

"It's us or him, Whilly. We can either settle down to be eaten and chewn, or we can skewer the beast, pack it in the hold, and sell it for enough gold that we all retire to the Annieran Riviera like kings. I don't know about you, but I don't aim to be chewn."

This plan was pure foolishness, and the crew knowed it. They began to wail and call out for their mamas. They cowered in their lockers, and crawled into the crannies of the hold to hide themselves from being et, so sure were they of their deaths.

"Turn her about!" cried Podo, and Hodd reluctantly obeyed. The ship heeled over and the hull creaked and groaned—it was heavy with the weight of all the sqwyrm we'd took and the *Gilded Whilly* had become a lumberous hulk indeed. When she'd got around and we were aimed at our quarry, we seen for certain how mad Podo's plan really was. The dragon was every bit as big as the ship—and then some—but it was nimble. In a shimmer of ruby-red scales, it danced through the water like a bird through the air, diving and cutting back and forth and leaping up and down—a creature born to speed and motion just exactly the way a turtle ain't. And the *Whilly* was a turtle indeed, so heavy was its hold.

"Steady," cried Podo. "Steer us right up her gullet!"

"Up the gullet, aye!" answered Hodd.

"No, no! We'll be crippled and sunk!" Whilly ran to the wheel and pushed the helmsman away. But before he could turn the ship, Podo put forth a muscular foot and kicked him. Poor Whilly flew through the air, landed on the deck, slid across it, and thumped up against the mainmast like a sack of totatoes. Podo took the helm in hand and aimed the ship toward the breast of the charging dragon. The look on his face was pure focus and determination. His jaw was set and the cords of his neck stood out like cables.

The dragon was having none of it, though. Before we'd got within a hundred yards, the creature dove. It slithered under the ship, and then it come up behind us. Its crimson head burst out of the water, jaws agape, and with one mighty flash of teeth took off the rail of the poopdeck and the three sailors standing near it. Then it darted away from the ship before anyone could think to toss a sharpoon.

Once away, it stopped and turned and opened its mouth and hissed at us.

"Arm yerselves!" ordered Podo. The crew that hadn't hid themselves took up whatever sharpoons and pikes and hooks they found nearest at hand, while Podo turned the ship to face the beast and pointed the bowsprit at its breast once more.

Again the dragon dove, and again it come up behind us. This time it took a bite out of the mizzenmast and what was left of it crashed to the deck in splinters.

"We'll be sunk!" shouted Whilly.

"Get over here, Whilly. I got an idea."

"You'll kick me!"

"I promise I won't kick ye! Now get over here and take the wheel."

Whilly obeyed with a suspicious eye toward Podo's feet.

"Now you just keep us aimed right up her gullet, you understand?"

"The beast is too quick! We've lost a mast. We have no speed."

"Leave it to me."

Whilly held his breath and nodded.

"Good lad."

By now the dragon had run out, turned around, and was diving as it come for us again. Podo grabbed up an eye-hook in each hand and took a ready stance amidships . . . waiting.

The air was quiet while every man wondered where the beast would attack. When it came, the beast rose up on the port rail. The great ruby head towered over us and its eyes flitted back and forth, looking for the target of the strike to come. The jaw dropped open and rows of teeth glimmered in the sunlight. The irises of the beast's eyes focused on Podo. They looked at one another, dragon and pirate, and seemed each to consider the other carefully and come to some dark conclusion. Though it all past in no more than a heartbeat, you had the sense that in a single moment an entire war had raged between them, though none could say who the victor was. Then Podo howled at the creature with an animal rage. The dragon's eyes, lit from within by an eerie intelligence, blinked and then it struck forward, jaws wide to seize and bite—but they snapped shut on empty air.

Podo Helmer leapt. The power of his beauteous legs carried him up and landed him neatly atop the dragon's head. Before the dragon could account for its prey's escape, Podo swung his arms and the hooks caught in the dragon's teeth on either side of its head.

The beast jerked and shook and tossed itself, but Podo held tight and wouldn't be unseated. He clamped his musculous legs into the dragon's neck and pulled the hooks tighter and tighter with every move the beast made. Then the beast fled and I watched as the maddest sight I ever seen took place before me eyes.

Podo Helmer *rode the dragon.*

And more than just rode it, he commanded it. He pulled on the right hook, and the dragon veered to the right. He pulled on the left hook, and the dragon veered left. He dug his boot heels into the beast and it surged faster and faster at the urging of those legs—those magnificent bronze appendages! We all stood in awe of his feat. There hadn't never been nothing like it before, and I reckon nothing like it since. "Scale Rider!" we cried, for such a thing had to be named in order to be understood at all.

We watched as Podo began to control the beast in ever finer detail, and then, when he had the knack of it, he turned it and drove it toward us—toward the *Gilded Whilly.* It took the captain a few moments to understand Podo's plan, but understand it he did, and he turned the ship, steering us on a collision course with the charging dragon.

The distance closed. The sharp tip of the heart-pike rose and fell as the ship pounded through the waves, and onward the dragon came,

onward Whilly drove us. Podo sat astride the monster like something
out of a storytale and a grim countenance was all across him. Closer,
closer, the dragon came, and the pike rose up, and up, and then—the
beast sounded! It dove beneath the prow and vanished into the deep.

"*AH!*" cried Whilly at the wheel.

Pea, who was still up in the buzzard's nest, clutched fast to the
mast, said, "That wasn't supposed to happen—was it?"

But just as we thought Podo was lost and gone, the beast breached
behind the ship. It came up making a racket of noise like it was
coughing and choking. Podo spit out a mouthful of seawater and I
heard him say, "Can't hold yer breath if I holds your mouth open, can
you? Now giddy up, dragon!" He dug his boots into the creature's neck
and they were off again, darting through the waves.

The whole crew was cheering now. *Scale Rider! Scale Rider! Scale
Rider!* All but Whilly, who had his tongue stuck out the side of his
mouth as he poured all his concentration into the steering of his ship.
Podo rode the dragon out and circled round again, and Whilly had the
ship aimed true. We all run back toward the helm to clear away from
the foredeck. The dragon howled and writhed. The heart-pike rose,
gleaming and sharp, stabbing into the air ahead of the ship. The two
giant forces careered toward one another until—

At the last moment, the dragon shimmied to one side. The tip of
the heart-pike caught the beast's eye, plucking it out, and scraped along
scales on the side of its head. But then the pike struck flesh. A great
yowl went up, and the dragon writhed past, raking the side of the ship
and tearing the starboard rail away. Timbers and splinters flew in every
direction, and men as was standing too close took them as wounds.
It was a shivered board off the rail that pierced me own eye. A stab of
light shot through me brain and then half the world went dark. But the
loss of an eye was little next to what was taken from others.

We was all staggered, none of us sure what had happened, until Pea
pointed and groaned in despair. We dreaded to turn and see what his

pointing portended, but turn we did, and we beheld a grievous sight. For skewered upon the heart-pike was not only the great dragon's eye, but a lone but magnificent, musculous, formidable, handsome, beauteous, bronze leg shoed by a single boot.

In horror, we spun to look after the dragon, and we seen Podo still clutched to the beast's head, but his face had gone pale and his eyes were wide with shock. Unable to clench the creature's neck with his one remaining leg, he flopped from side to side as the dragon thrashed. But he still had hold of the hooks, and he strove with the beast to steer it back around for a final approach.

Seeing Podo's plight, Whilly came into his courage at last. He cast all his caution overboard and clothed himself instead in the manner of the great sea captains of old. He muscled his ship about and braced himself hard against the bucking of mighty waters. He held fast to the helm and met the dragon's charge like a man before a storm. Howling a cry of defiance into the gale, he drove forth the heart-pike sure and true.

At the final moment, I beheld Podo Helmer, the Scale Rider, stand erect upon the dragon's head. He had but a single leg—though what a leg it was!—and he hauled on the hooks with all his might, drawing himself tall and straight, and pulling the beast's head up, up, exposing its supple belly and—

Calamity

Ruin

Havoc

—*Victory!*

The impact threw Podo across the deck and he landed near Whilly's feet at the helm. The beast, impaled upon the pike, thrashed and roared, and the ship trembled and shuddered under the weight of its captive. We scarcely believed we were alive to see the end of it. But as we watched the dragon begin to wane, we looked about us and knew the *Gilded Whilly* had lost its life in the fight. The collision had crushed her hull and sundered her along her keel line. Already she listed dangerously to port and the sounds of rushing water rose from the depths of her holds.

"Into the boats!" ordered Whilly. "Someone help me with Podo."

Whilly bent over Podo, but the old pirate paid no heed to anyone. Though he'd won a great battle, he seemed to take no joy in it, and he wore the face of a man defeated. A sailor inspected the stump of his leg, tying off the wound, yet still Podo gave no sign of injury or interest. He seemed unable to feel his own pain, but he was transfixed by the dragon in its agony and studied it grimly, as if in its destruction he might read omens of his own.

We launched the three remaining boats, enough to hold those of us who survived, and as Podo was carried aboard he said nothing. He kept his eyes on the beast behind.

We rowed away from the wreck of the *Gilded Whilly*, and we was silent and awed, pondering all we'd seen. As the sun was coming down, the sea went glassy smooth, and the dragon's roars turned to something like a song. It ran through the water, causing it to shimmer and eddy, and as the dragon and the ship was cloven together, the hull resounded with the creature's voice and magnified it. It was a doleful sound, a lingering and lonesome note. We all knew it for what it was—a lamentation thrown up against the sky to mark the ruin of one of the Maker's grandest children. And the sound of that lament seemed to catch up the unsung lamentations of all the sqwyrms we'd took for gold, and we felt as if their ghosts had risen from the deep to accuse us. The hairs of me neck bristled in the presence of that song, and in its echo I felt the weight of every questionable deed I ever did. The sound put us in mind of things we'd left behind, and things we'd left undone, and things we couldn't undo ever again. And Podo, I think, felt it more than all of us together, as if in his contention with the dragon, he had looked into the core of the beast and seen something greater and grander than himself— and at the same instant the beast had seen to the core of the man and knew it for the rotted and tasteless fruit that it was.

As the sun sank below the horizon, the dragon's song guttered out and the *Gilded Whilly* slipped beneath the waves. The water seethed and bubbled, and the ship plummeted down into Yurgen's Deep and took with it the dragon, and our livelihoods, and all we owned in the world, and all we'd harvested—and the tattered remnants of one magnificent and musculous leg.

As the dragon and the *Whilly* dropped into the darkness, I looked around at the faces about me, and I knowed we all felt the same. We'd been party to the ravaging of a thing that swum the sunken deeps since the mountains was young. We'd put our hands to the devices of death and plied them upon a creature that had life such as only millennia can fathom. We'd encroached where we had no leave. We'd took what wasn't ours to claim.

And for what?

The only prizes any of us gained from that cursed voyage were ghosts. For all of us that yet live are haunted men. Yurgen sees to it. Though we've gone our separate ways and fled to the four winds, make no mistake, there will come a day when the crew of the *Gilded Whilly* shall all be mustered together once more. For Yurgen knows our scent and he will not rest until we are gathered at last into his hall.

And then our doom: We shall haunt the seas aboard our cursed ship and pay at last for all we stole from the Deeps of the Dragon King.

And what of Podo Helmer?

He fashioned for himself a wooden leg, but it could not compare to what he'd lost. He was changed. And though many told the tale of the Scale Rider, and it certainly gave legs to his infamy, I think it also pained him. He'd have had the tales keep silent if he could, for they began to make of him something other than he was, other than he meant to be.

And he went forth ever thereafter with a limp.

The yarn now spun, the dragoneer leaned back and drew on his cup and nodded once to signify the end of his tale.

The man across the table nodded slowly and considered what had been said, then he raised an eyebrow and asked: "Yeah, but how'd you get back to Skree?"

The talespinner wiped his chin with his sleeve and called for a refill. "Another fine question. And *that* is the tale of how I lost me other eye."

THE BALLAD OF
LANRIC AND RUBE

Written by Jonathan Rogers
Illustrated by Justin Gerard

At the edge of the forest, where fazzle doves chorus
And the Keekle flows bubbly and clear,
Two farm families neighbored. Together they labored
Side by side, year after year.

The Rumley-A'Catos grew heirloom totatoes,
The Adoob family, shellery and charrots.
They shared what they grew to make prize-winning stews
And soups of incomparable merit.

The farmwives were cousins. Between them a dozen
Stout farmchildren filled out their brood.
So those dozen cousins I guess were fourth cousins.
No—first cousins two times removed?

Third cousins? Whatever. The point is, forever
These families had loved one another.
And the bond was the strongest between the two youngest—
Third cousins who seemed more like brothers.

Lanric Adoob loved his third cousin Rube
With a fierceness as fearsome as dread.
And Rube's love for Lanric was just as gigantic.
One soul in two bodies, folks said.

Two bodies, one soul, and yet, on the whole,
Those bodies were rather the same.
Both tall, strong of limb, and handsome and slim,
Each a credit to his family's good name.

When the day's chores were done, Lanric split on the run
For the Rumley-A'Catos' next door.
Excepting, of course, when Rube finished first
And arrived at th' Adoobs' house before.

They fished in the river, they went to discover
New marvels in the Woodlands of Linnard.
They hunted for thwaps and made treasure maps
And often came home late for dinner.

They loved Ships and Sharks, and Zibzy, and darts,
Handyball, Wiggle the Chicken.
But when they got older and broad in the shoulder
A competitive spirit kicked in.

They were evenly matched, so they struggled and scratched
And they usually played to a tie.
It was mostly good fun, but still either one
Thought, "Who's better? My cousin or I?"

"Who's better?" they pondered, and every day wondered—
"My favorite cousin or I?"

The Township of Torto fell quite a bit short
Of what you might call a great city.
But for Lanric and Rube and the rest of their crew,
The Township was city aplenty.

Each six weeks or so, a wagon would go
To the Township with produce to sell:
Totatoes and leeks, charrots and beets,
And twelve or so farmkids as well. [1]

In the middle of Torto stood a general store
Where candy was sold by the stick.
This was the reason, no matter the season,
Why Lanric and Rube made the trip.

But when they'd grown older and broad in the shoulder,
One day when they went on that mission
They rode to the store and strode through the door
And were struck by the same recognition:

They had come to this street to find something sweet—
Hard candy, perhaps taffy swirl.
But sweeter, much more, than all else in the store
Was Illia, the shopkeeper's girl.

Sweet Illia was neater, and quite a bit sweeter
Than anything else in the world.

They'd known the store-daughter since they were all toddlers,
But something was different this time.

---

1. The farmkids were not for sale. They made the trip for a different reason, as will
become apparent in the next stanza.

"Can I help you?" she said. Lanric stared as if dead;
Rube gabbled, "To see glad you I'm."

They rode home in a daze, unaware of the ways
They both had made fools of themselves.
They poked at their dinner, grew thinner and thinner.
Their mothers asked, "Are you quite well?"

Poor Ruben and Lanric, two lovesick romantics,
Both sighed and both pined for sweet Illia.
Each suffered alone; neither made his love known.
Sound silly? It's about to get sillier.

For a year and a day, the boys wasted away.
Neither knew of the other one's passion.
Then either young man came up with a plan
To resolve things in breathtaking fashion.

Fivemoon, Day Ten, as you already ken,
Is Declaration Day in Skree,
When secret admirers and bashful inquirers
Make public their love on one knee.

They go to their sweeties and get off their feeties
And speak of their love on one knee.

So each cousin-brother, unbeknownst to the other,
Took their fifth cousin Douglas aside:
"The tenth, at the town square, I need to be down there.
You think you could give me a ride?"

Doug wasn't too smart, but he had a good heart—
No wonder his cousins recruited him.
He said he'd be glad to. He'd do what he had to.
Keep quiet? Sure thing, that suited him.

When the tenth rolled around and Doug loaded for town,
Poor Rube disbelieved his dim eyes:
Lanric just climbed in and sat down beside him.
And Lanric was just as surprised.

The ride down the turnpike was silent—nay, ghostlike—
Except for the squeakles and jouncels.
The young men were caught in their innermost thoughts,
And each of them kept his own counsel.

When the wagon was parked at the Torto main market,
The boys separated in town.
They each had the notion to voice his emotion,
But not with the other around.

Lanric hiked up the block, turned left at the clock,
Then circled back toward Illia's store.
He focused his mind and practiced his lines
While he stood with his hand on the door.

He screwed up his hope then he swung the door open,
And what do you think he did see?
The lovely store-maiden with her face in her apron
And his cousin Rube down on one knee!

On one knee, and worse—spouting terrible verse!
As terrible as verse can be:

Illia, Illia, Illia, will ya
Be my sweetheart, Illia?
Will ya?

Lanric descended on Rube like the men did
Who smashed Orney-Permla to bits.[2]
Poor Rube went from kneeling to fairly careening
Through a wall, where he soon lost his wits.

Whereupon Lanric knelt for the lovely and svelte
Maiden Illia, who remained unimpressed.
He coughed and *ahem-ed-ed* with one hand extended,
The other hand pressed to his chest.

Oh Illie, oh Illie
I feel downright silly,

---

2. Proverbial. To wit: "Orney-Permla wasn't built in a day, but it was probably destroyed
in a day—a week at most." Collected in *Less-Than-Pithy Proverbs* (Fithyhoop, Skree:
Fithyhoop Bookery, 3/102).

All for the love of you,
Oh my Illie.

I am glad to declare that Illia was spared
The rest of that horrible poem.
For right about then, Ruben came to again,
And then the fight really got going.

They punched and they gouged and they bit and they scrouged
And they flung one another around.
The destruction was splendid—shelving upended
And merchandise littered the ground.

Glass jars went flying. Illia was crying
And howling and wailing extravagantly.
She took up a broom, ran the boys from the room.
It was an unmitigated calamity.

The prizefight continued in a new, outdoor venue,
And townspeople gathered to gawk
Till the Constable swam in and collared the young men
And invited them on a long walk.

He escorted them down to the outskirts of town
To the homeward-bound two-rutted track.
He said, "Boys, it's a long dig to the boondocks where you live,
So start hiking, and never come back."

The pugilists talked on that long homeward walk
And agreed that they still hadn't shown
Which kinsman-brother had outfought the other
And deserved to call Illia his own.

Together they lined out a way they could find out
Which one was the manlier he-man:
They'd fight every day until one had to say
He'd been thoroughly, verily beaten.

They felt ever-so better once they got that settled,
And walked with new springs in their steps.
They felt even more snug when they were picked up by Doug,
Who'd helped Illia clean up their mess.

The next day at sunup did both warriors run up
To the tater field, next to the lettuce.
They boxed and they wrestled and otherwise tusseled
Till the morning bell called them to breakfast.

The injuries were minor; Rube suffered a shiner
And Lanric a pair of fat lips.
Like two young tornados they'd trashed the totatoes,
But neither would say he'd been whipped.

When breakfast was finished, they resumed their scrimmage
By the Rumley-A'Catos' new barn.
Rube put Lanric's head through the wall of the shed,
Then they fought at the Adoob family's farm.

Day after day, it went on this way:
Every fight ended a draw.
For when one of the kinsmen was tempted to give in,
The face of dear Illia he saw.

It doesn't take long for two lads big and strong
To tear up two neighboring farmsteads.

The corncribs were smashed, the crops were all mash,
The animals frozen with harm's dread.

The paterfamiliae took both sons aside
And said, "Lanric, Ruben, my dears—
We don't know what's wrong, but you must move along.
If you must fight, you cannot fight here."

It made the boys sad to have upset their dads,
But this was more than a matter of pride.
They'd promised to fight until one proved his might
And won darling Ill as his bride.

If they couldn't fight there, they'd travel elsewhere
To fight for the love of a bride.

Their mothers both cried when they boys said goodbye
And threw them a big farewell dinner.
They packed up a tent, and off the two went
To live in the Woodlands of Linnard.

In the woods they had freedom to fight like two Skreeans
Had never fought ever before.
They leapt out of tree limbs without any prelims
And rolled on the green forest floor.

With shoves and with pushes and secret ambushes
And newly invented abuses,
With cudgels and sticks and a few dirty tricks
They covered each other with bruises.

But neither one slipped and said he was whipped,
So every day saw a new fight.
At every day's end, the young men—still friends—
Shared supper and then said goodnight.

Their skills were so even it's hard to believe in.
And this was the two kinsmen's curse.
For two years or three they fought every day,
Neither better and neither one worse.

One lovely spring night they sat in the firelight
Nursing their various contusions
When Lanric said, "Brother, don't you miss your old mother?"
And Ruben looked up in confusion.

He said, "Yes, she's a beauty. But, Lan, we're off duty.
This best not be one of your tricks.
Still, I've thought for a good while that maybe this lifestyle
Isn't all bubbles and bricks."[3]

"Listen," said Lanric, "this fighting's got manic.
A new thought to my mind occurs:
What if we left and asked Illia herself
Which of us two she prefers?"

Rube thought about it, and though he had doubted
His cousin's good faith at the start,
He soon saw the value of letting the gal who
They loved tell them who'd won her heart.

When the sun cracked the treeline the boys made a beeline
For Torto down the two-rutted path.
Lanric was limpy and Ruben was gimpy,
But they made it to Illia's at last.

They opened the door and went into the store
Looking very much worse for the wear.
Lanric's right eye was bruised (also was Rube's).
They were both missing patches of hair.

Rube's nose was a globe and Lan's right earlobe
Was missing (Rube had bit it clean off).
Their smiles were both gappy, but still they were happy,
For at least they looked manly and tough.

3. Proverbial. "If bubbles and bricks were henmeat and ticks, then every day would be Dragon Day." *Less-than-Pithy Proverbs*. Ibid.

Their noses were twisted, their knuckles all busted,
But at least they looked manly and tough.

"Miss Illia," said Lanric, "We're hopeless romantics,
And we've both chosen you for a bride.
We've been fighting it out, but we've changed our minds: now
We're going to let you decide.

"We both do adore you. We're standing before you,
And we've come here to heed to your voice.
The happy surprise is, we're both of us prizes.
You really can't make a bad choice."

Illia closed her eyes tight and her lip she did bite,
Apparently touched to the soul.
After a while she gave them a smile.
(But Rube thought he saw her eyes roll.)

Illia turned where she stood and hollered out good,
"Yoo-hoo! Can you come here, my dearest?"
To Lanric and Rube she said, "I hope that you
Don't mind, but my husband should hear this."

Sweet Illia's groom came into the room
Looking quite happy and smug.
Ruben and Lanric were boiling with panic,
For Illia's husband was Doug!

Illia said, "There you are. What in all Aerwiar
Made you two think either could woo me?
Did I ever suggest, in earnest or jest,
That I liked you? Just what are you, looney?

"But I must say I'm grateful to you for the fateful
Day you came in here and raised Dwayne.
True, you misused me, but you did introduce me
To your one kinsman with half a brain."

Thus reality's hand slapped Ruben and Lan.
They spoke at last, clearly bereft:
"Ill, we've been so wrong—we've acted like morons."
Then both of them cried till they laughed.

They said, "Cousin Douglas, it seems you've leapfrogged us."
Then both of them laughed till they cried.
"Such misguided fervor—but, Doug, you deserve her.
We wish you the joy of your bride."

We wish you, dear cousin, good things by the dozen,
And the joy of your beautiful bride.
The joy, the joy, the joy of your beautiful bride."

The Places Beyond the Maps

Written by Douglas Kaine McKelvey
Illustrated by Aedan Peterson

I.

The Night the Shadows Bound You

What are songs but remembrances of what has been lost?
—"The Ballad of the Hermit of Erwail"

The girl was gone.

The girl was gone and the night had run down cold and chill and silent and there was nothing he could do now because he could neither look at nor comfort his weeping wife nor untangle the knot in his own stomach. He kept his eyes mostly closed and felt the cool of the tile against his palm and cheek, wishing that the coolness would spread through his being like the inverse shadow of an eclipse, covering all and sinking even consciousness into a mute whiteness which would hold no knowing and no sound.

His head ached and the pain made him woozy and he was dimly grateful for the pain and for the gashed egg-rise of welt above his left temple now smeared with dried blood and oozing a clear liquid because it was at least a sign of resistance offered though he knew he had not truly resisted and the proof of this was that he was still alive. He had restrained his hand for fear that if he had acted the woman and he would have been shoved to their knees and claws drawn round their throats in a bright cascading of blood and the girl would have been the worse for witnessing such horror and still would not have been saved.

He rolled over to his stomach now and slowly worked his weight up to his elbows and knees, his pulse pounding furious waves through his skull like a blacksmith's hammer rung down upon an iron dome of sky. He buckled and retched and gagged, expelling whatever was left of the final meal he'd consumed in the hours before this world had so cruelly turned and he watched for a moment and then averted his face from the foamed and bittered contents of his stomach now splayed as if for the base divination of oracles, leaving those inscrutable constellations to pool and dry there on the floor because it seemed now a lie and to make one a party to a lie to polish those surfaces that were but part of a thin membrane drawn too wide like the plucked and tralucent skin of a thrush pulled taut over some great cavity of creation wherein darkness sloshed and reeled and men and women and children slipped that film and slid in as if drunk, slumping in to the slick maw of that abysm with mouths agape and eyes wide and uncomprehending.

Such were the tumbled thoughts of the man reclined in his own new ruin.

The man wiped his mouth on the back of his sleeve and pulled himself painfully to stand, supported by a hand pressed to the wall, doddering there a moment while the house seemed to spin round him. With his other hand he cupped his gut as if that steady pressure were what held his intestines in place.

He did not call to his wife for he doubted she would answer him.

Perhaps she would never speak to him again.

Perhaps she had good right.

He left her collapsed and shuddered by her own silent sobs, splayed there on the smooth, copper-inlaid tiles of their entryway and he made his way into the kitchen and stared from the window for several minutes at the darkness and the pale moonlight that fell like a thick gray ash upon the trees, as if the whole world were being slowly burned without flame, as if all that had been were collapsing like a jagged sink of water-cored shale, the emptiness of which would now become a chasmal and hollowed den of derelict beasts and creeping things.

Creeping things.

How he hated the creeping things.

Their venomous fangs. Their hard scales. Their fulvous eyes and flitting tongues.

Turning, the man gripped the edge of the table and for the searing in his gut lowered himself too rapidly, heaving his ungoverned weight onto the long bench so that his flailing elbow sent a blue enameled shaker clattering over the edge and plummeting to the floor where it shattered, scattering salt over the tiles.

The salt glowed stark and white in the scant moon and the cat—the girl's cat—ran to investigate the small calamity, licking curiously at the salt before shaking its head and backing away.

The cat had at least hissed when the creeping things had arrived.

What had the man done?

He had opened the door and let them in.

The Black Carriage, that great swallower of the innocent and of all innocence, had arrived. It had come creaking up the stone road that wound down and fell away towards the river, spokes dialing like days irreversible, a wheeled bereavement rolling round as the coopered hoops upon which the skins of wolves were tacked for curing. The man had awakened in the dead space of night because the dreadful creaking had stopped.

How strange to be awakened not by a sound, but by a silence after a sound.

He had rolled quietly from the bed and pulled the curtain back just enough to see the silvered movements of the fanged and disfigured creatures clambering down from the carriage that was spun of deeper darkness than the shadows around it. He could hear their guttural grunts and reptilian rasps desecrating the still, deep hours of night.

He felt the world turn to ice and stone and his own thoughts pinned and smothered like buzzing insects prehended in glacial flows of amber.

Spare the child, he had reflexively petitioned of a Maker whose mercies he had seldom begged, *and I will give you anything.*

As if there were anything left in this life to give.

Anything so precious as to counterbalance those scales.

The man turned and saw that his wife was awake too, her eyes wide with fear and locked on his own, years of dread focused in that silent stare. He had dropped his gaze and looked out the window again and had seen those monsters traipsing with their heavy, ungainly treads, trampling through the orderly bed of herbs and bright blossoms and to his door.

He had yet hoped they would realize their mistake, would divert from his own door and turn to some unfortunate neighbor's instead, taking some other child in place of his own and only daughter. Even as such thoughts spun in his head he knew it a horrid hope to wish upon another, but he could not help it. He felt in his bones himself capable of betraying the whole world if it would in that moment spare his own child.

The next sound was a jarring knock.

A shouted command. "OPEN!"

The woman had pleaded with him then not to go downstairs, not to unbolt the door.

"Hide her in the floor space!" she had whispered. "Hide her!"

"Have you any idea what they'd do then?" he had answered. "They'll smash their way in. Murder us. Find her . . ."

"Then fight them." Her words were cold, resolute.

"Three of them? And the driver? They have weapons! What do I have?" He realized his own voice was rising hysterically and he fell abruptly silent for the creatures were pounding at the door now with a vigor that caused even the walls and floor to shake.

His wife was quiet a moment. Then she thrust a hand beneath their mattress, grasped at something, and drew from that space a scabbard and an elongated dagger of some blued silver, nearly the span of a short sword. The etched form of some ornate, fruiting tree with a sun rising over it glowed in moonlight near the base of the blade. The woman held that cold coustille up to the man.

"Kill them! Kill them, husband, and then we'll flee!"

She kept the scabbard and pressed the blade into his hands, and he held it dumbly, staring at her, wondering from whence it had come and whether his wife had already put them all at risk by bartering for such an unlawful item at some black market in the seedy alleys of Dugtown.

Perhaps even now *this* was why the jackboots were at their door.

Perhaps they hadn't come for the girl at all!

His wife read his indecision and her eyes flashed a sudden contempt. She seized the weapon by the blade, clenching her fingers round it.

"Then give it to me and I will use it!"

She had always been a fiery woman when stirred. It was the back-side of her quick wit.

She tried to twist the weapon from his grip but in his panic he wrested the hilt, levering it from her, and then he turned to the open window of the bedroom and dropped it over the sill.

His wife gasped and struck her clenched fists against his chest. "You are a fool!"

The man stood a moment, his body drenched in sweat, his breathing pained and wheezing as the blade clunked against a stone pediment and settled somewhere in the hedges below. Only then did he turn and note the crimson roses blooming on his own shirt. Only then did he see that his wife's palms were freely bleeding, and realize that he had wrenched the weapon free while her fingers were yet tight round the blade of it. She held her smeared palms up to him and pleaded her agony.

"Do not let them do this to her!"

"By order of General Khrak, OPEN!" The horrid, croaked words boomed up the stairway, the consonants rubbed away by the intervening walls. But the same dire command spilled in more hissing and sibilant tones through the bedroom window, so that it seemed as if one fell spirit might have spoken with two voices, both from within and from without, one murky and muddled, one as presently manifest as a gnat's whine in the ear.

"Coming!" The man shouted and dashed downstairs.

The woman followed him in her now blood-splotched nightrobe, tugging the back of his shirt in her quiet hysterics, but he had not heeded. In his fear he yet convinced himself that there was a chance the creatures were here to search their home for the dagger or other contraband, and that all could be well if he simply obeyed, made no trouble.

When his wife darted round him to press her back against the door he thrust her roughly aside and watched his own hands then rising and fumbling to release the locks, fingers scuttling like wounded creatures. But his clumsy movements had been too slow for the scourge at their doorstep. The thick door had smashed down upon the man from its hinges, striking his skull a disorienting blow and then levering over him into the entryway where it upset a finely-wrought vase imported from Sylow, an old wedding gift from his brother-in-law and one of the few fineries that remained now of their former status. The vase had toppled from its pedestal and shattered into a thousand needlelike shards.

The man reached to feel a warm trickle from the gash over his temple where the skin had split against the hard brow bone beneath it. The Fangs stood upon the step and hooted. Violence was ever a base comedy to them. Sufferings and cruelty seemed the only wellsprings of mirth such twisted creatures could imbibe, and their degenerate reverie—so far as the man had observed—did not discriminate amongst species. He had seen a half dozen of the beasts hoot hysterically at the final writhings of one of their own who had fallen drunk in the middle of the market road, and whose back had subsequently been rolled over and snapped beneath the wheels of a horse cart. The driver of the cart had, of course, been hanged that same hour and in that very market square, pelted with old vegetables and pierced with arrows as he swung, but those sentient reptiles had found as much jeering pleasure in the death of their own comrade as they had in the execution of the driver.

They were creatures devoid of mercy and her benefits, wrenched and tangled and out of step and harmony with any nuance of creation. Why the Maker tolerated their existence was perplexing. Why he had ever created them in the first place was a question that toppled theologies.

The man recovered his senses enough to scuttle aside deferentially.

"Welcome to our home. We have nothing to hide here."

He allowed the beasts to pass in the hall with their hideous rasping jibes, their crude cacklings.

"We haven't tended our bellies since midnight," one of them barked to the woman who cowered pale in the moonlight, pressing her palms together to staunch the flow of blood from the dagger gashes. "What would ye offer as fine a trio of gentlemens as us?"

This set the three beasts to cackling again.

The one who had spoken was large and fat for a Fang and his snout was marked by a long, curving scar that twisted the set of his mouth and rendered his appearance even more leering than most of his kind.

"She aints givin' you the nicety of an answer, Cap'n Grumwold!" the second of the abhorrent beasts chirped. This one was smallish, and hunched as if burdened by some unseen load. "Shalls I give her a nice fat poke in the eye?" It quacked maliciously and prodded the shivering woman's shoulder with the staff end of a short spear.

The third Fang was lean and haggard and its eyes were not right somehow as it turned its head this way and that to scan their home, observing the ceiling and walls as if the dwellings of men held for it some sad and distant fascination. Instead of the rough, green hide typical of Fangs, this one had a brightly streaked and darkly beaded skin like that of a desert lizard, and the man had to look twice through the fog of his addled observations to confirm as the creatures marched past him that while the others slapped the tiles with their repulsively wide and naked Fang feet, this beaded Fang instead wore tall, strapped boots of a brown leather, so that he moved along with an awkward and stilted rhythm.

For the briefest of moments the man entertained the hopeful notion that this was all but a surreal dream, that none of it was actually transpiring, that his daughter was safe, but the illusion did not hold, and his head cleared and he saw that two of the ogres had begun to harass and gall his wife, calling for food.

Seeing that she was too rooted in her fear to respond, the man pushed to his feet hastily and nodded. "This way. Right this way to the food. Follow me, please. We don't have much but you're welcome to it!"

He led them to the larder. The Fangs knocked the man roughly aside and fell to rummaging violently through the family's meager stocks.

"Perhaps they'll just eat and leave," the man whispered to his wife who had followed and now stood behind him but she had shaken her head, her eyes wild with fear.

The Fangs jostled one another, scattering and spilling the dwindling totato and wheat stores in disgust.

"Not a maggot or a weevil in them!" the fat one who had been called Grumwold spoke disdainfully.

"Totatoes is only worth gulping when they's all rotty and fested over with gunchbugs, right cap'n?" the beaded one asked. There was something awkward and toadying in his manner.

"If we's had gunchbugs, you freak, why woulds we even need totatoes?" Grumwold responded, and the small, hunched Fang stomped his clawed foot hard upon the tail of the beaded one so that he howled in surprise and turned on his assailant.

"I tells you already, don't be a' stomping my tail!"

"Close your mush-hole, Beadsy!" Grumwold bellowed. "Or I'll close it for you and send you out on wilderness patrol!"

"He wouldn't last a week!" The little Fang snorted derisively and stomped the tip of the beaded one's tail again, and the beaded one called Beadsy winced, dropping the totatoes he held and then he whimpered and wrapped his tail round his legs so that it could be stomped no more.

The other two creatures sniffed their way through the larder, locating a gaunt hank of smoked hogpig and a dry wheel of crumbly cheese with a light blue mold growing atop it.

The oddkin Beadsy slunk behind them and nabbed a wilty turnip. He backed into the corner and gnawed it sullenly till the fat one yanked his nose and knocked the prize from his clawing grasp and then gave him a scraping kick to the ribs.

"Fresh vegetables? Don't be disgusting!"

Beadsy yelped and stumbled backwards trying to master his balance, but slipped in a spattering of the woman's blood on the tiles and splayed violently while the fat one and the small one guffawed.

The strange Fang scrambled to regain his footing and then, with a wild screech, darted across the kitchen where he seized a large hanging mirror, ripping it from its mountings and heaving it over the man's ducked head so that the silvered pane smashed against the far wall.

The beaded one then stood panting, as if in Fangs' abstruse and reptilian hierarchies the wanton destruction of a looking glass might bequeath some arcane power, but the other Fangs only sneered and returned to their work of rummaging clawfuls of dried onions, searching for ones with a dark, powdery mildew daubed between their papery skins.

With these confiscated foodstuffs they had arrayed themselves at table and slurped and burped and swallowed the family's provisions and had ordered the man to fetch them a cask of ale "under penalty of having your feet sawed off and your elbows hammered," and he had done so, even pouring the liquid into goblets for them and then he had offered them a little bow, as if he were a waiter, a serving slave in his own house, and they had laughed at this fawning behavior and all the while his wife had stood in her nightrobe with her eyes wide and her mouth parted in shock and then she had given a little scream and turned to run for the girl's room but then the smaller of those horrible reptilian-headed abominations had whipped his tail at her ankles, knocking her to the ground before she had gone two steps, and the fat one had laughed as the vile creature dragged her back to the kitchen and tossed her onto the tiles so that the wounds in her palms and fingers began to bleed again and then her eyes had looked up at his own, pleading, and he had just swallowed hard and looked away as if he had not understood.

I'm doing what I have to to keep us alive, he had told himself, and his desperate thoughts fell into the swung rhythms of prayers flung blindly upwards like the grappling hooks of beleaguered mountaineers: *Please, just let them eat and leave.* But those prayers had not been answered, though he had assured himself in the moment that it could happen, that the evening could still end well, that he need not act drastically, not now, not yet, but might still wait and see what would transpire and perhaps they would search for the dagger and not find it and leave with a threat and a warning.

He saw now that it had been a lie he told himself, and he knew that his wife had known it for a lie all along, and the Maker, for his part, had remained silent and distant as he had ever been. Once the Black Carriage had creaked to a stop below their windows there were only ever three ways this night might have ended and in no scenario could the man have hoped to preserve the life that he and the woman and the girl had known together.

The trick, he saw now, would have been to accept in the first instant—the moment the Black Carriage had arrived—that all was lost. Only in giving up any hope of preserving this life could a man have seen his way clear to act.

It was hope itself that had betrayed him. Hope that had made him weak.

It was the very fear of losing his daughter that had ensured her loss.

His wife had known it to a cold certainty, from the start.

And the woman would have interposed her own life between the creatures and the taking of her daughter had he allowed it. She had lifted herself a second time from the kitchen floor and run screeching at the smallest of the Fangs, lunging with bare, bloodied hands to claw for its eyes, but the man himself had intercepted her, catching her round the waist, and pinning her flailing arms to her sides as the creatures laughed and hissed and hooted, pointing and spitting and dribbling ale from their horrid maws except for the beaded one who had laughed at first and then had fallen silent and just stared dumbly at the woman struggling in the man's arms.

"Forgive us," the man had said. "She's been feverish. Doesn't know what she's doing. Settle down, woman. Stop this nonsense!" And all the while she had screamed "NO NO NO NO NO!" loud enough that he knew their child must now be awake and cowering in her bed at the cacophony below. The man had squeezed his wife so tight he was afraid he had bruised her ribs, but what else could he have done? Had she accosted the Fang, she would now be dead.

And so would he.

And their child would still have been taken.

So what could he have done?

What else could he have done except join her in the attack?

For what if the struggle had turned in their favor?

What if surprise, and the sharp blade, and the knowledge that they were fighting for their own daughter had given them an edge? What if he could even have held the creatures at bay long enough that his wife might have escaped with their daughter?

That would have at least been a noble death.

How had he not even tried?

Now that the creatures were gone and the girl with them and the house as changed and emptied as an abandoned theater stage, the man saw himself in a sudden, new light, and the settling realization struck him harder than the weight of the door that had smashed his temple.

If you live long enough, his grandfather had often told him in words that dripped with a farmer's quiet wisdom, *you might learn a thing or two about yourself.*

This night he had learned more about himself than ever he wished to know.

The man rose again and, supporting himself with one hand against the wall and one hand still pressed to his pained gut, he navigated the foyer, stepping over his wife's huddled form and through the gaping doorway to the stone steps where he sat again and for a brief watch of that splintered night gazed mutely at stars and shadows and glimmers of reflected light beyond the river that seemed now to divide the kingdoms of the living and the dead and he wondered if that were true which side he was now on.

Theirs was a tall, narrow house of the fashionable sort, built on a quaint, winding street that ran up the hill along the edge of Torrboro.

The man had before traded as a metals broker, negotiating and arranging deliveries from the iron and copper mines in the hills above Bylome to the merchants and craftsmen in Dugtown and Torrboro, pocketing the handsome profits. His trade had yielded a degree of settled comfort, though that comfort had eroded since the arrival of the first Fangs almost nine years past. What the family clung to now was only a veneered pretense of their former affluence.

The Fang General called Khrak had stormed in and seized the mines for the service and supply of the occupying forces, and as a result the man had lost his income and his family's many luxuries and also their land and animals—still tended in those days by tenants on the old family farm outside the town—had been confiscated "for the use of the troops," but they had managed to keep their city house and at least a shifting semblance of normalcy to their lives.

The man and his wife were both shrewd. They had understood the new order of things more readily than most and so had spoken carelessly to no one and revealed no confidences to any but each other and had taken to wearing clothes that gave the appearance of a near poverty and had resigned themselves at the start to certain losses and had bartered successfully for the things they most needed in the black markets of Dugtown.

They had sold furniture, sold their finer clothing, dispensed with two stylish carriages, bartered away their etched silver cutlery piece by piece. In their increasing leanness as the occupation stretched to its fourth year the man had even reconciled himself to the relinquishing of storied heirlooms: old silver bells forged by a great-great-grandfather; a small, rolled tapestry artfully woven by some ancient dame; and a dark and intricately carved scene of a man and a woman and a dragon in an orchard, rendered in some unknown wood and passed down from a time near the founding of his own nomadic line, having come east carried in the satchel fold of whichever storied ancestor had first ventured or been driven out of the western wilderness, spilling onto the bright, mapped lands and making camp in this river basin rich with fertile soils and sunlight and gentle rains.

The man had bartered these personal treasures to an itinerant dry goods merchant whose shop had some months earlier been ransacked first by Fangs and then by local ne'er-do-wells who had scavenged for what remained. So robbed of his settled livelihood, this merchant had yet a few hundred pounds of dried beans and a bit of corn and flour to trade from his wagon, and this merchant, as it turned out, had no wife or children of his own to consider the upkeep of, and so had also long been a collector of antiquities. When the man had climbed aboard the merchant wagon and unwrapped his barter goods, the collector's mouth had gaped and in the end he had paid him double what the man had expected, though it was still only a fraction of what such rare pieces might have brought in prosperous days on a fair market.

In prosperous days though, the man never would have sold them.

"I have only seen one other such artifact," the antiquities trader had told him only after the terms were agreed and the trade was complete. "The dark wood of this carving is beyond rare. If legends are true, it comes from a kind of tree called *gloamshadow*, which is said to grow only on the high slopes of The One Mountain in the West. Did your people come from the west?"

"Far back," the man answered, "but I don't know much to tell about The One Mountain, apart from yarns spun by doddered nannies."

"Ah, well, it is said to be one of the *old* places." The trader folded his hands and sighed, closing his eyes as if he were remembering the place himself, or as if memory were a thing that could be stored in the fabric of being and passed down from father to son for a thousand generations. "A great jagged summit rising from the plains, set there from the beginning of the world. A peak the first men climbed to meet with the Maker face to face, under the old order of things, when he taught his children how to live."

"I've recited a similar tale with sparkling embellishments for my own daughter," the man said, "for she loves the telling of myths."

"Oh, the mountain is real enough I'd wager. And if the mountain is real, who knows but that the old stories might have some truth in them."

The man feigned a smile and shrugged to say that he doubted it but would not begrudge his fellow man such fancies.

"Well, perhaps it is only a tale," the trader conceded and then looked away, his smile suddenly wan and his gaze distant. "But such wood must come from somewhere. And we both know that it does not come from any tree we have ever seen."

The man had agreed and tried not to seem unfriendly as they conversed after that, though he felt himself seized with a loathing then, not for the merchant who had bought his birthright for beans, but for the evil of the days that had required him to sell such birthright. Yet his child was growing thin, and they needed dry stores for the coming winter for there was no fresh harvest, and so he had traded even his own storied history for the hope of the girl's future, and by such desperate means they had somehow scratched by that year and even into the next.

Despite those harder times the girl had remained ever a cheerful child, bursting with hope and dreams and a sort of fierce poetry of existence that bound the man and woman together in common hope and common cause. He remembered the feel of his wife's hand slipped wordlessly into his own as they stood in the doorway of the girl's room one bright morning delighting together in their daughter's small delight as she overlooked the endless rushes and swirls of the river that could be seen in all weathers from her high window, and chirped and crowed at the distant ferry boat and the colorful scarves and bonnets of the women conveyed therein and remarked how like a box of tiny flowers they seemed. How like a box of bright and tiny flowers.

One did not ask for much in those days, just to be together, just to locate and cultivate and nurture those small moments that would spring in the memory like perfectly delicate blooms of joy in a private, walled garden.

Even amidst the tyranny that besieged their city, they had clung to their own happiness, and had laughed together at table, savoring their simple meals and treasuring the fierce and playful joys that flashed like sunlight on spinning waters from those pale blue eyes that were the wider windows through which their daughter watched the world.

If only he could live this night again.

Surely he would act.

Surely, now that he knew, now that he saw what had come of it, he would act.

For what good is a man who does nothing to allay his child's nightmares when those nightmares take on claws and scaly flesh and burst into her room?

The girl's capacity for wonder had ever moved him, even when she was a toddler and could not yet speak but would pause and stare at any mirabilia of light and shadow or coo at a softness of moss or smile at any song of sweeft or fazzle dove. She was the sort who was forever seeing little magics in the mosses of the forest and begging him for stories of the lost Shining Isle of Anniera (he often made these up for he knew so little of the legends) or of the great Lone Fendril that soared high in its glory round the world's skies with wings stretched wide as the roof of a house, drawing the turning seasons behind it, or of a thousand beasts and legends still rumored to dwell in the places beyond the maps.

"Oh Papa, can we go there one day?" she would ask. "To the Shining Isle?" And he would kiss her forehead and tuck the blankets tight round her and reply, "But say the word, my princess, and I shall make it so," and the girl would giggle and the man would bow comically and then catch her eye with a wink before he left her room.

His eye now fixed on something white catching moonlight in the trampled herb bed. It was roughly the size of a hen egg and he thought that he knew what it was and he leaned painfully forward and extended his fingers to retrieve it and it was soft against his fingertips. Lifting it closer to his face then he drew in a spasmed breath, for it was a thing the girl had carried and dropped earlier in the night.

It was a little tricorn, sewn of a silvery-white silk.

Of all the tales her father spun, the girl's favorites had always been of this, of the mythical tricorn who roamed the wilds and from whose alabaster horns and hooves peace and light were shed like golden lantern light upon a silvery wood.

Is it true, Papa?

Of course.

But I mean, is it really true?

As true as you can imagine it, princess.

He had steadfastly encouraged her belief in such fancies for he had loved the innocence of her wonder, knowing that he could not shelter it forever in a time of brutalities and war, knowing that innocence would one day collapse beneath a burden of knowledge and experience as it always must amongst life's sorrows, but for that knowledge vowing all the more to protect it so long as such was in his power.

"I will at least give her a childhood," he had told his wife one night, and she had kissed his cheek then and had rested her head upon his chest, and it pained him now to remember how it had felt then to be so trusted and to feel himself strong.

The man had wanted his child to believe in the big stories, the wide wonders, the legends and myths that would teach her to see beyond the fear and suspicion and decay that had become their town, but, he asked now, had he ever really believed such things himself?

It had not even seemed important enough a question to answer till this moment.

For what difference would it have made to their daily existence?

And now?

If ever he had believed, he realized, he would no longer.

Not now.

For it was now no longer possible to believe in anything good at all.

He stroked the tiny silk tricorn that had long rested atop his daughter's pillow, noting the ragged mane and cobalt horns and indigo dots of eyes. He had won this trifle for the girl as a skillgame prize at the Dragon Day Festival in the Glipwood Township barely a year before.

His lips twitched now in pained smile remembering how he had failed on his first attempt to toss three iron rings round a carved thwap, and he had told his daughter it was a rigged booth and their thin coppers would be better spent elsewhere. But because her eyes had been such a beautiful blue, more piercing than seas in sunlight, and because her laugh had always worked upon him like an enchantment, he had sighed comically and shaken his head so that his wife and daughter had goaded him merrily on, until he had handed over coin after coin, trying again and again, happily spending double what the trifle was worth to win it for the girl, just to prove to her that even in these tumultuous and dangerous times he was her protector and benefactor, and would secure for her a sheltered happiness.

What's more, he had believed that he could.

He had always believed his strength and his luck would hold because they always had.

And now this.

The man's chest began to heave and shake, wracking his gut with sharper pains. Tears brimmed and spilled his eyes and rode their curving trails southward along the creases of his face.

He should have been the one taken.

Not her.

Not his baby.

She should still be here.

Here, in the home where she slept every night of her life.

Here, where she begged for stories as her eyes grew sleepy.

Here, where she whispered to the Maker her prayers:

Watch over us all, even this night. May we wake in your care.

He turned his face upwards, as if that were the space the Maker must occupy and he stared long, seeking to focus even beyond the stars, and then he spoke aloud that same refrain that had always closed the girl's prayer—had closed it even that very night—and he spoke it quite slowly so that the Maker might have time to consider the implications. The accusation.

Watch over us all, even this night.

Even. This. Night.

When he had waited and there was no answer but the wind and the silence, he turned his face and wept again, wretchedly this time, for what was now left to believe in this world from which children were violently wrested and their fathers left to sit beside their empty beds?

"Don't fret, baby," he had stupidly assured the girl as two of the foul creatures had torn away the covers she had huddled under. "You'll suffer no harm!" He had rushed forward and clung to her for a moment, and she to him, even as scaly hands gripped her arms, and then they had wrenched her from his grip and dragooned her down the stairs, her eyes wide and her too terrified at first to scream, reaching out a desperate hand to him and then the mute panic rising to a heartrending shrieking *Papa! PAPA!* and him trying to calm her, running down the stairs behind those sidewinding abominations saying it would be all right while his wife at least had sense to wrap herself round the legs of one of the leering, unnatural beasts, pleading for her daughter until she was roughly kicked in the face so that she crumpled on the tiles and now bled from a deep gash that would surely scar her soft cheek forever.

"Might she stay long enough just to eat something, please?" he had appealed, not even knowing what he was saying as he trailed the odious and stinking creatures over the threshold and into the yard. "She'll be hungry on the journey!" He had even tried to negotiate his daughter's release with offers of more ale and hogpig for the Fangs until they had tossed the screaming girl roughly into the Black Carriage and had slammed the door of it and, tiring of his entreaties, the small, hunched Fang had folded him up neatly with the hard jab of a spear butt into his gut that felt as if something had burst or ripped inside him.

His breathless gasps had amused them all as the fat one swung his jiggling bulk up to the carriage seat and the other two leapt hissing to the footboards at the back, and the driver had cracked his whip and the horses had lurched into their harnesses and the Black Carriage had started and rolled away echoing the sound of his daughter's muffled shrieking and the wicked mirth of the small Fang. As the wagon receded the beaded one had fixed him with a slow and voided stare that was either pained or sadistic or perhaps merely purblind and oblivious.

If only the man still had his horse he could have followed to learn where the Black Carriage went. Surely he would have dared at least to do that, to ride at a distance behind and to spy out the final destination.

If he had seen where they had taken her, then perhaps he could have also rescued her. A resistance was rumored, fomenting in the shadows of Dugtown across the river. He could have made contact somehow then, gotten word to them, enlisted in their ranks, led them to rescue his child and the children of others!

Ah, how heroic his afterthoughts now.

Did he truly believe he would have ridden after them, when he had declined to resist them?

And why even ask such questions now?

They had confiscated his horse nine years earlier when the first fingers of darkness had groped their way into Torrboro, the first outpost of Gnag established this side of the river. The foul beasts had slithered in and taken whatever they wanted from the shops and homes.

"This horse is much too fine for the likes of you!" they had croaked.

"Of course," he had answered, and given a small nodding bow. "It is at your service."

"Ssservice, yesss," one of them had said in undisguised mockery of the man's subservience. "That's what we wants it for. For ssservisss. *Delicious* sservice."

The beasts had snickered at his helpless estate and then one of them had noticed and demanded his silver-buckled belt as well.

Maybe that had been the moment he lost himself—the moment the Fang had seized the bridle and the sweet little bay mare had whinnied in fright and cast her head round to find him and he had simply walked away holding his breeches up with one hand and had not looked back though she whinnied twice more before he could round the corner.

For a man who had grown up on a wide, rolling acreage, tending his father's animals in the rural outskirts of Torrboro, a man who understood and valued a good horse, it had been a painful loss. He could not but remember the mare with a twinge of guilt that he had betrayed her trust. But what could he have done?

Even then he had had no fight in him. For a man with a home and family, there was simply too much to lose. And so he had not resisted in the small ways that a man might, and in time the accumulation of such daily choices of acquiescence had hardened into a kind of moral muscle memory, such that resistance was no longer even a possible option.

For nine years the man had been rehearsing his surrender.

How weak and stupid he had been.

How weak. How stupid.

The moment the Black Carriage had rounded the wide curve of cobblestone in front of the house and was lost to view, the man bit his lip against the throbbing pain in his gut and crawled to the hedge to retrieve the silvered blade lest it be discovered by daylight and he and the woman arrested and hung for possession of it.

He absently slid the dagger from the scabbard at his belt now and turned it in his hand, testing the heft of it as he still gazed uncomprehending along the road where the carriage had vanished into blackness.

The hilt of the blade had a braided design, with a dark leather wrapped round the grip. It was an old forging, something from an earlier time. The emblem of the fruited tree and rising sun was probably the mark of some family lineage but it was not his own and he did not recognize it. The blade itself had been recently honed to a fine, sharp edge. He wondered again how his wife had acquired the weapon and decided, circumstances being as they now were, she would likely never tell him.

"What are you doing?" Her voice sounded sharp and small from the ruined doorway and interrupted his thoughts.

She had raised her head now from the tiles in the entryway and was watching him, her words an accusation mixed of desperation and disbelief.

It took him a moment to understand that she was speaking of the blade he held.

He turned his face half to her, but did not entirely meet her gaze. He could not.

He could not bear to see in her eyes the way that she must see him now, for he knew that it would be the truth about him that was written there.

"She's gone!" the woman rebuked. "THEY TOOK HER! What good is a weapon in your hand now unless you mean to turn it upon yourself?" Then she dropped her head again and clutched her sides and wept quietly.

"Would you rather we were all dead?" he said, suddenly angry, for he had no other defense.

He turned again to view cold moonlight reflected on the ripples of river below.

"Yes." The woman spoke after a long silence, but softly so that he almost didn't hear her. "Yes, I would rather we were all dead."

Scarcely a dozen sentences would pass between the man and the woman in the three days that followed, and none of these would be tender. They inhabited now the same desolate space but could no longer share it, drifting instead past one another as ghosts tied by grief to the same devastation but fixed each in their own ethereal plane and orbit without intersection to the other.

When the jail had been visited on the first morning and the corrupt authorities petitioned without remedy and the fixed certainty that no further word of their vanished daughter would be forthcoming had collapsed over them like a tottering wall, the woman had at last insisted on holding a small wake, though such public observances of grief were largely forbidden even if sometimes ignored.

The man understood that his right to protest any of his wife's decisions had been forever forfeit on the night of his failings, and so he said nothing, though in his own mind he believed it best to do nothing to provoke further scrutiny.

That night the man lay on the bed, scarce able to move from the lingering and now worsening pain in his gut, and he watched as the woman silently packed a satchel, taking hair ribbons and a little gilded book and tiny boots that had been the girl's when she was a newborn and tying them up in a wide silk scarf. He wondered if she were planning to leave him after the wake, but he was so strangely warm and the room seemed to be trembling and he thought that he must sleep for awhile so he stumbled to the bedroom that had been the girl's and he stretched across the foot of her bed as the pain in his belly increased and his mind clouded and the thought first occurred to him that he might be dying of whatever internal damage he had sustained, and he did not resist the thought.

The man lay on the bed for a night and a day and a night, drifting in and out of a fever delirium that he understood in his few lucid moments was probably an infection. His gut was painfully swollen and sensitive to even the slightest touch. He could eat nothing and only rose gingerly and painfully when he must relieve himself or gulp from the bucket of water beside the bed. The woman carried him water twice a day with some kind of salty herb crushed in it, but avoided his eyes and did not speak and there was no tenderness communicated by her touch nor was there any expected.

In his fever dreams the man was haunted by memory of that most horrible night relentlessly relived, only it was as if he were standing somewhere behind himself watching his own indecision and he would scream at the hesitant man to act as the girl was seized and handled by the black-eyed brutes, but the him that was in the dream either could not hear his entreaties or would not acknowledge them and then the man would turn towards him and would sometimes have the face of a Fang and other times it would be his own face and though he had dreamed the dream dozens of times he could never master the horror engendered at that reveal, and he found it no less horrible when it was his own face than he did when it was the face of a monster.

In his delirium the man was vaguely aware sometimes of wishing this sickness to end in death, but he knew it was only as an easy way to escape the burning blanket of shame that covered him, and so he knew that this was the wish of a coward and he imagined the joined voices of his forefathers echoing the same assessment of him in some spectral hall down which he must eternally walk: *coward*.

Only the dim thought that the girl might still be out there some-where, might somehow, someday, against all odds return, gave him a sense of obligation to rally his strength if he might, so that if she escaped she might find him waiting for her in the old house and he wondered if she did if she could ever forgive him, ever look at him again with the love and the trust she had always graced him, and he thought that in some way she might still love him but that he had probably lost her trust forever.

It would be ever so much easier just to die than to see her again, all things being as they now were, weaknesses exposed, secrets revealed, faultlines buckled, things done or not done that could now never be done or undone.

On the second night when the fever was at its worst the man dreamed he stood to his ankles in a wide, shallow river and might cross to one side where the banks were settled with a grey mist and a stillness from which no sound escaped, or to the other side which yet held light of day, and before him over the waters hovered a small, dancing light which he somehow believed was his soul or his life or some other thing that was equally unknowable and which seemed to tease him, darting here and there, first towards the fog, then towards the sunlight. He stumbled after it fighting for his balance among the tilt of slick river stones and when he captured it at last in his fist he looked round him and saw that he stood upon the sunlit bank and he woke then in the still and awful loneliness of his daughter's room to find himself soaked in sweat and his fever broken and his belly no longer on fire and the silk tricorn clenched in his fist as if it were the thing he had caught in his dream.

He drew himself to a sitting position to lean against the pillow, stinking and disheveled and emaciated and unshaven as he now was, and there he gathered his thoughts for the first time in days and discovered that the workings of his mind in that fevered state had not been without effect.

He woke with a clarity that had not been there before.

And with that clarity he saw that there was also still a course, still a pathway opened to him.

He had not known such a frail thing as hope in days, and this new swelling of it in his breast was almost startling, as if some magic bird had nested within his chest as he slept and had laid its egg there.

So long as he drew breath, he could still act, could he not?

The girl, after all, must be somewhere.

So in the quiet places of his own counsel he now began to weave a new story, some roughly patched hope of a life in which he might yet redeem his failings and resurrect his family from this ruin, and so on the morning of the wake, he rose from his sickbed and stumbled to his room and washed his face and drew from his wardrobe a dark, ragged longcoat not worn since his travel days and slung it round his shoulders. Then he took a weathered, black-brimmed hat from a peg in the cabinet and fitted it atop his unruly locks. Finally, he wiped cobwebs from the openings of the dark leather journeyboots not worn since the mines had closed and pulled them up over his calves, cinching them tight.

Whatever happened, he knew he would not be able to remain here.

Not as things were now.

He must go out and earn the right to return to this place.

Which was to say, he must find and save his daughter, or he must die in the trying, and either would be better than this.

Life had funneled him to this like a sheep through a chute. The sudden clarity was as bracing and unexpected as any accidental plunge through river ice.

He could yet become the man his wife had wished him to be.

It was not too late.

He would reclaim the honor that had been forfeit in his failing.

The man drew the blued silver blade and scabbard from where he had hidden them atop the wardrobe and fitted them through his belt, taking care to conceal them beneath his cloak, and then he descended the stairs to the sitting room where the wake was to be held, only to find that no neighbors had been brave or foolish enough to attend.

And who could blame them? If the Fangs had done one thing excellently in their governance, it was to recreate the culture of men in their own twisted reptilian images, so that now all relationships even among neighbors were amalgamated of fear and suspicion and sometimes of envy and greed and betrayal and none could trust the other and few were any longer practiced at sympathies, feigned or genuine, and compassion in any active form was now something like a distant mythology that one learned not to ever quite believe in beyond the bonds of one's own family and sometimes not even there.

And so in the end it had hardly been a wake at all. Just the two of them, the man and woman, sitting in a small, pained silence with several of the girl's favorite things piled between them and nothing to say to one another and no way to touch one another's pain. The woman wept quietly and the man absently scratched the head of the girl's cat until it bounded away from him and darted out the door and he wondered when was the last time it had been fed.

When they were done the man scooped up the girl's silk tricorn, slipping it into his pocket, and then he stood and tightened his belt and adjusted his cape and turned to the woman who raised her head to meet his gaze with a look that was aching and distant but also puzzled. The man drew his cloak back so that she might witness the blade and divine his intent.

"I will bring our daughter home. And if I cannot, I will bring our daughter justice."

The woman pondered him long before speaking.

"Swear it then."

"My word is my oath."

"Your words have been weak. Swear it now. Swear it by the Maker's hand."

The man removed his hat and ran the fingers of his right hand through his hair and swallowed hard, for such an oath was binding as law in that place, and the oathbreaker more reviled than the leper. "By the Maker's hand, then. By the Maker's hand I swear that I will bring our daughter home. And if I cannot, I will bring our daughter justice."

For a moment it almost seemed that something not unlike concern, perhaps even longing, played across the depths of the woman's eyes but if it was she had soon suppressed it behind the dark and impenetrable cloud of her own grief and then she answered him "Be it so. But what is justice? If you cannot bring my child home, I wish you never to return. This I also swear by the Maker's hand." And then she had bit her trembling lower lip and had looked away from him.

He had studied her a moment, hoping her hardness might break, or that he might think of a softening reply, for his heart still welled with feelings, and here at the last he saw the curve of her cheek that as a young man he had felt he was falling or flying over, as if it were the utter horizon of his world, and he longed now to embrace her again, to tell her he was sorry, to find her forgiveness before he walked through the door and away, but she did not soften, and no wise or tender word came to him that he might speak, and so he had simply nodded once in acknowledgement of her own severe oath and said, "Be it so," and had turned then, and pressing his dark hat to his head had stepped across that threshold and had not paused again to turn and see whether she watched him or no for he could not bear to know if she did not.

He pulled the brim of his hat low to hide the welling of his tears and tried his best to mimic the brisk but nonchalant pace of a man on common errand as he traversed his garden path, stepping out into the winding road and away from the last of the life that had been and making his way upwards till he crested the great hill of Torrboro and viewed for the last time the old town spread before and behind him, a panorama of homes and shops, of people and chimney smoke wisps and carts and carriages and clatter and clamor and cries and bells, and yes, of the distant castle and of slithering Fangs as well—a place of all such disparate things nestled together in a sharp bend of the mighty River Blapp. The man negotiated the long, downward sweep of hill, taking it in grim, purposeful strides without pause, and then he passed through the teeming streets, pressing his way towards the military quarters the Fangs occupied. His dark garb drew a few odd glances but no one hailed or questioned him as he passed, not even the bored-looking Fang sentries that loitered outside the jail.

It was deep shadows he now sought and he found them in the town's seedier quarter which had not so many years ago been a thriving row of well-kept shops and pubs and merchant stalls but which now was grimed and given to ever increasing degrees of neglect and disrepair the nearer one drew to the Fang barracks. He had not passed this way in some time and it seemed to him now as if several square blocks of Dugtown—with its strewn and stinking streets and its ramshackle facades and loitering swindlers and thieves—had been lifted whole and ferried across the river and dropped here in the midst of Torrboro.

Such was the imprint of Fangs within these square blocks.

Almost directly across from the barracks the man ducked into a place called *Wooster's Passable Ales (formerly Wooster's Fine Ales)* and, ordering a pint from a red-eyed and sullen barkeep, retired to a skein of shadows near the back of the place, a vantage that afforded a clear view of the murky room and also a line of sight through a smudged and spattered front window towards the Fang quarters. There he loitered for the rest of the day and long into the night, his hat brim tilted to obscure his eyes from the other patrons. Every so often the man drew the chipped brown mug to his lips and quaffed a draught which he deemed only *barely* passable and as he drank he scanned the rude features of every Fang that lurched or lumbered or skulked or slithered to or from the barracks across the cobbled street, for he knew those he sought must eventually pass into his view.

The floor and tables and counters of the pub were caked with a greasy film of dust and the place smelled of some rancid oil. In those slow hours the man never counted more than a dozen patrons in the establishment, and he suspiciously observed the motley assortment of citizens who did enter, some of whom even sat at table briefly with a uniformed Fang in the far corner and spoke in hushed tones and glanced nervously about them and then were handed coins and the man suspected these were surely informants betraying their own neighbors and so he tried to appear drunk or asleep most of the time so that they would pay him no mind, and even though they were not the quarry he hunted, his fury burned against them.

The place seemed never to close though he was sometimes the only customer in it and the dim candles still burning here and there atop empty tables in the darkness gave the illusion of signal fires flung across great distances. The town was under a midnight curfew, so when he judged it to be near the end of the second watch of night the man decided he must leave or begin to arouse unwanted curiosity so he pushed his chair back and made his way to the bar and settled his tab.

The sullen barkeep eyed him warily and asked, "So is Torrboro home, friend?" and the man had answered, "It used to be," and then he had stepped into the night and had wandered the streets until he found a cold stove pipe running up an alley wall and he had climbed it to a flat roof and slept there a few hours and woke with a stiff back and a sour mouth and a growling belly.

He had returned to the same pub in the early afternoon and it was a different barkeep this time, a broad-shouldered old woman with thrums of frizzed grey poking like spikes from her head and with fists marked by tattoos that were dark and smudged and indecipherable and which he guessed she had inflicted upon herself.

When he asked for a pint she only grunted and filled a greasy mug till it foamed over and did not wipe the spill from the sides before she plopped it down in front of him and grunted again. He sat at the same table and again tried to appear unremarkable as the hours trickled past and the scruffy clientele passed sporadically in and out through the doors.

It was a half hour before midnight and in his hunger and exhaustion he had felt himself suddenly wearied and had struggled to stay awake at the table but had just nodded when he was jarred by a peevish croak and looked up to see the fat Fang Grumwold with the scarred jaw shoving the peculiar monster Beadsy through the dark doorway of Wooster's.

"Because we drawed straws for it and yours came up short!" Grumwold bellowed. "Now does your duty and buy us a keg of eel squeeze for our night watch!"

"But it's *my* straw comes up every night!" Beadsy protested. "Not fair! It's cheating!"

The man was instantly and fully awake and felt his pulse quicken and he scooted his chair further into the shadows and drew the brim of his hat even lower and his right hand searched and found the hilt of his dagger beneath his cloak.

"Haw! It's not the rest of us faults if you're just unlucky!"

"But I doesn't even drink the nasty stuff!"

"Now what kind of a honest, Gnag-fearin' Fang don't love eel squeeze?"

"I loves kiffy insteads."

"You loves what?"

"A pot o' old kiffy. I dumps in eight spoons o' sugar and . . ."

Beadsy didn't finish the sentence. The fat Fang had reached out and pressed a clawed hand over his long snout, silencing him. "I'm going to assume you drink it with a handful of fat, black dung beetles tossed in and swimmin' around to make it nice and scrunchy and bitter cuz otherwise you're about to make me puke, you disgusting creature. Just buy us the eel squeeze and let's get out to our post!"

Grumwold gave Beadsy's snout a sharp pinch before releasing it, and the thinner Fang winced and whimpered and rubbed his nose before turning and reluctantly sliding his coin to the barkeep. The woman dropped the coin in her apron front and grunted and then disappeared into a back room. The fat Fang patted the other's back.

"There's a good boy, Beadsy-weedsy."

"You shouldn't call me that."

"Weedsy-Beadsy, then?"

The woman returned from the back room lugging a cask pulled two-handed to her belly the way a person might tote a portly child or pig for a short distance. She heaved it to the bar top with a grunt and turned away without a word. Beadsy sighed heavily and stooped and maneuvered the keg awkwardly to his shoulder and raised himself again and the Fangs turned to go.

The man marked their exit with his eyes and he stood and pressed a few coppers into the gummy residuum of the tabletop, and then he bowed his head to conceal his face from one haggard and lonely reveler who stared slow-eyed into the depths of his dark mug as the man moved past him wending amongst the vacant yellow hollows of candlelight that seemed in the coarse fug of that room to have acquired skin and to pulse with vital substance like some subterranean nursery of alien and pellucid larvae. He paused in a deeper gloom back of the open door to confirm that the beldam barkeep was retired to her back room and that the cobblestones beyond the boardwalk were empty of Fang sentries before he slipped forth and followed his enemies into that wide night.

The man hung in the shadows, holding his position a half block back and pausing to peer at the scant selections in shop windows here and there, should anyone be watching him. He kept the creatures ever in his sight though, as they negotiated a maze of half lit streets that were mostly unpeopled at that hour but that ran strange with distant sounds which dripped overhead from the roofs like thin rivulets of waters whose sources were somewhere higher up in the hills around the city, perhaps from within the courtyards of the castle where Khrak's personal guard must be bivouacked round their waning fires.

It was a night when the moon would rise late and set late and would yet be visible opposite the sun in the morning sky, like a specter given leave to visit again the life he had once lived, but for now the moon was dallying and the night was black as boiled pitch and lit only by vast plays of heat lightning tossed furiously between pillared clouds piled distantly to the east over the Dark Sea.

When the Fangs turned up a desolate and winding alley that seemed to lead in the direction of the castle, the man knew the curfew would sound ere long and sensed greater urgency to act and at last quickened his pace to close the distance. From the snatches of echoed conversation he could hear, it seemed the mismatched pair were still bickering the virtues of eel squeeze and the rank injustice—or the rare privilege, depending on the varied points of view being put forward—of being required or allowed to purchase for others a thing one would never oneself imbibe. And so the pair were altogether unaware of the man who ever more closely dogged their steps and they paid no mind even to the soft slap of his boots on stone. When he was ten paces behind them he drew forth his blued blade from its scabbard and, rushing up behind them, with a single stroke gashed deep across the lower left leg of the fat Fang so that the ankle tendon was severed completely and the portly beast wobbled and pitched forward to the stones, howling in his sudden collapse.

The man ripped the maimed Fang's sword from its scabbard and flung it clattering into the alley behind him before the Fang could even roll his jellied mass to perceive what had stung him, and when he did so, the fine point of the man's blade was already pressed to his throat so hard he dared not swallow.

"Cry out and die," the man said, and withdrawing his blade then from the rapid subduing of that first victim he turned his attention quickly to the second who stood shocked and trembling with the heavy barrel still balanced on his shoulders. With no hesitation or stuttering of his movements the man raised that razored dagger and cleaved down a deft and slashing blow that hewed the tail of the beaded Fang cleanly so that it dropped utterly severed to the street where it whipped and coiled like a headless snake and the beaded Fang, so unnerved by the sudden violence to its person, released its grip on the heavy keg, letting it roll from its shoulder and crash to the stones below, splitting apart so that a foul, reeking liquid that smelled both of rotting fish and sour beer sloshed and spilled out.

"You oaf!" the fat one shouted from his prone position, as if the loss of that nauseating grog were the worst of his concerns. Grumwold's breathing was wet and labored and something like perspiration glinted on his brow now and his foul blood seeped over the stones from his leg wound and the other Fang was trembling and gurgling like a snared rat though his stump bled little and the man hoped his wounded adversaries would now be of no mind to resist, but he did not know how to read their eyes and expressions in that darkness and intended to take no unnecessary chances.

"Up against the bricks!" the man hissed, fearing the noise of the barrel smash might already portend trouble. "You in the boots! Nose to the wall and keep your claws up where I can see them. And you," the man prodded Grumwold's throat again with the tip of his blade so that the paunchy Fang was forced to heave its bulk backwards until it was seated, propped against the bricks, panting.

"I knows your voice from somewheres recent," the fat Fang growled, "and that means I'll find you again. You ort to run while you can, little man."

The beaded Fang watched from the corner of a wide, black eye and it shuddered and trembled and something like a moan escaped its lips. "He murders us! We yabbed his babykins and now he murders us!" and here the miserable fiend yowled.

"Silence!" the man hissed and Grumwold narrowed his eyes at the pale face that hovered over his own.

"Took his babykins . . .?" The fat Fang's eyes went wide. "Haw! I members you now! The house on the hill with that crazy lady what tried to claw Scuzzy! You was the fellow kept bobbin' and bowin' like a scullery slave when we took yer little brat out! Oh, you've stepped in it now! GUARDS!" The Fang bellowed and tried to skewer the man's eyes with a sudden upward thrust of its claws but the man saw it coming and leapt back and then lunged nimbly in with a slashing riposte, his razored silver slicing across the beast's maw, cross-hatching the scar that already existed on its gnarled mouth. Grumwold's muzzle was now flayed open and a blackish ichor dripped heavily from the wound.

"Raise your voice or resist me again, either of you, and I will run you through." His voice carried that mix of unpredictability and of fear and of sudden resolve that left no doubt as to the veracity of his threat.

"What does it want from us?" the beaded one asked in a hoarse rush of exhaled breath that the man supposed was the Fang equivalent of a whisper.

"I want my daughter back."

"We doesn't gots it," Grumwold said. With each movement of the jaw a new flow of dark blood and slobbery strings of green bile or venom dribbled from its lips and threaded their way to its chest.

"But you know where she is."

"Do I?"

"You took her!"

"Well if you think I've still got her in one of my pockets, then search me, you miserable man-maggot!" The fat Fang snarled and its black eyes flashed wide and livid and the man saw that its claws trembled but whether it was from rage or loss of blood or anticipation of another attack he could not tell. He leaned in and pressed the point of the dagger hard against the creature's neck so that the tip began to slide between scales.

"Answer or die. Where is she now?"

"She's gone!" the Fang muttered. "Shipped off days ago!"

"Shipped off? To where?"

"Oh, I don't know. Let me think. Where do ships sail from Torrboro? Hmm. Oh, that's right. To the sea!"

The man felt his new hopes diminished, and his fatigue and his shames suddenly returned. If the girl was now ocean-borne what hope would he have of following and finding her?

The beaded Fang was mumbling fearfully and clutching his tail stump and whimpering while the fat one slavered and hissed and tried to draw breath with the knife pressed at his throat and the man could hardly think for the fear and the chaos and the weirdness of it all and he did not know if he should just kill them both and be done with it or if there were anything more he might learn before he took his vengeance.

"Silence!" he ordered the beaded one, striking its back with the flat of his blade before he addressed Grumwold again. "Shipped to where? To Dang? To the Phoob Islands?"

"Does Grumwold know everything?" the fat one croaked. "We take the brats and ride the carriage to the holding place and then we go home and it gets new drivers so it all keeps secret! Some maybe go to here, others go to there. Maybe to islands. Maybe across the waves. Does Grumwold know everything? No! They don't tell their everythings to Grumwold!"

"But we do knows where the babykins goes, don't we?" the beaded one whimpered, and the man saw the silencing glare flash from Grumwold's black eyes and he knew he was being played a fool and he heard then the great sounding of the horn blast from Khrak's castle that marked the start of curfew and the scouring of streets to follow and so he knew as well that time was now his enemy and that whatever truth this Fang held must be forced immediately from his tongue.

He pressed the tip of his blade hard against the soft cavity in the curve of the lower jaw, forcing the whole skull upwards so that the Fang was now staring wildly at the sky and breathing in pained rasps.

"Lie again and I will send you to your oblivion. Where is my daughter?"

The Fang seemed to take seriously his predicament only in that final moment, to realize that whatever afterward happened to the man, his own death was now imminent.

Grumwold scrunched scaly brows and lowered his voice. "Maybe it don't want to know what Grumwold knows. Maybe it only thinks it wants to know."

"Tell me." The man jabbed the dagger barely upwards, just skewering the tip through the leathery skin.

The man saw the sudden change then in the bulbous, upturned eyes, the precise moment when the Fang's loathing and fear glazed into something more malicious and taciturn.

"I killed her!" the creature shouted, thick, trailing beads of saliva and venom slinging wildly from its fangs. It scrabbled against the wall behind it, trying to push itself suddenly to a standing position. "I snaps her neck in the carriage and tosses her into the Blapp. We gets to kill the ones that scream too much and that brat of yours was a screamer!"

And then it opened its mouth and gave a horrid, howling laugh and reached forward to claw at the man, and before the man could think he had run his blade up between the jawbone arc and into the skull cavity of the beast and he felt the sudden cascade of dust pouring over him that told him the loathsome creature had sundered particle from particle and in its very being had ceased to be.

He turned quickly to the beaded Fang, still splayed against the wall, now sputtering and stuttering and stamping its boots in terror. To keep it from screaming he pressed his blade into its spine.

"And what was your part in this?"

His words held the form of a question but were not truly a question, containing as they did the settled weight of trial and of guilt and of verdict already handed down.

No words escaped, but he saw the beast's mouth working strangely, its eyes glazed and distant and fearful, as if the Fang were slipping into some dark sink and unable to find any handhold to stop his slide. An oily brown seep, like a tear, formed in the corner of the reptilian eye and spilled over as the beaded Fang raised his voice in a long wail. "It wants to go home!"

"Quiet!"

But the thing could not silence itself even to save its own life. It had slipped the precipice of some lunacy as a ship might tip the world's remotest edge waters and plunge into voids immeasurable. "Lets it go back hooooooooome! Leave here! Go home! Leave here!"

"QUIET!"

The man paused a moment in confusion and in that pause heard over the cries of the Fang the unseen voices and the slap of flat, clawed feet against cobblestones closing in round the corner and he knew his game was up.

"Murder! Murder!" howled the Fang as it grasped at its stump again and howled "Murder!" and hopped from side to side.

The man drew back his blade to kill the miserable thing for he had sworn the oath and as he could not bring his daughter home he would at least bring her justice, but as he raised his blade he heard the fletched hiss of an arrow and felt the tearing thunk as it ripped through the canvas cloak and passed harmlessly between his arm and ribs and he turned and saw the silhouettes of a half-dozen Fangs spilling into the alley.

He raised his blade a second time and hesitated for reasons he could not explain until another arrow zipped past the man's head in the darkness and then he heard more shouts and saw more troops rushing in and the man turned and bolted down the alley in a hail of blind arrows and he could never afterwards explain to himself why he had avenged himself of the one Fang and only maimed the other but perhaps it was because in the act of vengeance he had found no satisfaction but only a deeper hollowing of his own loss and perhaps it was because he did not know if the beaded Fang had played a part in his daughter's death or had only been there when she was taken, and he suspected now that it was a creature that was either an idiot or insane.

The man dashed those desperate streets, scabbarding his weapon and wrapping the cloak round him to hide it and weeping for the thought of his dead child, but knowing as well that those barracks would be emptied and the town swarmed and him now branded as an outlaw and a murderer of Fangs, so he knew also that he must make good his escape in these precious minutes else he would surely be discovered.

If he had simply killed the second one as well, there would be no witness who had seen his face. Why had he not killed it when the opportunity was present?

He cut right and left and right and left again, working his way southwest through the dark streets, never certain where the shouts that followed had their origins. Sometimes he witnessed shadows and torchlight played around corners and he reversed his direction and made wider circuits round and through.

At the end of this desperate traverse he had reached the edges of the city, avoiding the larger streets and still eluding his confused pursuit who perhaps had not yet been able to ferret from the screaming, tailless Fang any clear description of the man they sought.

Slipping into and crossing through the work yard of a barrel maker who stood bare-chested and sweating at his fire-lit labors and who barely raised his head and tilted a knowing fox-nod at the man's passing, the man opened a gate in the back fence and let himself through and then it was only woods and fields before him and the town behind.

A half moon had now risen and was balanced on its tip like a child's top in spin and he reckoned by it and pursued a westward orientation, though he jogged without purpose or destination, simply with the knowledge that he had only a few hours or a few minutes before his trail would be discovered and that if he were apprehended he would be punished by some measure of unspeakable skinning or torture followed by some ignoble death.

And so, even in the fog of this new grief of the knowledge of his child's demise, he sped himself along, the tears flowing and ebbing and flowing again, fixed as they were to the alternating poles of sorrow and of survival. He increased his speed and sprinted several miles through the woods without stopping though the exertion cost him dear in his state still weakened from the days of fever, and all the while he was yet tortured by the thought that a better man might have fully avenged his dead child and then stood his ground and killed all the Fangs that he could in that darkened alley until at last his own blood had stained the cobblestones too.

Even when his side ached and his legs wobbled so that he could sprint no more, the man yet willed himself to a labored pace for several more hours before his long hunger and exhaustion and the lingering weakness stemming from his recent fever brought him to his knees and he curled and slept like a wild creature for an hour in a field. Then, believing he heard voices and the baying of a hound in the distance, he rose and pushed himself on again, navigating by moonlight across the oddly fertile plains swept with tall nettles and pocked with burrows of dragonmoles and the scratchings of quill diggles.

When he stumbled into a shallow creek that ran parallel to his westward path, he paused a moment to drink and to consider and then he followed it north for a half mile, running along the middle of it so that any trail of his scent might be lost to casual pursuit. Leaving the creek some minutes later he read the stars, adjusted his course, and fled into the west again.

He had no destination now. No place to run to. Only a place and a great emptiness to run from.

So his daughter was dead, and he an outlaw.

Even were he not a fugitive now, he could never go home again.

Such was his oath, sworn by the Maker's hand and witnessed by the dead girl's mother, and now unfulfillable.

His small vengeance against the Fang had been hollow, and thoughts of justice, in light of his daughter's death, were but a meaningless abstraction, for the girl had been utterly innocent when murdered, while the Fang's death had been the death of a guilty creature that deserved to die.

How could he equate the two or remedy the one with the other or claim that an imbalance had been redressed or that any final justice had been meted out when his innocent daughter was dead and gone and would not return no matter how many Fangs were destroyed or tyrants overthrown?

Justice was just another of the old myths then, a shining and deceptive dream unattainable to the living. So long as death held sway in this world, justice could not exist.

Punishment? Yes. Vengeance? Perhaps. But justice?

Never.

In the hour before dawn the man finally halted and, expending the last reserve of his energy, hauled his wearied body up into the lower branches of a great, silvery-leafed tree. He dozed there lightly in the wide boughs and woke unnerved to the lowing of a toothy cow in the tangled undergrowth nearby and to the fresh memory of his own sorrows still so raw and ragged and new. Finding his daughter's silk tricorn still in his pocket, he drew it forth and stroked it tenderly against his cheek and thought he could smell upon it the scent of her hair like sunlight and lavender and he felt then most achingly the finality of her loss, and then, as dawn began to break, he quelled his mourning and pocketed the trifle and only then did he look around at the wide landscape and consider what path was left to him and he could think of none.

He had failed as protector for his child was taken.

He had failed as savior for his child was dead.

His oath was broken.

What was he now but an outlaw and a wilderness wanderer adrift without allegiance or cause or future or hope?

When he climbed down from the tree at the first pale infading of dawn he had in his mind that he would simply head west. He could not say precisely why. Perhaps because his people had come from there long ago and so the west might receive him back and he might simply vanish there. Perhaps because he might be pursued from Torrboro and the north was deadly cold and the south unknown while to the east were spread the ranks of his enemies.

That left only a vague notion of the west as the road he must travel, and so he determined to go west, and he would walk until he either died or came at last to the end of all things and he did not care which of those fates overtook him first.

And so he trod the wilds for weeks that became months, scavenging for roots and berries and sleeping in the open fields without concern of fell animals for having lost all that he loved he was now utterly careless of his own life. He did not bother to hide his tracks and crossed four hundred hard miles before the season turned, his face ever set against the current of the river somewhere to his north with that dark-brimmed hat tilted low over his eyes and the long dagger strapped swinging to his side beneath that black cloak.

All this time, he neither saw nor was seen by another human being, and his dark thoughts were turned ever and ever more inward.

II.

The Places Beyond the Maps

*I have gradually observed that it is not always the wilderness outside the
man in which he is most in danger of becoming lost.*
—Riggin Dagorma's *The Wailing Orchards:*
A Tanjerade Tragedy

Now *approaches the dark walker from the rising of the sun so that his
craned shadow cambers a mile ahead of him across the bister plains like a
shuddered distortion of his truer being.*

*He crests a granite-toothed ridge where spread below him in the dis-
tance gambloat herds mill amongst tall, windswept grasses, harried at their
edges by the lanky limberwolves.*

*When he is yet two leagues away he knows those wolves will have
spotted him, though he would be to them as a dark drip of blood raising red
trails of dust down the ribs of the sloping hills where they sink into swales
before spreading again upward into the plain.*

*Three of the hungry beasts lope from the plain. Distant grey dots like
flecks of bile hacked up from some waterless dragon's throat. They trot*

towards him and halt at the swale's edge, crouching on their haunches, dark eyes glinting the sunrise light back to his brim-shadowed eyes and he receives their scintillation like the winking of daytime constellations in blinding alien skies, but he neither slows nor turns from his present course for he is grown quite careless of how this or any other day might end.

Three months into his westward wanderings the man had waded into the waters of a mighty river lake and swum the dreadful length of it in the dark of night because it had been in his path and he had come to see any obstacle in his path as an implied provocation, and so the act of swimming it rather than skirting its banks had been his own unspoken declaration that if there was no redemption in this life he would as soon slip to an early death. He had very nearly drowned from the drag of his clothing and from the weight of the silvered blade strapped to his back and also from his own sorrow and exhaustion and desire to sink to the bottom, succumbing finally to the silting of grief. Three times he had ceased swimming and allowed himself to float downwards, tumbled by unseen currents, but each time he had fought instinctively for the surface again, gasping like a landed fish and had finally heaved himself up on the opposite shoreline and had slept a sleep too wearied for dreams collapsed half in half out of the water until the heat of the midday sun and the lapping of the waves against him had wakened him at last.

His emotions were ever raw in those days and he often wept and as often shouted at himself as he walked fen and woodland and his fears and shames were magnified in that lonely vastness and his woeful confusion soon folded itself tightly into a sullen certainty that all paths of goodness had been forever closed to him, that he was now unnoticed and unwanted and cast adrift, his former life wreaked to a havoc and him without purpose, without meaning, without friend. Deprived in this sudden, desolate exile of comfort and nourishment and community, the man's thoughts waxed dark and he buffed them darker still with the polish of his own coddled bitterness until all things were clouded by a thickening veil that had descended between the man and his own perceptions. It was a sort of madness in which he soon came to see all past joys and sufferings as meaningless, all past hope and circumstance as either haphazard or cruel, but it was a madness that did not begin in the mind but in the soul and heart and only worked outwards to the mind and body afterwards.

If this was the life the universe had offered him, he soon decided, he would sooner offer it back.

And so, when the swift but dwindling river led him to the base of a steep cliff that in his decreased state he could not hope to climb, he was forced to alter his course to make a hard circuit round it to the south, and in this he believed himself ill-used, imagining that in the wind that knocked along the half-walled canyon he could hear the mocking laughter of malevolent ghosts. Against such outrages the man in his emerging madness decided he would rather deprive those unseen spectators of their punitive pleasures than brook such affronts any longer.

He was done with life, such as it was, and would rather now die.

Laugh if you will! he had shouted to the emptiness around him and had shaken both fists into the wind. *But I will humor you no more!*

The man turned out his pockets there, spilling what remained of the small store of wild farnel nuts and withering bloomberries he had collected two days previous.

In the unseated turbulence of his soul, he believed he had won some victory that day, outwitting the wiles of his unseen assailants and robbing them of their sport by willingly choosing his own path to destruction rather than waiting for their trickeries and treacheries. If they sought to thwart his will now, they must somehow work to preserve his life against his own starvation, and he found this new irony hilarious, and trod the hard ground muttering and cackling beneath his sheltering hat.

Hardly a two hour's march from the scattering of his scant foodstuffs the man had already begun to lean and totter from weakness and from the heat reflected by the red cliff walls that worked upon him like the radiance of an oven. By evening he was tempted to abandon his sworn fast and to forage a sort of husky, spindly berry whose bountiful fruiting was out of sorts with the dry landscape, but no sooner had he picked a handful and placed one in his mouth to bite the tip and suck the juices than he recognized the temptation and the clear deception of the fruiting bush placed in his path and spit out the unsplit husk and kept walking lest he in his weakness turn back and surrender this battle so easily.

During the second afternoon of his three-day journey round the hampering cliffs, the man shuffled weakly through patches of ankle-high scrub and fell several times. Stepping over a jagged sandstone he pitched violently forward when something rolled underfoot. He cursed aloud and turned back to locate the provocateur and discovered it to be a straight piece of bleached wood almost his own height, oddly cast there in a place of no other trees or forest. He then thought to splinter the wood mercilessly against the rocks, but in the time it took to collect his failing energies and rise again, his anger had cooled sufficiently and he saw that the thing might be prized as a walking staff.

The man's mood brightened and, steadied with the aid of the stick in hand, he made the northward journey back to the river in much the lightened frame of mind he had once known as a merchant returning from the mines of Bylome with a well-bargained load of silver.

Such are the relativities of riches.

For a few hours, he forgot his besetting woes and wandered in a brief and careless happiness. It was not a mood he could long maintain though, for his fat stores were already far depleted and the compounded rigors of daily travel over hard terrain in the absence of sustenance had all but exhausted his remainders.

Yet more than a week he trued his resolve and suspended his daily foraging for nuts and berries and edible waterweeds, and as a result grew horribly thinner until his ribs protruded and the sockets of his elbows seemed too large for his arms. Had he a reflective surface in which to witness the sunkenness of his own cheeks, the dark hollows that his eyes had receded into, he would have recognized himself only vaguely as perhaps some primitive and ancient cousin returned from the house of the dead.

An odd clarity of thought emerged as twin of this prolonged fasting though, so that he traipsed a wide lake's undulant southern shore in a westerly direction for days, lucid enough to construct his own final defense and to rehearse his many grievances in a litany that echoed the endless rhythm of his steps. If he perished now, he would at least arrive at the gates of the next life well prepared to argue the righteousness of his cause before any gatekeeper or judge. If he were fated to die on this meandering pilgrimage, so be it. But he would die on his feet, acquitted beneath this cruel white sun, and his death would in the end become the final proof both of his sincerity and of his righteousness. To voluntarily relinquish his breath would be an act of protest that would so outweigh his own guilt that the greater sufferings imposed upon him by the heavens would then be proven unjust.

And so the man pushed his weakening frame to the outer frontiers of endurance and in that place where the body at last enters a waking twilight, he found himself strangely changed.

For there were days now when he felt possessed of an essential energy that required no sustenance save sunlight and on such days he might walk from dawn to dusk without rest, except to occasionally kneel and cup his hands and drink from the waters of streams or lakes. There were other days interspersed though, when his mortal frame revealed itself so weakened that he could progress no more than twenty paces before he must sit and rest a long spell, breathing in shallow gasps and feeling the rattling of his own straining heart like a wild, caged bird dashing itself against the bars of his ribs. But even this sensation was accompanied by a giddy lightness and elation.

On those days, when he sat long, he could hardly compel his being to rise again and if he had not possessed the staff to lever his limbs, he thought it likely he never would have. He sensed that he had somewhere crossed an unmarked line that portended he was now nearer to death than to life and as he sailed ever further beyond this equator of mortality he began to confuse the evidences of such passage with the measure of his own expanding holiness.

He was absorbed into a state that seemed entirely spiritual and in that thrall thought he could now glimpse the essence deep down of all things, like a bright shimmering of light that eyes could not focus on, that one could only see with the heart's truer vision and for which one must be separated from the constraints of the body.

In time he was no longer aware of any hunger at all. He became forgetful of the limits of his own physicality and sometimes tried to wave away the clouds or thought he might step beyond the horizon in one great stride and once he woke in the night and tried to pluck and eat the moon which he saw as a spiritual nourishment, sweet and pleasing.

He experienced himself as pure and ethereal and made of light and he rankled at the persistent witness of his own shadow, supposing it to be but a final illusion he must overcome to prove his own worthiness.

One day he could not remember his own name and he wept for joy, for he sensed his imminent release from all carnal miseries.

Even his grief and his memories of his daughter came to seem as insubstantial trappings of the former things, of the physical world. These too were a kind of airy fantasy, a temptation that when succumbed to bound one again to the material deceptions. He believed he had instead outgrown his sufferings and abandoned them beside the path miles and days ago, discarded as completely as those last remnants of nuts and berries, and he wondered if those ghosts that he first thought mocked him had actually been his guides to this new enlightenment, and he thanked them for their pains.

He had now consecrated and made himself holy by his chosen path of suffering and denial, and any impurity in him had dissolved in a bright gloaming that was all things and that filled all things and so, through it all, he pushed relentlessly westward in a great giddiness of waning light, staring unblinking at ravishing sunsets till he thought he had been absorbed into them and could feel their trembling joy within his own widening diffusion.

The man did not so much inhabit the landscape now as he haunted it.

The hawks that spiraled skyward spied him over their great and tumultuous distances and had no category for the species of paroxysmal, three-legged creature that he signified. Nor could the black carrion birds that lit heavily on high limbs round him ever seem to decide whether he was suitable fodder for their gluttonous covens or was a thing to be avoided.

His skin had grown leathered and his beard had twined itself to a wild scraggle, unbraided and unkempt. Likewise his neglected tresses had surrendered into a ropelike, clumped affair that no comb would ever unweave. They spilled from beneath the dark brim of his hat and over his shoulders like writhing clusters of snakes, and his dark eyes seemed to see impossible distances that even the bend of the earth could not impede.

He believed now that he would not die, but would simply walk into the afterlife, unbounded.

There was nothing of the merchant left about the man.

There was hardly even anything of the man left about the man.

When even the limberwolves who came to the river's edge to drink gave him wide skirt on those sandy deltas, confused by his strange scent and gait and appearance, he knew it as a sign that he had achieved a spiritual perfection and a blessedness that even the Maker himself could not call to question.

When the man had come far enough to sight the mountains south of Bylome in the distance, he slowly forded the waters at a narrow

shallows, annoyed to find that his feet sank beneath the tossing liquid rather than pressing weightlessly across its surface as he had supposed they should.

Surely this was the final test, he decided. Some last proving of his merits before he was to be utterly assumed into light.

Reconsidering the violent rush that would wet his legs to mid-thigh, he cinched the hat cord tighter beneath his chin and plotted his

course between large river stones and crossed then by leaning heavily
upon the driftwood staff, setting each foot with painstaking precision
lest his feeble legs be swept from under him.

He somehow achieved that dire crossing without incident.

But stepping up to the high opposite bank then he had lifted his
hands joyfully to the sunlight that it might receive him, and in doing
so had lost his balance so that he tumbled backwards into the river and
was tossed and swept helplessly along for a great distance, repeatedly
dunked by currents and abused by river stones as if he were a pile of
laundered rags. He felt himself endlessly rolled, his lungs half slogged
with water so that he sputtered and spewed all the way. As a further
indignity, the driftwood staff caught up to him and, violently spun by
the waters, struck the back of his head stiffly before careening away
beyond his grasping reach.

And so the man found himself viciously unmoored from his recent
ecstasies, all illusion of ethereal self vanishing as the river sped him
eastward mile upon mile, back the way from which he had come.

He saw himself carried into the canyons of those impassable cliffs
that he had detoured round days earlier and the torrents rushed fiercer
and he fought to draw more air than water into his lungs and would
have succumbed to the currents there but for a large and gnarled driftwood stump that he bumped against and was able to twine his arms
through the upturned roots of so that it seemed the man and the stump
traveled and spun together locked in some desperate embrace either
familial or conflicted or perhaps both.

In that channeled flood he was whelmed again by the uprushing of
his own anger, bitterness, bile and shame, now returned and redoubled
as he saw his hard progress undone.

Just let me die then! he said, and his gaze was fixed on the spinning
sky as the turbid waters tossed and whirled him, and though his invec-
tive was a kind of prayer, he could not see it as such, for he considered
it no more than a simple and reasonable demand.

Where the waters exited the canyon and the river bent again southeast some twenty miles downstream—a setback of more than a week and a half's journey in his present condition—the man found himself diverted at last from the frightful current into a lazy, sun-warmed, eddying pool and the sudden calm and pleasantness of it surprised and for some reason further angered him. Still, he lingered there for a time, drifting in slow circles with the stump, gathering feeble strength from the swirling warmth before he at last paddled weakly to the shore and dragged himself painfully half onto the mud, feeling then the full measure of the beating he had just taken over the stones.

He was weak and furious and spent and his shins and knees and forearms and shoulders and spine were bruised and aching, and after pulling himself completely from the water he found that he no longer had strength or will to rise again.

The little river cove he had washed into seemed to be the natural repository of driftwood from the swirling waters, owing to the winds or currents, and the shore around him was littered with the dreamwoven shapes, white and twisted as bones scattered upon the tidestones, and it seemed to him like a place that rested between worlds and in that way, it seemed not an unreasonable place to die, for it was perhaps already near to where he was going.

He settled his cheek on a flat, smooth rock and drifted to sleep, lulled by the lap of waves that whispered in rhythms like a mother's song to her newborn child. He slept all the day and dreamed in the night that he opened his eyes to see himself watched by a white horse whose forehead burst with horns of driftwood and he dimly resented its presence and knew that he had once known the name of such a creature but he could not find it now and closed his eyes wearily, convinced that he would never again open them upon this shore.

But he did wake again some hours later, and quite suddenly, when the nerves of his toes screamed alarms to his brain.

He opened his eyes to a dawning light surprised he was yet breathing and aware that some violence had been done to his foot inside the thick leather of his boot. A movement along the shore to his left drew his vision. He turned his head slowly to see a large snapping diggle rolling him with a slow and curious eye.

The man and the beast stared at one another warily.

The diggle blinked and the scarecrow man narrowed his eyes and flexed his injured toes.

He had resigned himself to dying here.

But even a half-dead man who wishes to be relieved of the burden of being will instinctively shun a fate that requires he endure the painful loss of a hundred chunks of his flesh before the aggregate loss of muscle and blood might finally achieve that desired end.

A man who has decided to die wants only to fade into a forgetful oblivion.

He does not want to be annoyed to death.

The man marshaled his reserves to kick his boot at the snapping diggle. The creature responded only by backing off ever so slightly and settling there to watch him with a greedy eye. Evidently it was rather hungry even by diggle standards, for the man was certain its standard prey were more along the lines of mudhoppers and glipperfish than humans.

The man tried to close his eyes again, wishing to float away unharassed, but as soon as he did he heard the scrape and stir of the animal slinking forward to assail his foot a second time. He kicked at its head and watched it edge tentatively backwards.

"You're not welcome here!" he shouted, his voice cracking and hoarse. "Go away!"

And then, after cupping a handful of water that cooled and soothed his throat, "Come back tomorrow and eat me then if you must."

He had squinted narrowly at it but the diggle had remained and cocked its head to watch him with an eye that seemed fixed in a confusion somewhere between the mammalian and the reptilian. The dance of approach and retreat endured for the better part of a quarter hour before the man cobbled enough anger to finally act, weakened as he was. He drew the silvered dagger from its scabbard at his side and pulled himself round till his head was towards the diggle, and he lay still with his eyes mostly closed then till the diggle gathered courage enough to approach. Eyeing the man's soft ear it thrust its neck forward, opening its wickedly tipped mouth.

With a quick jab the man drove the blade into and through the animal's unprotected neck and held it fast there with both hands till his unlikely assailant had writhed and scrabbled and perished, pulsing a hot dark blood over his hands and bathing the large stone beneath them as if it were some ritual altar.

Spent by this final exertion, the man collapsed and slept again the sleep of armies utterly defeated in battle.

He woke some time later to the pop and sizzle of fat over a fire, and to the meaty sweet aroma of roasting diggle, to the wafting smells of wood smoke, the warmth of fire, to a ravenous and maddening hunger such as he had not felt in weeks and, most surprising, to the sound of a man's voice raised merrily in song.

> *When a man dines on diggle, he dribbles and slurps,*
> *the diggle-meat jiggles, and squirts on his shirt;*
> *a man munching hen meat might cackle and chirp,*
> *but the man nibbling diggle just giggles and burps!*
> *Ha!*

The man opened one eye and saw that it was now dusk, and that a barefoot man with long, dark hair pulled back and tied off was tending a driftwood cookfire over which the entire diggle was now skewered. The singer's back was to the man and so the singer did not notice that he was awake.

The man worked himself to an elbow and studied the fellow. The voice was beautiful and somehow familiar, though the song was absurd.

> *The diggle will wiggle when basted with butter*
> *and pasted with peppers is better than others*
> *(I mean other diggles not pasted with peppers)*
> *the pepper-flecked diggle forever tastes better!*
> *Ha!*

The starving man shifted his weight on the sandy gravel and tried to sit up and found that he could not but the singer heard the noise and turned and smiled, seeing that the man was awake and the man instantly recognized the singer as the bard he had heard singing in the streets of Torrboro some year and a half earlier."

What was his name?

"Armulyn," the bard said extending a hand.

The man nodded once and allowed his hand a weak shake but gave no reply. His eyes were fixed on the savory diggle.

"Are you hungry?"

The man nodded.

"Well bring yourself to the fire, friend, and let's eat."

The man was quiet a moment. "I don't expect I could make it that far." And then, feeling the need to explain he added, "I haven't eaten for a few weeks."

The bard eyed him with concern. "I see. Well then, best take it slow. Here." He set within the man's reach a bowl that contained several longish yellow berries. "Break your fast with fruit and water. Sleep a while, and then we'll start you on a bit of meat."

The berries tended towards sour but the man decided few things had ever tasted so good. He took small bites and chewed each of them slowly, then drank two cups of water offered by the bard and closed his eyes and slept again and when he woke it was morning and the diggle now looked to be well roasted with a perfectly charred crust and the man allowed he was more famished than ever he had been.

He slowly worked himself to the wood fire which was now all coal and embers and the bard smiled a good morning and offered the man his own silvered blade with a small lump of diggle skewered upon it. "Chew it slowly. Once you're certain you can keep it down I'll give you another."

The man chewed as Armulyn flayed strips from the outer crust of the diggle and laid them on the stones to dry in the smoke. The man watched him at his long work and consumed a dozen small greasy gobbets throughout the day, with lengthy intervals in-between, the meat moist and succulent as that of a young, grain-fed hen, but stronger in taste.

The bard sometimes hummed but the men exchanged few words that day. The bard labored at his jerky making and went off now and then to forage for berries and waterweed, and the man ate his small portions and rested and slept and wondered at the abstruse meanderings that had brought him to this moment, coughed up not more than a mile east of the spot where he had first declared his intent to starve himself from spite. And now here he was, being fed the meat of a diggle that had all but begged to be butchered, and by a bard who had magically appeared in this vast wilderness.

The man kept his thoughts close and he watched the black smoke of the cook fire rising all that day from the edge of the lake like a thin prayer that seemed to dissipate unseen somewhere in the high tumult of clouds though he could not see its final end.

"I could patch your boots," the bard offered. "I'm handy with a needle."

"My boots are my own business."

That night the bard sat on a flat stone across the fire from the man and played a whistleharped melody that seemed to exist in the breaths between the lapping of the waves upon the shores of the backwater, embracing that constant rhythm and filling the hollows and the troughs of it in the ways that meanings fill words. The tune was lonely and lovely, sad and glorious, and it worked upon the heart and fancy of the man like legends and lost causes that even though lost are no less worthy of fighting for. The man felt himself transported to a landscape of light and dawn in a time of fierce beauty and he heard in that piping the footsteps of the Maker and that is when he turned away from the fire and drew an arm over his ear and hummed to himself as loudly as he could the fragments he remembered of the inane diggle song in an effort to drown out the spell of the bard's playing and of the stirring of vain hopes it sought to plant and when he could not drown it out, he rose tottering to his feet and wandered off down the shoreline as far as his legs in their weakness could carry him, but even this was not far enough and he still heard, drifting down to him as if it were winging from star to star through the wide universe, the piped melody, small and far away, and the man sat and bowed his head and wept, for to be alive again was to be alive now to his own loneliness and his hunger and his loss and he was, despite his best efforts, still very much alive.

The man woke at first light the following day and consumed two pounds of diggle meat and somehow kept it down, and then ate another pound of diggle ribrack that evening and he felt his strength returning.

He remained on that shore three more weeks with the bard, mostly silent, fishing the fertile waters and gathering the fleshy yellow berries that grew on flowery vines amidst the lake scrub. He did not know their name and neither did Armulyn, but as it turned out they were actually quite delicious when you found one perfectly ripened and sun-warmed so that the sour edge mellowed to a delicate sweetness.

"We've shared camp some time and you still haven't told me your name, friend," the bard finally ventured as they waited for clay-coated glipperfish to bake amongst the coals of their fire one night.

"Any name I had I shed and none has come along to replace it."

"Well I must call you something."

The man turned and spit into the sand. "Once we leave here and head our own ways, it would be better if you would just forget you ever met me."

"Surely it's not so bad as that."

"It's bad enough."

The next night the bard taught him to stew berries in their own juices so that you could pop them in your cheek and suck the hot sweetness from them, and as they enjoyed this wilderness delicacy the bard wheedled and cajoled the man into revealing at least the bare fact that he had been journeying west but had fallen into the river and been swept back here the day before the bard found him.

The bard listened to this tale spun vaguely and stared into the fire.

"Were you traveling the northern or the southern banks?"

"Southern mostly. Less thorny."

The bard was quiet for awhile longer and the man feared he would soon draw out his whistleharp and begin plucking or piping another of his Annieran tunes, but Armulyn eventually cleared his throat and said, "You might want to travel a little more cautiously in the future, friend."

"What do you mean by that?"

The bard shrugged. "Rivers are like highways. If a man doesn't want to be found, he might do well to stay away from the river."

"Did I say I don't want to be found?"

The bard picked up a narrow stick and leaned forward to poke the embers of the fire.

"Two days before I found you here, I was approaching the river from the northern side of the canyon. I heard fell voices and I knew what manner of creatures such tongues belonged to, so I squatted in the brush and soon spotted a Fang patrol headed west up the southern side. There were perhaps a dozen of them."

The man gave off sucking at the berry in his cheek and leaned forward slightly.

"What do you suppose they would be doing all the way out here?"

"Tracking something or so it appeared. Noses to the ground."

"You think it was me?"

The bard shrugged. "It doesn't matter. If they had found you, whether by intent or accident, you'd have been found. Tumbling into the river when you did likely saved you. They were behind you. This little misadventure of yours put you behind them. From their perspective, you just vanished."

"You think they'd come this far tracking one man?"

"And how far would that be, friend?"

The man smiled. "I see your tricks, bard. Where I hail from still doesn't matter. I'm asking would they come this far from where they all congregate back east along the coast in all the towns and cities. Torto, Torrboro, Dugtown. We're a far piece from there. Would they come all that way after one man?"

Armulyn hesitated. "I doubt it."

"Well I doubt it too."

"They might not come that far for one man, but they might come that far for men in the plural. And for women and children too."

"What do you mean."

"They might be out here for the same reason I am."

"Which is . . ."

"To hunt settlements."

"Settlements."

"Refugees. Folks who fled the occupation years ago." The bard raised an arm and waved it to the general south and west. "Men and women, some already with children, fled out here, even further than here. Just to live out from beneath the yoke and the fear."

"Well I haven't seen any of them."

"Good for them, then. Maybe the Fangs won't see any of them either."

"But they're out here."

"Could be a good distance further on, but yes. They're out here somewhere. Maybe they've even gone as far west as the One Mountain. Maybe they . . ."

"Hold on." The man lifted a hand to interrupt.

"Yes?"

"The One Mountain."

"Yes?"

"You say that like it's real."

"Of course it's real."

"I mean, we're talking now about the same One Mountain from the old legends."

"So far as I know there's only one *One Mountain*."

"The one where men are said to have met the Maker face-to-face."

The bard shrugged. "Those are the stories."

"You've seen it?"

"Me? Not yet. I've never been so far west."

The man raised his hand in exasperation. "So you don't even know if it's real!"

The bard looked at him strangely. "It's a mountain."

"It's a legend of a mountain."

"Others have seen it and spoken of it. People don't usually just make up mountains."

"So you believe all those stories about it?"

"That's a different question. Tell me a particular story and I'll tell you if I believe it. I've seen strange things in my life, often enough to remind me that I don't know everything. Who am I to say what might have been in the ancient days when the world was new? But if you're asking if I believe there's a mountain that stands alone out there to the west in the lands far beyond the maps, of course there is. Far too many ancient travelers wrote of it in memoirs and diaries that were anything but fantastic. Why would different people in different eras make up the same mountain?"

The man turned his own thoughts quietly. "And you think there are people who live out by it even today?"

"I don't know. Maybe not. I haven't been there. All I know is that frightened people are scattered out there somewhere in their free settlements."

"And you think the Fangs you saw are hunting them?"

"Have you ever seen a tyrant who could stand the thought of even one free man in his realm?"

The man ceded the point with a tilt of his head, then paused and asked, "Where do you suppose they come from?"

"The tyrants?"

"The Fangs. A decade ago no one had even heard of their kind. And suddenly, our ports and cities were swarmed by them."

"It is puzzling. I haven't met anyone who claims to know for certain, but I have my suspicions."

"Which are?"

The bard pushed a dangling strand of dark hair from his face and fixed it behind his ear.

"Strange as it might sound, I believe these Fangs are beasts that were made, not born."

"Made?"

"Formed by a twisting of some dark magic. Altered."

"From what?"

"Lizards? Snakes? Something reptilian. I've seen variations in their forms and skins that mirror those of natural creatures. Is that only by chance? One amongst that group I spied by the river just recently was darker, with bumps like one of those little desert dragons that scurry amongst the rocks. I know it sounds fanciful, and I don't have any answers. Just speculations."

The man pondered this notion a moment. "Well, they are talking lizards. That lone fact is pretty fanciful to begin with."

Armulyn chuckled. "I suppose so."

"So what will you do if you find these settlements of refugees?"

"I'll tell them the news."

The man waited for more thorough explanation but Armulyn evidenced no inclination to continue and seemed to be absorbed in poking at the fire. The man cleared his throat. "Would that be any news in particular?"

"Yes, it would be very *good* news."

The man saw now that he was being merrily played, for the bard's eyes were alight with some secret delight. "Fine. Make me ask. What is your very good news?"

Armulyn considered. "First tell me your own story, friend. How did you come to be out here in the wild? Then I'll tell you this good news of mine." He leaned back and folded his arms smugly and smiled.

The man turned his head and spit into the darkness. "You might be overestimating my curiosity about your good news."

"Well, so long as this fire burns my offer stands."

They both stared then at the flames as all firewatchers do, seeking in those burning liquid movements the reading of ancient words writ beyond their ken. The moon and stars had wheeled over the tip of a tall evergreen before the man finally broke the silence.

"Why did he close off the paths."

"Who?"

"The Maker. If he really did once meet men face-to-face at the summit of the One Mountain, if it ever was anything more than a story, why would he have stopped."

"What makes you think he did?"

"You know anybody says they met him there recently?"

"I don't know anyone who tried. Maybe it was the people who moved away, spread east, forgot the old paths. For all we know he could still be waiting up there for those who would seek him."

"Seems like it would be a whole lot more considerate and convenient if he came down and introduced himself."

The bard shrugged. "Maybe he hides his face so that only those who truly want to find him ever will."

The man drew a stick with a bright, flaming tip from the fire.

"Maybe. Or maybe he hides his face cuz he's got good reason to hide it."

"What do you mean?"

The man turned the flame down and snuffed the stick out in the sand.

"Not a thing." When the smoldering stopped the man drew the stick from the sand and tossed it back into the fire. "Forget I said it. I'm sure I didn't mean a thing in the world."

The man spread his cloak on the sand then and lay down on top of it and drew his hat over his eyes.

"Do you reckon the Maker has somehow offended you, friend?"

"If I said he had, could we leave it at that?"

The bard eyed the man long before answering. "If you wish."

"Well, seeing as that's also more or less the summary of my story of how I came to be out here, it looks like you're obligated now to uphold your end of the bargain and relay your good news."

The bard laughed and the tones of his amusement were almost musical. "Fine. Do you really want to hear it?"

"I brought it up, didn't I?"

Armulyn paused and then announced in tones both hushed and heralding, "The seeds of Anniera. The crown prince . . . the Throne Warden . . . the Song Maiden of the Shining Isle . . . they're alive!"

The man paused and then leaned up on an elbow and spat in the sand but never took his eyes from the other. "That's just stories, Armulyn."

"But I saw them. These eyes. They're alive."

The man eyed the bard for any sign heretofore unnoticed of euphoric hallucinations or general disorientation but found none.

"How would you know? Anyone could say anything. It's just stories."

"Some stories are true."

"And some aren't. You saw children. They could be any kids. You see me. I could be the King of Bylome."

"But you're not. Bylome has a mayor. I'm only telling you what I saw, friend. They're alive. It *was* them. And if they're alive, then Anniera is real. I can scarce believe it myself."

"Even if, even so. What does it matter? What does it matter now? What does it matter to you and to me, sitting out here? Alive or dead, child's fancy or true tale, what difference? Gnag wields the power in this world now. If there ever was a Shining Isle, there's not anymore so if there's a crown prince hidden away somewhere, he's the crown prince of charred rubble now and anyway, even if he's real and the Shining Isle is real, I'm from Torrboro so he's not really my crown prince anyway is he?"

"Torrboro, is it then?" Armulyn smiled. "Another week out here and you might even accidentally tell me your name."

The man shrugged off the comment. "All I'm saying is anyone could be anything I guess, but if it doesn't make any difference then what difference does it make?"

"That's where you're wrong." The bard lifted his hand and paused a moment before continuing. "It makes all difference. Because it gives hope where there was none. Anniera is not just one place. It is the heartbeat of all places. It is the beacon of beauty and the seat of good. From it our hope emanates. As Anniera, so the world. There are old songs of seeing that speak of times like these, and those foretellings might now hang by a slender thread, but they have not been clipped. If the heirs are alive, the hopes hang yet. I wander this wilderness to spread hope to those who have long ago abandoned it and fled. Those like you, my mysterious and still nameless friend. The Jewels of Anniera have survived. Can you believe it? I can hardly believe it and I saw them in the flesh. Victories have been won and kingdoms have been rebuilt from lesser hopes than this. Believe me! I tell you what I witnessed! Join me! Gnag will not sit his throne forever. Those royal children are alive. There is yet hope!"

"Not for me, bard. *My* child is dead!" The man spat the pulped berry from his cheek and saw its form printed upon one of the stones that ringed the fire, like a flower bloomed crimson, but the berry itself had caromed into the flames where it sputtered and wilted black. "So I ask you in light of that, what use have I for your distant hopes? Your prophecies are empty to me, even if they're fulfilled."

"I'm truly sorry, friend. Perhaps . . . perhaps in time you'll find a new hope."

"No thank you. I was rather fond of the old one."

"But the old one is gone."

"Don't I know it. And nobody even consulted me on the matter first."

He stood then and brushed the sand from his fingers and turned away and then turned back and added, "My new hope I guess is to never see the deceitful face of hope again," and then he trod away from the flames and paced down the riverbank till it bent and he could not see the firelight except as a flickering shift over the sandbars, and when the bard began to whistle his lonely tunes the man shouted at him from the distant darkness "Would you please leave the night in peace!" and the piping had immediately ceased.

The man lay on his back in the sand then and glared at the stars and shivered in the mist that came up from the river and in his mind great wheels were turned and great weapons forged and when he rose and returned to the fire some hours later his eyes had the wild look of a man who has encountered many ghosts and he shook the bard awake and told him simply "I'm leaving."

The bard yawned and sat up, rubbing his eyes. "But where will you go?" His voice held a genuine sadness and the man could not help but feel distantly moved despite himself and in the way of men on the cusp of parting he spoke more of his heart in the span of a few sentences than he had revealed in their many days together.

"When I asked for mercy I did not receive it. When I had love, it was taken from me. When I clung to hope it was ripped away. But when I prayed for death, it was denied me. So you tell me, bard. Where would you send such an ill-used man? Upon what course and what quest?"

The man half-feared the bard would give quick answer, vaguely referencing the unknowable ways of the Maker, but instead, and to his credit, the bard held his tongue. Both men were silent awhile and then the bard stood and staring into the other man's eyes he stepped forward and wrapped him in a strong embrace and then put his head on the man's shoulder and wept and wept and wept as if his own heart had been shattered, as if his own child had been lost, and the man neither resisted nor returned the embrace but stood and endured the tears of the bard and felt them at once as perhaps the nearest consolation he had yet been offered, but also as the worst of the weapons that had yet been fashioned against him.

Afterwards he packed some of the dried meat and some of the berries into his pockets and insisted on leaving half for the bard who tried to make him take them all and the bard asked him if he might not rest the night and then leave in the morning and the man told him his way was now clear and he would not lose another hour and then as the man fitted his blade to his belt something dawned in Armulyn's eyes and he pronounced, "Why, you're going to the mountain," but it was not phrased as a question and so the man looked at him but gave no answer.

Having fitted then his hat to his head the man turned and walked away into the darkness and as he crossed the river at its shallows he heard Armulyn shout, "Maker speed you," and then the lilting melodies of some song that was Annieran or perhaps even older found and circled him for the first hour of his journey, and the man longed for the melody to be true even as he refused to believe that it was and so he was both saddened and relieved when the sound of it had gradually faded away in the night behind him.

He had now but one purpose.

His face was set towards the utter west wherein rose somewhere the One Mountain, and he understood now that it was towards this destiny he had journeyed all along.

As he had lain alone upon the riverbank in that swirling mist earlier that same evening, pondering the fierce distances of the stars, he had seen at last who his true adversary was, and it was neither the Fangs nor his own misfortunes. He had named to himself then what he had in somewise known all along, and so he had renewed his broken oath, but he had renewed it on these terms:

I swear by my daughter's death that I will seek you out, O Maker. I will assault your high summit and there will I demand you give answer for my loss.

III.

If Wishes Were Horses

*You would be surprised how much a man can accomplish
once he gives up hope.*
—Colonel Quentrice Trollrender

As morning dawned the man reluctantly adjusted his course in a hard southerly bend to avoid overtaking the Fang patrol in the weeks to come. He had dispensed with only one of those fell spawn in his brief career as an outlaw, but he had been then a man desperate to recover the child he had then believed was still alive, still in terror, and still in reach of ransom. Hope and fear had rendered him rash so that he had risked all for her return in a great casting of the dice and had come up empty though his own life had not been forfeit for it, scant consolation that it was.

He had grown more hardened in the grabbled wayfaring that followed and his form and frame had reworked themselves more resilient in those lean months, but still the man was no inveterate warrior and did not fancy himself as such. He would not now seek confrontation with a dozen of the despicable lizards, for he knew the outcome of such a meeting. The tradeoff for avoiding them and remaining unseen now was that he must at last abandon his reliable water source and trust that springs and pools could be found further south as well.

Wishing to keep all ledgers balanced and to be no more beholden than he must to any man, he had weeks before declined the bard's kindly offer to repair his journeyboots. In less than two days' walk now he felt sorely the folly of his pride. The toe of one boot had been pierced through by the diggle so that water entered it from stream and rain and the soles of both were wearing so thin that his feet which had softened in the last weeks of his rest and recovery with the bard were become more and more blistered and bruised by the miles he crossed.

Within days the more southerly course took him out of sight of any woodlands and into a land of wet weather gulches and barren scrub. The stark hills were stony, weather-swept rises that jutted up sheer from the land, revealing bright and layered swaths of reds and umbers and yellows and purples, the slow, unfolding dreams of old geologies splayed upon a dry, gashed land.

Shatterings of flint and pumice filled vast tracts, cutting hills like waterless cataracts halted in their sharp cascades. Some paths were impassable. Others demanded in payment for passage some diminishing of leather, some bruising of flesh, some sluicing of cruor.

He stumbled and started and sent sliding clinks of rock behind him that chimed like ceramics till their capricious physics were played out against more entrenched tessellations further below. He used the dagger to exsect leather strips from the bottom hem of his cloak and wrapping them round his palms he navigated tenuous and motile terrains configured on hand and foot like a man enchanted by sunlight to a form half-beast. He crossed miles of prospect laced with formations as slick and sharp as broken glass that warbled in the curving designs of hardened liquids, and these crazed rock fields so shredded the casings of his boots and flayed the soles to near uselessness that by the time he reached less hostile territories, his injuries were already profound. His boots remained but as ragged remnants dyed dark with his own blood, soaked and dried and stained and soaked and dried and stained again. He cut more strips from the hem of his cloak and wrapped these hard round his feet to shore them against the disintegration of the boots, but this new remedy came with fresh excoriations for the leather strips chafed in places previously untouched so that distended and cloudy blains emerged within hours upon his skin, like moons pressed hard against their own risings by horizons malignant and thick.

The heat of the days wore him steadily down so that he could not take rest in any coolness but night and the misery of his feet was enough that he woke from his light sleeps deviled and exhausted. It seemed a land designed either to kill men or to spit them out for there was no shelter and no shade in all of that baked expanse. Even when the blisters that staked his feet began to break open and to rub into raw ulcerations against the blood-and-salt-soaked leather of his boots he marched grimly on, for he knew himself to be a trespasser in those waterless wastes, and unsuited for survival in them.

And so he hobbled along, gritting his teeth against the torment of his abscessed wheals, tilting his head into the wind so that the brim of the hat shielded his eyes against intermittent blasts of volant sands, unwilling then either to beg for mercy or to relinquish his quest.

If you're trying to keep me from reaching You, he finally muttered against a hot wind that swept north from some distant desert, *it won't work. You'll have to kill me.*

Limping to the edge of a storm gulch two afternoons following, and thinking to slide down the sandy side and shelter there to escape the high heat of day, he spied in that deep, red rift a saddled and bridled horse, tangled by reins in thorny scrub that jutted like horns from the hard arid walls. There was a dark stain of old, dried blood on the saddle and an arrow shaft protruding from the leather padding at a skewed angle.

The horse was white or pale but layered with a red dust and was laid on its side so he thought it was dead at first and wondered if it might be either fresh enough to scavenge for meat or preserved enough to scavenge for leather, but at his approach the animal raised its head and tried in alarm and in vain to stand.

The man shielded his eyes to the sun and surveyed the open scrub land for miles in every direction, and seeing no movement, he maneuvered himself over the edge and slid down into the gulch and knelt beside the horse at last and slipped the bridle from its mouth, then loosened the saddle cinch and removed that too along with a saddle bag half full of dried groats. He was pleased to see that the arrow had angled sharply enough into the saddle that it had hardly penetrated the horse's skin and the wound had already closed itself in a knotted scar.

He left the horse where it lay and explored the ravine downwards, wincing at every step, and found at last in the bottom of it the water he sought. In his upturned hat he fetched drink from a small spring pool and carried it a quarter mile back to the horse.

He was well acquainted with the care of livestock from his own rural childhood and immediately judged the horse a fine animal, despite its sorry condition. The owner had likely been affluent once, at least before abandoning his or her former life to challenge these forsaken spaces.

The creature's owner was also likely dead, felled by an arrow as black as the one the man now worked free from the saddle, else why would the horse have been alone and perishing here? It had probably smelled the water and been searching for it when the reins had become tangled.

The man built a sheltering roof of scrubwood across the ravine over the beast to shield it from the worst of the sun and every couple of hours he brought it another hatful of water, pacing the hydration knowing that a thirsting horse offered too much water at once might drink itself to death. The next morning he was able to coax the beast to stand, and he led it to the small pool without use of a bridle. The grateful creature followed him down the gulch like any trained hound.

He squatted to watch it drink, and then it raised its head and shook its pale mane and looked at him.

The man pulled up a clump of dry weedy grass and offered it to the horse and the horse took it and ground it between its flat teeth, then nosed round and found another clump on its own.

"I know you've been ridden before," the man said. "But I'll give you a few days yet."

He eased his boots off, teeth gritted against the raw friction of the leather and eased his bloodied feet into the pool. The spring water had the taint and taste of minerals, and there rimed a whitish deposit round its edges. Perhaps there would be healing properties in it.

He soaked his wounds for an hour and then walked the horse slowly back up the ravine to the shelter. He opened the feedbag and poured out a small mound of groats which the horse munched up greedily, then nosed the feedbag.

"You'll get more tomorrow," the man said and patted the animal's soft muzzle.

He rationed the groats for two more days, soaking his feet in the mineral pool many times and feeling his heart strangely stirred at the desolate night cries of limberwolves and filchdarters beneath the clear starry skies on the chill nights. The horse would lay down to sleep and the man took to reclining with his back against its belly and welcomed the shared warmth which was of benefit to both.

He spoke and sang to the horse softly and appreciated the companionship, and when he thought the horse was asleep, memories of his daughter rose like shapes in the shimmer of heat released from the sands around him for he thought how she would have loved the horse and he reached into his pocket and drew forth the silk tricorn then and clenched it and rehearsed aloud his sworn oath as if that silken creature or somehow the legend whose image it echoed might be summoned to bear witness in that desert night, and then he returned it to his pocket and he slept.

The saddlebags had contained other sundries as well as the groats: a long coil of rope, several rocks of salt, a tattered and illegible map, a soot-grimed tobacco pipe, a spring-loaded trap for snagging small game, and a sturdy needle and a spool of stiff thread ample for the amateur repair of the man's boots which he patched with mending strips of leather cut from his cloak.

They rode up out of the gulley headed north and in two days they found streams and woodland again and over the next month the horse grew fat on marsh grass and the riding allowed the man's feet to quickly heal, now calloused over where they had once been so raw.

The man could see no visible progress day to day, but after the first two weeks of riding the ground began to incline gradually more upwards.

In his third week in the company of the horse he woke on a bald hilltop. The haze of morning had burned away and in a remarkably clear refraction of light he sighted in the distance what might have been the blued serrations of a mountain ridge placed at some infinite remove and his resolve strengthened again and he knew what he must do, though he could not judge the distance, whether it was a hundred miles, or a thousand miles, or a thousand lifetimes away, and though he looked for it each sunrise and sunset afterwards, he did not sight the mountain again that season.

They explored the terrain ever further west and made camp in a region of wide and verdant hills. His mount relished the tender green shoots of grass emerging in thick clumps amongst the hill dips and also the small, tight buds of a crimson flower the man had never before seen. The man pulled hundreds of wild onions and harvested the last of the bright red crambleberries from their thorny thickets. He carved a straight shaft from the trunk of a small hardwood and bound his silvered blade to the end of it and then spent days hunting speedy flabbits by spear from horseback and roasting them three at a time and smoking some of the meat to preserve for the remainder of his journey. He became strangely adept at intuiting when one of the cantankerous varmints in its headlong flight was about to cut left or dart right. There was a pattern to it that he could sense but could not articulate. They made camp there several days and both the man and the horse grew fatter.

They afterwards resumed their bellicose pilgrimage, pushing further west towards that shimmering rumor of mountain he believed he had sighted but which had not yet curved round the horizon towards him to allow for any stark delineation.

Along the way were wonders the man had never heard rumor of. Great plumes of steaming water that blasted upwards from barren rock. Small silverish creatures that looked as if they were made of molten metal and slid over rocky terrain like dripping rivulets. Swarms of glowing nightmoths that numbered in the millions and wrought the fields strange with luminance where there should have been shadow so that it seemed as if he rode at times the underside of some other world in which darkness shone and those things too solid for darkness to pass through cast about them instead shadows of fluttering light.

One night the man and horse were followed by a dozen lithe limberwolves more inquisitive than aggressive and the man gripped his blade unsheathed and kept alert to their movements in the field but was more curious of the bearing of the pale horse when it was asked to hold its nerve in such a hostile surround.

The horse rolled its eyes and laid its ears back but trusted the man's calming voice and did not spook and after more than a league of such tense company the wolves caught some other scent and wheeled away to the north, leaving the travelers to their journey.

They slept that night in a meadow illumined by nightmoths and when they set out the next morning they crossed into a dead forest of blackened, moistureless trees and rode it for three days till the horse's hooves were smutted by the passage over an endless carpet of ash that muffled all sound in that stillness. They slept in the ash and they breathed in the ash and they saw no creatures stir in that grey place save an unkindness of ravens alighting on spindly branches from which dark cinders dispersed and floated downwards like snow misremembered.

The man had begun almost to entertain the possibility that they now walked an eternal shadowland of death that would stretch to the world's rim when without gradation one morning they stepped beyond the stark border of that place and passed again into bright lands cool and shimmering with a now almost unbearable greenness, though the season was late and already near its turning. They soon found themselves plying a corridor of violent weathers such that morning might break pleasant and at noon one might be overtaken by great walls of windswept dust that curtained the sky and bleared the sun to a dim whiteness. Behind these dust storms at evening the temperatures could plunge mercilessly amidst a great dumping of rain and hail that assaulted all living things unable to find shelter and then the next day might break pleasant again as if begging for another chance to be trusted. The man and the horse traveled west when they could and sheltered from the dust and the storms when they had to and their progress was slowed but remained steady.

The Lone Fendril bent the sky repetitively round in its glorious coursings and the man once heard its piercing cry spilling down from some invisibility in the high tumult of clouds. Months turned upon the great wheel of seasons and for an insensate span the man simply existed, surviving as a wild creature among wild creatures and he indulged in no conscious thought of the former things and made no effort to divine meaning from his griefs and he no longer drew the tricorn from its place in the depths of his pocket. He obliged his mind instead to ponder nothing save the immediate burdens of shelter and sustenance and considered the days to come as beyond his knowing and therefore of no consequence.

He would turn his attentions again to the One Mountain when he reached it. Until then, all that mattered was the surviving of the journey. Having dulled himself to the pangs of hope and disappointment alike the man also no longer gave thought to whether he was happy or sad.

He was simply alive, one of many parts of a landscape that was both hostile and eloquent.

He survived, and the horse with him, and for a time, as he journeyed ever further west, that was enough. He relinquished many of his former human comforts, sleeping often without fire and sometimes waking soaked by dew and eating without revulsion locusts and larvae and the flesh of things that had not been cooked, and there were long stretches of days when he could not have conjured the image of his own daughter's face if he had tried.

Perhaps especially if he had tried.

The chill suggestion of a hard winter had already swept over low hills to swirl around them as a thin layer of white and beaded sleet, and the man understood that to be caught unsheltered in this windswept landscape would mean almost certain death at the first furious and blinding winter storm. And so he had already begun to search for a suitable winter camp that would afford natural protection from wind and cold when they chanced suddenly upon a lonely, abandoned structure hidden by an overgrowth of scrubby trees. It was small and round and constructed of dark stacked stone and wood and there were three arched doorways without doors. In the now-brambled courtyard of the structure he saw that a well had been dug and the mouth was covered by a flat, square-cut stone.

The man called out and there was no answer so he dismounted to scavenge the ruins of the place for anything useful but he first shoved back the stone and drew up water for the horse and for himself and it was sulfurous to the taste but seemed drinkable. When he entered the structure he saw that the roof was mostly caved in, and that a dense clot of tiny, brown bats had colonized the underside of the topmost beam and these were now surveilling him with dark globose eyes and swaying like witches' pendants in their agitation.

The place stank of something foul, and fat green flies lit everywhere on the floor and walls. Low rails were fixed to the floor and arced round a central stone that was either pedestal or crude altar, and behind that plinth rested something large and covered with a rough canvas cinched round with rope. The man drew his blade and sawed through the rope and pulled away the coarse covering.

Ensconced beneath it was a hideous, man-sized blackstone sculpture of a crouched Fang with its claws raised and its jaws splayed wide and its forked tongue extended to its feet in horrible exaggeration.

The man felt fingers of fear wrapping his spine and wondered what manner of place he had stumbled into. He looked round him but he could not long abide the maniac stare of the gruesome figure and so he cut short his exploration and retreated again to the untended courtyard. He drew the cold air into his lungs and saw then with clarity the deed that was in his hands to do and so he took his rope and tied an end round the saddle pommel and then he reentered the strange ruin uncoiling the rope as he went and he wound a noose at the other end and slung this over the head of the stone Fang and cinched it tight round the neck.

Returning to the horse he took it by the bridle and asked it to walk and the horse stepped forward till the slack was taken up and then understanding there was a load to be moved it heaved into the resistance until the carved figure dislodged and toppled so that it cracked against the floor stones and shattered into three pieces.

The man left the arms and body where they lay but the grim head he rolled to the well and cast it in and then he covered the well again with the flat stone and he rode away from that unholy place shaking his head at the idiocy of men who would prostrate themselves even to their own nightmares.

A light swirling of snow was falling when he crossed a descending stream and located a large cave sunk into a quandary of stony foothills to the north. Upon entering it, the man discovered that it had been utilized by other men before him. Animal bones were strewn about amidst evidences of twain fire pits and the remains of a crude smithy. Some two dozen bundles of hay were piled against the back wall, baled he supposed for the care of oxen long dead in some winter that had already passed.

The man searched the place and found protruding from damp, piled ash beside the crude forge a blacksmith's straight-peen sledge, a heavy, long-handled hammer with one face flat and one face wedged. The balance and heft of the tool was pleasing to his hand. He tested the swing of the thing against a large bone in the firepit and the bone split vertically along its length and he knew that the instrument would be useful as both weapon and tool.

The hay was well preserved.

Two of the outer bales showed evidence of rot, but most had been protected and appeared to have remained dry. He pulled out several handfuls of the silage and offered them to the horse and watched it eat and the horse seemed to judge it still edible and nuzzled the man's arm for more.

The man tossed more hay to the floor and then went and stood at the cave mouth and surveyed the stream below and ran his fingers through the hoarfrost already accruing in the tangle of his beard and considered his options weighted against the coming freeze.

He had earlier hoped to push on another week or two towards the mountain but he knew he would likely find no camp so accommodating as this one. They would winter here, he finally decided, as others clearly had before them.

The next morning he climbed the great stones at dawn to survey the land roundabout, and positioned with his back to the rising sun as the near fog burned off the man deciphered at last there the certain rising of a lone mountain to the west but at that distance it appeared no larger than a solitary jagged rise of rat's tooth jutting from a jawbone of horizon.

He was tempted to saddle the horse and ride at the mountain full gallop then but he knew that they would not make it and that it would be a fool's charge across weeks of open ground when even the ice was at his adversary's command.

The man felt himself again thwarted and lamented that he must endure a cloistered winter here when he was at last within sight of the fulfillment of his oath.

But he had come this far and had endured this long.

He could yet abide a winter more.

The man turned his considerations then to the details of their winter provisions. He calculated the days of their coming sequester and deemed there would be just enough hay to keep the horse through a short winter.

To keep fat on his own bones he created a fish trap of woven saplings, installing it beneath a shallow fall in the stream that ran below the cave, and he also set and obscured the metal trap and stripped the branches from hale saplings and leaving them rooted bent their resilient trunks into snares along the stream banks. He also explored the forested hills above the cave, using his spear to dispatch selbrils and other small game, and some of these creatures he roasted and ate and others he skinned and flayed and smoked for later.

While the meat hung curing the man spent days scavenging firewood which he piled and stacked into tall mounds of branches and kindling just inside the mouth of the cave.

One morning as he labored a spitting freeze howled over the hills above him, stinging the skin and glossing the world with a thin coat of ice and the next morning the man woke to a snow tossed so deep that he had two hours of exhausting labor just clearing a path down to the stream and then he had to dig out and reset each of his snares. He returned to the cave and the small fire with his cheeks bloodless and deadened and his fingers and feet too numb to be of service. That afternoon and evening he cut and sewed rough fingerless gloves of the selbril skins he had collected and turned the fur side inwards and this brought some relief for his hands, but his clothes in general were tailored for a different climate altogether and were thin and unlined, and he had at night only the shortened cloak to pull about him and he wondered if he would yet die here of the cold and he wondered if he might not have been better off in a mad fool's dash for the mountain before the winter had set in.

If not for the fire and for the warmth of the horse that he slept against, he would have certainly perished in that first brunt of glacial chill, but even so he shivered uncontrollably and woke to the chattering of his own teeth before dawn in that startling cold.

He saw that he must make a warmer den of it or die for the lack and his first thought was to employ the bales of hay. So the man set about unpiling them, architecting in his mind how he might restack them into a sort of walled enclosure at the back, a simple structure that would trap his body heat and block the freezing winds that sometimes burst savage and howling through the mouth of the cavern, raising sparks from the fire and swirling them down the hollow throat of the passage.

The horse nosed at the hay and watched the man as he pulled bales down from their haphazard piling. He had removed perhaps ten bales when the horse snorted and laid its ears to its skull and shied back from the man's work.

"What is it then?"

The man went to the front of the cave and looked out but saw no movement and so he returned to his work and the horse observed him from a distance, planing its body to the rocks of the side wall.

"If it's something you ain't happy with, why don't you just tell me?"

He pulled down another bale and stopped for he saw now that the forage had been piled over a second dark passage at the back of the cavern and he could not see what was beyond it, but he could smell an old stale rot of things excretory and organic and when he stuck his head inside and sniffed he inhaled a more acrid stench as well that seemed to sit heavily in the mouth of the passage. He covered his nose with his shirt and coughed and backed away and then held his breath and pulled the remaining bales down so that the passage was fully exposed.

"I guess we know why they piled that hay up anyway. Wouldn't wanna be smelling that all winter. Whew! I think I'd rather freeze to death too."

The man used leather strips to bind a selbril skin over his nose and mouth, preferring the fetor of that gamey half-cured leather to the miasmic reek emanating from the cave wall. Then fetching a burning limb from the fire he carried it to the back of the cave and heaved it into that second passage and saw immediately that it opened into the remove of another chamber, the floor of which sloped downwards.

The horse turned and clopped over the rocks and stepped into the snow outside and stood there looking back at the man in what seemed like irritation.

"Don't run off. I might need you."

The man breathed deeply several times and then held his breath and plunged through the short passage and into the second chamber.

His eyes adjusted and in that flicker of firelight he knew the place immediately for what it was.

This was not any shelter that men had employed.

Here was an old lair of beasts.

Here some sizable creature had lodged itself, dropping foul dung and dragging in its many kills. Later scavengers perhaps had done the work of unsorting and democratizing hundreds of white and ashen bones so that they were now strewn here and there, spines and hips and shins of things, origins uncatalogued.

This rear chamber was much warmer than the front cave, but the fetid corruption hung so heavy in the place that the man could not remain long in it. He soon retreated to stack the bales again across the opening, and then he built of the remaining bales the wind break and heat trap he had first intended, hoping as he did that whatever foul predator had once resided here was not a migratory thing that might return.

The days to follow crawled in a white and grey sameness, often without sound, and the deep snows hushed the world and closed it in and the man slept in the hay barrier sometimes twenty hours at a stretch like the lingering of a child in a womb, giving no thought to the world outside, and sometimes he woke to find even the floor and walls of the cave glossed with a thin ice that was the residue of his own breath and of the horse's.

Without human companionship, the man became tuned to the moods of the horse; a nicker of unease, a snort, an agitation, a flattening of the ears to the head that signaled he should increase his own alertness and most often in such moments he would peer into the night and find that there were wolves padding about somewhere in the vicinity and once he thought he spied across the hills a great, shaggy bear riffling through patches of blue moonlight and forest shadow and he wondered that it was not dormant in winter, but none of these creatures ventured to harass the horse and the man in their cave.

Never before this had he considered that a man might endure such intense and unremitting cold for so long. The hay barrier served to keep him alive, but it could not fully counter the slow dolor of what it meant to be a man in a winter such as comes only once in a hundred years, and to be clothed only for the spring.

Unmarked days and nights the man shivered and slept and pulled blankets of hay over him and lived in dream and shadow and memory, and perhaps the horse did as well, for it too ate less and also slept most of the day. In the long darkness the man sometimes saw things that were not there, familiar silhouettes of chair and window and he thought he was in his bed and called out to his daughter or rolled over to drape an arm gently round his wife and then he must remember again where he was and what had become of happiness and how those things were no more and how the world and his existence had all come down to nothing but this cold.

He sat shivering before the fire and because he had no other task to occupy him he constructed cut-by-cut and log-by-log in his mind a quaint cabin and when he had finished that he also built by that same fancy a sprawling meadhall as the thanes who dwelt in Tyho and Nellok across the sea were said to have erected in eras now past. For days he searched the storehouses of his own memories and retold to himself each of the myths and stories and legends he could remember from his own childhood, and also the real histories of the peoples of Skree he recited for the benefit of the horse, sometimes mulling for hours to retrieve the name of some ancient king. He long pondered the nature of Fangs and considered whether there might be any truth to the bard's suspicions that they were creatures made rather than born but he could not reconcile himself to the idea for in the end it still seemed an abomination too astonishing and too vile even for the wickedest of men to have undertaken, and it also seemed a thing beyond achieving and he could imagine no way in which it might be done. For days he mentally retraced the steps of his own journey and then painted a detailed map of them in his head, adding flourishes and embellishments. He set before himself the task of constructing a ship and, though he was altogether unversed in the art of boatwrights, after several nights pondering he believed he had devised a detailed and workable process by which a craftsman might achieve that end. By these and a hundred other such diversions of the mind did the man cling to his sanity in those cold dark days in those close, quiet quarters without human company.

He gave off checking his snares for days at a time because the boreal clime without could no longer be contended in his thin rags and because few animals were equipped with hides thick enough to keep them astir for long in such temperatures and so the snares were usually empty and when they were not the creatures caught in them were frozen solid and would keep that way till collected and thawed near the fire. The man thought many times that the winter must soon turn but as many times as it did turn, it only turned colder still.

The horse grew visibly gaunt and the man knew that the hay was no longer robust and so he increased the creature's rations and as the weeks wore on, the hay barrier that stood between the man and the elements was being eaten away so that he was continually reconfiguring the bales that were left.

The man woke one night in the chill stone darkness, alert to the fear of his horse, aware of its snorting, aware that the fire had gone out. He shuffled towards the mouth of the cave and listened. Something large was snuffling at the stream below, grunting and splashing round the fish trap.

The man seized the heavy sledge and crawled forward until he could see over the lip of the cave and out into the cold light where the deep snowfields glowed like the surface of the moon.

Something rose near the stream below him, itself white and luminous and massive, with brutal tusks jutting from lower jaws, tusks long and upwardly curved as scimitars.

A low, deep growl.

The man felt suddenly awake after this sleep of weeks, and a new kind of fear thrilled in his most inward parts.

He had never witnessed such a beast with his own eyes.

Hadn't even known if they truly existed.

What was it children called them in their little rhymes?

Bomnubbles.

He had heard trappers trading in Bylome call them snowbears.

His grandfather had told a story of his great-great-grandfather encountering such a creature on his journeys through the wastes and had called it "a most odious snowbeast, a bully of up-pointed tooth and belligerent disposition."

The man watched the thing for a moment as it clawed a fat fish up from the trap, snapped its jaws over the head and gills, and tore the fish in half with a wet rip.

It was then that he caught the mephitic scent of the beast, malodorous fumes drifting foul and acrid in that polar cold, and he knew whose migratory lair he had unhappily occupied, for it was the same stench as haunted the sealed passage.

He did not wait for the snowbeast to notice him for he knew that it would soon enough.

The man raised the hammer and charged the hulking form.

He was three steps from it, planting his foot to bring the wedged face of the hammer against the base of its elongated skull, when the creature raised its head, bellowing foul breath and striking him full in the ribs with a smash of its powerful claws. The man was thrown backwards to the cave entrance and for a moment was stunned, though he did not loose his grip on the hammer. The creature rose to its full height and bellowed again and the sound rolled out over hills and snowfields, there resiling from rocky rises and caroming from trunks of trees and so returning in staggered bursts from a dozen points afield that gave the dim beast momentary pause as if in the sound of its own echoed cry it recalled and longed for a lost companionship. The man meanwhile scrambled backwards into the cave and there took up his spear, and the horse whinnied wildly all the while.

The snowbeast lurched forward, raging, and the man fixed the shaft of the spear against a stone and braced for the impact, angling the tip at the charging creature's throat. The monster's brutish gait was unpredictable and so the blade pierced wide, plunging into the left shoulder instead, but stopping the bomnubble for a brief moment as it clawed at the thing that had suddenly pained it.

The horse spun, seeking an exit, and finding none, reared and kicked and shied backwards deeper into the cave.

Rather than retreating from this first wounding, the snowbeast was only stirred to greater rage and yowling its fury it clawed the air, striking rocks from the cave roof and clambering forward towards the man, driving the spear deeper into and through its own shoulder as it did.

The man saw that the spear would not save him and pushed to his feet, taking up again the hammer that was beside him.

He stepped in, ducked the beast's raking claws, and swung with all his might for the nearest tusk.

He felt the contact shudder through the head and handle of the great hammer, as the upward pointed ivory cracked and sheared apart. The beast was stunned. The man did not wait for this new pain to funnel again to a wilder rage, but returned a two-handed backswing that jarred and snapped the remaining tusk from its mooring in the jawbone.

The dazed creature now retreated backwards, shaking its head in a confused flurry, then spinning its massive form round as best it could in the narrow cave entrance with the spear protruding awkwardly from its body. The man gave rapid chase, screaming now for the heady rush of battle, and overtaking the confused monstrosity just beyond the entrance he brought his weighted hammer down hard against the hind leg of the thing. He heard the crunch of bone and the miserable, shocked howl of the predator that for the first time in its years of life tasted wrenching pain and fear. It tumbled down from the entrance of the cave, splashing into the stream and from there he watched as it limped and dragged itself away through the snow, the silver blade still pierced through its shoulder and levered ever deeper there by the creature's own lurching movements.

Twice in that infinite night he heard it howl mournfully from out in the flatlands and he felt it as the most desolate sound in all the world's long history, for when had such a fell and towering beast ever been asked to spend such a long night rehearsing its own demise?

The man kept awake lest the thing return, and he occupied the cold hours binding the monster's great fangs to the sides of his dark hat with a weave of twine so that they jutted up ominously from the hatband, curving slightly outward like horns from his head.

The next morning at first light he mounted the horse and they followed the convoluted and blood-dripped trail two miles through the deep snow and rode the crippled thing down with a final cavalry charge, stoving the great skull in with a crushing blow.

The odious snowbeast had been too forlorn to lift its head or even defend itself in that final encounter but had seemed to track the horseman's approach with a slow movement of eyes from which all fire and instinct had already been extinguished.

Retrieving his blade, the man skinned the creature for its thick coat and carved free several cuts of meat. That night the man determined that bomnubble was edible, though a foul, dark, greasy, gamey meat that stank of liver and cooked apart like tough cords of twine.

The horse was dissettled even by the scent and the next day the man threw out what was left for it was all congealed with a cold and gritty grease that made him retch just to smell it again.

The thick coat he stretched and tanned over a smoky fire in the cave entrance for a full week until it lost the bomnubble stench and then he wrapped it round his shoulders as a cowl and fashioned crude leggings of two long pieces and used the odd remnants to line and patch his cloak and shirt and the larger scraps he sewed into a blanket which he tied over the horse's back.

Rolling himself tightly in those new furs he slept warmer than ever he had, even in Torrboro in summer.

The man and the horse remained in the cave several weeks more until the hay had run out and the muddy snowmelt of approaching spring had swollen the stream to a narrow river and washed away the fish trap and this small loss, though in hindsight it was to be expected, had rankled the man's ire because it was like a rude retelling of his own life and by the next morning they had broken camp and rode out with their faces set and their purpose renewed, preferring the risk of a late blizzard to the certain monotony of another day waylaid in that cold cavern.

The man had no mirror to observe the changes that had come over him. His merchant skin had weathered into a permanence of soot and leather. His muscles were tightened and gathered into bunches of taut leanness. His black hair swung about his shoulders like a wild mane, and the horns that protruded from his dark hat and the thick beastly cowl of the vanquished bomnubble imbued his appearance with an ominous talismanic power, as if he were a not a man but a dark archetype conjured from the fabric of the myths of this unsettled land. His senses were ever alert in the way of animals, and distant sounds and smells now told him of things he would have missed in his former life. He had become a creature more of instinct than of reason. Even his thoughts were no longer primarily envisaged as words, but came to him often now as fully formed hunches, impulses, intuitions which he had no reason to question. The distance between thought and action had worn spare, and his entire being was now pointed like the tip of a honed blade towards the one action that still held meaning in his flattened existence:

I will seek you out, O Maker, and demand you give answer for my loss.

After only a few days' ride over lands piebald with patches of muddy greenness and blanketing snow, the peaks of the One Mountain had ascended to permanence beyond the natural horizon, rising there like some broken fragment of a wrecked moon and the man paused and stared and at last believed the witness of his own eyes. As the bard had told him, some of the stories were indeed true. The place he had so long journeyed towards was as real as water and stone, and was rooted and fixed in the hard landscapes of this world and not just in some shimmering aura of myth or of the spirit. How his daughter would have thrilled to see it.

His daughter.

His daughter who was dead and was no more and would never rise to witness such wonders again.

The One Mountain did not yet loom near enough to lord over all of earth and sky but the man saw its increase day by day, and he traveled now with the sensation that he, and the land itself and all it contained, was being inexorably drawn and inevitably lifted towards that one place. He crossed leagues of alien terrain teeming with bright and stunning floras and faunas unknown to him—fields of small, furred creatures with dark, bulbous eyes and coats almost crimson that perched on rocks and hooted and scurried into tunnels at his approach; droopy feline-types with velvety, membranous wings that took to the air in short, swooping glides and then slumped amongst branches overhead, feasting on gulpswallows and altogether unalarmed by the man's presence; colonies of azure spiders that seemed to be tribally banded and that scurried the terrain together in their communal hunts like a bright spilling of jewels. The man passed amongst these wonders and ten thousand others and noted them scarce at all some days, so fixed was his sight upon his destination, and his thoughts were pulled always towards it and gyred round it as it rose and expanded in his field of vision.

Even the grey swell of wintry storm clouds that had risen behind him some days earlier was still of scant concern, for it was piled in the east, and the east was the past, and he did not yet reckon that it would overtake him.

Such was his orientation that he was only dimly distressed when he rode up on the charred remains of a sizeable settlement of some dozen cabins and garden plots now grown weedy and uncultivated and haunted by a speckled parliament of annoyed owls. Save for one split log structure off to the side, the dwellings had all been burned and heaved down. The well at the center of the village was fouled with the carcass of a large animal. A stacked stone wall round the hamlet stood either half finished or half destroyed and would now always be so. The place was a hush and a void and a great rounded sepulcher open to the grey sky. The habitation had been desecrated when the snow was deep and now that most of it had melted there was scant readable sign in the mud paths outside, though it was obvious who or what had sourced the desolation. No beast of the wild would destroy an entire village with such intent.

This was the work of Fangs, and the man knew it to a certainty. Perhaps it was the handiwork even of that same patrol the bard had warned him of months earlier and more than a hundred miles to the east.

Entering the one cabin that still stood the man wavered a moment allowing his eyes to adjust to the murk, and then glancing downwards he observed dried and crazed footprints stained of mud and blood spread across the floor as if there had been a mad dance. Some of the prints were of boots and some were those of Fang claws, and for the first time in months his emotions returned to him and he felt his throat constrict when he saw that some were also those of a barefoot child.

The man sought to read the narrative of senseless calamity written on those rough hewn boards and though he could work out only a small phrase here or there as if translating from a lost and ancient language, he read enough to know that he did not wish to read the whole.

Unspeakable dread was hallowed here and the lingering sense of it permeated even the grains of the wood and it brought back the palpable taste of fear, the helplessness, the shame of his own bereaving.

The man felt his anger rising, unchecked, and the righteousness of his oath again confirmed.

Here was an accusation to add to his own.

Had the Maker noted in his ledger that he must one day supply a debt of retribution to this forgotten village, unmarked on any map? And if so, how, when he supplied it, would it not then already be too late? Would he bend time to undo what had been done? Or would he bend instead the bounds of good and evil to somehow justify such negligence?

The man exited the cabin and drew the door closed softly behind him, noting the progress of the soft, grey forbode of storm clouds that piled the eastern sky. He had begun to feel the cold breath of it purling at his back and had pushed the last three days to keep this freezing storm behind him, but he could see now that it had gained and threatened to overtake him.

When he had quit his winter quarters two weeks earlier, the winds careening over the hills had lured him forth with a deceptive warmth and with the wet smell of root and soil and he had believed the killing cold was ended and the steady warming underway. But now he knew that the winter had not yet relinquished her claims on the land and intended this one last assault, and that he must outrun this front or be waylaid another fortnight in some dank hole or else be caught out on the open plains when the blinding storm and killing cold overtook him.

He considered the cabin before him. It would be warm enough, though with the horse sharing the space it would be cramped.

But the Fangs that had ravaged this settlement could still be nearby, or might pass this way again. He would not dare to light a fire here, for fear the chimney smoke would give him away.

Which would be worse? To be overtaken in the open by murderous storm, or to be trapped in a cabin surrounded by murderous Fangs?

He would opt for the mercies of the storm, and would ride now, the sooner to fulfill his oath and to carry his cause before his adversary and his judge.

The man stood a moment in silence, drawing the burned air of the village deep into his lungs, tasting the acrid taint on the back of his tongue. He turned and knelt then in the mud where coagulated the lost memory of that place, but he did not kneel to pray. For by what entreaty would one petition a Maker who had so thoroughly forsaken this remote corner of his creation? No, it was rather to sanctify himself a final time to his own purposes that the man bent low. He would collect the burden of this injustice too, he thought, and would bind it to his own accusation, and would carry it there to the One Mountain. Thrusting his fingers into a wet dissolve of ashes that contained what wretchedness he could not know, the man wiped them across his face and across the backs of his hands in three dark lines, and he did not even ask himself why, for the doing of things had long since become the why, and there was no more distinction for him between action and reason.

As he rose his eyes roved to recent tracks in the mud near the corner of the cabin and hearing the horse snort he was only a little surprised to see limping towards him an old man whose skin was of a dark, coppery hue and who was draped in loose, unfamiliar raiments more ragged than his own, approaching from the direction of the woods, waving his hands in some ambiguous gesture of greeting or warning or entreaty. The grandfather fell to his knees in the muddy dirt while yet some distance away and spoke words that were unintelligible, then clasped his hands together in a gesture of supplication. The man stood his ground beside the horse and scanned the wood before and the horizon behind for any additional movement while the old man repeated his senseless pantomime three more times, running forward several steps, then falling to his knees and opening his hands to show he had no weapon, meant no harm.

"I know you got no sword," the man said sharply, losing patience. "What do you want?"

The grandfather rushed across the remaining space between them then and dropped to his knees before the man. His bald head bore three raking scabs across the top of it and the man did not have to ask but knew without asking the manner of story scribed hard across that scalp.

The stranger looked up at the man and his tongue was suddenly loosed in a torrent of exotic syllables, but it seemed as a mad fit of ecstasy, for the words were but suggestions of words with no fixed meaning, and then the man realized this settler had not come from any land in the East, but had arrived here from far north or south or west, from some land and some people altogether unknown. He was an outlander.

"I don't know what you're saying." The man's own words struck his ears as strange, hoarse, croaking. The last conversation he had engaged in was more than a year past, and that had been beside the river with the bard.

The outlander paused a moment, then spoke a second time, but slower and louder. He gestured round at the ruined village, then at the woods.

The man shook his head. "I told you, I don't speak your language." He motioned to his own ear and mouth and shook his head again. "I can't help you."

The grandfather furrowed his brow, then gave a sharp whistle and a clap.

A moment later the man spied a red-haired boy of perhaps eleven or twelve rising from the tall grass at the edge of the forest and moving warily towards them.

The man and the grandfather eyed one another till the boy arrived and at the old man's command dropped to his knees in the mud as well. The boy's skin was pale and splotched with freckles and his lower jaw receded so that he had a pronounced overbite, but his eyes were a piercing grey like they had been cored from some glowing stone and he was a lanky child who appeared to be on the verge of sprouting into a tall, broad-shouldered man.

The old man said something in his strange tongue and the boy replied haltingly, then looked up curiously at the man. "He says can you help us?"

The man observed the look of the boy and the rural chop of his speech and naturally mirrored the manner, as it was near the same cast as of his own agrarian boyhood and he knew that such boys are raised with instinctive distrust of the ease and sophistication of more cultured speech such as he had over the years acquired the habit of in Torrboro but had mostly shed now piece by piece as he had traveled west.

"Help you with what?"

"We got attacked. Fangs."

"I can see that. Looks like a few weeks back now."

"Last full moon."

"How many of you's left?"

The old man said something and the boy gently hushed him and then counted on his fingers. "I'd say about twenty of us."

"How many men can fight?"

"Ten I guess?"

The man leaned and spat in the dirt. "Then you should be fine."

The boy hesitated.

"Tell your granddad you all should head back east. Go to Torrboro or somewhere."

"I heard Fangs run all them places back east."

"Yep, they do." The man looked at the ruined cabins. "But your place looks more runned than anyplace back east ever did. Go on now. Tell him you'll be safer back there. You got ten men, you sure don't need me."

The boy spoke to the old man and the old man raised his voice in response and spoke directly to the man, then to the boy, all the while moving his hands like the last flutterings of palsied birds. The old man and the boy carried on a conversation in that strange tongue for more than a minute, the odd intonations rising and falling in sonorous cadence from the man's lips, but breaking off more like chunks of rough stone spat out from the boy's less practiced tongue. While those two argued, the man further studied the landscape and noted a shock of blond hair moving at about the height of the tall grasses and figured it for a child of perhaps six.

"What it is," the boy finally said, "is we don't really got ten men."

"Why'd you say you did?"

"In case you was thinking of starting something."

The man gave a mirthless laugh. "Tell that old man to get off his knees."

The boy spoke and the old man rocked from his kneeling position and gingerly extended his legs till he was standing again.

"So how many men you really got besides grandpa here?"

"Nobody. Just him and me and he ain't even my real grandpa. He come here from somewhere over the sea. Come out here two years ago tryin' to sell us his tailoring services and then stayed on cuz he was good with goats. He makes cheese."

"Who else is left? Anybody?"

"Nossir."

"Then who's that little 'un yonder?" He nodded towards the blond crown of hair that kept popping up amongst the tall weeds.

The boy looked over his shoulder. "Oh. She's my cousin. She don't count though. She's too little to help. Me and her was off picking berries when them Fangs come through and I kept her there till they left but she eats most of the berries she picks so her bucket's always empty."

"Tell her to come on out. And any others with her."

"It ain't but her."

The boy whistled a passable imitation of a flitwing call and the girl immediately burst from her hiding place in the weeds and ran towards them on little legs that bespoke no hint of wariness, and the man could see even from the distance that she was beaming some smile at odds with all relevant circumstance. The three of them studied the girl's progress without speaking, and for a moment the man revisited in her movements some echo of his own daughter at a younger age than she had been when taken and he turned and spit again to hide this dismay and then cinched at his saddle and busied himself with other details in order to not observe the child any more and so was unprepared for the sudden impact and embrace she gave him at her arrival.

The man recoiled from the touch of the child as one might from the winding of a snake round their belly, raising his arms rather than returning her hug and the boy noted this and acted quickly to pull the girl away.

"Sorry, she likes everyone," he said, peeling the girl's arms from around the man's waist. "She can't talk though. I mean, she *can* but she stopped . . ." The boy's words trailed off as if he was unwilling to speak some memory and the man noted the sudden puckering up of the face and the faraway look in the boy's eyes. The confusion passed almost instantly though, like the snapping of a sheet from a clothesline, and the boy's face unpuckered and he looked at the girl and then at the man again. "I think she thinks you're Old Woller."

"Who?"

"Old Woller. He's a trapper. Used to come in here once a year to trade pelts and he always brought some wild honey for the kids. Say, you got any wild honey?"

"No, I don't have any honey."

"Well, anyway. His beard looked like yours and your horse looks a awful lot like his too." The boy seemed suddenly taken by the idea and eyed the horse more narrowly.

No one said anything for a while till the man finally answered, "Well I never met no man named Woller."

The old man said something that approximated the sounds of the word *Woller* and the boy touched the saddle and then drew his hand back. "He says that looks like Old Woller's saddle too."

"Well it ain't. And if it used to be, then there ain't no good news about Old Woller left to tell. I found this horse half dead caught up in a gulch a long ways south and east and it was shot with a arrow and I waited three days and nobody turned up."

The boy conveyed the gist of this to the bald outlander and the old man squatted and picked the girl up and said something.

"He says you got Old Woller's horse so you got to carry the girl and me to somewhere else."

The old man tried to set the girl in the saddle.

"What are you doing?" The man pulled the girl roughly from the saddle and placed her in the mud again without ever looking directly at her. "I need that horse to get where I aim to get to and it ain't any kinda place to take a child."

The old man snatched the girl up a second time and tried to set her astride the horse but the man thrust his arms out to block the way. "No!" he said, and then turned to the boy. "How does he say *no* in his words?"

"Koo-ha."

"Koo-ha?" He turned to the old man and then pointed to the girl. "Koo-ha! I can't help you. I got nowhere to take her. I got nowhere to take any of you. Koo-ha!"

The old man argued and the man waited impatiently for the boy to translate.

"He says . . ." the boy started but the old man interrupted him. After another rapid volley the boy raised a hand to silence the old man. "He says he's too old to take care of us out here if the Fangs—he calls 'em something else I don't know what the words are, something like *Song People? Song Singers?* But he means Fangs—if the Fangs come back. And he says winter's not over yet and we ain't got any stores left. He says you can leave him behind if need be but you need to take me and her out of here." After saying this the boy looked away nervously and then down and traced a line in the mud with the toe.

"Well tell him I got nowhere to take you and I ain't got any stores left either. There's been enough hard times to go around lately."

The boy spoke to the old man and then the three of them stood several seconds in a ructious silence. The man turned and opened his saddlebag and pulled out two strips of dried flabbit. He handed them both to the boy. "You and the girl both get one. Go on."

The boy held the jerky and studied the man's wild appearance more closely now. "You ever killed a real Fang, mister?"

The man peered at a ragged association of evergreens bowing wildly in the wind along the hilltops and adjusted his hat brim. "Only one."

The boy's eyes widened and he relayed this information to the outlander. The man could see in his peripheral vision that the girl had crouched in the muddy grass and was poking at a little flower bud just emerged from the thawing edge of a snow patch and he glanced again at the pending storm and considered it was a bud that had emerged too optimistically.

The old man tilted his head as he listened to the boy and then he gestured with both hands and seemed to respond with a longer narrative of some sort. After this had gone on for several sentences the man interrupted. "I ain't got time for this. What's he going on about now?"

The boy pulled himself from the narrative. "He's saying that where he came from is where the Fangs came from too. He told me that before."

"So where's he from?"

"Across the ocean somewheres."

"Dang?"

"Yeah. I think that's it." The boy asked the old man and the old man shook his head and said something.

"Not Dang I guess but somewhere close to it. Up above it or something. He says . . . I don't know how to say it. It's like he comes from people who move around and they have a chief but it's not a real country."

"Rovers?"

"I don't know. That's not the word he used."

"Sounds like rovers."

"He says they're people."

"The rovers?"

"The Fangs."

"The Fangs. He says the Fangs are people."

"No, he says they *were* people. They got taken and then they got turned into . . . the way he says it is like *song people* . . . people of the song . . . into Fangs."

"What does that supposed to mean? *People of the song*?"

The boy asked and the man replied. "I guess they make them sing a song that does something to them and afterwards they turn into a Fang. There's a stone."

"A stone."

"Something magic, I think. Like the stone does the changing."

"A magic stone." The man shook his head at what seemed so likely a spun tale. "How do they make somebody sing a song they don't want to sing?"

The boy asked and the old outlander wrinkled his face up and made violent twisting gestures with his hands as he answered.

"He says they hurt them until they want to sing it. He . . . "

The old man interjected before the boy finished speaking.

"And he feels sorry for them." The boy paused and looked at the outlander and then back at the man. "Do you feel sorry for them Fangs, mister? Cuz I sure don't."

"No I do not, son. Sympathy for a Fang." The man eyed the outlander. "Well ain't that a thing then." The man spit and paused and spit again and addressed the boy. "You see this coat?" He gripped and shook the snowy cowl draped round his shoulders.

The boy nodded.

"The fellow wore this skin here was born a monster. He couldn't help it. I guess it's reasonable to feel sorry for him if you want. But if one was ever born a man and choose to become a monster? You telling me he wants we should feel sorry for that one? Anyway, you believe what he's saying? You believe Fangs were people?"

The boy shrugged. "They talk like they coulda been, I guess."

The outlander spoke again and the boy waited.

"He says his own brother got made into a Fang. But he says he could still tell it was his brother. That's how he knows for sure. He says they tortured him bad. It's why he ran off and came over the ocean, but then the Fang army followed him all the way to Skree and even out here halfway to nowhere."

"Well, I ain't gonna stand here arguing with an old man about what he might or might not have remembered correctly from his own life," the man said. "Not while I got that diggle of a storm to keep ahead of. Tell him it's been nice talking but I'm about to be leaving now."

"That one there was my house," the boy said, obviously trying to delay the man's departure with conversation. He turned and pointed to a burned out shell over his shoulder. "When the Fangs came my mama and papa was—"

"I don't need to know any of that, son." And then, when the man saw the boy was about to cry he said in a softer tone, "Look, it ain't easy, I know. But we can't live in what was. Can't none of us do that. Awful things has happened and will likely happen again. You have to buck up and be strong and move on."

The old man launched into some new argument but without an opponent this time as the boy had ceased interpreting and was now just standing with watery eyes and quivering chin. In his peripheral vision the man saw the little girl move towards and cling to the boy but the man still did not look at her for he did not want to know the color of her eyes or the shape of her mouth or whether she had dimples or freckles or delicate little fingers as his own child once had.

It was bad enough just to know that there was a girlchild immotile in this desolation.

He intended to ride away, and once he did he did not want to be haunted by her either in memory or in dream. He did not want to look at her and discover that she looked like his own daughter but he also did not want to find that she did not. If she must exist for him, she must exist in some dim borderland as a featureless motif and not as a little creature of flesh and blood and bone and bright radiance.

"He says you have to take us with you. I told him you wouldn't but he says you have to."

"Look, I know he wants me to do something about it and I'm sorry about whatever happened here but I don't have nothin' to do with any of you. I've got something I have to do so I'm about to be on my way." He gripped the saddle pommel and prepared to pull himself up.

The boy relayed a shorter version of this and the old man barked back a single word.

"He wants to know *what*."

"What?"

"What's the thing you have to do?"

The man stared off towards the western horizon and shook his head. "Now that's my own business, ain't it?"

The boy translated and the old man responded.

"He wants to know before you leave if you know the difference between a Fang and a man."

"What?"

"He wants to know if . . . "

"I heard the question." The man eyed the outlander. "I'm just a bit suspicious of the asking." He pointed to the charred cabins. "You can tell him if he's confused on the matter, the Fangs are the ones who do stuff like this and the people are the ones stuff like this gets done to."

The boy started to translate but the outlander interrupted and spoke.

"He says whatever you said was wrong. He says the difference between a . . . a Fang and a man . . . is mercy."

"Mercy?"

The boy shrugged. "That's what he said."

"Well whose mercy are we talking about again? As best I can see it," the man continued, "mercy was done away with some time ago from the top down." He opened his palms wide to encompass the utter ruin of the settlement. "Does this look to that old man like a world where mercy means a blessed thing? When the Maker makes it a point to show some mercy to folks like you, maybe we can talk. Till then, it looks to me like he's got a thing or two to answer for." The man leaned and spit. "What does that old man think mercy even means out here? I got nothing to give you and no safe place to take you to and I'm sorry but that's just the bone of it."

The boy had fallen silent and turned and watched the girl patting her palms in a snowmelt puddle until the man prodded him. "Go on. Tell him what I said."

Then the boy turned and parsed the general meaning into some choppy paraphrase and the man wondered how much of the meaning had seeped out from the edges of the translation and he suspected most of it but he could see from the old man's face that whatever parts of his sermon had been delivered had in nowise been well received.

The outlander responded with a raised finger and with rising emotion in his thin voice.

"He says the Maker did show us mercy."

The man kicked over a pile of ashes at his feet and looked towards the storm and shook his head. "And how does he figure that?"

"He sent us *you*."

The man's eyes flashed beneath the brim of his horned hat and he opened his mouth to say something and then thought better of it and closed it again and finally he just said, "Well, tell him he's wrong about that. I wasn't sent. I just happened up here. If I know one thing for sure, I know I ain't fit to be anybody's mercy. Look at me, boy." He lifted the hat from his head. "I'm as stove up and wrung out as any man out here, the recently dead included. And with that I will take my leave."

The man replaced his hat and set a hand on the saddle and the old man divined his intent and babbled something.

"He says it ain't your choice. You was brought."

"Look!" The man was losing patience. "Ain't nobody brought me here but this horse and my own thoughtless choices. Now the smart thing is for you all to set up shelter in those woods. Today. Before this big storm hits. Tell him you can't stay in that one cabin anymore. It don't matter how cold it is. If the Fangs come back and find you there that'll be that. I know it's got a roof and a stove but you got to forget about all that. If you got any rope or twine go lash you up a lean-to inside the woods and I ain't saying it's gonna be easy but that's where you need to stay till this passes through. There's plenty of fallen wood you can gather for fire to get you through another couple weeks. You'll have to make do on roots and berries. You know how to find those?"

"It's what we been doin'."

"Good. Then keep doin' it. And keep that girl hid in the woods. You'll be all right."

The boy took a while explaining and the old man didn't say anything else immediately and the man took the outlander's silence for resignation.

"I know it ain't what he wants but it's the best I can do for you. I can't take anybody anywhere. I ain't going anywhere that's any better or any safer than this. Come full thaw you need to go back east is what you need to do and find some people but for now you just need to hole up in them woods."

The man gripped the pommel and surveyed again the destroyed settlement, all parts of him warring against all other parts to legislate what if anything was owed this scraggled detritus of humanity.

"Look."

He let go the saddle and grabbed the old man's wrists in exasperation and twisted the frail arms so that his hands were cupped together palms up. Then the man took hold of his saddlebag and turned it upside down so that the contents spilled into the old man's shaking hands. It was mostly a mixture of nuts and shriveled berries and a few remaining strips of smoked flabbit.

"Tell him that's all I got. I just give you everthing. Do I look like the mayor of the wilderness or something?"

The boy struggled dutifully to relay the man's words but the old man interrupted him with a curt jabbering and then the old man and the boy both seemed to lose patience with each other and halted their conversation at some angry impasse, the old man still awkwardly cupping the piled foodstuffs.

The man pondered and nodded before gripping the pommel and swinging himself up to the saddle. "If I live through what I'm about to do, maybe I'll make it back through to check on you."

This action set the old outlander to ranting wildly again.

The man adjusted his saddlebags and shook his head, not at the old man, but at the situation in general. He had done what he could. Which was more or less nothing. He could not be the arbiter of misfortunes such as had happened here. There were times when a man just needed to leave. The longer he stayed, the worse it was becoming for all of them and the smaller his chances of outpacing the cold.

He would ride for the mountain while he still could.

He had sworn an oath and he would no longer be dissuaded from its fulfillment.

An oath sworn against the Maker himself.

If there was a measure of shame in turning away from the old man and the boy and the girl, it would be less than that which he already carried. He did not think they were in any immediate danger. It would be unlikely the Fangs would pass this way again soon, and even if they did, these survivors would probably be unnoticed if they stayed in the woods. This was not his place. These were not his people. This was not his fight.

And whatever fight it had been was already well over now anyway.

He could see again that the mute girl was watching him and smiling and he did not want her to smile at him and he did not want to see her smile.

He reined the horse round towards the distant mountain so that his eyes would not accidentally be drawn to her face. "You all just need to head east and take your chances there. That's the bottom of it. I wish you well."

He felt a pattering of grapeshot against his back and he knew that the old man had hurled his own insufficient food stores back at him and he heard the old man now cursing him in words that required no translator to denude meaning.

"He says the girl's blood is on you."

"I figured as much." And then, after a moment, "Tell him she might have to get in line."

When he turned a last time to nod his farewell the outlander thrust the girl into his arms and for a stunned moment he held her there and then he dropped her as quickly and as gently as he could, sliding her down the side of the horse dangled by her left arm.

"Koo-ah, koo-ah," he barked, but it was too late.

His wild eyes had locked on her own.

It was like seeing his own child reborn but with fairer features so that he almost spoke her name but reined away instead and heeled his horse in the flanks and he rode out without speaking again. When he rounded the collapsed wall of the ruined village and set out along a now almost imperceptible path that had only weeks earlier been trampled by Fang hordes drunk in their blood reveries, he did so at a gallop and in a choking blindness of his own sobs and tears.

He sprinted the horse several miles before ever he looked back over his shoulder at the slow violence of the storm whose charcoal clouds curved down to the horizon angled like the prow of some ship larger than the world but advancing forever upon it or like some great grayed pestle pressing down to grind all living things in the wide mortar of the plains that stretched before him for days yet to come.

IV.

The Ascent

I have seen your mountain, O Maker, and I will go up to it.
Now chop the onion finely and fold the egg into the crust.

—*Pilgrim Songs and Traveler's Recipes,* Anonymous

For the first uncertain day he lamented the hour he had stopped to indulge the bereaved settlers, believing it might be the undoing of everything. He fled before the howling of the cold northeastern winds that harrowed the land and coiled and swirled round him now like a silvered twisting of serpents, seeking any entry into the gaps and folds of his boots and clothing where their sharp bites would numb his skin. He paused on a slight plateau to water the horse near sunset and looking back could see beneath the slow and towering storm darkness a polished glint of golden light glaring back from the eastern curve of horizon as if that sextant of the world had been recently turned to pure glass. He beheld as a blurred and darkened smear like a thumbprint grimed upon that glossy swath the patch of forest he had forsaken hours before and though the details had long since been swallowed at such distance he could yet fix in his mind at its edge the position of the ruined village and having done so he sought to push away again the intrusive remembrance of the girl's soft and piercing eyes.

What right to set her in my arms?

What right?

He realized he was speaking aloud to the mountain and turned his face away. The world to the east was now dissolved and abandoned and all that remained was his westward course and the end to which it drew him. As he rode down from that plateau, behind him lay his own history and origins now cased in a thick ice whose slow march might continue until it covered all things in a frozen silence and he too would also finally be still, and in the knowledge of his losses he wished it to be so.

He rode on in urgency and in fear that the heart of the storm would overtake him, assigning it in his mind a kind of cunning, as if those dark clouds moved with a will or at the bidding of a will that had unjustly arrayed itself against him and that sought even now to cut him off and divert him from his chosen path or if he would not divert, then simply to destroy him on those unsheltered plains so that all his days and his injuries and his fury would at the last amount to nothing and he would be fixed in his last unfinished movement as a cold effigy of himself, eyes locked on the mountain, perched upon by crows and mocked by the snows till the thaws came and his form collapsed and was picked clean by dark birds descended upon the plains.

For two days and nights the storm neither sped nor slowed but followed steadily in the wake of the horse and the man, not overtaking but always compelling his flight as if by choosing this course the man had engaged some unseen mechanism whereby all other courses and all other choices had been forfeit, as if the entities that judge such things had seamed this fate behind him so that he now could not turn back even had he repented of his sworn course, which he did not. Driven thus, he paused only an hour or two each night to allow the horse sleep and the man himself ceased to slumber at all but kept watch and sharpened his blade on stones and sharpened his arguments, both his defenses and his accusations against the coming judgment and he wondered at times why he did what he did and if he had ever really believed that a man might approach and challenge his Maker upon some high summit or if he was now mad or half-mad and in the end he realized that he did not care whether he was for it was the will and the act itself and not the reasonableness or the outcome that mattered.

The horse held up against all reason, laboring heavily but neither stumbling nor dropping from exhaustion and on the third day the great mountain that had been creeping towards them had loomed up suddenly like a distant wreckage of skyward spires and the whole land had tilted upwards attaining a scale that the eye could scarcely reckon.

They had then labored along worn switchbacks in the steepening foothills for the better part of a day, rising in elevation but scarcely gaining forward movement, and the dark front had pressed its advantage against them, rapidly closing the distance until the man felt a cold spitting against the back of his neck and with a shout drove the horse yet harder upwards and the horse had strained till it was trembling and foamed with sweat even in that chilling cold.

At sunset they had split lowline ridges to the north and south of them and had tilted the passage between granite outcrops so that the ground momentarily leveled off and he had seen there silhouetted against the setting sun—and still many miles beyond the plateau rim upon which they sat—the abstruse and recondite mystery of the One Mountain ascending heavenward in its greater glory. The form rose from the plains so large and so sudden from that vantage as to be beyond comprehension, as if it were the hub of the axis of the world's spinning, the immovable center that all stars and planets wheeled round.

The man forgot for a moment the storm at his back and he stood the horse and lowered himself from the saddle and settled to his knees upon the rocks and simply stared.

The reach of the mountain before him far exceeded the ridgeline where he was now perched but because of the angle at which he had ascended the switchbacks he had not till now glimpsed the measure of the towering rise that lay beyond so that it seemed to him as if some elemental cataclysm of earth and stone, of forest and cloud and fire, had simply appeared ex nihilo, a colossal conjuring from the void. The foot of the great mountain seemed to encompass vast kingdoms of earth and the lower slopes were green and umber with thick forest that opened to a paler green of mountain meadows and then rose sharply to sheer cliffs that seemed themselves as tall as any mountain might ever be and where they at last resolved he could not now determine for the head of the mountain was shrouded in dark cloud that rose upwards in a towering column and that was lit by ominous, flickering charges and by great strikes of lightning that played both upwards and downwards and across the sky.

The man remained knelt in the shadow of that immovable and ancient form and so awesome was the sight that for the first time he faltered in his fiery resolve, and did feel some urgency to unmake his quest, and instead of continuing on his way half thought to prostrate himself and to turn his eyes ever after to lesser things, his heart to lesser purposes.

But he would not be so swayed.

He had a foreboding sense that his presence here was already marked by unseen witnesses, and as his retreat was cut off by the storm and as what had been set in motion and sealed by the invocation of the Maker's name could not now nor ever be repented of, so had he rather whispered in that dread shadow that gulfed the eastern world a restatement of his purpose, and with this dread shoring of his resolve he stood again and heaved his beleaguered form up to the saddle and there took the reins and began the last long gallop across the intervening plain even as the storm piled against the hilltops at his back and falls of cold cloud began to spill the plateau's rim and stream westward across that flattened expanse on chill currents of air.

By morning of the next day they had arrived at the furthest foot of the great mountain, a jagged, stony outcrop like a dragon spine flung mightily into the land round it, and for wide distances before and around that base no life had seemed to stir. There were scrub and flowering plants, but all was shrouded in a heavy silence and the man judged that all canny creatures had sensed the portent of the coming storm and already fled or hunkered low into their dens underground, but still, he found the stillness of the landscape eerie and could not shake the insinuation of himself in violation and trespass of it.

He skirted the great mountain hastily northwards, seeking ahead of the storm a passable route across the lower wooded slopes whose rockiness and pitch and deep gullies suggested no clear line of ascent to the meadows that he could not now see but knew rested somewhere above for he had noted them from a distance the previous evening. Such was the cloud and haze that the man and the horse passed between the blocked and tumbled remains of ancient precipices long since thrown down and cast no shadow upon those faces of rock, as if they were themselves bodied of that same occluding cloud. So impenetrable did that sheer base now present itself and so looming and final the sweeping line of storm and the drizzling clink of ice that now overtook them that the man almost wept with relief when he rounded an escarpment of speckled and weathered granite and spied there the collapsing ruin of a small archway of stone beyond which had been wrought by some primordial mason a clear succession of steps carved upwards into the mountain itself.

Judging this crumbling escalier too precarious for both man and horse to ascend mounted, the man swung from the saddle and taking the reins of the horse in hand drew it along the upward course with all urgency and haste. As the storm pillared against the mountain thick clouds enveloped them so that the man soon had to resort to feeling his way along the carved steps with his left hand and in certain breathless spans he sensed by sound that to his right there was nothing but sheer drop, though he could not see it for the dark fog. In all of this the horse hardly balked but remained fixed to the man's own will and climbed with unnatural gait, ribs pressed hard against the rising mountain at their left hand as if the beast also felt the peril of the emptiness that hemmed and held them there.

The man drew his cowl and cloak tighter against the fierce, needling wind and climbed through that undefined gray light till the unbroken repetition of movement and his own infinite weariness folded together so that it seemed this blind climb from nothingness and into nothingness was all that had ever been or ever would be and that there was no true past and no terminal attainment offered by such existence but only an illusion that there had been a life before and only an illusion that any would yet come after and even the closed sound of his own exhaled breath, even as that same breath compounded to slags of ice in his beard, pushed him deeper into that remove of space. The remoteness of his own numb and distant hands in their ungoverned movements and the shuddering that began in his core, spasming his spine and then traveling outwards like last throes of death even after he could no longer feel the cold—so senseless had his touch become—all piled and converged to supplant his knowledge of the measures of the places where he began and ended and even of the memory of earth and sky so that when the man and the horse stumbled at last upwards into bright sunlight and a spring warmth and open meadow pocked with goldish trees and gentle spring pools that spilled to tiny streams and all of this but a step above the pressed top of those ashen and opacus cloudfields stretched backwards like endless roils of ocean, he at first had no category to reckon such change and he and the horse simply drank from the pools and then folded in a numb collapse and slept more than a day as blood returned to their ice-burned flesh and the clouds pushed and diverted slowly round the rocks below them in an endless sweep that had no visible genesis and no evident end.

Waking again in pleasant light upon that lush island that rested so nearly on clouds the man lay on his back and yet beheld still far above him the darker cloud and storm that clung to the invisible summit of the One Mountain and he appraised that the climb ahead remained still greater than the one behind them. The black thunderhead above columned up over ridges and outcroppings he could yet barely perceive and he felt muffled and dim the distant reverberations of the thunder above him and realized he had felt them for some time even as he slept, like a primal speech mumbled endlessly from above and he imagined it an impenetrable conversing that had always been but was heard without awareness or understanding.

He turned his head and saw that the horse was also awake and peacefully cropping golden grasses and he saw also that many of the trees there were fruited, and he half expected to see shimmering spirits, bright and translucidus, tending the grove. He rose and put forth his hand and plucked a strange fruit, small and golden, and found it sweet and so he breakfasted there and washed in a pool by cupping his hands and bringing the water to his face and the water was startling and clear and cool and was also itself sweet and as he rested the afternoon in the cool and mossy grasses beside those whispering waters he felt himself restored of weariness and found here yet a hungry desire simply to believe that such beauty and goodness might be at the heart of all that was ever intended, and to bask here in placid content for the remainder of his life.

His clothes were stiff with sweat salt and stank and he had given this no consideration for months but in this place he felt the offense of his own stench and so removed his outer garments for washing. But once he had done so his right hand chanced into the pocket of his submerged breeches and his fingers closed on the tattered silk tricorn and he drew it again from its long dormancy and stared at it sopped and dripping in his fingers, and his thoughts fell mute as any animal, mute even to himself, until he realized he was weeping and then did all his sorrow overtake him again in the stirring beauty of that place only this time it was because of the vast and irreconcilable gulf between the word spoken by the beauty of the meadow grove and the word spoken by his own loss, and he knew himself then as alien to this landscape and without purchase in the bliss of it and sensing his own exile he wondered what airy creatures unacquainted with sorrow could ever dwell long in such a place, and then he wiped his eyes and looked upwards and fixed his intention a final time towards that clouded summit and the great question he was sworn to ask there.

When the man's laundered clothes had dried upon the branches of a tree, billowed by those sweet winds, he bid the horse a nuzzled farewell and lay the hammer in the grass and strapping the daggered spear to his back he approached the dizzying stone face that distantly had appeared so steep and sheer but which he could now see was riddled with small hand and footholds. This pocked face he began to climb knowing that life itself would dangle from the fissures his fingers found and from the rough ridges of each tenuous toehold, and that the odds of perishing in this ascent were nearer now than the odds of achieving it but in this he also saw the righteousness of his case distilled to a manifest purity for what man—he imagined the heavens asking this and bearing witness when he confronted his accuser in that lofty courtroom at last—what man would risk life, what man would offer his life seeking redress, were his cause not utterly righteous?

The man was hours at the ardor of it though he could not reckon the passage of time for all existence had collapsed into an attentiveness to the smallest motions of his trembling body: the reach, the grip, the pull, the stretch, repeated and perpetual and from which hung all time and meaning.

He attained a height such that the meadow below seemed insignificant, and he could no longer discern the location of the pale horse anywhere in it. He briefly considered were he to fall now whether his body would plunge to that remote purchase of meadow, or arcing wide of it would plummet like a star hurtled through ice and storm to the wide plain fathomless distances below.

Though dark cloud and churning wind still buffeted the heights far above him, he believed he could just discern the lip of the summit as a great verge of rock that promontoried over an abyss of sky. This he angled towards and made a steady progress through the afternoon, twice attaining thin ledges of stone he could just stand on till the quivering strain of his arms was relieved enough to go on.

The afternoon was passing and the shadow of the One Mountain stretched at his back beyond the eastern horizon before the man at last heaved himself over the lip of the promontory and sprawled on his stomach wheezing and trembling from the long expense and from the thinness of the air in that impossible reach of sky.

His eyes were closed and his thoughts dizzied, and only when they had settled and his breathing had eased to a sane rhythm did he open his eyes and peer round him to see what purchase his climb had finally achieved and he saw then that his earlier vision had been far too hopeful.

He stood and surveyed the rock and saw that this promontory was not a pathway to the summit, but only an outcropping that had eclipsed the still higher reaches from view.

The storm-wrapped summit was yet somewhere above him, though the lower clouds were near enough that he might have met them in an easy walk had the distance been merely along a sloping ridge.

But it was not.

At the root of the promontory grew a thin line of black trees and over them rose a face of slick obsidian so nearly sheer in its incline that no hooves of craggy goat had ever found purchase there, nor ever any feet of man.

Downward rushing winds swept the promontory and lightnings cracked horribly overhead and the skies even roundabout where the man stood were charged with an anticipation of unseen things as if new wonders were set to be called into being there. Thunders pounded downwards against the stones and their repercussions struck as physical blows against the man's chest.

It was not so difficult to believe that a great power dwelt here.

It was not difficult to believe the Maker himself dwelt aloof in that high tower.

The man looked round, taking account of his options and saw that he had none.

His way had been hemmed.

He had come here by a hard path but here all hard paths ended, still short of the summit and the nebula.

He craned his head and pondered the wild heights, his mind hardly yet able to compass this finality.

So his oath had always been a preposterous futility then, doomed to incompletion, and his journey had been all along only a journey towards that grim realization at this last marooning upon this inescapable promontory of soul.

He saw then that this was also the place his own story would end.

After the losses.

After the sorrows.

After the scars.

After the crucible of years and the hard roads and sleepless nights and the hunger and the thirst and the fury and the shame.

The man he had been had been slowly worn away and was now finally vanquished by his elusive adversary.

The Maker sat yet ensconced in that towering and impenetrable cloud and the man had been shown he might approach only thus far and no further.

He felt himself so near to that unreckoned and terrible holiness but he would never be suffered to enter it and there was nowhere and nothing left that he might return to. His course had been run and he had no recourse. His case, his argument, his plea for justice, for explanation, for answer, even for bare acknowledgment of loss, would now never be heard, would never rise to the heavens but would die within him and sift downward to be silted over by the sediment of days, silenced and forever unremembered by those who would come after.

Was that mocking laughter carried down upon the swirling winds? Roiling in the thunder?

Or was it in the silences between those sounds that the mockeries were implied, so that even those eternal ridicules he was not privileged to descry and to defend himself against?

This, then, was it.

And so here the man tarried at last, defeated and stripped of any power, fixed upon this tapering promontory that jutted out over empty sky, the habitable places of all other peoples so far below but now so unreachable, and the habitation of the Maker so nearly overhead but more impassable still and more defended in its heights than are the unseen aeries of eagles, than are the storehouses of the lightning and the hail.

Here is what it means then to see the shape of what will never be, to reach the end of a thing before the completion of it, to witness, after a lifetime at war, oneself vanquished and to know in that moment of final defeat that there had never been a chance it might have ended any other way, that one's defeat had been written before the war began.

If ever a game was rigged, it was this one.

The man dropped to his knees and covered his face with his hands and for a time was engulfed in his long sorrows. His fury and his ache there mingled in a strange alchemy that formed within him a hollowed and hungry space so that he lifted his face at last to the storm above and violently rending the front of his garment he shouted up to the swirling storm.

So is this it then?

And then, after a moment, he bowed his head and shook it in disbelief and turned away and then he pushed himself to stand again and

walked to the tip of the promontory and raised his arms outward like
some eagle preparing for flight.

What else might a man do, when he has sought audience with his
Maker and has been denied and has prepared his righteous accusations
and has been prevented from bringing them?

What else might a man do when cast upon a high mezzanine fixed
between earth and heaven with no way to reach the one or to return
to the other?

Is this not in a way like the place all people dwell, whether they
know it or not?

He did not consider the morality of his action for he no longer
believed he was making a choice. It seemed to him rather that all other
paths of life had been closed to him, and this one act alone remained
and was perhaps even now expected of him.

There where winds swept that naked rock and thunders shook the
very stones, he shut his eyes and breathed deep and releasing all claim
on life he resolved himself and made ready to tip into the arms of
gravity. But just as he inclined his balance forward towards that great
gulf, his ear caught a distant note that he had heard but once before
in his years, and it was far off and piercing and sweet and lamentable
and eternal so that he started backwards and gripped the rock to stay
himself and he opened his eyes upon that precipice to search out the
source of that sound.

Far to the east the cry rushed together and took form, first as a
grey speck wending upward into his vision and then moments later as a
bright and winged thing whose feathers gathered and replied the light
that streamed golden from the low, western sun.

The great bird coursed towards the man on unseen highways of air
and behind it, round the rim of the world, rode green and gold and
warmth in wondrous and holy transformation. Ice melted and storm

dissolved, and curving over that distant landscape now sailed the visible approach of spring.

It was the Lone Fendril crying its glad, eternal circuit round the earth.

For a moment the man forgot his despair.

For a moment he forgot himself entirely.

Such is the power of beauty in its wildest exultations.

But even this glad invitation to gladness the man could not long abide, and its spell wore quickly thin, for how could such a thing ever be reconciled to his own devastations? He pulled himself from the stupor of it, and remembered his grievance.

For what place had joyous beauty in a world without justice, without mercy?

In a world whose Maker gave no answer?

In such a world all beauty must be a lie, however glorious its deceptions.

And if it were a lie, the man would have none of it.

He peered over his shoulder at the unapproachable mystery of the storm-shrouded summit as if calling it to witness his intentions and then he turned again to mark the Fendril's flight, for his hands had already plighted what they must do and had begun to move in preparation, reaching for the spear hung at his back even before his heart had divined and named its own dark intent.

The man sensed more than understood that the great bird sailed a singular course of sky that must carry it past the forbidden peak of the One Mountain for he reckoned the creature a fixed sign and an emissary and in some way a seal of the designs of that One who had in some secret council decreed the man's own utter ruin, and who had now hemmed him to this place without passage, without future, without hope.

And so his grief and confusion and suffering and anger were sharpened to a fine point and were focused into a rage that burned against the Maker and so by proxy against that Lone Fendril and the beauty of that Lone Fendril that converged from that limitless expanse of sky.

Hefting the daggered spear in his right hand he stood and he waited for that one moment to arrive which he now saw rushing towards him as if from the beginning of his days.

The Lone Fendril did not waver but soared onward towards the mountain even as the sun stepped slowly down the staircase of sky and the distance between the man and the great bird closed and closed and closed and then it was all but upon him.

The mighty creature was a marvelous wonder in the azure shimmering of its long, trailing feathers that now broke sunlight into a radiant resplendence of dazzling colors and in the mighty span of its magnificent wings stretched across clouds in exultation.

No person had ever seen it so near as this, so none had ever reckoned its true size, but the man knew it now as the largest of creatures in sky above or sea below, larger even than dragons of the deep.

The Lone Fendril was still wilds above the man as it swept towards the hidden peak, and in its appointed round seemed as oblivious to the man's presence as ever the Maker had been.

Tensing his muscles the man started forward five steps to the utter edge of the jut. He timed his throw and flinging his spear upwards at the sacred bird he loosed a rending cry that he intended as defiance but that erupted from his gut and throat sounding somehow more like the wailing of a lost child.

He watched the shafted blade rise in its poetic ascent and he knew even as it left his hand that such a feat was beyond him, was beyond all mortal strength. The gulf of sky between the man and the bird marked a span that might have been achieved only by the heroes of legend who were said to be half man and half monster or half divine. He knew that his strength alone would not deliver the spear a quarter of the distance to its mark, but he hardly lamented this now, for the act itself was his clear and final word to the Maker.

The flinging of the blade was his last declaration, and when it arced and turned and fell, so would the man take one small step in his final defiance, following the spear to earth, and by his own death upon those distant plains so pronounce judgment that he had weighed and found wanting this Maker's world, this Maker's ways.

But the spear did not fall.

As that silvered blade rose, the bird tilted its resplendent head ever so slightly, folded its great wings to its shimmering body and dove like a fall of lightning towards the oncoming spear, and thus that impossible distance was closed against all reason.

As the projectile reached its zenith to hang there a moment balanced between intent and gravity, the gloried bird there met itself to the malice of the man, colliding with and taking the spear into its own breast and screaming then with a great and deafening cry that was neither avian nor human but that seemed to draw in and envelop the man's own rage and anguish and then to release it outwards, and as it did thunder cracked and lighting coursed from mountain to cloud and the mountain itself shuddered and the warm winds that either drove or followed the Lone Fendril arrived with a force that struck the man full on, knocking him backwards and tearing the horned hat from his head and carrying it into the line of dark trees where the promontory met the higher cliffs and rippling and whipping his wild hair and beard so that his cheek and chin felt the small, sharp pains of it even as the wounded creature now tumbled downwards as if in unhinged dreams to the rocky promontory and swept horribly in, piling to a heap and a half crash, clinging briefly to that edge of rock.

The man drew back from what seemed now a terrible vision and cried out without knowing it, for the beauty of the bird was a sign in itself, and the glory of the bird was as awful as the splendor of kings.

The massive wings beat three times, thrumming against the sky as the great talons clawed for purchase upon that perch of stone and found none. Even as the creature struggled its great open eye was fixed

woefully upon the man so that he could not escape that sad and pen-
etrating gaze. And then with a groaning exhale the giant body shuddered and the Fendril fell suddenly still, the wings going lax, and the
pierced creature slipped from its tenuous hold and plummeted away
from the rocky promontory leaving the man both astonished and alone.

He flung himself forward to the cragged edge and witnessed in
some awful unfolding dread the long and broken spiral of the lan-

guishing Fendril, and he could see the bright and anguished eye of
it still marking him as it spun downwards wobbling in its limp gyra-
tions like an unspoked wheel until it had swept so far into the reaches
below him that he could discern its form no longer, and even then he
strained his own bleared eyes to find it again for he was too stunned,
too disbelieving to move then, to speak, even to breathe, and he knew
the sudden torment of one who has destroyed worlds that cannot now
be remade.

At their edges his eyes took in the vast circle of the horizon, how
before him to the east was a new greening of the lands, and behind
him still rested the white stillness of winter, and below him where the
beautiful creature had plunged by his hand to its ruin there had halted
now a fixed and unmoving boundary between the two, as if warring
armies had drawn up their lines, or as if the world were halved like a
clever toy a child has cracked open and spoiled in his eagerness to view
its inner workings.

And all the while the man could not accept what his own eyes had
seen.

Nor fathom what his own heart had intended.

Nor undo what his own hand had done.

He was as one who wakes from a dream too late and sees that
the sun has already set and the day is gone. Or as sailors stormblown
to strange waters where phantom constellations wheel arcane skies
without bearing.

Events having exceeded all categories.

Had the Lone Fendril coursed high over his head, taking no notice
of him, the man would afterwards have shaken his fist at its passing
and then stepped from this life coddling the flames of a fury he would
have held to the last moment as righteous and justified.

Or had it rather swerved down from its course to meet his blas-
phemous defiance with violence, had it seized the impudent man in its

massive talons, sweeping him from the promontory, bearing him aloft to heights more dizzying still and then releasing him to be plummeted and dashed against the rocks far below, then he would have thrilled across that long plunge to the dark satisfaction that he had finally rankled the ire of the Maker, had forced his hand at last, had drawn his attention and provoked his wrath by throwing in his face righteous accusations that he could not answer.

But the Fendril had done neither of these things.

And what it had done and what the doing of it might mean, he did not know.

Only this did he know with some final certainty:

That his right to speak had died with the bird upon the point of his own spear.

For he had transgressed both law and beauty.

And had been left with only sorrow and mystery.

A heart, it turns out, could be fanged though the body might still appear whole.

And he saw now that he had in his own way been singing the fanging song all along.

That night the man sat long in the horror of his own company, peering out into the windswept darkness and the void, and when he finally curled upon the rocks in his sorrows he slept as those shipwrecked upon moonlit islands haunted by the spirits of forgotten tribes and he dreamed finally of fire rising from the distant meadow, a great and roaring burn that was somehow alive and that flamed outwards and then coursed upwards enveloping and swirling past him and away to the west leaving behind it a conflagrant trail like the green and luminous tail of a coursing meteor angling over the shadowed and endless stretches of open country.

When he woke in that heart of night, he sensed that there was a small stirring of some undefined and alien hope that had not been there before, and he peered down from the promontory and saw no more reflection of light from stormclouds or snowfields below to the west and he wondered at the change and the portent of it and he wondered if the line of spring had simply traveled on again without its constant herald.

Crawling to the edge of the outcrop and blinking against the warm and swirling wind, he traced the line of promontory pointing east as if in sign, and he allowed his eyes to be drawn out along it so that below the line of stars he saw on the easternmost rim of horizon a tiny point of light that at first seemed an unknown star but that did not rise to wheel and turn with the other celestial displays. This he pondered for some time and determined finally that it was surely fixed to the earth and was in fact a blazing conflagration of fire viewed over a great distance, and he could not then unburden himself of a vague sense of unease.

He waited upon that high edge of nothingness until dawn emerged in the east and he calculated and considered the topography and the journey that had brought him there and the dawning of a cognition of a thing he did not want to know worked its way upwards from inarticulate instinct to unwelcome suspicion and finally to a dread certainty.

Where the pinprick of light had danced on the curve of distant horizon, the man now saw in that almost infinite distance a thin and almost imperceptible blackness that he squinted long at until he knew that it could only be smoke.

Ah, his heart. His heart.

The mind could not have known with certainty, for at that distance it could have yet been anything.

But his heart already knew the one thing it was.

That dark and distant smoke was rising from a reburning of that same settlement he had encountered already in ruins.

For what else lay in the middle of that wilderness that might be consumed in such great but limited conflagration save that standing cabin and the ruins of those other dwellings already fallen round it.

The girl.
The boy.
The old man.
The boy.
The girl.
The girl.

He thought of the girlchild and he rubbed his eyes and watched the rising of that tiny smudge against that impossible horizon and at last he bowed himself to the burden of it because he saw that it was also a burden of his own making.

What could he do now but attempt a downward climb, though he believed it impossible to negotiate those sheer walls when he could not even see where to place his feet beneath him?

And yet he must try.

The man searched for his brimmed hat amongst the line of black trees at the base of the obsidian cliffs and found it snagged in the tangled lower branches.

He must try.

If he died, so be it.

But if he died, he would die with his hat on.

He studied the smooth, dark wood of the trees a moment and realized it was the same wood from which that ancestral carving had been hewn, the wood that the antiquities dealer had called *gloamshadow*.

He ran his hand over the smooth trunk and branches and he found what might have been an old scarring of initials carved there.

Someone had been here before.

Hundreds of years past.

Someone had been here and had returned from this place to the living world.

But how?

He scoured the base of cliff behind the gloamshadows where the promontory met the sheer rise, but found nothing hidden there, no covered passage or secret keyhole in the rock.

He had ascended to the promontory on its southern side, and so he knew with certainty there was nothing there.

That left only the portion of the mountain's face that lay on the northern side of the outcropping unexplored. The man lay down upon that edge of the rock and leaned his shoulders and arms forward, looking and feeling for anything that might be hidden there.

All he could observe was that the face of the rock just beyond his reach rounded away from him so that he could not know for certain what lay beyond it. To all appearances though, there was only the curving face of the sheer stone.

He walked to the tip of the promontory and stood, only this time he faced the mountain and gave it long consideration.

And making his decision at last he ran the length of the promontory and then leapt from the righthand edge over that chasmal emptiness towards the blind curve of wall, and passing beyond it saw that his desperate guess had been correct, and that the curve indeed masked an edge, and that there was carved here as well a concealed staircase and he dropped twice the height of a man into the well of it and sat for a moment as his heart pounded and surged and his knee pulsed with the pain of a wrenched landing.

He saw that the staircase continued both up and down from here, and he paused a long moment, viewing the way to the very summit he had once sworn dire oath to achieve.

But that was before the Fendril.

How could he ever approach the Maker now?

And so he turned and chose the downward path, and he gathered strength to himself as he descended limping towards the meadow where the horse yet waited and neighed in welcome when it finally saw him clamber over the lip of the hidden staircase and drop to the meadow some two hours later.

In the midst of that meadow the grass had been burned and there was a great pile of ash that the winds now billowed, lifting layers and flinging them outwards and the man approached the burn slowly and fell to his knees when he saw the blued silver of his daggered spear half-augered into the earth though the shaft of it had burned up in some intense conflagration. At first he thought to retrieve his blade and then he thought better of it and did not set foot in that circle, but taking a pittance of the ash from the near edge he took it to one of the spring pools where he knelt and mixed it to a paste in his palm and painted lines with it upon the backs of his own hands and upon his forehead, and upon the forehead of the horse, and then he rose and ate of the fruit that was there and plucked more for the journey and then he saddled the horse again and led it to the stairs and the horse seemed reluctant to go and tossed its head many times back towards the meadow as if to persuade the man to return and when he also glanced wistfully back he saw blown against the rocks one of the brilliant tail feathers of the Lone Fendril and it was five times the height of a man so he gathered it up reverently, coiling it like a rope, and he thrust it inside his shirt.

Neither horse nor man afterward required food or drink or rest but raced at a gallop three hard days and nights eastward somehow sustained by the pooled waters and the golden fruit that both had consumed in the meadow of the One Mountain.

On the first day of that journey they paused a moment at the edge of the plateau to find the trailhead down, and rode on from there, and did not stop again as the fires of heaven and the days and nights, the clouds and the winds and the woodlands passed over or beyond or beneath them, as if man and beast remained stationary, and the horse's hooves were the spinning gear that turned the world westward beneath it and cranked the sky overhead.

When they reached the village ruins on the third day, a light rain had dampened the forest and fields and only small, sheltered pockets of crumbled coals still smoldered here and there, sending up tailing wisps from that twice-burned fuel.

The horse shied from the smell of the place and the man spoke gently to it and encouraged it forward again.

The one cabin was now a reduction of charred log and blackened stone and within the wreck of it the man thought he glimpsed a grimed color of the cloak of the old outlander and this grim discovery did not bode particularly well for the girl and the boy.

When he had earlier met the old gypsy he had viewed his unintelligible demands only as an irritation, but now he paused to consider who was this man who had taken on a task that he knew was beyond him, simply because there were no others left alive who could do so. Was that not a courage worthy of a song, even if resident in one too feeble to win whatever battles courage had required? Beneath these blackened ruins rested perhaps a better man than himself. He accepted this truth now without bitterness and removed his hat and paid his respects.

The man called then for the children and receiving no answer he kicked through the collapse for any sign of them but did not find it, and so he rode on to the woods and dismounted and entered it.

The signs of human passage were obvious and it was not long before he found the red-haired boy sweating and shivering in a crude lean-to, his eyes closed and his left arm bent unnaturally from the shoulder.

"Boy."

The kid tossed his head and mumbled something.

"Boy!"

The eyes opened, then widened. Pale, freckled cheeks pinched into a pained grin.

"You come back!"

"How about that shoulder."

"It hurts."

"I bet it does." The man gently unbuttoned the boy's shirt and drew it back over the discolored and swollen shoulder. "You been stove up like this for the last three days?"

"Yessir. I guess. I don't know how long. I keep fading." The man prodded the injury and the boy winced and gritted his teeth and tried not to cry but tears slipped the corners of his eyes.

The man had seen similar injuries on his family farm and also amongst the miners of Bylome. "Well, the good news is it ain't broken, it's just all outta joint."

"The good news is I took care of the lizard that done this to me." The boy pointed to the old man's ax, laid on the ground beside him.

"Good boy. I need you to hold real still and just let your muscles all go limp now. Can you do that?"

The boy drew in another shuddered breath and nodded.

"Right. You see that big limb yonder? The low 'un?"

"Yessir."

"I'm about to carry you there and drape you over that thing belly down like a fat cat and you're just gonna let that arm dangle while I gently pull it back into place. You understand?"

The boy nodded and the man did as he had said.

"Now just close your eyes and turn your head the other way. No, other way. Away from the shoulder."

The boy sobbed but did as he was told. "That hurts like fire!"

"An arm outta joint ain't so bad if you get it fixed right away," the man told him. "But this has set up for a couple days. I'm sorry it hurts like it does but there ain't no help for it."

"It hurts more'n a bite from a toothy cow!"

"So you'd have me believe you been bit by one of them, have you?"

"No, but I bet it wouldn't hurt no more than this."

The man laughed, but there was no humor in it for his thoughts were elsewhere, fixed on the thing he had to know but knew he did not yet want to know.

"So tell me all what happened here since I left."

The man gripped the boy's bony freckled wrist and began to pull gently on the arm. He steadily increased the tension.

"Ow."

"Just dangle it. Don't go tight."

"I know you told us to stay out here in the woods—Ow!—but we got hit by that blizzard and it got so intolerable cold we was freezing to death out here. My little cousin was all shivered like a icicle and we couldn't keep the fire goin' cuz the snow kept dumpin' on it out of the trees so we went back. Me and the old man was afraid she'd lose her fingers and her toes if we stayed. I'm sorry."

"Nothing for you to be sorry about, son. It was me that was wrong. I shoulda stayed put here like the old man asked me to. You did what you had to. You was just pressed between a fire and a flood."

The boy looked surprised at first but then seemed to accept the man's assessment.

"One of 'em come up on me, see. I come back out here the next day cuz we needed wood to burn and we'd forgot the ax the night before. I didn't know nothin' about what was going on till I heard a bunch of shouting and my cousin screamed all like . . . well, you probly know how little girls can scream. Anyway I run to the edge of the wood and saw they'd lit the place on fire and the Fangs was running all around and . . ."

Here the boy stopped speaking and his eyes welled with tears.

The man placed a hand on the boy's head. "It's all right."

"It ain't all right. They took her! I saw 'em ride off with my baby cousin and I ran to find the old man but they'd already . . . they'd already knocked him down. There was too many of 'em. They had their spears and clubs and there wasn't nothin' I could do. She was all I had left and I was supposed to watch out for her!" The boy closed his eyes and wept hard and the man kept working on the arm and tried to quell his own fears and stay calm for the boy.

"Here we go. I think she's about to pop back in any minute now. We just had to get those muscles stretched out again. So what happened to your arm? You still ain't told me that part."

The boy heaved a breath and slung snot from his nose and his sobs subsided.

"That happened the next day. I was hiding out here and I had lit a fire for the cold and then I heard someone kinda like creeping up through the woods."

"A Fang?"

The boy furrowed his brow. "Yessir, kind of."

"What's that mean?"

"Well it weren't green and it didn't have a tail. It had this awful dark lumpy skin with orange marks on it. It was—ow!—it was a sight but I sure didn't wanna see it."

The man had stopped the boy's treatment without realizing it. A moment later he resumed his work. "Was this Fang by any odd chance wearing boots?"

"Yessir. You seen that kind before?"

"I'm not sure it's a kind. It might just be the one. So it come after you?"

"Well, not exactly. It just stared at me a long time like it didn't know what it wanted to do, and then it made a . . . it waved its hand at its mouth like it wanted something to eat. Can you believe that? They come in and burn Dubble's Stead for the second time and take my cousin and then that one has the nerve to come back and ask me for some of my food? I was about as flat-footed as I ever been. And it had some kinda letters carved on its skin too."

"What did they say?"

"I don't know. I can't read."

"Did you give it any?"

"Any what?"

"Food?"

"I acted like I was. I told it to wait, and then I come in here and I took the ax. While that Fang was turned to the fire getting warm I snuck up behind it and whacked it pretty good on the side of the back. It hollered and it caught me and thowed me on the ground and grabbed my arm and dragged me and that's what done this cuz I twisted back over while he still had a holt of me and I gashed him again on the back of his leg so he dropped me and limped off a howlin' and a growlin' with his leg kinda flopping where I'd cut him—HEY! How'd you do that?"

The rounded end of the arm bone had popped back into the socket of the shoulder and the boy gently tested it, then sat up on the limb. "Well that sure feels finer!"

"So they took her then. The girl. Your cousin."

The boy's countenance went cloudy and he looked like he might cry again.

"It's not your fault, son." The man lifted him from the limb and held him for a long moment as the boy wept. "None of this is your fault. You understand?"

The boy nodded and leaned back and wiped his nose on his sleeve and the man set him down.

"Good. Now let's talk man to man. I'm about to leave here and go after her."

For the first time the boy's expression turned hopeful. "Are you gonna kill all them Fangs?"

"I'm gonna do what I have to to try and get her back. I don't know yet what that's gonna look like. But right now, we need to talk about what you're gonna do."

"Well I'm gonna go with you! I got that ax."

"I admire your spunk. But I need to ride fast and your arm won't be useful for a few days yet."

"Well I don't wanna stay out here anymore."

"I understand, but all I'm asking is for you to wait here for about a week."

"Wait for what?"

"Wait for me to get back. If I don't make it back in one week with or without your cousin, you pack up whatever nuts and berries and anything else you got and you start walking towards the sunrise. You get up and you walk every day. You understand me?"

"Yessir. But where am I trying to get to?"

"You follow the sunrise you'll eventually hit the ocean. But before you do you'll likely run into people. If you come across a path or a road or a river that runs east, you follow that long enough and it'll surely take you into a city or a town."

"But ain't it all Fangs there?"

"There are some Fangs in the towns but they don't just go around murdering like this bunch out here. Mostly in the towns it's people. You can't just stay out here all alone. There's still good people left in some of those places. You need to find a family who'll take you in or a tradesman you can apprentice to who'll learn you a trade and while you're waiting to be grown up you just learn to lay low and not attract any attention till you're old enough to make it on your own."

"I can make it on my own now."

"It's not a life for you out here by yourself. Now which way did they take the girl when they left here?"

The boy pointed south and west. "They took some old wagon wheels we had and built some kind of a cart before they left here. I was watching from the woods. They put my cousin in it and tied sticks around it like a cage."

"Did they have a mule or something to draw it?"

"No sir, not that I saw. They strung a couple ropes to the front and they was a pushing and a pulling it themselves."

"Well, they'll be leaving ruts then. That should make them easier to find. I'll head off that way and start cutting for sign."

Before the man stood he took the boy's face in his hands.

"What you did when you fought that Fang was nothing but brave. Braver than most anything I ever done."

The boy stared at the hardened and grizzled warrior who gripped his chin and hair, and his face bore a doubtful expression.

"You keep that fight in your heart and one day, when the time is right, I believe Skree will be free again."

"You really think it could happen?"

"I have it on good authority. The prince of the Shining Isle has survived and he's out there waiting for the right moment to take back his throne. With boys like you about to become men? I don't see how Gnag has a chance."

The boy's slight chin dropped so that his mouth hung open. "Durn," he said, and then after a moment of silence, "You think I could find him? That prince, I mean. You think he'd take me on as a Fang fighter?"

"I think he'd be lucky to have you."

The man kissed the top of the boy's head, swung up into the saddle and then reconsidered something. He reached into the saddlebag at his right leg, drew out three of the last four golden fruits from the meadow of the One Mountain, and set them in the boy's hands.

"You can eat one now. I suspect it'll help you heal. If I don't come back, you eat another one directly before you start walking east and then you can eat the last one whenever you need it most. These are powerful. They'll keep you going for a long time."

"And if you do come back?"

"You can eat 'em anyway. I'm giving 'em to you."

The man reined the horse around then and raced through the woods and out and past the overthrown village and turned then south-west and did not even slow to scan for sign of the loathsome spawn because he saw that the sign was everywhere.

Considering themselves invulnerable in this unpopulated domain, the twisted creatures had given no thought to the possibility of hostile pursuit, and so they had trooped the wilderness careless of their tram-pling and of the conspicuous witness of their rutted wagon tracks, and further on, of the sullied lingering evidences of their rude encamp-ments.

The man encountered such evidence of Fang passage almost hourly, even from that first day, and because they would travel on foot, he knew that he must be gaining on them, though where they would be taking the girl he did not know.

He hoped only that their purpose involved keeping her alive.

He located the remains of one of their camps under the overhang of a low cliff and guessed from the signs that there were something like a dozen of them but perhaps as many as twenty. The contents of their shallow and filthy latrine pit had not yet been washed away by rains. He scoured the ground till he found in the mud amongst grasses at the edge of the camp the toe prints of the little girl, and he sat for a long time then and breathed a temporary relief.

He spurred the horse on and rode hard for two more days, stopping only often enough for the mount to crop grasses and sleep a stretch while the man mostly lay awake staring at the cold stars and the play of heat lightning in the clouds, sometimes drifting off lightly and dozing for an hour or two and once he even managed to bag a brace of sleeping flabbits with the flat face of his hammer.

Four nights out he witnessed the fire of the Fang camp far off amongst the loneliness of the low sweeping hills and plains, and when the wind carried it towards him he briefly heard upon it the faint and cackling sound of their voices, or something that in those wide and desolate places he could at least imagine were their voices.

He resaddled the horse in the third watch of night and began his long approach, guessing the marauders now but a day's march ahead of him and anxious for the whole matter to be settled.

V.

A Late Remembrance of Things to Come

"I remember you now," he said,
for the spell had broken at last.
And as the waters rose he pressed her hand to his heart
that they might never be parted again,
and he told her
"You were once my everything."
                                        —"The Bright Woe of Hadrell & Simi"

When the man came upon the straggler the next morning, the sun was just rising behind him. He spurred his mount forward so that their long conjoined shadow overtook the limping Fang upon the plain several minutes before the horse and man did, their dark adumbration overreaching him like some herald of doom.

He saw the booted Fang turn and shield its eyes against the light, the venomous curve of the teeth visible in the red gleam of sun from a half a league's distance. The twitching monster increased its speed to a jittering limp, and the rising light glinted from its dark, beaded skin.

And how have you now come to be out here alone? the man thought. *And the two of us to be met again in this life?*

The creature veered from the trampled path his fellow troops had taken over the sloping grassland, as if such misdirection might throw the horned rider from his trail.

A small, cracking squeal sounded from its throat.

As the man bore down upon the hideous lizard he could hear the thing snuffling, wheezing, gasping. The grotesque left leg of the thing flounced all but uselessly as it dragged itself through the windblown terrain.

"No!" it shouted at the last, wheeling on him and raising its spear. "Don't hurt! Don't hurt!"

With an easy backhanded swing of his heavy hammer the man dislodged the spear from the craven Fang's grip so that it fell to the side and sifted into the tall grass and then the man saw the animal terror rising to crescendo in the eye of the beast.

He had known it from the first sight as the same creature that had desecrated his home and taken his child and he suppressed the instinct simply to kill it.

It wore now a scar that ran diagonal above and below its left eye, and that same eye was a milky white clouded by blindness of some injury.

But it was the same Fang.

These years later. These hundreds of miles distant. It was the same that had ushered his ruin.

"Mustn't kill!"

The creature cowered, putting its claws up in front of its face in a gesture like that of a frightened child. In a gesture much as his own daughter had once made in a child's effort to ward this very Fang.

The man saw also that the boy's observation had been accurate. Words had been carved by knife or claw into the skull and arms and back of the beast and were fixed there now, permanent as welted scars.

Coward. Fool. Worm.

The thing remained in its shielded crouch and winced anytime the horse moved and the man realized suddenly that it did not recognize him in his changed form and wild attire.

"Why are you out here? Why did they leave you?"

The Fang cocked its head like a pup and shielded its eye from the glaring wash of sunrise light that spilled past the man.

"They?"

"The other Fangs." The man leaned and spit. His loathing was almost a palpable thing that could be tasted and smelled.

The pitiful creature looked away towards the horizon, as if it hoped to see that help was on the way, but those grasslands were devoid of any other movement.

"Were you abandoned?"

The thing puckered its mouth, pinching its bottom lip with its sharp fangs and making a pitiful sucking noise as it breathed in.

The man stepped the horse towards it and raised his hammer. "Answer me!"

"They treasons me!" it shouted.

"Who?"

"The others! They comes out here with me and then leaves me all alone."

"Why are you out here at all?"

When the thing flitted a look at him, he read the enmity and disgust that flashed briefly in its one good beaded eye, before those emotions crumbled again to fear and the creature sucked at its lip again.

"Tell me why you have traveled out here beyond the maps at all." He shifted the grip of his hammer to hold it in both hands and this menacing gesture was not lost on the Fang.

"Because they say I don't fight back when I oughts!"

"And when was that?"

The Fang shielded its eye and studied the man silently, horns and beard and bomnubble coat.

"I said when was that?"

"When some awful man cuts off my pretty tail!"

The man instinctively backed the horse a step so that the blinding sun would fall fully in the Fang's eye and then he drew the brim of his hat lower over his own.

"So you were sent here to be punished?"

"Not punished! No! Khrak orders me find that man and kill him and bring back his hands and ears and tongue, or if I don't he says to stay and die out here in these awful places." The beast dug a claw thoughtfully round the inside of its nostril and flicked something away, then looked wistfully after it. "Too many questions! I don't want to talk to you!"

The Fang fell to a pitiful weeping then, such as the man had never witnessed from a Fang. Thick, oily brown tear secretions squirted from its eye and it hid its face behind its claws.

"And this man who cut off your tail. Where is he now?"

"What?" It peered through its fingers and seemed annoyed that the man was still there.

"The man who cut off your tail. Did you ever find him?"

"Gone! Gone! He is no one! He is a ghost! I tracks him for weeks and months and my tail stump swells and hurts me awful. Up the river. Up the river he goes and then he is gone. Vanished away! If we go back Khrak will kill us for not catching the awful man. For not showing the people Fangs cannot be murdered and their tails cut off and got away with. But the man poofs away and so we has to stay here in these nasty places so the others say it's my fault and pokes my poor eye out and cuts awful words on me. They pokes me and cuts me!"

The Fang burst to sobs again and the man looked up wondering if the sound would carry and bring trouble upon him before he was ready, but he saw no movement or sign of the other Fangs.

"They won't sits with me or eats with me," the weeping creature continued, sounding like a child eager to spill its woes to any listening ear, "because they hates me and I haven't got a pretty tail. They starves me and beats me and sends me away and when I asks nicely for a nice bite of flabbit a wretched boy hacks at my leg so I falls further and further behind. Alone! Alone!"

The thing buried its face in the crook of its arm and the man determined he had likely gleaned all of the information from the miserable creature that he was likely to get for the moment.

"Join your hands behind your back."

The man dismounted and with cords of leather bound together the wrists and the shins of the languishing creature, noting that the ax wound at the back of its knee was swollen and oozing pus. He did not want it to die yet for he believed he would yet have use for it, so he washed out and salted the deep cut and then wrapped it with a strip of leather though he was loathe to touch that unnatural skin at all and throughout the procedure the Fang winced and cried out repeatedly that it was being murdered.

The man rolled the beast onto its back and gave it a hip joint of raw flabbit which it chewed voraciously and swallowed with a slurping noise the man was revolted to hear.

"If you don't cause a fuss, you'll get more when we stop later," he said and then he secured its long jaws with a rope cinched round its muzzle. He lifted and threw the miserable thing across the pommel of the saddle and then found its spear in the tall grass and swung himself up to the saddle and they rode that way for several hours, the creature grunting all the while in jostled discomfort and sometimes squirting the oily tears that stained the horse's shoulder. They made steady progress, resting only in the high heat of the day beneath a spreading shade tree with silvery leaves that swayed in the wind and that seemed to captivate the Fang as if he were an infant staring at some spinning trifle fixed over his crib.

The man unmuzzled the creature and poured water from his hat into its mouth upturned and opened like a baby bird, and he tried not to show his disgust at the fetid breath, damp and foul, and at the chunks of food that rotted between decaying molars.

The thing whipped its wet tongue round the rim of its mouth and coiled it round the base of a long fang.

"There was a girl," the man said.

"Who?"

"A girl. You burned a settlement a few days ago and took a girl."

"No! Not me! I doesn't take anybody!"

"Never?"

"What?"

"Never? You've never taken a child?" The man gripped the handle of his hammer.

The Fang started to respond, then fell silent and sucked its lip nervously again and the man took note that while it did not answer, it also did not try in this instance to lie.

"Why did they take the girl?"

"Who?"

"The Fangs."

"What Fangs?"

"The ones you were with. Are you an idiot?"

The Fang creased its beaded brow and the carved letters there curved fancifully. "If you calls us names I doesn't answer."

"Why did the other Fangs take the child?"

The Fang was quiet a moment before drooping its shoulders. "They were scared."

"What do you mean?"

"The cry! Didn't you hear it? The cry from the sky that shakes us to our bones. It comes from the mountain far away but we still hears it and we hates it! The ground shivers. The Fendril falls. Far away but we sees it. We sees it somehow. And then the green fire rises from the mountain in the night and whooshes up and away. More strangeness. We don't likes how it makes us feel. Maybe the end of the world, we say. Maybe better to go home. But we can't, they say. Because Beadsy never found the man! Then one of them says what if we leaves Beadsy here and says he died? And another one says what if we collects brats? What if we brings a cart of brats back to Khrak? Maybe then we leaves this nasty wilderness and Khrak takes us back and doesn't hang us for Beadsy's fault!"

"So they abandoned you then, and they returned to the settlement and found the girl?"

"They say I loses the man and so I can't ever go back."

The man turned his head and saw that the Fang was studying him intently now, and for a moment the man wondered if recognition were dawning, but then it asked, "Are you a man or are you something else?"

And the man tossed it another joint of raw flabbit and replied, "I am nothing anymore but a kind of ghost," and the Fang studied him a moment longer and then turned its full attention to the devouring of the flabbit.

They remounted and followed the cart trail of the Fangs till darkness fell round them and then they stopped and the man leaned the captive Fang against a tree and bound it against the trunk for the night. He removed its muzzle and then he gave it water and built a small fire and the two of them stared distantly into the curling blue-tipped flames without speaking while the constellations burned in the clear expanse and the man finally began to nod and then he found himself suddenly alert and listening to a hissed and rhythmic whisper.

Flicker fire, flicker flame,
Pot grow hot and stew is made.
Little baby, warm as wool,
Sleep abed with tummy full.

The man half-opened his eyes but did not move.

The Fang, unaware of him, stared drowsily into the fire, its eyelids heavy, but its mouth moving in whispers.

Goodnight kitten, goodnight bed,
Goodnight pillow, here's my head!

The man leaned up and the Fang's eye jolted and followed his sudden movement, breaking from some distant and stupored mooring.

"What were you just saying?" the man asked.

"Nothing."

"You were speaking a rhyme. Some sort of a child's verse."

"No. Was sleeping. Don't know any child rhymes. Fangs don't rhyme."

The man considered the creature for a long time, turning in his head remembrances of the bard's strange suspicions and then of the old outlander's narrative of how the twisted creatures came to be.

"You are repulsed by what other Fangs eat and drink, yes?"

"I has particular tastes."

"Yes, but does something like eel squeeze makes you queasy?"

The Fang crinkled its brow.

"And you weep, but other Fangs do not. You have a different skin. You wear boots. What Fang wears boots? And just now, you were speaking rhymes as if to a baby."

"I don't! I just hiss in my sleeps and it sounds like rhymes."

"Why do you wear boots?"

"I like boots."

"What do your boots conceal?"

He saw the creature's eye go wide in the firelight. Something like panic. Then it closed it tight. "I'm sleeping now! Done talking!"

"Your boots. What do you hide within them?"

"No hiding! Nothing! Like boots! Like to wear!"

The creature squinted to see if the man was still watching and the man held a grim, unblinking stare until it squeezed its eye shut again.

The man stood then and went to the cowering creature and knelt and seizing a boot began to unstrap it even as the Fang dissolved into chokes and frenzied sobs, drawing up its legs and trying to kick at the man with its bound feet.

"NO! Mustn't undo! NO! NO! NO! Like to keep boots ON!"

When he pulled the boot away the thing had howled mournful as any dumb and dying beast and when the man had begun to unwrap the rags round the foot, the creature had twisted itself violently against the bonds that held it but could not get away, and the man had already known even before those filthy cloths came away that the foot when revealed would not be the foot of a Fang but would instead be the foot of a man.

He rocked back and tossed the rags behind him into the fire and then sat and considered the implications of the chimera writhing before him.

The creature sobbed and contorted and then opened its eye and stared at its own foot, in a sort of mute bewilderment as if it were a deformity so monstrous and surreal as to be beyond all reckoning.

As if there were no sane explanation for what was appended to its leg.

"So it's true." The man stroked his beard. "You were a man once."

"No!"

"You were a man, but something happened and made you a Fang."

"No! Always a Fang!"

"You sang a song, didn't you?"

"No! No song!"

"Was there a stone? There might have been a stone where you sang. Try to remember!"

"No! No song! No stone!" But the Fang's eye had focused distantly in the darkness as if he were seeing perhaps something that had been.

"Yet you chose not to finish the singing. At the last you resisted. Some part of you stopped short."

"No! Beadsy always a Fang!"

"Then where are you from? How old are you? Who was your mother? Do you remember your childhood as a young lizard boy? Do you remember anything beyond a few years ago?"

The thing stopped, stunned, and its jaw went slack and worked loosely against its tongue and its mouth puckered in nervous agitation.

"Do you not wonder why you have no older memories?"

"I just have the wrong remembers! Addled Beadsy. Beadsy-Weedsy. Bonked on the head! I am Fang! Fang! Fang! Fang!"

"You are almost a Fang now. But you were also a man, once. Do you really remember nothing? You were a man like me."

"You not man! You monster! Stinky! Horns! Stinky ghost!" The Fang began to weep and the sound of its weeping rose over the sweeping plains and into the night. "I am Fang! Beadsy is mean, terrible Fang!"

"You wanted that, but somewhere in your heart, what was human in you held out. I wonder is there any flicker of the man you once were still within you."

"Liar!"

"It is no lie, and you must know the truth of it every time you see your own feet."

"NO!"

"Maybe you even had children of your own once. Little babies."

"NO!" The thing struggled against its bonds.

"You would have tucked them in at night and kissed their foreheads and told them those little rhymes."

"NO!"

"And then the Fangs came."

"NO!"

"And somehow you lost what you loved and when hope was gone and nothing remained but fear you might have decided in the end to become what you feared rather than to go on fearing and remembering such horrors."

The Fang was reduced now to a slobbery blubbering, though it still protested weakly through its cries. "No! Doesn't happen! No!"

"Then where did that foot come from?"

"Beadsy will chew it off! Beadsy hates it! Chew it off and then be all Fang!"

"I wonder could you ever now unchoose what you once half-chose?" the man mused, staring into the fire and ruminating more to himself now than to the disfigured creature before him. "And if you could return home again, in your present condition, would they even know you? Would they even want you back?" Whether he was speaking now of the Fang, or of himself, or perhaps of both, he did not pause to sort out.

He looked at the Fang again. "We met once, you know, though I was also a different man."

The creature studied him, half fearful, half curious.

"It was after midnight. You forced your way into my house."

The Fang suddenly looked more frightened, eyes instinctively darting for a path of escape, though it was bound and could not have run.

"You rode the Black Carriage."

"Following orders!" it cried. "Your own fault! Not what I wanted! Don't blind its other eye! Please don't blind it forever and leave it here to die! I didn't hurt your little boy!"

"I didn't have a little boy!"

"Your big boy then? Or your girl? Was it a baby? Twins? Triplets? I didn't hurt them! Beadsy no hurt!"

"How many children did you take during your service? Was it so many that you don't even remember them all?"

"ORDERS! FANGS FOLLOW ORDERS!"

The man rose and took up the spear and, advancing upon the Fang, he pressed the tip of the blade to its throat, and holding it there with his right hand, he reached up with his left and drew the hat from his head.

"Don't kill it! Beadsy is sorry! So sorry! ORDERS! Followed orders! Didn't want to!"

"You took my baby."

"What baby? Beadsy never hurt babies! NEVER! Don't like hurting things!"

"You took my daughter, and with her my wife and my home and all that I had. You it was sent me out to wander this wilderness alone. As a beast. As a beast hardly better than yourself."

The Fang began to shake visibly now, and a long moan like the push of wind through a crack in a door rose from its gut to its throat, escaping over the tongue and hissing as it issued between the teeth.

"Never hurt the babies! Beadsy doesn't!"

"Kneel!" the man commanded and he lashed at the cord that held the Fang to the tree, severing it with the spear tip. "KNEEL!"

The Fang scrabbled and fell forward, then righted itself and balanced trembling on its knees.

"Please! Doesn't kill it! Beadsy will help find brat Fangs took!"

"Bend your face to the ground!"

The Fang still knelt, watching the man with wild eyes.

"BEND YOUR FACE TO THE GROUND!"

The Fang obeyed, whimpering.

The man set a boot on the hideous creature's back and lay the tip of the spear against its spine. "Let me hear you say it."

"Say what?"

"You were once a man like me."

"Never! Never was!"

"But you were. And you must know it. And I need to hear you say it."

"Why? Why does it torment Beadsy?"

"I need to hear you say it."

"Why does it makes Beadsy say hurtful, hateful things before it stabs him?"

"Say it." He pressed the spear harder into the creature's back.

"Beadsy was a man!"

"Louder!"

The creature was spewing venom and saliva and tears now. "BEADSY WAS A MAN!"

"Do you remember?"

"NO!"

"Yes you do. Do you remember?"

"Yes."

"What do you remember?"

"Sheep! Sunlight on sheep and sunlight on snow."

"What else?"

"It hurts me!"

"What else?"

"Things like dreams. Like dreams I don't stop having! A boy by a gate when sheep go in. A girl rolls dough and a woman who watches me and smiles when I see her. And then I look down and see my hands are claws! Not hands! CLAWS!"

"Do you remember their names?"

"NO!"

"Do you remember your own name?"

"NO!"

"Where you lived?"

"NO!"

"Anything?"

"A little blue pond pool with silver fish. A girl makes a wish. But it's all only dreams! Not real!"

"You fool! These are the few memories you still hold of what *was* real. Don't you understand? Perhaps they could even bring you back. What else have you seen?"

"A hill. A gate. Red stones stacked to be a house. . . . And one in my arms."

"A red stone?"

The creature turned its head and looked up at the man desperately, a horrified mournfulness at the remaining measure of what had been lost distorting its already monstrous features.

"A baby," it said quietly, as if this realization had only just occurred to it.

And then it dropped its head and shrieked and shuddered and wept in the dirt for all that was lost. "Little Sweets. I called it Little Sweets! Kill Beadsy now. Poor Beadsy! He can't be anything! Torn! Torn inbetweens! Why? Why did the cruel man make him remember what are always gone? Why?"

"Because I couldn't risk releasing you until I knew you could remember and yet feel something." With that, the man jerked the spear downwards and cut the cords that bound the wrists of the monster, and then jabbing further, he split the leather binding from its shins as well.

The creature scrambled away from him, to the other side of the fire, and from there crouched, looking back at him with a wounded expression.

"You let Beadsy go?"

"I have let you live. In return there is a thing you must do for me."

The miserable creature watched him and did not respond, so the man continued.

"You must carry a message for me."

"Message? Who for message?"

"For the other Fangs."

"No! Fangs leave Beadsy to die! Not want him back!"

"You can at least approach them. Surely they will still allow that."

"For why?"

"I want the child. But if I attack them unannounced, who is to say that in their panic they might not kill their prisoner? Or that she wouldn't be struck by a stray arrow? I cannot take such a chance. So I will send you ahead of me to carry my terms."

"Terms?"

"I am coming for the girl. Before I get there, you will tell them about me. You will tell them of the horror that I bring. Tell them if the girl is harmed, if she is even scratched, I will hunt down every one of them and destroy them on these open plains."

"Man can't! Too many Fangs!"

"Tell them they are to leave the girl in the wagon, in the camp. They are to lay down their weapons there, and they are to be gone before I arrive. Any that I see will die."

"They will laugh at me. There are too many!"

"There are not too many. I am mounted. They cannot catch me. And they are like ants without a queen. I will harry their heels day and night, plucking off the stragglers until there are too few left to defend themselves. They cannot be in good fighting shape. Not after so long scrounging and half-starving in the wilderness. They will never make it back to Torrboro. And if they do, they will not be accepted by Khrak as they hope. All of you have failed in your quest and all will be punished if you return. I am offering them this one opportunity to turn the girl over to me unharmed. If they do not, none of them will live to see the next full moon. This I swear to you by the sacred memory of my own daughter whom *you* took from me."

"They won't believe me! Mean Fangs beat Beadsy and cut his skin again!"

"Then you must make them believe you, you pathetic creature!" The man was losing patience. "You will tell them I am more than a man. Tell them I am the fury that rides from summit. Tell them I am bone-breaker. Fang-cracker. Monster-hunter. Tell them I wear the teeth of my enemies upon my head. Fangs are not brave. They only believe they are brave when they wield power to be cruel. Make them believe that they should fear me and they will melt away. And fear me they should!"

"They will say one man has never stood against them and no man is more than a man. Even all the men of a village could not stand against them!"

The man shook his head, uncertain of what he was about to do, uncertain as to whether it was right, or a grave, grave wrong to present what was his greatest shame as if it were a feat of glory.

"You told me before that you heard the rending cry and saw the Fendril fall?"

The Fang gave a barely perceptible nod.

The man hesitated a moment and then reached into his saddlebag and uncoiled the long and glorious tail feather of the Lone Fendril.

"And why do you suppose it fell?"

The creature did not answer but eyed the feather with a mixture of desire and disbelief as one might a rare jewel unearthed in a neighbor's yard.

"I tell you that the very seasons were halted because one ascended the One Mountain, to stand upon it, and with his spear he smote that great bird, the messenger of the heavens, and brought it down from the dome of sky, from those pathless heights. It was I who caused the Fendril's cry and the quaking of the ground. It was I who stopped for a time the seasons in their turning. So I ask you, am I but a man, after all? If I have done such a thing to the Lone Fendril, what do you think I would do to a Fang?"

The Fang stared at him, in mute fear and wonderment.

"Here." He coiled the feather again and held it out to the creature. "Take this as a token and a proof. Take it and show them and tell them the awful wonder of what I have done. Tell them I am half man and half monster, and you will be closer to the truth than you imagine. Tell them I will arrive at the dawn and will bring with me thunder and fire, and war and death are at my heels and my spear will pierce and my hammer will crush and any that hold their own lives dear would do well to leave the girl and flee and not even to dare look upon me."

The creature timidly took the feather and held it in its hideous claws and stared at it, and the man wondered if it was ashamed to see the profanity of its own beaded scales against something made of such fierce and pure beauty and light. It shrunk back, almost as if it were burned by the resplendence it held.

"Go now. Go ahead of me. You should reach their camp before morning. Walk towards that distant fire on the horizon."

"I leave?" The Fang seemed still frightened, uncertain.

"Carry my message as I have charged you, and after that, I care not what you do so long as you vanish into the hills and forests and never trouble this world again. Swear it."

"You let Beadsy go?"

"Swear it."

"I swear."

"You swear what?"

"Whatever Fendril-Smiter wants."

"That you will harm no more."

"Yes."

"That you will cease living as a Fang."

"Yes." It bobbed its reptilian skull rapidly.

"That you will deliver my message?"

"Yes."

"Swear on the memory of your Little Sweets."

"Beadsy . . . " The creature faltered.

"Not *Beadsy*. I. Say *I*. I swear."

"*I* swear."

"On what?"

"The memory?"

"Say it."

"I swear on the memory . . . " Here the creature faltered again and its face twisted into something like a snarl. "But I don't wants to say it!"

"That is exactly why you must."

The beast muttered and made several pitiful little noises and then it snarled and shouted in a rush of words, "I swear it on Little Sweets!" and then it whimpered but the whimper ended in a small snarl.

"Good. Now leave. I don't want to see you again."

"Beadsy leaves now?"

"Yes."

The creature started to skulk away, then turned back. "Why?"

"Why?"

"Why does he find Beadsy and doesn't kill Beadsy if Beadsy took his babykins?"

The man sighed and looked at the fire, and sighed again before he answered.

"Because I do not know if what was wrought in you might ever be unwrought. And if you are part a man, then to kill you now would be part a murder. And though I hate you, I also pity you. And though I despise you, I also am ruined and wrecked, though I do not show it the same in my skin. Now go. I do not know if the mercy I claim presently will sustain through all moods and thoughts."

The hunched and wondering form of the creature receded then from the circle of light and slipped into the shadows and away, and the man followed a few minutes later, followed silently for a quarter mile until he was certain the creature was on its way to do his bidding, and then he returned to the fire and sat again and did not sleep, but remained alert and considered what morning might bring. Two hours before first light he rose and poured sand over the embers of his fire and catching up his horse he saddled it and rode away with his face to the west, passing over a depression that was a wet weather creek lined with succulent plants that had unfolded wide flowers the color of butter in the moonlight and he considered whether this might be the last new wonder he would ever see.

As he rode out of that wash, he cut again the tracks of the Fangs and of the wagon cart sluicing through tall grass in long lines that curved away over the low hills and he followed it in that gray and silver light till dawn.

The man rode down a ridge from a bloodstreaked sunrise and he could see now the makeshift cage and wagon, lonely amongst the tall grasses and the low sweeps of hills dotted with rocky juts that cut like dragon's teeth from the hills. He paused and scanned for movement but saw no Fangs.

Drawing closer he could begin to see the little bob of the fair hair of the child, sitting in that prisoner cart, and also the sparkling of the Fendril feather coiled in her small hands like a circlet of emerald and indigo and azure stars, and also the dark curving lines and the glints on steel that were weapons laid upon the ground just as he had commanded.

But he could see as well the form of the dark and beaded half-Fang, which seemed to be still and kneeling before the wagon, and this was not at all as he had commanded, and he slowed his approach for a moment, wondering what it might mean.

The man digs his heels into the horse's flanks now and spurs it forward to a full gallop across that last stretch of prairie, and as he does he notes here and there, scattered distantly amongst the stones, scaly heads half raised to behold his passage. He observes their brief confusion as they shield their fulvous eyes, trying in vain to discern the manner of horned creature that thunders past, and he knows his position is now precarious, and so he does not pause.

He can see well before he reaches the abandoned camp that the beaded Fang kneels now with a rope about its neck. It hears the approaching hoofbeats and raises its head to watch him close the final distance, its one good eye blinking against the rising sun that silhouettes him.

"They beat me!" it screams. "They beat me until I showed them the feather . . ."

"Quiet!" and then "Child! I am here. You are safe."

The little girl looks slowly up from the mesmer of the Fendril feather in her hands and stares at him almost without emotion. Her fear too deep and constant now. She has retreated to a place within, and roams it as a child lost in a deep wood.

The man leaps from the horse, and taking a short sword from the surrendered arsenal of the Fangs he severs the rope that latches the cage, flings it away from the wagon, and lifts the child out. "I've got you, child. No more nightmares."

"Don't leaves me here," cries the Fang. "Others will kill me when they come back. Please! Mustn't leave Beadsy. Please!" It raises it voice to a wail.

"Silence!" The man sets the child gently on the horse, taking the feather from her and sliding it into his shirt, and then he places her hands upon the pommel, surveying the landscape as he does and noticing that several Fangs are standing now, their gazes intent upon him.

"Beadsy begs!"

"Silence, you fool!"

The man turns and with a swift hack of the sword he divides the rope that binds the Fang to the cart by its neck, and then with a rapid sawing he cuts also the cords that fetter the miserable creature's hands behind its back. "Flee while you can! Do not let me see you ever again!"

The man drops the black sword and slides the hammer from his back to have it at the ready must he run a gauntlet of enemies to deliver the girl to safety. He places his left hand upon the saddle to swing himself up behind the girl.

And it is then that he feels the bone of his rib snap, feels the thunk and the bite of the arrow that has pierced into his back.

He turns.

There wobbles the half-blind and man-footed Fang, not twenty paces from him, notching a second black arrow to a black bow he has seized from the splayed weapons.

"BEADSY IS STRONG!" the half-Fang shouts for all to hear, though the voice quivers and falters and the clawed hands tremble. "DO YOU SEE? BEADSY KILLS MAN WHO CUT OFF BEADSY'S TAIL! CAN GO HOME NOW!"

"No!" the man shakes his head. "Not this. Not like this. Let this girl go. You gave your word. You swore by your own Little Sweets."

But the Fang raises his voice to drown out the voice of the man speaking a name he does not want to hear. "Beadsy is smart! Beadsy knows who you are and doesn't tell. Ha!"

And the miserable Fang looses a second arrow that flies wide of the mark and it fumbles now to notch a third, and the man sees that his gambit has collapsed, for the other vile creatures are now showing themselves emboldened, slinking from their hiding places amongst the rocks, and he sees as well that some of them are armed with bows.

Giving scant heed to his own pain he is yet fearful for the girl lest she be struck by an arrow, errant or intended, and so he sweeps into the saddle and reins the horse round and charges directly at the beaded Fang who yelps and drops the bow and turns to run but because he has no tail to balance him, he falls, and the man raises his hammer as he nears the creature, but when he might strike he suddenly checks his rage and does not bring down that death blow.

He pulls up instead so that the horse leaps the cowering figure cleanly and as it does the man leans down and declares only, "You called her Little Sweets. Can you remember that?" and then he pulls the horse round and they go thundering back across the prairie plains, and he hears the thrum of strings as the archers on the slopes round them release a first volley and then a second and the man leans forward over the child and covers her and he feels it grim when he is struck a second time in the back and he hears afterward again the whistle of fletched shafts and ducks his head ever and ever lower, waiting for the piercing and he feels it this time in the meat of his thigh and he knows also from the sudden shift in the horse's gait and from the disconsolate whinny it gives that it too has been struck though it scarcely even slows and then it finds its pace again with speed increasing as if it would outdistance that pain.

The man glances behind and sees a dark arrow shaft buried at the base of the animal's back, just behind the saddle, and when he turns forward again he sees ahead both to his left and his right three large Fangs loping now, animal-like, towards him, their tails undulating, serpentine as they run, spears in hand, seeking to cut off his escape. They have broken off from their fellows, a vanguard flung down the slope towards him and he spurs the horse and leans and spurs it again and begs from it every reserve of speed still quartered within that belly and the horse responds, now perceiving the Fangs with its own eyes, and it leans into the race and pulls hard but even so will not be able to outpace the angles of their hostile descent so the man now in more desperate maneuver cuts the horse to charge directly for the lone Fang rushing down at them from the southern rise so that the Fang slows momentarily, confused, and then raises its spear and the man

presses the girl to the neck of the horse, closing ground, and as the Fang draws back its arm to fling the spear, the man rises in the saddle, and heaves his hammer in terrible spiral at the body of the beast, and lands a punishing strike hard in its chest, driving it backwards so that the spear sails high and errant and then the Fang must dive away before the sharp hooves of the charging horse and by the time he can roll to recover his spear the man and the girl and the horse are beyond him and his breastbone has been cracked by the hammer so that he cannot raise his arm to throw again and the pursuers descending the northern slope have been outpaced by the diverted angle of escape and so they pull up at last and give off the chase, and then the man and the horse and the child are passed beyond the gauntleted slopes and beyond the immediate danger though they yet do not slow and the man leans back and sees that the child is unharmed and he weeps at last for the relief of that and does not think yet of the portent of his own wounds.

"I will get you home," he tells her, "wherever that may be," and the girl looks up at him with eyes that scarce seem to remember anything beyond the harrowing of recent days.

The land had grown fogged or it might have been his sight that was compromised.

The man held the girl before him and rode for hours without slowing and he knew he was losing blood and must stop soon to staunch his wounds or he would pass into a delirium and the girl would be left alone and unprotected in a wilderness that would not long suffer the survival of innocents such as her.

He knew that the horse's wound also would be stiffening and must be tended and so they rode along the middle of a shallow stream for a time to throw off any pursuit and climbed up out of it only after the stream had cut its way into thick forest and there the man slumped from the horse and leaned against it a moment, steadying himself against the pain of his own wounds, and then he gently lifted the girl from the saddle and she smiled at him before he set her amongst the leaves on the forest floor.

"You still think I'm Old Woller, don't you?"

The man saw that the horse now trembled and that there was a blood flecked foam at its mouth and that it had taken a second arrow that he had not seen before that was angled in near the middle of its wide breast and he wondered that they had made it as far as they already had.

The man sat with his own wounded leg splayed in front of him, and though he longed to lay down he could not for the arrows protruding from his back and he wondered if it were not better that way, for if he lay down he did not know how likely it was that he would soon rise again and he sensed that they must not rest long. He felt his breath shallow and labored and there were several ways he could not move for the sharp pains those movements produced inside him. He groaned and then saw that the girl was studying the arrow shaft lodged in his thigh, and the wide seep of blood round it, a puzzled worry on her little face.

"It's not so bad," he told her, laboring to keep his voice steady. "I'll take it out in a little while, after I rest a minute."

He closed his eyes and tried again to find any upright position that would allow him relief, but there were none. He willed his lungs to contain the coughs that he knew would be attended by excruciating pains and for a stretch he succeeded.

"Are you hungry?" he asked the child, and she nodded, and the delicate beauty of that upturned face so pained him now that he soon looked away. Why must it be that each new generation was fated to be born swaddled in rags of a glorious hope that would never be suffered fruition in this life but would be worn down, ground away, scattered to ash well before their own life's end? Was it somehow better in a way that his own child had died young, and quickly, while she yet carried that glory unselfconsciously? What was the deeper meaning of this poem that was ever newly written in the wide faces and doe's eyes and tiny hands of babes? The girl who watched him was scathed by horror and was caked and grimed and matted and smelled of old urine and her dress was spattered about the hem with the blood either of the man or the horse, but the lustre he saw in her was no less obvious for any of that, and the contrast of the rags and the ruin of her condition somehow served to stoke his awareness of it.

He wished to give her the world, but he had no world to give.

"Can you reach up into that saddle bag? There's a piece of fruit there. Sweet. Sweet and good like you."

He watched the little girl, her small, deliberate movements as she pushed her tangled hair back from her face and stretched her arms up and grunted when she could not reach the buckle of the saddle bag.

"Here," he told her. "Hold on a minute. I'll fetch it for you," and he worked himself to his knees and then stood, pained and wheezing and he coughed for a moment like he was choking and doubled over and the outrage of those spasms screamed through organs he could not identify and when he spit several times it was mostly blood.

Standing slowly he smiled at the watching girl for he did not want her to be afraid, and he unbuckled the saddle bag and drew out the final piece of fruit and handed it to her as if she were a princess and the fruit some gift of royal garnet.

"Never forget," he told her, cupping her fingers round the pome, "however so long you live, that you ate of the fruit of the golden meadow of the One Mountain."

She smelled it and smiled and then took a small bite, briefly mulling it on her tongue. The man saw the sudden delight in her eyes and the eagerness of her second bite and he watched the juice drip down her chin and he was pleased to see it for he wished to please her and to divert her worries.

While the girl was thus occupied the man limped round the trunk of a large oak so that she could not see what he must do and he prodded the wound in his thigh so that he flinched and felt the tears rise smarting in his eyes.

The tip of the arrow had penetrated deep, and was now but a small finger-length from the back of his leg. Removing his hat he folded it and clenched the doubled brim in his teeth and then he clutched the shaft of the arrow with both hands and steadying himself he counted and then thrust the projectile forcefully downwards, and felt it tearing through the muscles of his thigh and how he restrained himself and did not scream but only moaned, he did not know but he did this for the sake of the girl and he had to ram the shaft of the arrow a second time to break the skin at the back of his leg and push the arrowhead free and when it ripped through the skin he felt the warm rush of blood that accompanied it.

He covered his eyes with his hands and rested a moment, trying just to breathe, to gather and collect himself, and then he snapped the arrow shaft below the fletching and drew the remainder of it from the back of his thigh and then he lay on his stomach and did not move for some time and might have passed out or might have slept from exhaustion and the weakness of the loss of blood.

When he woke some minutes later the girl was knelt beside him watching his turned face and softly stroking his hair and he remained there with his eyes closed for a time, holding in his mind a picture of his own daughter, as if it were her, in the days before, waking him now to sunlight and happiness, and it was only when he heard the horse snort and paw the ground in its discomfort that the fantasy was broken and he opened his eyes, and labored through his own pain to smile up at the tender child who was not his daughter but who had certainly once been someone's.

"We'll get you home," he promised her again. "Back to your cousin. Both of you back to some relative . . . an aunt, a grandmother. Torrboro or Bylome or wherever your people came from. Don't worry, child. We'll get you to a home."

He felt the stiffness of his leg wound and he sat carefully and saw that he had lost a great deal more blood from it and he knew that he should heat metal and cauterize the wound, but he couldn't risk a fire now for they had not distanced themselves enough yet from the Fangs.

They must move on, while they yet could, and hope that by some providence they might happen upon a sheltering place, or better still a kindly person, with implements and medicines and skill to remove the arrows from his own back, and from the flesh of the horse, and to sufficiently clean and address their wounds.

And even then, he did not know if they could or could not be remedied.

"Did you like the golden fruit?"

The girl's eyes widened and she smiled and nodded and he saw the dimple take set in the pudge of her cheek and he almost wept to think of her constant fear when she had been taken by the Fangs, and in the days that had come afterwards.

"What is your name, child? Do you know that I once had a daughter as bright and pretty as you?"

The girl did not answer, but studied his eyes intently and he saw the pursing of her lips and movement of her tongue as if she were trying to form some word that would not yet be shaken free.

He reached out a hand and stroked her soft cheek and she clasped his hand in both of hers almost hungrily and for a moment he saw in her again some echo of his own daughter and such seeing was sweet and bitter and he gasped and drew his hand away. The man worked himself carefully to his knees and then pushed from a crouch to stand and taking the girl's hand he led her back to the horse and lifted her up into the saddle, suppressing as best he could the moan this produced from his lung. He leaned against the side of the horse a moment and then he examined its wounds more closely and saw that there was nothing to be done which he might now set about to do for the suffering beast, and that they must push on while they could and hope to reach the ruined settlement and the boy and after that they would see.

They rode two more days, stopping only to drink, or to sleep an hour at a time. The girl slept in his arms as they rode and seemed to be sustained by the flesh of that golden fruit so that she did not suffer from any hunger and for that he was grateful for he had no means to gather food for her now.

His thigh still bled and oozed and was swollen and crusted and he feared it was now infected, and the horse's wounds showed the same telltale ulcerations and dark discolorings and he wondered if the Fang arrows had been dipped in some filth or some poison.

He could not see the wounds on his back nor could he bear the twisting required to prod them but he sensed that they too were setting up badly and were probably also swollen and putrefying and the smell that seeped through his cowl was unpleasant. He found that he must bend lower and lower as the hours passed, if he were to have any relief at all, and the horse could no longer trot but pressed forward at a walk and even the rhythms of its walking were strangely varied as if it too were trying find some new cadence that would pain it less.

The morning of the second day dawned and the man had drifted in and out of waking fever dreams in the saddle and had almost dropped the girl. They stopped at a small pond and he dismounted and as the horse waded out to drink the man knelt and removed his hat and thrust his face into the water to cool the burning and he fought to clear his head and he coughed and spit up mouthfuls of blood with dark clots in it and he tried not to let the girl see.

He estimated they were still a day and half ride from the burned settlement where the boy might be waiting.

Perhaps he could not get the girl to Torrboro.

He knew now that the horse could never make it so far.

But if he could deliver the child safely to her cousin, then even if the man did not survive beyond that, at least the child would have a chance.

The boy was barely old enough but he was resourceful and brave, and under his protection the girl just might be able to survive the arduous trek back to civilization.

It was a hope at least, even if a slim one.

He turned and saw the girl watching him, and her lip was trembling as if she were near a burst of tears, and he wondered why and then he realized she was staring at his back, at whatever visible evidence of his wounds was there and he knew that it must be very bad.

"Don't worry, child. We'll get you there. We'll get you to your cousin. I won't leave you."

He dipped his whole head in the pond now and felt the cool fingers of water as they pushed through the great mats of his hair and stroked his scalp with lingering sensation that was suspended and pleasant.

"I won't leave you," he said again when he had raised his head. The girl rushed to him then, throwing her arms wide around him and he embraced her and held her close and felt the rapid beating of her heart against his own chest while her long-stifled tears were at last released and he allowed his own to cascade round her then, spilling upon the crown of her head, and even the horse came to them from the pond then with halting steps and lowered its head and closed its eyes as if it too were an initiate in this communion of griefs.

Before he rose with the girl in his arms the man had a thought, and reaching into his pocket and finding the old silk tricorn still there, he drew it forth and held it out to the girl.

"This was my little girl's. I think she would have wanted you to have it now."

The girl took it and stared at the silk head and the ragged mane and the blue eye dots a moment before drawing it in and cradling it close, even as the man cradled her and now rose and set her again upon the saddle and then pulled himself painfully up behind her, mindful not to jostle the arrow shaft that still protruded from the horse's back like some obscure and unreadable sundial that perhaps reckoned mortality.

"You should name it," he whispered to the girl. "Give it a good name."

And the girl had whispered back, "Stormflower," and he had asked her to repeat it, but she had fallen mute again and he wondered if she had spoken at all, or if it had been his own delirium, but he thought that she had spoken so he said, "Stormflower. Stormflower is an honorable name."

All that afternoon and night they rode, for the man was well-tuned to the hints and the harbingers evidenced in the movements of the horse and in its breathing and he feared that when they next stopped the horse would lay to rest and would not afterward rise again, for he could tell that it was played out and dying and even now was moving forward driven only by loyalty and as an extension of the man's own will, and also perhaps because of some rare strength the fruit of the meadow had given it but which was now reaching the end of its ability to sustain in such extraordinary circumstance.

Through the night the horse plodded steadily slower while the man had frights and was aware sometimes of the shivering of his own body and he tried to press the girl close that she would not tumble from the saddle as she slept and the man saw things that were not there, or that he could not determine and sometimes things magnified of the shadows and sometimes things woven whole of an unseen cloth appeared before him and so he was ever disquieted and felt himself accosted by spirits and pursued by Fangs that were not truly there, and before the dawn the horse at last came to a halt and stood a moment upon a hill swept by wind and over which a scattering of stars were still faintly visible and upon which a lone, spreading tree had found purchase for its roots, and the horse lifted its head as if it smelled something in the wind and then it turned and looked at the man with one dark eye as if to say it were sorry that it could do no more and then the creature's legs gave way and it buckled and fell with a gentle moan and settled there for a moment so that the man leapt to draw the girl from the saddle and slid away falling onto his side to protect her and wincing and groaning

from a piercing pain within as he did, and then the horse also groaned
and rolled onto its side and stretching its legs out almost straight began
to move them in a way that seemed as if it were still trying to carry
them a bit further on, and the man wondered if the horse too were in a
delirium and thought itself upright and racing through a field, and all
the while its eye roved wildly as if it were taking in the stars.

The girl woke sometime after dawn and the man by then already
knew that he was unlikely to rise again either and he lay in that stillness considering how one could reach the end of a story without having
finished. The horse was not yet dead, but must be nearly so, and only
twitched now and then and the movements seemed mostly involuntary.

The girl blinked her sleep away and sat up and looked around to
see where they were and smiled and plucked a pink flower near at hand
and turned and offered it to the man and he could neither reach for it
nor even return her smile. But he concentrated his thoughts to form
words that slurred from his tongue.

"What is your name, child?"

The girl held the flower out to him a second time and when he did
not take it, she placed it in his beard and leaned back and studied his
face.

"Layna."

"Layna."

She had spoken.

"Pretty. Pretty name."

She was breaking his heart, kneeling there, still trusting him, waiting
for him to rise, to set her again in the saddle, to ride on to the home the
man had promised her would await. What could he tell her now?

He had failed her so utterly and she did not yet even know.

After all this, he had failed to deliver her.

"Layna."

She watched him closely now, the way he blinked slowly, the unnatural position he had bent into as he lay, the steady seep of blood from his mouth. She tilted her head in a small dawning of concern.

"Layna, do you see those berries just budding on that vine beneath the tree over there?"

She turned and squinted and nodded.

"You can eat those wherever you find them. They're still green and will be hard and sour, but it's okay. You can eat them if you're hungry enough. They'll turn purple in a few weeks and then they'll be sweet. Do you know where the sun rises?"

She turned to find the rising sun and pointed.

"Yes. Each morning you must look to see where the sun rises, and walk towards it. No matter what happens to me, you must do that. Can you do it?"

The girl looked suddenly disturbed, and drew the stuffed tricorn to her breast, and then lay down and curled against the man without answering him.

She is frightened, he thought. *She begins to understand the things that I am not saying.*

"I'm so sorry," he told her then. "I promised to bring you home. And now I don't think I can. And I'm so sorry."

He concentrated his attention for a moment on the movement of his arm and managed to drape it round the little girl and then he coughed hard and groaned and spit blood again and she reached and gripped his wrist.

"But you can find your way back. I know you can."

He did not want her to abandon hope, but in truth, his own hope for her was already lost. She was two days walk yet from the burned settlement, and with her little legs perhaps it would be four. And that was if she could walk to it in a straight line, if she didn't get lost. And of course she *would* get lost. She would walk in circles.

And even if by some chance or miracle she found the place, her

cousin would likely have abandoned it days earlier if he had followed
the man's instruction, setting out east on his own after a week, and so
the girl would never reach him, but would wander alone, falling further and further behind him till she was taken by Fangs, or wolves, or
hunger, or one of a thousand other beasts or fates that would swallow
any child who straggled alone in that vast and hostile wilderness which
he had barely survived as an adult and which, in the end, he had not
really survived after all, had he?

"When you find a stream, follow it in the direction the waters run,
but not too close." He coughed and tasted more blood and bile in his
throat. "You mustn't fall in." His teeth were chattering now as he spoke
and he felt deeply cold, though the sun was rising and he was still covered in the snowbeast skin and huddled against the girl. "Follow stream
to river. Follow the way the river runs till you find a town, a city. It
might take a long, long time walking. Many days. But don't stop. Keep
going. Hide when you see big animals. Can you do that?"

The girl didn't answer, and he knew his advice could not save her,
for she was too small, too young to follow such instruction. Had she
ever seen a river? Would she know one if she did?

"What was her name?"

It took the man a moment to realize Layna had spoken, and this
time in full sentence.

The girl held up in front of his face the tricorn gripped in her little
fist. "What was her name?"

"My child?"

The girl nodded.

"Sara. Her name was Sara Cobbler."

Layna mouthed the name and repeated it. "Sara Cobbler."

"Yes. My sweet little Sara."

"Did Fangs take her too?"

The man paused, uncertain how to answer, and then he decided
that poised as he was upon this mortal rim, and by the light of what

was sure to be his last sunrise, he could not but speak what was true.

"Yes. It was Fangs."

"And you didn't get to save her?"

"No. I didn't."

"Did you try?"

"I tried. But I was too late." He coughed, and swallowed the blood this time so that the girl would not see it. "I tried too late."

The girl fell silent and seemed to be mulling this thought, and the man found that tears were spilling the corners of his eyes though he tried to hold in the sobs that painfully spasmed his lungs.

"But you got to save me."

The man didn't respond and the girl turned to look at his face.

"You wasn't too late to save me."

And then she had raised her head and kissed him once on the cheek, as a child might her papa at bedtime, and afterward she turned to look again at the silk creature in her hands.

And then was the man overcome and wept a great weeping that he could not contain though it racked his body and raked afresh at the fell wounds inside him. He pulled the girl close, and his weeping was for her tenderness and her innocence and for the ache of things that could not be set right and for his own Sara, and he wept too because he knew, and because the girl did not, that he *had* arrived too late to save her.

Once again, he had arrived too late.

And he blinked his eyes at the clouds scattered against the firmament above him and he knew that he was no longer angry with the Maker but he found that he was perplexed to the core of his own existence and could not fathom the whats and the whys of this world and of his own journey in it because nothing lined up and nothing had been tidy and nothing had ever been met.

Nothing but the point of his own spear.

And in that mystery, and in his own failure and his fear he must now close his eyes.

Must close them and rest, accepting that any fight yet to come was not his own, and his own fight was ending and that this end of his own story would almost certainly mark the end of the girl's story as well, though hers might linger yet a few senseless days in this wilderness.

Perhaps she would have been better off a captive of the Fangs.

At least then she might have been delivered alive to Torrboro.

He heard the horse exhale a long breath and he believed it must be its last but he could no longer turn his own head to see.

I have seen your mountain, O Maker, he recited finally, not knowing where he had heard the line or whether he now spoke it aloud or not, *and I will go up to it.*

The man was curled on his side in the middle of a shallow river whose waters rushed dark and behind him the darkness grew while before him a clear light spread like the refractions of diamonds and yet there was no source to it but it was everywhere, and he knew that he had been crossing that river though he had no memory of his first steps into those waters or of why he had lain down in it.

He tilted his head and listened now because there was a lovely music, and at first it had seemed far away but it drew steadily nearer and the man felt himself stirred by the melody fierce and joyful, and he sensed in it the beginning of something like a kindling of a flame in his bones, a stirring that was both within and without and that was calling him to rise and he thought that it must be the music of the whatever-came-next, the music of the forever wild and unmapped lands, of the places beyond all maps, urging him on across that last river, and it came to him with a sense both of nostalgia and of expectation that it was a music he had known before or perhaps always known and had always heard in the wind and the stars and in the beating of his own heart like a melody that had never ceased playing though he could not quite yet name it, and he craned his head towards the source of it and opened his eyes.

He was lying on his side precisely where he had been, upon that grassy hill with the still form of the horse stretched before him, and a dull pain still evident in his wounds, but the girl was now standing, peering to the next hill as if she too could hear that eternal music that echoed and beckoned from the other world.

And then, in a beautiful confusion that could not be sorted by his mind, the man beheld as if in vision a great crowd of children like a surge of bright sea waters suddenly rushing and spilling over that far hill.

He saw children laughing, somersaulting in the grass, running and skipping and playing as if there were no Fangs in the world and no troubles to weigh their hearts. This bright reverie of blue sky and green hills and companionship and laughter and joys multiplied was so utterly unexpected that he could only describe it as the radiant advent of the next life, as the glittering approach of the paradise to come and he tried to rise and run to them, to join their glad company, but he could not rise and he could not even move his hands.

He was confused and lay half in joy and half in fearful anticipation.

He saw the girl Layna clap her small hands in delight and heard the chirp of her hailing and he watched her then as she sprinted forward on those cherub's legs, away from him towards the others in his vision, and he could not reconcile these events, for he knew she was yet alive and should not yet be joining him thus in the afterlife, and then the other children seemed to see Layna as well and there were happy shouts of greeting and several of them rushed forward to meet her as the music that had been playing all along welled louder.

The man now knew the voice of the thing as a whistleharp, and perceiving that, he suddenly remembered the tune as the same played by the bard to send him on his way at their last parting by the lake. It was one of those lost songs of Anniera which he had before struggled against even as he had longed to embrace it but now he could not remember why he had ever resisted, and he blinked again and saw that same bard who had been his friend step over the hill and pause in his playing to shield his gaze against the sun and to see little Layna rushing towards him on her short legs and to cry out to her in welcome and to open his arms and then the girl was taken by the hands of other children and passed forward to the bard upon the far hill who lifted her and kissed her face and then she pointed, pointed back towards the man who lay atop the hill opposite them, and Armulyn the Bard shielded his eyes again and looked and even at that distance which seemed to be both near and far and seemed to be a vision stretching and stretching across worlds the man believed their eyes had met, if only briefly, and the bard had raised his hand in both greeting and farewell and then the man heard at hand the horse he had thought dead whinnying expectantly and he turned his head from the vision of the children and the bard, and marveled to see how wonderfully that handsome creature had risen, and now stood tossing its spirited head in great eagerness and seemed to be waiting for the man to rise, and he noticed for the first time ever the three cobalt horns that protruded magnificently from its forehead and he wondered how he had so long missed a thing so splendorous and marvelous and plain to the eyes.

The glorious horse now nickered again and lowered its head and pawed the ground and light flashed from the striking of its hooves and the man felt that wave of light wash over him as a deep peace, and surge through him as a healing stream and he found that his injuries had not been so bad as he had earlier thought and the pain and the weariness of the years had fled from his limbs so that he knew he could move and could stand again, and he rose and thrilled at the awakening of his own strength, returned as he had not felt since his youth, or even in his youth.

He breathed that glad air and shouted because he could and his cry came echoing gladly back and he laughed to hear it and then he ran and fairly leapt onto the horse's back and the horse reared and when its hooves struck the earth again there was another great showering of light. Turning to look back at the far hill the man saw now that the children and the bard had been separated from him by an intervening cloud that glowed with impenetrable flame, but he could not now be grieved at this, for he sensed that the light was a greater good than could be named and that those within it were held now by that glory and so he was free to beg their leave and need no longer fear for the girl or for any child.

Thus released he wove his fingers into that wild mane and leaned and spoke into the horse's ear a new word that was now held in common between the two of them and that magnificent tricorn reared and snorted its joyful response and clashed its hooves and leaned into what the man felt as a full gallop and he tightened his hold and thrilled to the rising of that furious speed. But he soon learned that it was not a gallop, and it was not even a canter. It was only a trot, and the thundering canter and the calamitous gallop of that glorious tricorn were yet to come.

As they coursed the wide and shimmering earth in that merry charge the man was amazed at stretching his gaze to discover that his eyes might now perceive events revealing themselves beyond the visible horizons of this world. His vision spread suddenly wide and far even into other times both past and future for he was in a place where all was somehow becoming *now*. He peered behind him and he saw there the woman who had once been his wife sitting long ago at the high window of their daughter's room, weeping, and lamenting the oath she had in her bitterness bid him swear, and he saw that her heart had afterwards softened towards him again and she had prayed his return and so he now blessed and released her even over that distance of years for time had grown both large and small in that place, and he turned then and gazed to the days yet to come which soon would be and also had already been and he saw yet farther away the receding of the Fangs from all of that land he had known, and he was heartened to see it and his eye roved further still and passed over the waters of the Dark Sea, and was drawn towards a bright and shining isle that gleamed like a vast diamond amongst the waters and he saw how battles had been fought and tyrants thrown down and even old enemies redeemed and he saw how it was being rebuilt to a new glory amongst its former ruins but his eyes did not rest there, for they were drawn on to a castle newly risen, and his vision rushed ever on now towards it and through its gates and doors and then along its hallways coming to rest at last in a room of thrones where he paused and saw that upon one of those sat a young and beautiful woman whose soft features and blue eyes were so familiar and yet so beautifully changed and he saw that she held something tenderly in her palm and as he drew nearer he saw that it was the tattered silk tricorn he had so long carried in his own pocket and he raised his eyes then to the face of his own dear Sara and he wondered then and he marveled and he wept for his joy at the mystery that she was yet somehow alive and not merely alive but also a princess and though he could not explain how it might be and though the mystery of it was not then opened to him, yet he beheld it and knew it to be true.

As this vision began then to fade and he to feel himself drawn back across that great stretch of sight, he thought that she raised her eyes, with tears in them, tears of tenderness and of memory and of mercy, and met his own across that distance of time and worlds and raised her fingers to her lips and kissed them and held them out to him and blessed him as a father and a pilgrim, and he blessed her then as a daughter and a princess, ere she receded at the last from his view and he knew himself again to be borne astride that hurtling tricorn.

Lifting his face into those wild winds he scried the horizon and hearkened there to the rising brightness of the eternal immensity of the One Mountain and he knew it instantly in his heart as their lasting destination and the true home to which all of their journeying had led them and of which the mountain he had partway ascended in the other lands was only an echo.

They rushed onward then in a wonder and a mystery that did not lessen but only increased the closer they drew, and the Mountain was near enough now to fill the man's vision and to capsize his heart but was also yet far enough away to give jubilance to their shared journey and as they journeyed together that joy and that mystery and that wonder were ever unfolding around them, giving way to deeper wonders and deeper joys and deeper mysteries that could not be answered in words for in words their questions could never be framed, for these were living mysteries that were not hidden in impenetrable darkness but were blazed in unfathomable light and the man knew then that it had never been answers he had sought in his sufferings, but presence, and that presence was here and was itself the thing that had always stood—from the foundations of the world and even before and even after—in the place that answers could not.

Before the questions had been asked, the presence had already been given.

It was only here in this place gradually unveiled that it might be ever more fully known and increasingly reflected by all things as all things were drawn upwards towards the One Mountain where the greater glory of it dwelt and from whence it streamed eternally. He saw the light of that presence shimmering upon the horns of the tricorn now, and shining from his own skin, and showered across cloud and waterfall and forest and field, till the very air around them had become radiant and he drew it into his lungs with every breath and that presence felt then as a kind of constant communion that one must grow in capacity to bear the ever increasing joy of, for the increase of it would never cease.

Hearing a great cry he had known twice in that other world as well, the man looked up then and spied above him the Lone Fendril with wings unfurled in joyful coursing, bearing still the wound of his spear, but crying out in wild exultation and in welcome of the man and his steed. He marveled that its feathers had become flames blazing all the colors of sunset as it swept wide circles round him, drawing so near that the man reached into his shirt and finding the feather still there he brought it out and offered it up in his hand to the Fendril but the Fendril only trilled a festive song that was most like a glad laughter and that gave the man welcome leave to keep that bright token of his own former estate and of the journey that had brought him to this place, and then did the great bird beat its wings and rising skyward gave cry to bid them follow, and so they did, racing it towards the One Mountain and towards those unreckonable reaches that were already rising to tower over them, the summits and heights of which would now be forever open to them and yet would never be exhausted for the man understood now that the Mountain was infinite in its reach and would never cease ascending and so ever upward into the boundless depths of that greater and more joyful presence would they run.

Epilogue

The straggler had found his way here from the Field of Finley but it had not been easy for he remembered so little of these lands and had searched for any familiar outline of hills or lanes across the continent and several islands as well, and so had wandered the years away in his long search for anything that might match his tattered memories and so give sign. He was now an aged man and for the wear of his journeys looked a beggar and more or less was when he finally limped up the hill on his crutch and found this place and stopped at the gate bent on its hinges and pondered the empty sheep pen and the little blue spring pool and the red stones in sore need of mortar and repair.

But for the wisp of grey smoke that curled from the chimney he might have thought the homestead abandoned.

He stood and pondered the place with his one eye roving beneath a scarred brow and he stroked and worried his grey beard and found at the last that he could not bring himself even to enter, to knock upon that door again, for his shame was too heavy upon him, and his iniquities too great to ask or expect forgiveness.

And so he had watched awhile in compounding sadness and then he turned and began to hobble away, hunched and hopeless now.

He heard the door unlatch distantly behind him and then the sound of running feet and he tried to go faster but his crutch sank in mud and he pitched forward and lay in the road.

He turned and saw the beautiful, grey-haired woman running towards him, her eyes pained, but her expression kind as ever it had been in any of his haunting dreams, all deep questions long since etched to lines upon her face and she stopped yet twenty paces from him and stared and her mouth opened and her lovely hands, frail and worn, clasped together.

"Karl?" and then her eyes went wide and her voice broke with a release of more than thirty years and she lifted her skirts and ran to him crying *"Karl!"* only it was no longer a question this time, it was his own name.

She stooped to throw her arms round him, and then she turned over her shoulder and shouted, "Sweetness! Bring your babies to meet their grand-pa! He's come home as I always told you he would!"

About the Authors and Illustrators

Andrew Peterson

www.Andrew-Peterson.com

Andrew is the author of the Wingfeather Saga (which feels really funny to explain here, but there it is). He's also the critically acclaimed singer/songwriter of more than twelve albums, including *Light for the Lost Boy* and *The Burning Edge of Dawn*. In addition to writing books and songs, he's the Proprietor of The Rabbit Room, a non-profit organization dedicated to the flourishing of art and community. He lives in Nashville with his wife and three children in a house called The Warren and is currently plotting to unleash the Wingfeather Saga on the world as an animated series.

Cory Godbey

CoryGodbey.com

Cory Godbey creates fanciful illustrations for picture books, covers, comics, editorials, advertising, animated shorts, and films. His work has been featured in a variety of esteemed annuals and publications including *Imagine FX*, *The Society of Illustrators*, and *Spectrum: The Best in Contemporary Fantastic Art*. Cory seeks to tell stories with his work. He also likes to draw monsters.

Nicholas Kole

www.behance.net/NicholasKole

Nicholas Kole is the son of two mimes. He is a wandering bard-type Halfling sellsword working out of a backpack, most often in the vicinity of Rhode Island. From his various coffee-shop homes he draws dragons and wizards and pigs that can fly for clients like Disney, Hasbro, Riot, EA Games, and The Flight Anthology! In between adventures, he takes occasional breaks to write stories of his own and to sit under trees looking wistful.

Jennifer Trafton

JenniferTrafton.com

Jennifer's first novel, *The Rise and Fall of Mount Majestic*, received starred reviews in *Publishers Weekly* and *School Library Journal* and was a nominee for Tennessee's Volunteer State Book Award and the National Homeschool Book Award. She teaches writing classes, workshops, and summer camps in a variety of schools, libraries, churches, and homeschool groups around the Nashville area while the world anxiously awaits the publication of her second novel, *Henry and the Chalk Dragon* (coming from Rabbit Room Press in 2017).

John Hendrix

JohnHendrix.com

John's work has appeared in numerous publications, such as *The New Yorker* and *Rolling Stone,* and he has drawn book jackets for the likes of Random House and Penguin. His drawings have won many awards including the Society of Illustrators' Silver Medal in 2006 and 2008.

His first picture book, *Abe Lincoln Crosses a Creek*, was named an ALA Notable book of 2008 and won the Comstock Award for read aloud books. His book, *John Brown: His Fight for Freedom,* the first he both wrote and illustrated, won the Oppenheim Toy Portfolio Gold Seal and was named one of the "Best Books of 2009" by *Publishers Weekly.* His most recent book, *Miracle Man*, has been highly acclaimed and will probably win him fourteen more awards (which it absolutely deserves).

N. D. Wilson

www.NDWilson.com

N. D. Wilson is the author of *Leepike Ridge* (a children's adventure story), *100 Cupboards* (the first installment in a multi-world fantasy series), The Ashtown Burials (an adventure series), *Outlaws of Time* (yet another adventure series), and *Boys of Blur* (yet another adventure—though not a series, because authors do require sleep). He enjoys high winds, milk, and nighttime (partly because of the sleep). He received his Master's degree from Saint John's College in Annapolis, Maryland, is the managing editor of *Credenda/Agenda* magazine, and is also a Fellow of Literature at New Saint Andrews College. His writing has appeared in Books & Culture, The Chattahoochee Review, and Esquire. He is also very tall.

Joe Sutphin

www.JoeSutphin.wixsite.com/JoeSutphinArt

Joe Sutphin illustrated *The Warden and the Wolf King* (the fourth book of the Wingfeather Saga), the *Dr. Critchlore's School for Minions* series by Sheila Grau, and *Word of Mouse* by James Patterson. He lives with his wife Gina, their cat lil'Miss, and their fish, Jerk Fish, in a big red barn in Ohio. He has been drawing and creating stories since he was little, though he's still not very large.

Joe spends as much time in nature as possible, getting scolded for picking up too many creatures. He is an avid collector of kids' books, loves playing vintage video games and is quite possibly addicted to black licorice and root beer.

A. S. Peterson
www.RabbitRoom.com

A. S. "Pete" Peterson is the author of the Revolutionary War adventure *The Fiddler's Gun* and its sequel *Fiddler's Green* as well as a number of short stories and at least one stage play (*The Battle of Franklin*). Among the many strange things he's been in life are the following: U. S. Marine air traffic controller, television editor, art teacher and boatwright, and progenitor of the mysterious Budge-Nuzzard. He lives in Nashville with his wife, Jennifer, where he's the Executive Director of the Rabbit Room and Managing Editor of Rabbit Room Press.

Doug TenNapel
TenNapel.com

Doug is an animator, writer, cartoonist, video game designer, and comic book artist whose work has encompassed animated television, video games, and comic books. He is best known for creating Earthworm Jim, a character that spawned a video game series, cartoon show, and a toy line. His graphic novels include *Cardboard, Ghostopolis,* and *Tommysaurus Rex.*

He also likes Chesterton and pipes, and is somehow taller than N. D. Wilson.

Jonathan Rogers

www.Jonathan-Rogers.com

Jonathan received an undergraduate degree from Furman University and holds a PhD in seventeenth-century literature from Vanderbilt University. He calls his fiction "fantasy adventure stories told in an American accent." The Wilderking Trilogy (*The Bark of the Bog Owl, The Secret of the Swamp King,* and *The Way of the Wilderking*) and *The Charlatan's Boy* are fantasy stories, but they owe more to Twain than to Tolkien. Peopled by boasters, brawlers, bumpkins, con men, cowboys, and swampers, his novels draw deeply from American vernacular storytelling traditions. They harness the humor of that tradition in the service of divine comedy—a worldview in which the sorrows and hurts of this world, as true as they might be, aren't nearly so true as a vital joy and love that will one day sweep everything before them like a flood.

Justin Gerard

www.GalleryGerard.com

Justin began painting after finding a Step-by-Step Graphics guide on Peter de Sève. Armed with this and inspiration from the works of Arthur Rackham and the Golden Age illustrators, he began creating narrative-driven images to inspire himself and others. He has a special love for the Golden Age illustrators and has made a long and detailed study of their brains in an effort to distill their collective genius into a drink, which he might sell for millions.

While Justin has always derived a great deal of inspiration from nature and human history, his favorite source of inspiration is story. The works of J. R. R. Tolkien and C. S. Lewis have remained constant sources of inspiration for him throughout his career.

Douglas Kaine McKelvey

www.DougMcKelvey.com

The remote descendant of Scottish horse-thieving ancestors, Douglas Kaine McKelvey has already bested the dubious achievements of his predecessors by authoring six published books and penning lyrics for more than 250 songs recorded by a variety of artists including Kenny Rogers, Switchfoot, and Jason Gray. He is currently completing the manuscript for a sci-fi/fantasy novel, developing a feature film comedy-drama project with Ruckus Films, and recently released an amazing picture book, *Wishes of the Fish King*, in collaboration with Jamin Still.

He also has a small, fearless dog that believes it can fly (but cannot).

Aedan Peterson

www.instagram.com/AedanPeterson

Aedan Peterson is about to graduate high school and is weighing his options. He plans to study either art, literature, or theology, and will let you know once he decides which. Aedan is already in high demand as an illustrator, having created most of the illustrations for *Pembrick's Creaturepedia*, posters for the band The Gray Havens, an album cover for artist Galen Crew, illustrations for Porter's Call, as well as several commissions for his church. He loves stories, he loves art, and he loves when the two come together.